UNTIL THE SUN RISES

To Henry,

Curiosity can be our strength and our weakness. Which will you discover?

Thomas Whitaker

UNTIL THE SUN RISES

ONE NIGHT IN DRAKE MANSION

BY

CHANNING WHITAKER

Oak Tree Press Hanford, CA

Oak Tree Press
Publishers Since 1998

UNTIL THE SUN RISES, Copyright 2015, by CHANNING WHITAKER.
All rights reserved. Printed in the United States of America. No part of this book may be used or reproduced in any manner whatsoever without written permission except in the case of brief quotations used in critical articles and reviews.

For information, address Oak Tree Press, 1820 W. Lacey Boulevard, Suite 220, Hanford, CA 93230.

Oak Tree Press books may be purchased for educational, business, or sales promotional purposes. Contact Publisher for quantity discounts.

First Edition, April 2015

ISBN 978-1-61009-163-3
LCCN 2015934062

Dedicated to Kristy, without whose love and support this book would not have been possible.

Before the Sun Sets

Two TV crewmen, Brian and Jeff, stood on the front stoop of an aged, Dutch Colonial mansion in severe disrepair. Both men placed large lights onto stands directed at the boarded-over front door. Jeff inspected the nearest window for a glimpse inside, but the glass was veiled with filth.

Jeff shivered. "This place gives me the creeps."

"I'll be glad when the night's over."

Seconds later, a muffled, cracking noise caught Jeff's attention. He stopped and surveyed the area. The noise faded. As Jeff returned to his work, a large wood beam fell from the overhang three stories above and slammed on the steps striking mere inches from the men. Both fell backward and tumbled to the ground. Neither could stand. They stared at the debris silently. A soft voice from behind broke their shared stupor.

"That's exactly where the young couple died. Where you're lying now, that's where their bodies were found." The men locked eyes then scrambled to their feet. Turning, they found a woman standing, her face and features hidden in the shadow of the house.

Jeff squinted. "Are you that psychic?"

"That's right." She stepped forward. "Madam La Claire."

"Can you sense anything here?" Brian asked.

La Claire closed her eyes and reached for the stoop. Both men were mesmerized with anticipation. She let her fingertips gently dance on the wood. "Oh that's terrible," she uttered under her breath. The men grew further excited.

Jeff couldn't wait any longer. "What? What is it?"

"It's—" she began, but before elaborating she opened her eyes. "Maybe I should save it for the cameras. Don't you think?" She smiled. Jeff and Brian sighed. La Claire turned and spoke over her shoulder as she walked away, "I just wouldn't stay up there any longer than you have to."

As turbulence interrupted what had been a smooth flight, Walter Resnick awoke among twenty passengers aboard a small charter jet. Walter, a handsome gentleman in his fifties, had salt-and-pepper hair, a dominant jaw line, and wore a pristine, custom-made suit. Yawning, he slid one hand over his hair to ensure nothing had fallen astray. He straightened his tie and scanned the cabin, exchanging nods with sleekly dressed television, marketing, and advertising executives while skimming over assistants and below-the-line crew—the less important people in his view. Many seats were empty.

Eventually, Walter's gaze fell on the smooth and flawless medium-brown legs of the knockout actress seated across the aisle.

Audrey Donahue was tall, trim, and curvaceous with long, straight black hair. Her features and skin tone suggested she was of Asian descent, but her natural blue eyes indicated this was only partially true. Her clothes were tight and revealing, which only encouraged Walter's attention. Oblivious to Walter, Audrey methodically thumbed through a tabloid magazine. Walter's gaze lingered as she shifted from one crossed leg to the other, then licked the tip of her finger and flipped another page. Walter smiled, checked his watch, and then let his eyes drift closed again. The designer fragrance Audrey wore kept her impression fresh in Walter's mind long after his gaze had strayed.

Less than a minute passed before the jet lurched once more, this time severely. Irritated, Walter abandoned hope of catching further shuteye. The aircraft's intercom interrupted the cabin.

"This is your captain speaking, folks. We'll be landing in approximately 30 minutes. As we descend through the cloud layer, we're anticipating a few more bumps and shakes. It'd be a good idea for everyone to make their way to their seats and buckle up."

Walter glanced out the cabin window seeing only a complete saturation of thick, fluffy white. Beside him sat Jason, a young man dressed in a cheap suit who, in spite of all the disturbances, remained in slumber. With a frown, Walter jabbed his elbow sharply into the young man's side. When Jason jumped to attention, Walter's expression grew innocent as he feigned another yawn. "Oh, excuse me." Jason's hair was flattened where it had rested on the wall. Still groggy, he slid a cellphone out of his jacket pocket and futilely checked for messages, forgetting he'd turned off reception prior to takeoff. Walter interrupted him. "We've still got a little time. Why don't you hand me those scripts?"

"Sure thing, Mr. Resnick." Jason pulled a briefcase from under the seat to his lap and fumbled through a cluttered jumble of documents. Scraps of paper escaped the chaos and drifted to the floor. Walter rolled his eyes and sighed. Not expecting the pages anytime soon, his attention fell on black and white images dancing on the laptop set before the passenger seated across the aisle one row ahead.

Harlan Holt, a man just shy of 30 with a collared shirt tucked into a pair of jeans, paused the video playing on his computer. He minimized the viewer window revealing a music player program. The last track of a playlist was highlighted. Harlan double clicked back at the beginning and straightened a pair of headphones on his ears. As a down-tempo, hip-hop tune began, Harlan restored the video player. Immediately, a frozen man in sepia tint snapped into action. The picture was choppy with vertical streaking, characteristic of worn film prints. A title card broke the action reading, "For my next trick, I'll require a volunteer from the audience." Harlan couldn't help but grin at the contrast between the modern soundtrack and the pre-sound era visual that he'd inadvertently paired as the magician executed a basic disappearing ball trick from the grasp of a child's hand. Harlan daydreamed, pondering whether there might be a market for old silent films scored by one of today's rap mogul producers: the RZA presents Charlie Chaplin's "City Lights." Harlan dismissed the notion with another chuckle, for now, and refocused on his work.

The figure in the old film was dressed in a black tuxedo, along with dark, mysterious eye makeup. The look made his facial expressions distinct and exceedingly sinister, though he performed for an audience composed entirely of children. The character pointed to his shadow on the wall behind him. The movie cut to another title card, and then to a close shot on the dancing silhouette. First, a few shadow animals were created: a rabbit, a dog, even a gorilla, but soon the entire shadow turned from a man with extended arms into the silhouette of a medieval knight, complete with sword and shield, and mounted on a horse. The video cut out momentarily, then stuttered and resumed as a blurred shot that slowly returned to focus.

A folder containing documents, periodical photocopies, and a half-filled notepad rested in Harlan's lap with a pen clipped over the front flap. Harlan moved the notepad to the top of the stack. The exposed page was filled top to bottom with handwritten notes. The last stood out larger than the rest and was underlined, "Death Shows?" On the next fresh page Harlan scribbled, "Thank Tom at the Film Institute for digitizing the Malvern archive." This too was underlined before Harlan went on to write, "Magic show filmed 1925."

On the screen, the shadow knight encountered the outline of a dragon twice as tall and wider than him. The shadow dragon's mouth opened and tendrils of fire rolled outward. The shadow knight raised his shield, and the flames bent around it. When the blaze subsided, the knight thrust forward, impaling the dragon. Its silhouette melted away. The figure of a long-haired, long-gowned, and buxom woman with a crown atop her head was revealed in its place. As the knight lifted the princess to the back of his steed, all the shapes blurred and returned to a single simple shadow of the magician. "And They Lived

UNTIL THE SUN RISES

Happily Ever After" followed on a title card before the film returned to a wide shot of the magician and audience.

The children applauded. The magician paused for their accolades, briefly, then contorted his body. His shadow took the shape of the dragon, larger than before. Harlan leaned toward the screen to see the poorly focused shape. Abruptly, the magician dashed forward, and the dragon appeared to spring toward the crowd. The children jumped. Many hid under their seats, others cried. Even Harlan jumped in his seat, snapping back from the screen.

The magician broke his dragon pose, laughing, and proceeded to comfort the youthful audience, luring them back to their seats. A beautiful woman, smiling broadly, joined the magician on stage rolling a waist-high metal hoop. The audience settled and clapped, welcoming her.

Behind Harlan, Walter's attention drifted, but he caught the appearance of the woman out of the corner of his eye. His interest was reinvigorated. Harlan and Walter both observed as the magician instructed the beauty to lie down on the floor before him. He waved his hands over her and, after another title card bearing a few nonsense words of spell casting, the woman rose from the floor. Her body remained horizontal and rigid. The magician continued waving his fingers until the beauty had levitated above his head. He lowered his hands and grinned. The woman remained aloft. The audience was motionless in wonder. Next, the magician grasped the metal hoop at his feet, lifted, and proceeded to slide it back and forth over his assistant's body, never touching her or any other noticeable obstructions.

"No Wires" cut in from yet another card. The audience in the film applauded. Behind Harlan, Walter chuckled faintly, but Harlan didn't notice over his headphones. Harlan yawned while he wrote a note reading, "standard tricks." As the magician passed the hoop over the suspended beauty again, her feet and legs slowly disappeared up to the position of the hoop. When he reached her waist, only half a woman remained hovering above. Harlan paused his writing. The magician quickly slid the hoop back to the woman's feet so most of her legs reappeared, but just as swiftly he reversed and slid the hoop all the way up and past her head. Again, her body disappeared as the hoop passed over, resulting in her total absence from the stage.

Harlan stared at the screen in awe. This time he heard "Wow!" from behind him even over his music. Harlan glanced over his shoulder and caught Walter wincing in embarrassment. His sudden outburst had drawn every other passenger's attention. The moment of tension was broken when the jet took another hard lurch and everyone's concern shifted to the nearest window.

Harlan grinned and turned back to the screen. The magician brought the same hoop up above himself, holding it with both hands, like an oversized halo. He then released the hoop, allowing it to fall over him. Just as with the beauty, when the hoop passed around him, his body incrementally disappeared; first his head, then his shoulders, followed by his torso, legs and feet, all in the second it took the hoop to fall to the stage floor.

With the stage empty, the audience on screen was stunned, but soon broke into ovation. There was no sound of cheering, only the backs of children barely able to stay in their seats as they clapped and appeared to shout. Soon after, two hands appeared in the center of the hoop on the floor. The disembodied appendages split and slid right and left, then gripped the hoop. The magician's head, shoulders, and elbows followed as he lifted himself from the hoop's center as if it were a hole in the stage floor. When he finally climbed out and onto the stage, he kicked the hoop with his toe as he took a sliding step toward it. He stumbled, off balance, and flailed as if teetering on an edge. With the impression of a hole remaining it appeared the magician would fall in the opening. Surprisingly, his feet found only solid floor where the hole had been.

The film's crowd jumped up and down, and the magician bowed several times before he drew a single finger up to the side of his mouth. His smile became perplexed. A title card interrupted once more. "Have I Forgotten Something?" The children spilled into the aisles with excitement, yelling. "The Woman" popped up on the next card. Nodding his understanding, the magician lifted the hoop beside him, looked at it curiously, flipped it one way then the other, and finally lifted it above his head, but to the side. As he slowly lowered it from ceiling to floor, the beauty reappeared from head to toe. Another round of applause began. The magician and woman took a final bow before a curtain dropped.

The video ended and cut to a selection menu with a few other clips. Harlan slid his headphones down around his neck. After a moment of contemplation, Harlan looked over his shoulder and locked eyes with Walter, who simply shook his head, impressed. Harlan nodded his own veneration, then turned to his notes and rapidly filled the rest of the page. Walter stretched forward to peer onto Harlan's notes, but from a distance, Harlan's hurried cursive was impossible to decipher. Walter did manage to make out the last word on the page as Harlan printed it in all caps, "KILLER?"

The jet made one last lurch, then every window snapped from white to blue. Harlan stowed his computer and shifted his notes off the top of the file. Opening the first document, he flipped through a few pages of text then slid the report to the bottom of the pile. The next had a close-up photo with the face of the magician, titled "Malvern Kamrar." After reading the single-page of biographical text, Harlan flipped this document to the bottom as well and proceeded to skim several newspaper clippings. One bore the headline, "Magic Show Appears Spectacular" and was followed with an action photo of the magician, mid-illusion. Next was an old advertisement with "Malvern Kamrar, Master of Shadows" on top, with Malvern in a spooky, spell-casting pose, surrounded by shadow figures in the middle, and with "Tonight Only" written beneath them.

Harlan passed through several similar clippings regarding the magician. The final clipping was a front-page article from the Des Moines Register dated 1933. The headline read, "Heir to Drake Fortune and Family Missing." The photo included was a family portrait with a father and son seated, a mother and daughter standing behind them, and another toddler son on the father's knee. All were dressed in stiff, uncomfortable-looking clothes. Harlan noted there wasn't a smile among them.

After skimming the article, Harlan moved to the last document in his file but was disrupted by a commotion in the cabin. Most of the passengers across the aisle abandoned their seats to lean and peer out windows on Harlan's side of the jet. Behind him, Walter leaned over the actress Audrey's seat and casually placed a hand on her shoulder, seemingly to steady himself. She, too, leaned toward the window to see the spectacle. The window seat beside Harlan was empty. He unclipped his seatbelt and slid over. However, Harlan took the time to fasten his belt in the new seat.

The jet descended rapidly over a small town. The surrounding area was filled with neatly shaped acres of crops. Harlan smiled. He'd always appreciated the geometric aesthetic of farms from high above. In the town, many houses and small buildings were organized on a neat grid of north to south and intersecting east to west streets. At the center of town, however, the pattern was broken by a large, clock-tower-topped courthouse, surrounded by a courtyard of green grass and a town square filled with storefronts. Besides a stream running through part of the town, only one other anomaly stood out from the ordered landscape—a huge three-story mansion, complete with a long rear courtyard and a carriage house, all surrounded by a tall, wrought-iron fence. The vector of the jet's landing brought the mansion estate closer and closer to view, on course to pass almost directly below them.

As the motors of the landing gear engaged, the jet vibrated and increased its downward slant. Many of the unseated passengers stumbled and had to grab for something to steady their stances. Walter's something was Audrey's lap. She squealed in surprise as Walter exclaimed, "Oh, pardon me," but they both laughed off the awkwardness.

Harlan mumbled to himself, "This is why we have seat belts." He turned back to the window. The mansion property was very clear. The house had patches of missing roof tiles and appeared terribly rundown. Harlan flipped open his file to that last document and found several photos of the same mansion among pages of text. He glanced back and forth from the images to the property outside.

The photos spanned decades, each with a different degree of dilapidation and overgrowth. On the ground outside, however, there was also a buzz of people, cars, camera trucks, trailers, and broadcast equipment populating the mansion's front and rear lawn. In the shadow of the grand house, crewmen ran cables between production vehicles to a massive generator trailer just outside the back corner of the property. The mansion slipped out of sight behind the tail of the jet. Moments later, the tires found the pavement of a runway, and the charter jet slowed to a meager, taxiing speed.

Audrey was the first off the jet. She removed a pair of sunglasses, nearly equal in size to her tank top, from a handbag and covered her eyes as she descended a mobile stairway. Lenox, a young, female production assistant with a walkie-talkie in hand, directed her to three rental vans waiting beside the runway.

"All my bags are up there." Audrey spoke without looking at Lenox directly. Walter, his assistant Jason, and many of the other passengers impatiently packed in at the exit, trying to edge in front of one another. Harlan waited for the rest to clear the aisle, seeing no need to rush to the exit just to wait in line to get out. Calmly, Harlan organized and re-filed the pages into a bag with his computer. Once he had the cabin to himself, he stood, pulled a small piece of luggage from an overhead compartment, and stepped to the front. A narrow closet was near the doorway with a single green sport coat draped on one of two-dozen hangers. Harlan grabbed the jacket and put it on before exiting the aircraft.

Outside, Harlan noted the small size of the airport. There were several crop-dusting propeller planes but no terminal. Lettering on the front of one hangar read, "Shadows Bend Municipal Airport." Nothing Harlan could see, not even the buildings, were as large as the 30-seat jet they'd just flown in on. He found it odd such a small facility would have a runway long enough to accommodate this aircraft. Harlan smiled and took a moment to holler, "Thank you," back to the exiting flight crew. After leaving the airport's drive, Harlan and the other van passengers were greeted by a bullet-dented road sign: "Welcome to Shadows Bend."

The convoy of vans arrived at the mansion estate and all the passengers from the jet filed out. On the street, a truck with a mast on its roof held a satellite dish forty feet in the air. Harlan's attention was drawn to the rotting wooden planks nailed across the mansion's front door. Many shutters were askew, broken, or missing. Several windows were cracked and one corner of the roof overhang was crumbling. As he surveyed the ominous manor, his eyes landed on the topmost window, tucked away between the pitches of the roof on either side. Unlike all the other broad rectangle windows in the lower floors, this one was small and round. Its placement made it virtually unnoticeable, yet when Harlan examined the features carefully, the window stood out as an architectural misfit. Harlan's gaze lingered until the sound of a low-flying jet interrupted him. He turned to see a charter, almost identical to his earlier transport, on a similar path dropping over the property, bound for the local airstrip.

Harlan stood alone, just outside the bustle of activity on the mansion grounds. The vans were gone. Having lost the group, Harlan looked around, not sure where to go, but Lenox came running back. She arrived out of breath. "Mr. Holt," she paused for air, "let me show you to your trailer."

"Trailer?" he asked.

"You can settle in there until they're ready in makeup."

"Makeup?"

"Yeah, we're only about an hour from going live, and they'll have to get you prepped with the equipment, too, so it won't be long."

The thought of gunk on his face was the opposite of thrilling for Harlan. Resistance was his immediate impulse, but he decided not to protest. He would concede, and let this young woman get back to the long list of tasks he figured she was swamped with. "Lead the way."

After stowing his bags and taking a seat in the small chamber, one of three dressing rooms in this particular trailer unit, there was a rap at the door.

"Yeah?" Harlan hardly got the word out before the door swung open to reveal Walter. He showed himself to the only other seat in the room. Walter carried a bound set of pages. His face appeared different than on the plane. Close-up, Harlan concluded the addition of makeup had altered his complexion and masked some age.

"I don't think we were introduced on the jet." He extended his hand. "Walter."

"Of course, I'm Harlan."

"Holt, right? The archaeologist?"

"The name is accurate, but it's anthropologist."

With a nod, Walter made a note in his pages. "Right, right, my mistake, I just wanted to get all the facts straight before we go on the air. Is there anything more to be said for your studies? Do you have a specialization or something like that?"

"My research involves supernatural and occult beliefs. Mostly I examine western civilizations in more recent periods, limited to the last 200 years, though in many instances, veins of cultural beliefs go back to the beginning of western religions. I think anthropologists are equal parts historians, scientists, and psychologists, so my work deals with people's beliefs from all three angles."

Walter bore an expression of deep concentration, complemented by a nod of understanding he had perfected over many years of TV interviews while paying almost no actual attention to Harlan's elaboration. "Now, let's see, you...are...the skeptic, right?"

Harlan smiled. "I'm many things, Walter—academic, lover, critical thinker, gourmet coffee aficionado, microbrew enthusiast—but I suppose in this instance skeptic is as practical a label as any."

Walter rattled off another dozen biographical questions to Harlan. Once concluded, he thanked Harlan and moved to step out.

Harlan raised an open palm. "Hold on a moment, Walter. I have a couple of questions for you."

"Fire, buddy." Walter returned to his seat.

"As both executive producer and host of this show, whatever happens it seems to me you'll be the one with the closing words, right? You'll be summing up the night." Walter agreed. "I have a fair idea how paranormal-themed shows use camera tricks and editing to create the impression of seeing something which was never actually on screen. I'm also quite familiar with how shows can spin even the most minimal suggestion of something eerie into a statement of lingering mystery."

Harlan impersonated a television host. "Like seeing a simple shadow and exclaiming, 'was it just the cameraman's silhouette or was it something more? We may never know.' When in fact, there was no actual question about it."

Walter grinned and nodded again. Harlan went on. "The way I see it, you and the other producers brought me in here to provide a voice of skepticism as a contrast to the abundant voices of speculation. Of course, I am prepared to be shown something that is truly beyond the scope of normal scientific understanding. I'm always open to it, but I suspect that will not happen, and should it not, I'd like to request that you compose your closing words... I don't want to say truthfully, but... straightforwardly. Since I happen to know you are a veteran of TV journalism, and had a long career in broadcast news before you became an entertainment producer, I'd just ask you to comment like a journalist, only on the facts, and don't spin the events to imply the show had more mystical significance than it did. Can you do that?"

Walter looked him in the eyes. "I don't have an agenda on the matter, Harlan. I'm just interested in seeing what happens and getting to the bottom of this mystery if we can. That's all. I'll call it straight. You have my word on that." Walter extended his hand and Harlan shook it with a satisfied smile before Walter left the trailer.

Lenox waited outside and escorted Harlan to the dreaded makeup trailer. Before stepping in, they waited for Audrey to step out. Her hair was curled, makeup perfected, and she'd changed into a shimmering blouse, short skirt, and heels. "Not very practical," Harlan commented to his escort, who was delighted but held her chuckle until Audrey passed out of earshot.

Lenox shouted, "Stepping!" as she guided Harlan in.

Upon sitting, Harlan requested, "As little as possible."

Harlan's next stop was a truck set outside the village of trailers. He sensed uneasiness among all the crew people he passed along the way, though many words of "Good luck" and "Be careful in there" were uttered. As the sun dropped in the west, the shadow of the mansion engulfed the entire camp. Inside the truck, a burly man showed Harlan to a workbench full of parts, wires, and tools. "The name's John, son, but everyone around the set calls me Bomber. Don't ask."

"Bomber it is."

"Now, when y'all are in there, you'll be outfitted with one of these babies." Bomber pulled a chaotic-looking jumble of parts out of a plastic crate. "I built 'em myself. It's a hard hat that's for your protection, but here on the front we have an LED flashlight. It's small, but at least it can run all night on one charge. Of course, the best part is this." He pointed to a lens above the forward brim. "It's a high-def camera, right here on the front, that transmits wirelessly. You'll each have one, so basically we'll see what you see, as long as you're wearing it, and the whole thing weighs less than two pounds." Bomber plopped the helmet onto Harlan's head. "Comfy?"

"I'll live."

"There's a good sport." He slapped the hat twice, apparently checking that it was in fact hard, and jammed it farther down on Harlan's head. "Now let's try 'er out." He flipped a switch then leaned over to adjust a channel selector on a small monitor near the workbench. Video of the inside of the truck came up on the screen. "Looks good," Bomber announced with satisfaction. Harlan looked over at Bomber as he spoke and immediately Bomber's smiling face popped up on the monitor. "That's enough of that." Bomber switched the camera back off. "Now if ya feel right up here on the side," he grabbed Harlan's hand and guided it to another switch, "you'll notice the button for your light."

After flipping the switch, a dim beam projected a circle from Harlan's head onto the wall. It moved left and right as Harlan turned side to side until he reached back up and switched it off. "All set." Bomber patted the helmet again.

"Will these be the only cameras in the house?"

"Not on your life. Here, I'll show ya." He beckoned Harlan to follow him out of the truck and into a semi trailer beside it. With the press of a button, lights snapped on inside, revealing an entire mobile shop, at the center of which sat a pillar with a wide base which was as tall as a person. Bomber pointed as he spoke. "Four HD cameras, each with 90 degree left-to-right and 180 degree up-and-down movement for a full 360 by 360 view. They have lights built in on all sides. Each camera has a night vision mode, heat vision mode, and a few other modes. And, of course, the entire shebang is mobile and self-propelling by RC. We can control 'em from the booth up by the house. We'll have eyes everywhere. I built these custom, and we'll have a half dozen following you guys." Bomber patted Harlan on the back, then flipped the lights off, and showed him out. As Harlan headed back toward the trailers, Bomber called to him, "Good luck," though his words were followed by a notably sadistic chuckle.

Harlan had to meet with several other crewmen. He signed releases, received a tetanus booster, had photos taken, gave another brief interview—recorded on camera this time—and even stepped into a small cylindrical, green-screen booth with a series of cameras all along its perimeter. Harlan was impressed with the high-tech setup as they latched the door closed on the coffin-sized chamber. Moments later, the whole unit shook, tipping him off balance. "Hey, you're not going to toss me in the nearest lake, are you? I'm not Houdini, you know. At least you didn't cuff and shackle me, so I might have a fighting chance."

An unamused voice cut in through a speaker above, "Hold still, please." Harlan stiffened and held his breath as all the cameras snapped in unison. Seconds later, a computer just outside the cylinder rendered out a moving image of Harlan, with a very cross expression, seemingly frozen in time with the appearance of a single camera tracking around him in free space.

By this point, Harlan had grown fatigued with all the preparatory obligations. He'd thought he would be nervous when the show began, but by the time Lenox tracked him down to announce, "They're ready for you up at the house," Harlan welcomed it warmly.

7:00PM, Sunset

"One million dollars. One night in Drake mansion." Walter spoke with intensity into a handheld microphone. Behind him, the boarded-up mansion front entry was vacant. One bright light shining on Walter cast a shadow figure on the front steps. A crewman with a shoulder camera captured his monologue.

The nearest truck to the mansion entry had its back and side doors wide open. Inside, one wall was covered in small monitor screens, forty in all, each with a different video feed. Several showed the house from different angles while others showed the grounds or incidentally captured the behind-the-scenes work of the crew. Walter's image filled one of two larger screens in the middle, which was labeled "on-air," while a crew of five manned the computers, camera selection board, and audio controls. Nora, a woman in her thirties, directed the broadcast from a center chair. Walter could be heard faintly, but Nora's voice dominated. "Standby deck three. Roll deck three."

On the screen, Walter continued, "I'm standing here in the small town of Shadows Bend, Iowa. More than eighty years ago, the family of five that resided here, in this mansion—"

On the large screen, an aged photo of the family replaced Walter. His voice continued. "—A man, Vinton Drake, his wife, Martha, their 13-year-old daughter, and their two younger sons set out for a night of wholesome entertainment, attending a traveling magic show starring the mysterious Malvern Kamrar, master of shadows." The screen faded to another image bearing a vintage publicity photo of the sinister-looking magician. "As far as anyone knows, the family never returned home and neither they nor the magician were seen or heard from again." The screen cut back to Walter. "At that time this was a small coal-mining town, the kind of small town where you rarely run into someone you don't know, and Vinton Drake was the president of the mine. He and his family were well known by all. Malvern, on the other hand, was that rare stranger."

The on-air image shifted again, this time to a montage of historic photos of the Drake mansion. Walter's voice accompanied it. "The story, however, doesn't end there, and neither does the tragedy. Here at the family's manor, a series of deaths began. The first was a pair of police officers investigating the family's disappearance. Both suffered unusual, yet separate, accidents and perished in the mansion within hours of one another. Next, the family's live-in nanny returned without permission, supposedly to collect her personal effects. She, too, met her end in the house, poisoned either accidentally or as a suicide, though no container, pills, or note were ever discovered." The broadcast shifted to modern footage of the mansion, including helicopter aerials. "The last was here on the front steps of the manor. A young couple passing by was caught in a violent thunderstorm less than a month after the family's disappearance. They sought refuge under the eaves of the entry and were inexplicably and most disturbingly electrocuted." The screen cut back to Walter. He gazed down to where the couple's bodies would have lain.

Outside the static composition of the camera's narrow frame, the area was drastically opposite. Workers, the TV execs from the jet, and representatives from the city all crowded the area, watching Walter's opening. The campus of trailers and trucks was brimming with activity. Bomber, along with a crew of 10, prepared a line of six camera pillars identical to the one he'd shown to Harlan. Piles of equipment and crates peppered the cable-laced grounds. Other crewmen readied huge lights, cameras, and microphones. A squad car with a pair of officers was stationed nearby, with an ambulance next to it. Additional officers manned each of three gates to the property.

Harlan waited near the back of the broadcast truck. He followed the images on the large screens through its open door. Another crewperson strung a remote microphone from Harlan's collar, under his shirt, to a transmitter clipped to his waist. Along with Harlan, four others equipped with the helmet cameras received similar wiring. Harlan scanned the line of people. One was the actress, Audrey. She shouted heatedly into her cellphone while she snapped her fingers, beckoning a makeup artist for another touchup. Beside her, a young and very muscular Latino man wearing jeans and a heavy metal band T-shirt meddled with a case of small gizmos, flipped some switches, and replaced batteries in one of his devices. Another good-looking, twenty-something woman was next. With sable skin and brown eyes, she wore durable, broken-in jeans, an athletic jacket, work boots, and a rugged, tucked-in shirt, though the top two buttons were unhitched, showing traces of cleavage.

As she tightened her bootlaces, Harlan's eyes moved between her and Audrey, contrasting Audrey's ready-for-the-club outfit versus this woman's ready-to-get-dirty ensemble. He laughed to himself. The last of the five sat with her legs folded on the ground. A candle flickered before her. Harlan estimated she was in her late forties, though she had youthful, fit, and attractive features. She had blonde hair and a fair complexion and wore a long, colorful skirt straight out of the sixties, as well as a blouse and knitted sweater draped over her shoulders. Her scarves and jewelry were abundant. At no time during Harlan's appraisal did she break from her meditation. It was obvious to Harlan that their mix of genders and ethnicities was intentional, designed to market the television event, just as the relative physical attractiveness of each was also by design. "Show business," he snickered softly.

"Six missing and five dead in a matter of weeks," Walter's introduction went on, "it was then that the town's leaders decided to suspend the investigation into the Drake family's disappearance, abandon the Drake mansion completely, and seal it off for a duration of 100 years. In the more than three quarters of a century since then, the legends of the Drake mansion abound. Few people remain who remember those original occurrences first hand."

The broadcast cut to a shot that slowly zoomed in on the attic window, the same that had caught Harlan's attention earlier. "Many say that they've seen the figure of a man in the attic window at dawn, while others claim it's a woman, and some insist it's a child, again in the window at dawn. Equally, there are claims of hearing screams, howls, or sobs echoing from the abandoned mansion at night. If you were to ask any resident of the town for their experiences with the Drake house, most could tell you a bone-chilling tale, each different from any other."

After moving to Walter briefly, the broadcast cut to the mansion from a distance with the western horizon behind it. "Behind us, the sun approaches dusk. Tonight, you, me, and five brave contestants will break that seal, decades early, and the Drake mansion will be vacant no more. Will we discover the tormented spirits of an age-old crime? Will clues to solving the mysteries present themselves?" He paused as the camera returned to him. "Will anyone last through the night?" Walter smiled devilishly. "We will find out together, broadcasting live through the entire night, both on television and online. If any of our five daring investigators lasts through the night to when the sun rises at dawn tomorrow, they'll earn their share of a one million dollar prize. Please stay tuned." In the broadcast truck, eerie theme music accompanied Walter's final words, and then both image and sound faded into a commercial.

The crew was given a signal that they were clear from the broadcast. The area around the mansion entrance erupted with action. Harlan and the other four contestants were ushered up to the steps. Bomber, all the camera crew people, and the camera pillars were lined up behind them. Lights cast on the doorway intensified, illuminating it thoroughly. As the chaos returned to order, Walter and two police officers took their places at the boarded-up front door. Each officer bore a crowbar in hand. Small screens in the broadcast truck showed the five helmet camera views, witnessing the action at the mansion steps.

The on-air monitor faded back from the commercials and into a pre-edited introduction. Music led into the title: "One Night In Drake Mansion," along with the network logo. Walter's voice, recorded this time, briefly reviewed the mystery of the family's disappearance and the questionable involvement of the magician Malvern Kamrar. The video included clips from the same film of Kamrar's performance that Harlan had researched. Next, the intro package restated the terms of the million-dollar contest to last through the night, sunset to sunrise, in the spooky mansion. Finally, the five contestants were introduced, giving their names and biographical information. Their stories were accompanied by shots of the five in their regular lives, and followed by footage of each preparing before the show at the mansion. The sequence finished with shots tracking around their statuesque bodies, just as Harlan had posed.

The new-age woman's bio was first: "Madam Galva La Claire, career psychic of more than 20 years, known for hosting popular online reading events where she communes with lost family members, hailing from Sedona, Arizona."

Recorded footage rolled of Walter interviewing Galva. "What do you hope you'll see or discover in the mansion tonight?"

"I'm hoping to make contact with the tormented spirits here. If I can speak with them, and give them a voice, then perhaps they can finally leave our world in peace."

The Latino man's bio was second. "Baxter 'Ax' Cruz, professional paranormal investigator, a veteran of paranormal investigation TV, born in San Juan, Puerto Rico, but now residing in New York, New York." Ax responded to the same question from Walter. "I'm hoping that using my custom spirit detection equipment, I'll be able to show that spirits are in fact here and confirm this as a genuine haunted house, as I have before with many other inhabited sites. Then, myself and others can study it, refine the methods of spirit detection, and continue to further understand the paranormal sciences."

"Very ambitious," Walter added.

Audrey's bio was next. "Audrey Donahue, an actress, model, former Ms. Texas, and recent star of several low-budget, independent, and popular cult horror films, now hailing from Los Angeles, California."

She also answered Walter's question. "I think many of my fans will be watching tonight, and I'm just hoping I'll be able to hang in there until morning, so I don't disappoint them." She smiled and winked to the camera.

Fourth, Harlan. "Harlan Holt, an anthropology Ph.D. student at the University of California, Berkeley, a published paranormal skeptic, an authority on U.S. spiritualism and magician heritage, and a Scientist, Magician, Skeptic Foundation research fellow hailing from Berkeley, California."

Again, prerecorded interview footage followed. "Walter, I think some mistaken assumptions, creative theories, and even wild interpretations of whatever happens tonight will fly abundantly. The history of the house is no doubt intriguing. I'm just happy to be present to offer grounded logic and reasoning when extraordinary speculations do arise, and to ask the critical questions which often go unvoiced."

The athletic, outdoorsy woman was last. "Genevieve Freeman, recent Pre-Med graduate from the University of Iowa and four-year scholarship NCAA soccer player, born and raised right here in Shadows Bend, Iowa, living just blocks away from the Drake estate, considered a local authority on Drake mansion lore."

The final interview rolled with her response to Walter's question. "This puzzling tragedy has been a black mark on our community for so long, an eyesore literally and figuratively. I wouldn't mind shedding some light on what happened here, or at least opening the door for others to thoroughly investigate and finally put to rest this long standing mystery."

"Very admirable, Ms. Freeman. Good luck." Walter's interview concluded.

Near the Mansion, activity continued to race until a crewman yelled, "We're live in thirty!" Everyone made a few final adjustments before they quickly came to rest. "Twenty," the crewman shouted. Walter met with a makeup artist for a quick touch-up, then hurried back up the steps, stopping briefly next to Audrey. "Remember what we discussed. If you do, you'll send this show's rating into the stratosphere and secure your career for another decade." He finished with a wink. Audrey grinned and nodded agreement. When the broadcast faded back, a handheld camera swept up the steps showing the five contestants in line and ready to enter, then landed on Walter and the officers.

"In just a few moments, these planks will come down, and our contestants will cross this threshold." The camera zoomed in on the foot of the door. "If, after that time, any one of them chooses to come back outside or is rendered incapacitated and must be evacuated before sunrise tomorrow morning, just about 12 hours from now, then they forfeit their claim to an equal share of the million-dollar purse." The camera refocused on Walter. "There's only one other stipulation. The attic. Since legends place the spirits there at dawn, our contestants are only allowed to open and venture into the attic during the hour preceding sunrise. That means you'll have to be here, with us, through tomorrow morning in order to see it opened live, no matter what lies in wait." He paused dramatically. "The stakes are high. The potential for danger is even higher. Challengers, are you ready?"

All five confirmed they were prepared to enter. Nearby, a pocket of local townspeople looked on, including the mayor, chief of police, fire chief, as well as city council and chamber of commerce members. Genevieve's parents were present as well. When she nodded in agreement, her eyes darted over to them and found her father smiling, giving her a thumbs-up while her mother, wearing a worried expression, squeezed his hand.

Walter looked directly into the lens. "Are you ready? We'll be here broadcasting live, straight through until dawn tomorrow and don't forget, you can enhance your viewing experience with live feeds from every camera online through our website, so you won't miss a moment of the action." He listed the names of several corporate sponsors, then his gaze shifted to the distance. "This is not only a great American mystery for the ages, but one that has gone virtually uninvestigated all these years. I can see the sun is only minutes away from disappearing. Without further ado, officers, please open the door."

On his cue, the two police officers jammed their crowbars under the edges of the rotten wooden barricades. With an anticlimactic lack of cracking or splitting, the first few boards fell away with ease, hitting the ground dully. In the broadcast booth, however, the audio operator clicked a button and slowly raised the volume on recorded sound-effects of wood planks cracking and popping.

When the last board dropped away, the officers stepped aside. Walter pressed the latch and pushed the door open. The thick mahogany groaned as it resisted swinging freely. "Your chambers await." Walter beckoned them. The five contestants filed forward. Ax elbowed in front of Harlan to be first. The broadcast took Ax's helmet camera live, showing the first footage from inside. Each of the five bore a backpack of personal and safety items. Ax also toted his case full of detection equipment. The crew's bright lights bombarded one side of the house while the subtle glow of dusk embraced the other. Years of dirt had accumulated on each windowpane and restricted the outside light almost completely. Rectangles were distinguishable on the walls, but virtually nothing cast through to the floors. One elongated streak of light penetrated from the wide-open front door but dissipated ten feet inside.

Harlan and Genevieve followed Ax. Harlan pulled a flashlight from his bag and scanned the ceiling for potential dropping hazards. He nodded to Genevieve that the coast was clear, or at least appeared to be, as indicated by his raised eyebrows. A decrepit and musty smell overwhelmed everyone's senses once inside. Audrey hesitated at the doorway. Walter put a reassuring hand on her shoulder. "Are you going to be all right?" She nodded, struck a determined expression, and finally breached the entrance.

Madam La Claire was last. She clutched a pendant strung from her neck as she entered. Bomber's team of camera operators rallied their equipment, ready to follow behind her. Harlan continued to scan the foyer and front hallway for falling or tripping hazards. Several framed photos had fallen to the floor, along with eroded plaster, which had dropped from the ceiling. Harlan swept the larger obstructions to the corners with his foot. "This place is creepy." Audrey said.

Harlan didn't turn to face her. "That's the point, I believe."

A woman's shriek drew everyone's attention. Ax, Harlan, Genevieve, and Audrey each spun back toward the entryway. There, Madam La Claire convulsed feverishly with her eyes clenched shut and one hand grasping for the wall. They rushed to her aid. When Genevieve and Audrey reached her, she fell into their arms. Gently, they lowered her to the floor. She continued to spasm. A cameraman quickly filled the door behind her. He framed La Claire and followed her without stepping inside.

"Spirits, the spirits," she murmured. Ax dropped to a knee, opened his case on the floor, and withdrew a device. Once powered, he began scanning the air in Madam La Claire's vicinity. Harlan calmly observed from a distance. La Claire struggled to speak again. "I, I can feel the spirits. They're, they're here at the doorway, several of them." Audrey and Genevieve gave her their full attention.

"I'm not getting any unusual reading." Ax switched to a different gizmo.

"They're not here to welcome us. No, they're, they're here to warn us." La Claire's eyes snapped open. She grasped Audrey and Genevieve's hands with force. "They don't want us here." Her body went limp.

Bomber waited impatiently behind the cameraman in the doorway. He looked toward Harlan, "Can we get her out of the way? We need to get these camera units in A.S.A.P." Harlan stepped toward the women, but no sooner than Bomber finished his request, La Claire began to rouse and brace herself to stand. "The presence has passed."

"Good timing." Harlan assisted in bringing La Claire to her feet.

He guided all three women to a nearby bench where La Claire could compose herself out of the way. Bomber's crew stormed past with a pair of the camera pillars in tote. Several assistants with bright floodlights accompanied them to show the way as they hefted pillars to separate points on the ground floor. Harlan and Ax stepped aside, near La Claire, to allow the progress. Bomber himself stood just inside the doorway and unclipped a 2-way radio from his tool belt.

"Check one," squawked from the radio. Bomber looked outside. A crewman just outside the broadcast truck gave Bomber a thumbs-up signal. Bomber replied into the radio, "One's good."

"Check two," immediately followed from the radio. The camera-checking process was interrupted, however, by another scream, this time from a man somewhere inside the house. Harlan, Ax, and Genevieve rushed forward with Bomber close behind. The howl sounded again, this time followed by a distinguishable, "Damn it!" just around the corner in the living room. As they turned in, they spotted Brian, the camera crewman, on the floor beside one of the pillars with both legs of his pants ripped below the knees. Blood streaked down the exposed skin. To Harlan, he seemed more angry than injured. The pillar was tipped over on its side. Ax impulsively rushed toward him. Harlan hesitated and blocked Genevieve and Bomber with an extended arm. Ax stumbled and fell almost on top of the crewman, letting out a yelp of pain at the same instant.

In the broadcast truck, everyone worked frantically. They punched up one of the cameras from the overturned pillar and watched the scene from a skewed angle.

"Be careful and don't move." Harlan scanned the floor with the beam of his flashlight, revealing a minefield of tiny spikes. The nails from nearly every floorboard were rusted over and standing more than an inch out from the floor, each with only a very small head pointed up, though they were dull. "It's just nails from the floor. Years of expansion and contraction must have pushed them out." More crewmen joined the scene behind Genevieve and Bomber. Harlan called for one of the floodlight operators to brighten the space. Once lit, they could see that the extent of the spiked area spanned nearly the entire room. "There's a clear spot over there." Harlan carefully navigated the narrow areas between spikes to a portion of floor at the foot of a staircase, which was clear of protruding nails. From it, he could reach Ax and the downed crewman. He aided one after the other to their feet and back out to the hallway.

"All right?" Bomber asked Brian.

"Yeah, just scraped up." Brian turned to Harlan. "Thanks."

"What about you?" Harlan asked Ax.

"Fine." He was curt, and his cheeks blushed.

Harlan pointed to a hammer on Bomber's tool belt. "Can I borrow that?" Bomber relinquished the hammer, and Harlan began to pound down the nearest nails. Audrey and La Claire joined the crowd watching the action. The next set of camera pillars were ushered in, but were forced to wait for the path to the stairs to be cleared of the protrusions. With a nod from Bomber, six of his crewmen sat down their respective equipment and joined Harlan at hammering in the flooring nails. Several chairs, a couch, and a half-dozen tables were spread about the room. Many were draped in dust cloths. The men didn't bother moving anything. They focused on the nails in the walking areas. A few more joined, and they finished the entire room in a matter of minutes. As Harlan returned Bomber's hammer, Genevieve drew her flashlight and surveyed the hallway in both directions and the entry to another room across from this one. She spoke toward Harlan. "I wonder why this is the only room where the nails have crept out like that? It doesn't seem the others have."

"Could be the wood variety, age, maybe they treated lumber with less reliable chemicals back then, or perhaps something has been contributing significantly more water vapor under this area over the years, exaggerating the natural expansion."

"Maybe the spirits didn't want us in there," La Claire inserted. Harlan shrugged, but Ax nodded in agreement, disregarding Harlan's conjecture, as he moved to his case of devices. He took additional readings at the living room doorway. The crewmen returned to placing the camera pillars, ushering the next set past the contestants and up the staircase. Bomber resumed checking off each as functioning. Harlan returned to the front and retrieved his backpack. Audrey, Genevieve, and La Claire did the same. When they came back, Ax was still waving his devices.

Brian lifted the pillar in the living room upright. He placed a slate of multicolored and gray-scaled swatches before one of the pillar's four lenses, then spoke into his radio, "check five." Moments later, Bomber's voice confirmed the camera was operational. The pillar's lights slowly brightened, though they only added the illumination equivalent of a few candles to the room. La Claire pulled a container of white powder from her bag and dispersed it around the perimeter of the room.

"What's that?" Audrey asked.

"Sea salt." A puzzled expression from Audrey followed. "I'm purifying this room, establishing a safe area so we'll be protected from the spirits in here. If you get into any trouble, retreat to here." Audrey nodded in understanding and smiled. Harlan began exploring the features of the room further with his flashlight. The ceiling was vaulted, at least 15 feet high, and tapering inward near the top with exposed wood beams. Elaborate plaster molding transitioned from the ceiling to the walls, including leonine busts in each corner. The walls were paneled with wood and adorned with a dozen paintings.

Harlan admired a beautiful oil landscape. "You have to wonder if there's anything valuable in here."

Genevieve explored another corner but hollered in response. "A better question might be, what isn't valuable? The Drakes had plenty of money and didn't mind showing it."

An intricate chandelier hung at the center of the room. Harlan stood under it. It was only a few inches over his head at its lowest. "It looks like this once held candles, but was refitted for electric lighting, probably already an antique even back in the Thirties." Harlan continued to explore. He noted doorways into other rooms on both walls adjacent to the hallway door. Through one, he could spot part of a dining table and chairs; the other had an ornate desk and bookshelves. On the fourth side, an outside wall, there was a large fireplace in the center framed by an expansive mantle. Closer inspection revealed a series of framed photos. The largest, at the center, was a family portrait of the Drakes, similar to the one in Harlan's research but older as the youngest son was an infant, cradled in his mother's arms.

Harlan lifted and blew on the image, generating a cloud of dust. Genevieve drifted toward the mantle as well and skimmed a few of the other photos. She stepped next to Harlan and looked over his shoulder at the portrait. Just as in Harlan's newspaper clipping, the family notably lacked smiles. Vinton, the father, was cross. The mother, Martha, had a fatigued expression, while their daughter and elder son both looked as if they'd just been scolded.

"I wonder if their formal clothes were terribly uncomfortable, or if sitting for a portrait photo was just a long and miserable process?" Harlan asked.

"Maybe they were just a miserable family."

Harlan turned to Genevieve. "What do you mean?" Genevieve took the portrait and studied it.

"I've always figured theirs was a marriage of convenience or function." She licked her thumb and polished a patch of dirt away, which had partially covered Vinton's face. "The Drake family had an empire, including banks, rail, and several coal-mining assets here in Iowa, but Vinton used college and then the army to avoid getting involved with the family's interests. He only stepped in and took over control of the mining branch when he married Martha, who just happened to be the only child of the largest landowner in the state back then, Ely Stanton. She was heiress to the Stanton fortune in Iowa farmland."

"Couldn't the Drakes just buy the land they wanted? Not all of Stanton's land could have been valuable for minerals. Maybe Martha and he met and married due to their equal social status? Martha resisted her family's wealth by living humbly and teaching school children prior to marriage, if I have my facts straight." Harlan pointed to a small photo on the end of the mantle depicting a young Martha in a class photo with a dozen children. "She and Vinton had many things in common."

"One couldn't say for certain, but Martha's father definitely wasn't selling. Stanton publicly opposed coal mining in Iowa, after seeing how a few early strip mines affected the land. He was a self-made man who began with a single farm and built it into an empire. He was also a conservationist. In fact, without Martha and her family to inherit his land, when he finally passed, he trusted everything to the state. No, I think marriage was the only way for the Drakes to open the door to all that land." She looked up to Harlan. "Can you imagine being a child raised in more of a business than a family?"

Harlan shook his head. "You certainly know a great deal about the Drakes."

"Every kid in town has to take a half semester in fifth-grade history about the town back then and the Drake mystery." She smiled. "I suppose I might have brushed up a little." Genevieve replaced the photo on the mantle. "There's one man still living in town who was a teenager back then. He's over ninety now, but as a kid he worked as a men's room attendant at the country club. He overheard Stanton say he was going to kill Vinton if he ruined a plot of land where Stanton liked to hunt. Maybe it was just a figure of speech, but it was one of only a few leads the police dug up before the investigation was halted. Perhaps Stanton offed Drake and snuck Martha and the kids out of the country."

Harlan thought for a moment. "What does the magician Kamrar have to do with it then? He disappeared too."

Genevieve grinned. "Maybe Martha and the magician were lovers." Her eyes widened. "If she and Vinton weren't in love, Martha may have looked elsewhere, and when Stanton whisked them away she took the magician along. It's almost Shakespearean."

Harlan laughed. "That's one theory. So what happened to Stanton after the family disappeared?"

Genevieve's eyes sparkled. She smiled wider yet. "He stuck around about a year then he moved away, just up and moved from his life-long home. With the investigation suspended, no one tracked where he went, or at least the police didn't. They only learned of his death and his bequest to the state many years later when his will and death certificate were sent from a New York law firm, but there was nothing to suggest Stanton had been in New York himself. Pretty suspicious, huh?" She continued to grin as Harlan absorbed her ideas.

From the hallway, Bomber could still be heard confirming camera functions. The crew had already vacated the living room. The pillar sat on rubber wheels and steered itself toward Harlan and Genevieve's conversation. The hum of a motor drew their attention to the camera facing them as it turned to frame them both. Harlan noticed lights dancing in the hallway. Moments later, it returned to darkness. In the same instance he concluded the last of the crew's floodlights were gone, Bomber poked his head into the living room doorway. "We're all set and heading out. You're on your own now. Break a leg."

"Thanks." Only Harlan and Genevieve acknowledged him. Harlan moved into the hall and watched, as Bomber was the last to exit. A large, gray crate remained in the middle of the entry hallway. It contained provisions for the night: clean water, food items, a first-aid kit, a seat-topped bucket, toilet paper, hand sanitizer, and the like. Outside, Walter stood at the entry, addressing the camera. Harlan couldn't make out his words from the distance but could still pick up the intensity in his tone. Finally, Walter leaned in and pulled the door. As it closed, his voice became muffled until it was virtually gone. The bright light cast through the door grew ever narrower until it was nothing more than a sliver on the floor and finally disappeared, leaving only the five contestants in the once again cold, dark, and lifeless mansion.

8:00PM

The five gathered in the main room. Harlan broke the silence, "I think it'd be prudent for us to look for some candles or oil lamps." Genevieve and Audrey acknowledged him. La Claire and Ax didn't bother. "There's no reason we can't make use of objects we find in the house. Power back in the thirties, I imagine, would have been less reliable than today. With a huge house like this, I'd guess there's a large stockpile somewhere, the kitchen, a pantry, or a workroom. If we can get more lights going now, we'll have a much easier time the rest of the night."

"Who the hell made you the boss?" Ax finally looked up from his gear. Harlan was taken aback, then it occurred to him Ax's ego was bruised from needing rescue within the first five minutes inside the house.

"No one. I was merely offering a suggestion for cooperation and for getting started. I'm open to alternatives." Ax said nothing, searching for a better idea.

"I think it's as good a place to start as any." Genevieve eased a long moment of tension. "I wanted to take a look at the bedroom situation anyway."

Audrey gasped. "You're planning to sleep in here?"

"They said we had to stay in the house all night, but they didn't say we had to stay awake all night. The night will pass faster with a few hours of sleep, and I figure I might as well be comfortable."

Audrey squirmed as if an icy hand had been placed on her neck. "Eew, I can't imagine closing my eyes for more than a second in this place."

"It's probably not a bad idea to at least check it out," Harlan said. "Let's get some better light going, then it will be safer to check the bedrooms upstairs."

Ax pulled out his flashlight and pointed to the provisions crate out in the hallway. "Yeah, well, anybody wants to go hunting for lamps, go with the boss man, anybody wants to help me unpack the provisions crate can give me a hand pulling it into the living room. This should be our base of operations. I need to unpack my equipment anyway. After we're all settled in, we'll start investigatin' the place."

"Great plan, divide and conquer," Harlan said. Ax was more patronized than appeased. Genevieve joined Harlan while La Claire and Audrey moved toward the crate. Harlan nodded. "Looks like it's settled then. We'll be back in just a bit. Holler if you need anything."

Harlan and Genevieve moved to a door branched from the living room. Harlan reached up and flipped his helmet light on, giving him double coverage together with his hand flashlight. Genevieve followed his lead. They came first to the very large dining room, complete with a long oak table and seating for 12. They surveyed the room, tracing their intended course around the furniture with their lights. On the opposite side, an open, waist-high window in the wall showed an adjoining kitchen.

They could hear murmurs from the others behind them, but the sounds faded as they crossed the room. The living room camera pillar drifted to the passage between rooms to gain a view into both. "You know, none of us were ever really introduced to one another. I'm Harlan." He extended his hand to Genevieve.

She smiled as she shook it. "Genevieve, but you can just call me

Vieve. Most my friends do."

Harlan nodded. "Vieve it is." Across the room, Harlan stopped at a wooden china cabinet. "There's a pair of candelabra on the table; there might be candles around here." The first cabinet drawer was heavy to move. Once open, they saw it brimmed with tarnished silverware, hundreds of pieces. They exchanged a silent glance, both understanding the high value of the contents. Harlan slid it closed and continued to search the remaining three drawers, but to no avail.

As they proceeded, Harlan felt compelled to fill the silence. "I'd prefer to get substantial light going, if for no other reason than to combat the mind's tendency to see what isn't there when it's dark."

"What do you mean?"

"People have a peculiar way of letting their imaginations run away with them when they're anxious or frightened. It's no coincidence virtually all reported paranormal experiences take place at night, with the lights off. No one ever holds a séance at high noon."

"True, I guess?" Vieve checked a series of kitchen drawers.

Harlan opened the higher cupboards. "In the 1850s, two brothers from New York, Ira and William Davenport, performed shows in which they were tied tightly together with ropes, both arms and legs, while in a seated position and then closed in a large cabinet. The lights were then lowered on the audience and in the darkness, tambourines would rattle, horns would sound, and drums would beat. When the trick was over, the lights were raised, the cabinet opened, and the brothers were revealed to still be tied together. They sometimes had a Spiritualism minister present, assuring the audience the spectacle was executed through the power of spirits and not trickery."

Vieve slowed her searching, paying deeper attention to Harlan. "Audience members would swear that in the dark, they'd heard the instruments flying through the air, sounding from behind them, that they'd been touched by the hands of spirits, and all sorts of fantastic experiences. The brothers performed that trick, or variations of it, for their entire careers. The great Harry Houdini used to investigate and publish on magicians who claimed spirits were involved with their abilities. Years after William Davenport's death, when Ira was long since retired, he admitted to Houdini how the trick was done. One brother could adjust his ropes to give slack to the other to free himself, and vice versa, special knots were sometime also used, after which they simply played the instruments themselves from right there in the box, never having left it. No spirits, just escape artistry."

Harlan paused his own searching and leaned in toward Vieve, letting his flashlight point up to his chin like a child telling a ghost story. "Houdini of course asked how the effect of spirits and objects moving through the audience was achieved. Ira reportedly grinned and simply commented, 'Strange how people imagine things in the dark!'" Vieve smiled. Harlan broke his spooky pose. "All they had to do was let the audience use their imagination and natural apprehension in the dark. The infamy it added to that one trick provided lifelong careers."

Vieve shook her head. Harlan resumed searching. Vieve moved past the drawers to inspect a tall, double-doored pantry. As she opened the doors something sprang out and struck her face. She yelped and fell toward the floor. Harlan was close enough to scramble, catch her partially, and ease her fall. She opened her eyes. At first, she struggled to focus in the dark. Something was an inch from her face. Once she could see, she screamed at the top of her lungs. Their limbs were tangled from the awkward way Harlan had used his body to soften her collapse. Vieve couldn't get to her feet. She dug her fingernails into Harlan's forearm and calf.

In the broadcast truck outside, everyone lurched backward in their seats as the image of a skull filled the large screen on Vieve's helmet feed.

When Vieve's shrill bellow finally waned from lack of breath, another sound filled the air, laughter. Still virtually paralyzed with fear, she managed to turn enough to see Harlan in stitches. She scrambled to get away from him, unraveling the knot of their limbs. At last she could see broadly. The skull belonged to an entire skeleton, though it was no larger than a cat's. Vieve frowned as she caught her breath. Harlan managed to suppress his laughter. "It's from a little raccoon." Then he cracked up again.

Vieve stood all the way up, stomping her feet and huffing in the process. "Is it really that funny? Wouldn't you be freaked if some ghoulish critter sprang out at you?"

"I definitely would. That's not the funny part." Harlan chuckled. Vieve interrogated with a scowl. Harlan pointed with his flashlight, highlighting her chest. "It's the baculum." Harlan bit his lip, but tears built in the corners of his eyes. Vieve looked down and discovered a thin bone lodged in her cleavage. As she withdrew the bone, she looked to Harlan.

"Baculum? That's familiar from biology, but I can't quite place it. All I've had is human anatomy the last couple of years, and I don't..."

"Humans don't have them." Harlan closed his eyes, continuing to resist. "It's the penis bone." His laughter got the better of him once again.

Vieve rolled her eyes, "Childish." However, tomboy and scientist that she was, she took a moment to examine the bone in the light from her helmet before she discarded it. Inside the cabinet doors, one dismembered paw of the animal had its claws dug into the wood. "The attached leg must have propelled it forward."

Among the kitchen storage, Harlan and Vieve discovered pots, pans, and dishes; corroded canned foods, rotted goods in jars, and eating utensils—nothing of use or interest, until Harlan opened the last cupboard. Pushing aside tins for flour, sugar, and cornmeal, he reached to the back and pulled out a clear glass bottle full of brown liquid. Harlan was excited. "Have you ever heard of Templeton Rye, Vieve?"

"Of course, it's the pride of the state dating back to prohibition and bootlegging." Vieve's excitement grew as she crossed the room.

"I've only read about it."

"Does the bottle say Templeton?"

"No." Harlan pointed his light on a simple piece of parchment taped to the bottle. "All it says is 'The Good Stuff.'" He smiled.

Vieve's eyes lit up. "Could it still be good? Safe to drink?"

"It's been sealed and kept out of the light. At worst the alcohol might have evaporated, and it would taste bland and watery, but I don't think it could hurt you. If you can still smell alcohol and sugar, it's drinkable." Harlan uncorked the top with a loud, suctioned-popping sound. He inhaled the aroma and grinned even wider. He held the bottle out for Vieve to sample the scent.

"Mmmm, it's sweet. This might just be authentic."

"A one-of-a-kind opportunity. We should take this for later." Harlan replaced the top. "Our search hasn't been totally wasted. I suspect this will be the only spirit from the Thirties that we find all night."

"It's weird having all these cameras around and never knowing if you're on air." Audrey sat along with La Claire on a sofa they'd uncovered. The contents of the supply crate were spread out on the coffee table before them.

"Always assume the cameras are watching you." La Claire looked around the ceiling of the room. "If they're not, someone is."

Audrey leaned in, examining the pendant on La Claire's necklace. "That's very pretty. What's it made of?"

"Quartz crystal. It channels positive forces to me, balances, empowers, and allows me to stabilize emotions even when dealing with dark and evil spirits." La Claire was matter-of-fact, showing no appreciation of the aesthetic compliment.

Ax stood at a taller table behind them. The cloth that once covered it had been crumpled and discarded below. He unpacked several gadgets from his open case. Audrey joined Ax. "What are all these gizmos?" She reached to pick one up, and Ax instinctively blocked her hand. She pulled back, frowning.

Ax smiled, embarrassed. "Here, ah, let me show ya." He placed the piece she'd reached for in her hand. "That's an EMF detector."

"What's it do?"

"Everything that has energy emits electromagnetic fields, EMFs—powerlines, batteries, you, me, the earth—they all emit EMFs. This happens to be a very sensitive detector." He turned on the screen and put his hand under hers, cupping it to guide her. "When ya have it out in the open you pick up ambient fields, like the globe's, but then when ya move it close to a smaller emitter, like me for instance"—he swung her hand, with the device, close to his chest—"then ya get a small variation of the reading, because my field is adding to or altering the reading. Since ghosts are made entirely of energy, they put off a similar field, or even a stronger one. You might not be able to see them when they come right up to ya, but this will detect their EMF. You use it to detect spots where the EMF reading changes suddenly and then ya know where the spirit is or where it's been." Audrey smiled. They lingered touching hands another moment, then Ax let his hand drop. Audrey tested the device, swinging it back and forth from Ax's body.

"Pretty cool. Very hi-tech." Ax fought to conceal his elation. "So what else ya got?" she asked.

He selected another item. "This is an instant read thermometer." He pointed it to the wall and squeezed a trigger button. A red laser pointer appeared briefly on the wall then the screen gave a reading of 66 degrees. "Spirits can both emit and absorb energy, and heat is nothin' but energy, so we look for anomalous cold or hot spots to indicate their presence, too." Ax sampled three more locations around the room with similar results, and then pointed the thermometer at Audrey. The laser pointer showed up on her rear end. He held the device so she couldn't see the reading. "Wow, that is hot!" Audrey smiled, charmed. Ax was proud of himself.

"Besides that, I've got an HD digital camera with night vision, heat vision, and a couple other modes, plus an added infrared illuminator to cast more infrared light, aiding in picking up somethin'. My computer records the video feed and data streams. Normally I use a wireless mic to record myself as I'm investigating, but we're already wired, so I left that out. Oh, and this is an EVP recorder, electronic voice phenomena, to catch any paranormal noises."

Audrey nodded but looked puzzled. "How is the electronic voice phenomena recorder different from a regular audio recorder?"

Ax was thrown. "Umm, well, it's not really, I mean the recorder is a consumer recorder, but it transmits to my computer wirelessly to record. Sometimes you can't hear the spirits directly through the recorder, but they show up as interference between it and the laptop." Audrey nodded again but with an eyebrow raised. "Oh, I also use this to enhance its ability." He picked up one of the last devices. "It's a white noise generator. Many spirits can't make noises themselves, but when you provide the steady stream of background sound, they can distort it, and that's what ya actually pick up."

Audrey pondered, looking over the equipment. "So you use a regular get-it-at-the-electronics-megastore recorder, and if it doesn't pick anything up alone you fill the room with noise, and then it picks up ghostly sounds?" Ax nodded and started to respond, but she continued. "And you don't always get the sounds directly on the recorder, but only after it's transmitted to the computer?"

Ax thought she was ridiculing him. He nodded unenthusiastically. To his surprise, Audrey grinned. "So this is something even an amateur like me could set up for not that much money and start doing some ghost hunting of my own, huh?"

He was reinvigorated. "Most definitely." He lowered his voice for a suave quality. "Although, you may not want to do it alone."

"That's really cool." Audrey turned to La Claire, still on the sofa. "Did you catch any of that? Pretty advanced and impressive, don't you think?"

La Claire didn't look over. "Using a machine to make bread when you cannot cook, or a camera because you do not have the talent to paint, will never gain my admiration. I suppose those who are not blessed with a natural gift for perceiving spirits must fill the void as best they can, but I see no cause to applaud it."

Audrey looked to Ax. "I was only trying to be nice."

There was another doorway in the kitchen opposite where they'd entered. Beyond the door it was pitch dark, even when Harlan pointed his flashlight. He abandoned the whiskey on a counter corner. Once at the doorway, he noticed a few steps down leading into the next room. Vieve followed him down. With her light shining left and Harlan's right, they revealed windowless brick walls lined with large shelves and more freestanding shelves filling the room. A path continued from the steps with three aisles of shelves partitioned on either side. One had to step into the rows to see onto the deep storage racks. "I think it's a huge pantry," Vieve said. The wall adjoining the kitchen was also lined with dozens of pipes above the shelves, which protruded through the bricks.

"Where are all of these coming from?" Harlan asked.

"The coal furnace and water heater are in a separate shed outside. These probably fed water and steam heat to the entire house."

"Wouldn't those normally be in the basement?"

"The Drake mansion doesn't have a basement as far as I know."

"Isn't it a little strange, for a house this size, especially with the tornados Iowa gets?"

Vieve shrugged but agreed. She moved into the first row on one side while Harlan began searching on the other. Her side was filled with more stockpiles of food items while his bore kitchen extras including oversized pots, stacks of plates, a meat grinder, and other specialty utensils. The next row for Vieve stored laundry items: baskets, chemicals, and folded linens, along with a wealth of other household cleaners from the period. "There's silver polish over here if you were thinking about snatching anything from the dining room," she shouted. In the middle row on Harlan's side were boxes of decorations for every holiday and season of the year.

In the last row, Vieve struck pay dirt—boxes and boxes of candlesticks. "You were right. There are hundreds of candles here, plenty to light the whole house." She waited, expecting Harlan to show up, or at least reply with praises for her discovery, but she heard nothing. Concerned, she took care to be perfectly quiet. She didn't even hear Harlan checking boxes or shuffling items across the way.

She stepped out of the isle and anxiously scanned the third row across the way. Panic mounted as she checked the other isles. The small light cast from her helmet and basic flashlight hardly lit the room, but Harlan was nowhere to be found. As she double-checked the isles on both sides, she shrieked his name again and again. Finally, she dashed to the kitchen doorway where she was abruptly grabbed from behind.

Vieve screamed primally. She instinctively brought her arms up to protect her face and midsection, ready to fight for her life.

"I'm here, I'm here," Harlan said. "I didn't mean to startle you."

Vieve shoved him away. "Where were you? You scared the hell out of me! I was worried you'd—"

Harlan drew closer and grasped her trembling hands. "Calm down. Everything's OK. I'm sorry. There was another door in the corner, obscured by the shelves. I stepped in, just for a minute, but it seems we couldn't hear each other." Vieve was slowly calming. "Let me show you." He released her flashlight hand and took his own light out from under his arm. Still grasping her with one hand, he led her down the end isle on his side. At the very back, blocked by the shelving sides, was a small section where racks were omitted. Behind it, a narrow door was sunk into the brick wall. The door was peculiar compared to the rest of the house. With a half dozen vertically running planks, it was rough, had no finish, and looked more like a makeshift fence gate than a door in a mansion. They opened the door and stepped through.

Harlan pointed his light to the ceiling. It was completely glass, though all that could be seen were piles of leaves and accumulated debris outside. The walls of the room were windowless and lined with rugged, unfinished benches and cabinets. Harlan opened one, showing Vieve it was filled with tools. He pulled out a chisel. "I think this was a wood shop. Maybe Vinton was a woodworking hobbyist."

"Or someone in the house was. They had more help than just the nanny."

"Look down here at the end." He escorted her to the far end of the room, where a hodgepodge office was arranged. Papers were pinned on the wall, a desk was cluttered with documents, a file cabinet was jammed so full it couldn't close, and there was a small couch and record player in the corner. "I bet the office up front was for show, and well-kept, and this is where Vinton really did his work." Vieve agreed as she skimmed through the loose papers. Harlan shined his light on a large hand-drawn map on the wall. At the bottom, "Entrance" was marked, then a narrow hall or shaft began with long rooms extending off it, both left and right. Immediately after, another pair of chambers started, and so on and so on for ten rooms.

Vieve looked up to see what had caught Harlan's eye. "It's a coal mine. Room-and-pillar format. They mine out all of these long chambers, but they leave enough material between each room to support the ceiling. If you go too wide, they collapse. If you go too narrow, then you lose out on the mineral resources you didn't mine out."

"Must have been one of the Drakes' properties." Harlan panned the wall with his light. There were dozens of smaller maps throughout. Then Harlan looked down at Vieve and the desk. "Anything interesting?"

"Business contracts, state permits, progress reports, nothing unexpected."

Harlan scanned the desk then made a very audible "Hmm" sound. Vieve turned, waiting for his thoughts. "This desk looks hand made."

"Wasn't everything back then?"

"True, but the Drakes could have afforded a master craftsman's piece. This seems to have a number of little flaws, like the work of a novice. If Vinton dabbled in woodworking, I have to wonder if he made it."

"Could be."

"When I was a kid my father loved to woodwork, and I always helped. I still do when I get home to visit." Vieve smiled. "I've always planned to take it up myself once I'm out of school for good, and actually have free time." Harlan saw Vieve was growing impatient. "Whenever we made a piece of furniture like this, we always added a secret compartment, a drawer with a false bottom or something similar, for fun mainly, but something only the builder would know about. My parents' house has several dozen hiding spots."

"So you think Vinton might have put something like that in this desk?"

"A secret second office through a concealed door in the pantry—

there's no reason not to check." Harlan handed Vieve his flashlight. All lights shone on the desk. There were three drawers along the side. Harlan pulled the top drawer completely out. He sifted through its contents briefly and then upended it, scattering objects and notes everywhere. Vieve jumped. Harlan shot her an apologetic smile as he knocked on the bottom of the drawer both from inside and outside. He repeated this inspection with the second and third drawers but found nothing.

Next, Harlan pulled out the pen tray just under the top of the desk, the last drawer in the piece, but found nothing of interest there either. Finally, Harlan cleared the jumble from the desk surface, placed one ear down on the desktop, and proceeded to knock on it gently, moving his knuckles steadily to span the entire surface.

"A-ha." Harlan ceased knocking. "Let's see." He slid his hands inside the cavity where the pen tray had sat. They barely fit. He had to strain to press them in far enough, but after a few moments a mechanical click sounded. Vieve looked on curiously as Harlan grinned with satisfaction and a hatch swung down, up underneath the desk where one's legs would fit. It was hinged at the back and folded up flush with the bottom of the pen tray. When hanging down it had a file compartment, open on top and positioned at the very back, against the wall. "It wouldn't be much of a haunted mansion without hidden rooms and secret hiding places, huh?"

Harlan leaned down on his knees and beckoned for light. He reached back to the compartment and came out with a leather-bound volume. Both of their minds raced with anticipation. Harlan started to open it, but paused. "I hope it's not just an accounting ledger."

"Will you open it already?" When he turned the cover, a slip of paper fell to the floor. It was jagged along one side like a page torn from a small-bound pad. Harlan thumbed through the first few pages, each filled with handwritten paragraphs, as Vieve retrieved the scrap.

"It looks like a journal of sorts." Harlan looked to Vieve, but she didn't respond. Her focus was locked on the note. "Vieve?" She finally looked up with wide eyes and handed Harlan the slip.

No one heard my voice. Panicked screams had filled the air. I stood and declared, "Dead. He's dead." When I released his wrist, it too sounded the drum as it landed on the stage floor. "That's the second time he has died in my hands.

They looked at one another, both drunk with excitement. Harlan grabbed Vieve's hand and pulled her to sit on the small couch. With both helmets and flashlights compounded, the pages of the journal lit up brightly. The first page had a title in all caps:

FOR THOSE WHO WISH TO FOLLOW IN MY FOOTSTEPS: THE NOTES OF VINTON DRAKE.

A byline below read: "By Vinton Drake."
They both leaned in eagerly as Harlan turned the page.

In the broadcast truck, Nora punched through several cameras showing all the contestants over and over from different angles, but with two reading the journal and the others still lingering in the living room, there was no visual action. "Let's cut to commercial. When we come back, we'll open on a thermal camera." The commercials began. She punched up a camera from a pillar in the main hallway. The walls blocked its view into the living room where Ax, Audrey, and La Claire were waiting. With the click of a button, the camera switched into an eerie derivative of the previous image and immediately the features of the room turned black and indistinguishable. However, three human-shaped red, yellow, and orange figures appeared, floating in the darkness. Two stood next to one another while the other appeared to be seated.

FOR THOSE WHO WISH TO FOLLOW IN MY FOOTSTEPS: WHAT I DISCOVERED PART 1

Dear Reader,

The following is intended to guide those who may choose to retrace my footsteps or to investigate the exceptional outcome of my life, through my having met the magician Malvern Kamrar, what I subsequently discovered of him, and the results that followed. For the sake of understanding as deeply as possible, I will attempt to recount the details, not limited to what simply occurred so many years ago, but also of thoughts, rationales, and sensations so that the events can be relived and experienced, not merely retold and accounted for.

Signed,
Vinton Drake

It has to be pushing four in the morning. I hate this kind of drizzle, this slow drizzle where you can't see any rain falling, but the drops accumulate on you. It's just wet enough to conjure an array of stenches from the grime in the gutters, but insufficient to wash any of it away.

"A dime says I can put it right between the legs of that mailbox." I kick the rock at my feet sending it up the sidewalk and far right of its target; again. I start walking forward. "So what do I owe you now, forty cents?" I didn't always talk to myself. "I don't think I started until the war. No, no it was before that."

"Excuse me?" says a very expensively dressed man, as he and the sumptuous woman on his arm pass me by. I just shake my head and let my eyes drift away, settling back on the rock that is now, once more, at my feet.

"All right, double or nothing, I put it in that gutter across the street." I let it fly. The rock strikes the metal casing, producing a surprisingly resonant toll as it bounces away. I resume walking, wondering what that couple was doing out so late? "I know, I know, eighty cents. I don't have it on me, but believe me I'm good for it."

I've taken to walking the streets late at night long enough to know the type of people who wander the streets late at night. Either they're on their way to work; milk, newspapers, bakery and the like; or they're up to no good.

"Which are you?" I'm carrying a damp, stuffed bear and kicking rocks around, and no one is paying me for either. Working or causing trouble, either way it's unusual to cross such genteel individuals at this hour.

"Where are they going?" I hope they don't realize I'm following them and have been for several blocks. I didn't realize it myself until they cut through an alley and I had to jog ahead to keep them in sight. It would be hard to miss me if we hadn't walked into a uniquely bustling street at four in the morning. Though it's dark, there are small groups of men scattered about, lackadaisically dismantling tents and stages, booths and kiddy rides. "How did I pick up this habit of talking to myself?"

I soon encounter a vacant, wooden booth. "This was where I won the teddy bear." Hours ago this street was abuzz with activity. Strands of lights trimmed every structure. Children whizzed by chasing one another with sparklers or toy weapons; game workers and food venders shouted at passersby as young men tried, mostly in vain, to win their young ladies prizes, or just to show off, took to a challenge of strength among their buddies. Organ music dominated the foreground while, in the distance, the snap of detonated ladyfingers was punctuated with juvenile shrieks and giggles.

Your feet were as likely to find spilled popcorn or peanut shells as clear ground. The far end of the carnival bore the shadier attractions, with shows of human oddities and burlesque. "Behold, the most naked giant in the world," or something like that. Ignoring their beckoning, I stepped up to this shooting game.

The operator said my hands were steady and asked if I'd fought in the war before he handed me the gun. I said, "No," and proceeded to hit the bull's-eye five times in a row. "We have a winner!" he shouted. Several onlookers clapped. That's when he leaned close and asked if I was certain I wasn't in the war. I told him, "I was 'in' the war; the army saw fit to make me a medic. I never fired a shot. I've just always been able to shoot like this." "Their loss," he responded as he awarded me the bear.

It's odd that I should follow my curiosity only to be led back to where I began. "It is furthermore odd that I now find myself staring blankly at an empty carnival booth, and talking to it." I scan the area around me. The subjects of my investigation appear long gone.

"It was none of my business anyhow." No sooner than I finish my thought, I spot another pair. Two men dressed to the nines making their way up the street. "Gentlemen," I utter with a solitary nod as they pass. With hurried steps, they ignore me. It's unlikely coincidental discovering two sets of such out-of-place society types. I make the decision, this time consciously, to follow them.

It's unclear to me whether it's simply survival instincts or something deeper and more sinister that I have called upon to dictate my actions, but I manage to lurk just out of sight, yet remarkably close to the men. "Well–" no, I must stay quiet, but well within striking distance, were that my intention. I stealthily shift between shadows, always staying in patches darker than theirs. We emerge from the carnival's exhibition area and cross a set of railroad tracks, the means by which the group travels, I surmise. We even pass trailers, the mobile residences that accompany such traveling attractions, until finally the men turn into a dead-end alley. I recognize it as such a few steps in and jump back around the corner to observe as the men proceed.

The alley is narrow between two tall, brick buildings and terminates at a solid wall. No doors open into the alley, and no windows overlook it. It also lacks the garbage cans and debris one expects, at least if one spends much time in dark alleyways.

More curious yet is the small yellow and red striped tent positioned near, not next to, the wall at the alley's end. The tent appears to have a curtained door with an usher poised outside. Candles are lit atop two freestanding posts on either side of the tent's doorway. The men, now out of earshot, engage with the usher, who proceeds to draw the curtain back, and allow them entrance.

The tent is hardly large enough to offer standing room to two grown men, let alone to additionally house whatever it is the men are seeking, "And worthy of the anticipation I've developed through the recent events of the evening."

"I beg your pardon?" A startling voice draws me to turn. Two couples, as eloquently dressed as their predecessors, approach the alleyway.

"Please excuse me. I was muttering to myself."

One of the women interjects, "We mustn't dally." The group continues past. They too gain admittance to the usher's tent.

Dressed for a symphony in a tent for a flea circus. "It's a flea symphony!" I carefully scan up and down the street. It's empty. I turn back toward the alley, and after a long pause in contemplation I approach the tent.

The usher remains stoic as I draw near. Next to him sits a narrow table only large enough to support a worn wooden box no bigger than a loaf of bread. His posture is statuesque, his clothes are immaculate, but his face; his face is unsettling. It's worn, scarred, and ugly along with, as best and as simply as I can describe them, scheming eyes. Beyond the saturation of shadows in his features and the blackness of extremely dilated pupils, which would add an eerie element to any face, his face strikes me as truly sinister.

The usher breaks his stance. He reaches into his front pocket and withdraws a watch. "Good evening, sir." He speaks without looking up.

"Good morning, taking for granted your watch is functional." Now his gaze migrates to me, first with his eyes and a contemptuous reading, followed by his head.

"Indeed, but perhaps time is too short to belabor the point, sir. With your keenness for precision, I'm sure you are aware you've only three minutes for admission."

I add "pompous" to my mental list of descriptors for the usher. It should be well worth antagonizing him. "Thank you, I didn't realize?"

"Given the exclusive limit on guests, the let's say lavish ticket price, and the nature of our show, promptness is expected, sir. I'm afraid it's quite strictly enforced." His eyes fall back to his watch.

"Of course, and remind me, what was the price of admission?"

This time his gaze snaps up. His eyelids narrow with suspicion. "One thousand dollars, of course."

"Ah yes, that's right. I was thinking that is a little steep." Though it explains the aristocracy of those before me. "One doesn't grow wealthy through frivolous expenditures. You'll have to forgive me, but I've grown accustomed to never paying the asking price, and had my mind set on paying no more than seven hundred. How many seats are left anyway?"

My guise is weak, but he relaxes. He continues to search my face.

"There is one seat remaining, sir. The price is not negotiable."

"One seat, and less than one minute to fill it?"

"Correct."

"Wouldn't you rather sell one seat for seven hundred than have one empty?"

"Excuse me, sir, but let me assure you first, only a select few of the most affluent individuals share our audience and that thinking of it as simply paying full ticket price hardly does justice to our exhibition. Second, we find rather than requiring identification or special invitation, the extravagant price provides us the insurance that those who can afford to attend risk just as much as we do should any ill consequences arise, while at the same time ensures our distinguished guests their anonymity. Given the nature of our show, I'm sure you can understand."

That's the second time he so ominously avoided divulging any details as to the orientation of the show. My brimming curiosity gets the better of me. "Remind me, what exactly is the nature of your exhibition?" That was a foolish question.

His reaction is instant. Our eyes lock. His face bears an expression I've been subject to only a few times, but one never forgets. I've known too many killers to mistake that combination of rage and panic, but his is momentary. I've got the upper hand. His hesitation suggests he still has control, and furthermore he either has too much to lose to act, or lacks what it takes to act. Either way I know I'm already out of danger.

Already his passion is subsiding. That, however, doesn't put me any closer to walking through the tent doorway, so I go for the only thing I can think of that can drastically redirect this situation; any situation for that matter. I reach into my pocket and pull out a twelve thousand dollar roll of cash, give or take. I was at the carnival earlier, and I think I spent upward of four dollars.

The usher watches me, and as I'd hoped his disposition calms and swings closer and closer to my favor with every bill I count out. "My apologies, just panhandling for advanced particulars. Curiosity, I'm afraid, but that's why I'm here." I extend thirteen hundred dollars. He's still cautious.

"Of course, sir. I understand."

"Was it one thousand, you said?"

"That is correct."

Withdrawing the money, I count back the extra three hundred and return the surplus to my pocket. "I guess I'll just have to wait and see like everyone else." I place the thousand in his hand.

"Thank you, sir." He lifts the rickety lid of the wooden box and adds the money to an already bulging stack of bills then looks at his watch. "Not a moment to spare." He draws the curtain open. As I step inside, I immediately drop below street level onto a step. The tent only houses the open top of a staircase to some basement-level location that is currently cloaked in darkness. The stairs are old wood planks. Some are broken, most are off kilter, and each produces a ghostly creak when used. I have to search with each foot to blindly locate the step before trusting my weight to it. As is my habit, I count them as I submerge myself.

When the usher seals the tent, dampening the street and candlelight, a faint illumination on the floor below takes dominance. It trims the fronts of the last few steps in half rectangles, enough for me to proceed to the bottom with normally paced movement. "Nineteen."

The guiding light is escaping a bright room down a narrow hallway. Before entering, I hear murmurs of conversations and body movement. The doorway sits at the backright corner of the minuscule venue. The floor slants toward the front where a tattered and faded maroon curtain conceals a stage. With narrow aisles on all sides, there are five rows of six stationary, fold-down seats. Each chair is upholstered dark red with gold embroidery; only one is vacant. My demeanor is neither obtrusive nor covert, but no regard is paid to me by the aristocratic 29 occupants, deep into their own trifling conversations. The open seat is on the end of the back row, conveniently nearest to the door. I slip in, my presence detected only by the woman now seated beside me, and only with a disdainful glance, not at my face, but solely at my inconspicuous clothing.

I catch the movement of a shadow from the corner of my eye, and turn in time to see that stoic, scheming-eyed, sinister, and, oh yes, pompous usher reach for switches on the back wall. He proceeds to fade the house lights. The murmurs of the crowd diminish in volume in proportion with the lighting until both are extinguished. Only four stage-mounted lights that cast up onto the curtain remain. In the darkness, I'm unable to see into the back of the room. I can't be sure if the usher crept back out, but with the silence of the audience I am able to hear the door latching, closing the entryway.

The curtain raises and a lone performer is revealed. My self-proclaimed extraordinary awareness for my surroundings is immediately replaced by total mental saturation of disbelief; disbelief and only disbelief, for a long, long moment.

I've come to pride myself as having exceptionally gated my emotional responses, as having the refined ability to effectively suppress my responses in favor of continuing to function calculatedly. I'd never claim to be without fear or anger, or a bevy of emotions, positive or negative, that can temporarily consume an individual. In fact, it is the keen perception of one's emotional onset, conditioned awareness of associated external effects, and systematic emotional counters that grant me the capacity to function this way. This has served me in life and certainly in the service of country. I've often considered some degree of this ability to be a defining line between capable and deficient soldiers. This is the only reason I do not appear radically hysterical at this very moment.

My breathing is steady and my body is still as I reel my thoughts in for evaluation. The man revealed behind the curtain speaks. Slowly his words begin to infiltrate the select stimuli allowed into my currently perceived world.

"Again, thank you for coming ladies and gentlemen. I realize this is an exceptionally peculiar hour for a magic show, but you'll soon find, as I imagine you're already anticipating, this is an equally peculiar magic show."

He's dressed in black, slim-fitting clothes. His speech is reserved, not at all the flashy and boisterous personality one expects of a magician. The stage is dim around him, lit only by the stage-level lights. The performer's dark clothes flow indistinguishably into the shadows and then into the abyss.

He raises his hands as if lifting an invisible platform, and two spotlights brighten in matching pace. The stage is barren with the exception of some sole, draped monolith in a corner and two grand shadows of the magician now cast on the stage wall. He lowers his hands back to his sides deliberately, and it appears that one of the shadow men behind him follows his actions more slowly than the other.

"My name is Malvern Kamrar—"

I knew this man. Not as Malvern Kamrar, and I didn't know him well in the sense of knowing what his dog's name was when he was a child, or whether he prefers blondes or brunettes. We weren't even friends, but I did know him well, well in the sense of knowing exactly what he was made of, of knowing he could work with calm, steady hands while the entire world around him was bleeding to death or exploding, and knowing how he faced death. He served as a stretcher-bearer, a medic just as I did, rushing forward with the troops for the first time, and he died as a medic. It wasn't my habit to comfort men as they passed; it never seemed prudent to waste precious time on lost causes. As it happens, after an undoubtedly mortal wound to the spine, I had to lift him off another injured man, and in that moment he died in my arms.

"—Malvern Kamrar, the Master of Shadows."

Momentarily, his shadows morph into larger figures with devilish horns and crisp fluttering peaks emanating from their shoulders, like black flames, and then return to matching his form.

"I won't burden you with conventional tricks that build toward a climactic finale nor will I squander with any further delays. For you, I have prepared this single spectacle."

He crosses to the cloaked device behind him. His shadows follow, one step behind. He takes hold and pulls the prop to center stage. Though the object's shadows match its form, his shadows become first pillars, and then elongated pyramids.

"Ladies and gentlemen, I give you death. In this instance as made famous by Revolutionary France." His shadows both come to rest as Eiffel Tower–like shapes. He whips the covering away, revealing a guillotine. The audience communally gasps.

"I will require the aid of one volunteer from the audience. Is there anyone present with a medical background?" One woman in the second row raises her hand. "What type of experience do you have, Miss?" The woman is bold.

"I was a nurse, a boarding school nurse for three years, before I was married." She glances at her husband beside her.

"I see. And in your three years as a school nurse, how many patients in life-or-death peril were subject to your treatment?"

She responds humbly, "None, sir."

"I don't mean to belittle your professional history, but aid training is not as relevant for our purposes as is familiarity with...mortality. Does anyone here believe himself to be well versed in...such life experiences?"

For a long moment, no one moves or speaks. Considering direct confrontation summons anxiety, I push it aside as I have my fright and confusion, and instead concentrate on curiosity—on bringing curiosity to the surface. That is an emotion I'm comfortable with exhibiting. "I was a medic in the war," I understatedly offer.

"Ahh, then you have both. Would you join me on stage, sir?"

I stand. As I approach, Malvern removes his jacket and neatly places it on the stage floor. With no steps, I must place my back against the front of the stage and hop up so that I am first seated on its edge before I stand to join him.

"I'll ask but one favor of you, sir. Oh, your jacket, would you mind removing your jacket first, please?" As I comply, I wonder if he recognizes me, though that seems the trivial question of the situation. Malvern rolls his sleeves back, so I emulate his preparation.

"Very good, sir, now all that I ask of you is to check my wrist for my pulse." He closes the short distance between us and holds his arm out. It is unmistakable. Under face-to-face review, I can see the scar above his right eye from a gash I personally stitched closed. I take his wrist. "Can you feel my heartbeat, sir?"

"Yes."

"Excellent." He pulls away and then steps offstage into the minuscule wings briefly. He returns with a wooden stool. "I'll ask that you continue to monitor my heartbeat while I"—he strikes a smile with one eyebrow raised—"execute this trick." Dropping the stool behind the body platform of the guillotine, he pats the seat twice, beckoning me.

From the seat, I watch as Malvern proceeds. Through the entire performance, his shadows continue to defy him through off-time reactions, independent movements, and shape distortions. Often, one shadow will precede his action while the second follows a beat behind like ballet choreography, rhythmic and beautiful, though they move to the horrific guillotine and, pulling the cord hand over hand, draw its blade toward the peak. Malvern strains as though the blade is heavy and won't budge, but when his shadows assist they manage it more easily. As the last of the steel withdraws from the neckclamp, a metallic vibrato, like that of an unsheathed sword, pulses through the room. Many of the onlookers quiver. Several have captivated faces; others shake their heads with suspicious smiles. One man in front kneels from his seat and stretches left to right searching with his eyes. No doubt, he's trying to identify a clue to how the trick will be performed, a mirror, trap door, or the like. From where I sit, I can detect no such tools. Though their faces speak loudly, the room is perfectly silent. With the blade raised, the Malvern Trio, man and shadows, lock it into the triggering arm.

Malvern produces a dark hood from below the device. "Once I'm in position, I'll ask our friend to once again update you with the status of my heartbeat then I will engage the device. From experience, I have learned that for both our sakes it is best to conceal my head, neck, and shoulders with a covering. We wouldn't want to ruin any of your elegant wears." This elicits a few snickers as he turns to me. "Particularly yours, sir." He pushes an arm into the hood and holds it up for examination.

Malvern draws a long slender knife from a pant pocket. "There is nothing special about this material which would alter the damage of the blow." He demonstrates how easily the knife cuts through an edge of the material with a small slit. "Please trust that in a few moments there will be no question of that fact." One shadow places a hood on its head as it moves to the guillotine. First Malvern, then the second shadow, follow. The hood is long with ample excess that bunches into a pile around his neck. He lies on the bed of the device, face down. I believe this is authentic. In the event the blade is unable to cut clear through, it's better to cut the spine for instantaneous death than to cut the throat and risk death from bleeding out.

Malvern slides up, closes the neck clamp around his throat, and then extends his arm to me.

"My pulse again please."

I wrap my fingers around his wrist. "It's a good, strong pulse. A little elevated from before." Adrenaline, I suspect.

"Please continue to monitor it."

Everyone in the crowd is holding their breath. Malvern reaches with his other hand to the triggering arm and with no delay, he grabs and jerks it back. The blade is swift. It drops in an instant with a slicing wisp. There's barely a difference between the sound of its cutting of air or its cutting of flesh. It's smooth and crisp in motion and stops with only a slight collision; hardly indicative of the blow it delivers. Malvern's head drops to the floor along with half of the hood material, cleanly cut from the rest. It bounces once, up a foot, then lands and proceeds to roll over twice before the slack in the material retards the momentum. These thuds are the first audible sounds in the room since he spoke.

I pay close attention to my fingertips. On the moment of impact, the pulse ceased. I adjust and wait for another beat; I detect none. I expected the heart to have a few residual beats; simply carrying out the last message the brain sent the muscles. I was desperately honed to this in my attention and could not have missed it. His arm is now limp weight in my hand. As my other senses seep in, I pronounce the verdict. "Dead, he's dead." No one notices my declaration. The crowd panicked. Most scramble in the dark for the exit. There are screams of terror as well as pain. I assume people are trampling one another to escape. I stand, releasing Malvern's arm. It raps thunderously against the floor. When the sound echoes back amidst the screams it draws my attention back to Malvern. I look down upon him, his head four feet from his body. The hood wicks the bloodshed. Stains travel upward in the material. "That's the second time he's died in my hands."

"The door is locked, we're trapped!" are the only decipherable words from the audience. I surmise from the lasting darkness that

I'm the only one who was paying attention when the house lights were lowered and accordingly decide that I should move for them to assist the panic. As I leap down from the stage I announce, "Calm down and clear the way. I can find the lights." My progress is immediately impeded by the struggling mass of bodies.

One man finds me with a hand on my back. I can't see his face, but his voice is unflustered. "Lead the way, Slick." Moving with me, he assists by pulling people up out of the way as I push further toward the switches.

"Indeed, do please calm down. Everything is quite fine." The words come from behind me. I turn to find Malvern. He is upright and moving, his neck intact and unmarred. The guillotine is empty and the split hood discarded. Malvern lifts his and my jackets and dusts them off.

"Please, quiet down and return to your seats. The door will be unlocked in good time. Now please compose yourselves." Slowly, members of the mob look to the stage and start to settle. Malvern tosses my jacket to me, straightens his shirtsleeves, and slides his own jacket back on. Finally, the crowd returns to order. I notice Malvern's shadows now appear in sync with him, only they lack their craniums. "Very whimsical."

"The doors have only been locked for your own protection." Malvern raises one hand deliberately, proportionally the house lights fade up. I glance to the switches and find no one controlling them. "Thank you for coming," are Malvern's final words as his other hand commits an inverse action and both the stage-front lights and spotlights drown to black. People look around at one another. I can now see the man next to me who tried to assist with the lights. He stands out from the others, not only in his collectedness, but while his clothes are expensive, they're sleek and dark, quite opposite the frills and ornate attire of the others, like a man of means, but who wishes to blend in rather than flaunt his status—a notion with which I can identify.

We lock eyes after he looks me up and down. He smirks and gives me a single nod. There's nothing particularly distinguishing about the man's build or face except for a nose best described as flattened; the effect one might expect from a career boxer who would have had it broken several times in his life. I can't help but suspect he may have a part in all of this. Was he the one who directed everyone's attention to the locked door and away from Malvern's body? Perhaps he's a planted conspirator of Malvern's, or even just security mixed into the crowd to prevent panic from turning to violence? Sometimes desperation encourages uncharacteristic behavior, one of many observations I developed during my time in the service. Then again, he might very well suspect me of the same subterfuge.

After a few moments pass, the man nearest the door attempts it again and discovers it's unlocked. Everyone, including the flat-nosed man, move to the door. I wait back. Of course, the door is congested with too many people in too big a hurry, but my hesitation is calculated. I search the stage darkness for indications of an explanation. My, and everyone else's, attention was drawn away from the stage for a long time. Our concern was on the locked door.

Malvern's performance was unmistakably authentic as far as I can tell. I was holding a man's arm with a heartbeat, and I am quite convinced that someone died in my hands tonight. He wasn't the first, and it's not a feeling easily synthesized. However, with this post-execution redirection of our focus I can surmise it would be more than sufficient time to clear the stage of a body and return a man from hiding.

"This, unsettling as it may be, would only explain one of Malvern's resurrections."

9:00PM

Vieve and Harlan were enthralled. A digital beep broke the silence. Harlan's watch read 9:00PM. "Maybe we should head back and meet up with the others."

Vieve agreed. Harlan gently closed the aged volume. They passed back through the pantry and gathered a box of candles. Through the kitchen, Harlan collected the whisky bottle along with a stack of saucers from the cupboards. Finally, they crossed back through the dining room. On Harlan's request, Vieve retrieved the pair of candelabra he'd noticed earlier.

They found Ax exploring the living room with his digital camera, watching the night-vision screen as he panned side to side. Audrey followed him with the EMF sensor. La Claire ignored the others. Only Audrey noticed Harlan and Vieve. "Find anything good?"

"And then some," Vieve said. Harlan pulled the dust cloth off of another table and proceeded to lie out his haul of goods. Vieve did the same, then picked up the leather-bound book. "We found Vinton's journal. It's full of some very intriguing accounts."

Harlan took a small lighter from his bag and lit one candle. "They did have a fire truck outside, right?" He chuckled as he tipped the burning candle over one of the kitchen saucers allowing several drops of wax to splatter in the center. Next, he planted the base of another candle in the wax and held it a few seconds. Once cooled, the candle stood independently. Within minutes, Harlan replicated twenty candle saucers and loaded both candelabra with three fresh sticks. Harlan lit and dispersed five of the saucers through the room.

Vieve studied the journal. "It might be worth it for us to read through this. There could be some crucial clues."

Ax glanced over the book briefly, noting its length. "Nah, I don't want to burn any time on this. We can read it any time after tonight. For now, we need to take advantage of our exclusive opportunity to search the house." Audrey agreed. "You can stay and read it if ya' want, though."

Harlan slid a chair under the chandelier in the room's center, climbed, and affixed another dozen candles to the antique's still intact holders. "He's right, there'll be time for that later, we need to put on a good show for the cameras." Harlan continued to light the chandelier candles. Combined, all the flames lit the room well. "Where should we start?"

"The study," La Claire butted in. "The spirits are loud." She put a hand to her temple and closed her eyes. "It's difficult to isolate one voice, but it seems many are telling me to start there." She pointed toward the office doorway. "Wait. There's one, one louder than all the others. He is shouting, telling us to stay back. Stay out."

Harlan looked up to Ax, but Ax only shrugged. "No argument here," Harlan said. "To the study." Harlan lit the sticks on both candelabra then handed one to Vieve. Madam La Claire led the way through the entry of the office. Ax followed with his camera as well as a thermometer. Audrey continued to scan with Ax's EMF sensor. Vieve followed while Harlan leisurely took up the rear, though the last to the door was the glacially moving camera pillar striving to keep them in view.

The room sat in the corner of the house and had windows on two sides. The walls were lined with shelving, almost completely filled with books. At the center of the room rested the ornate desk and chairs Harlan had spotted earlier.

"Hmm." La Claire crossed the office. "Yes. This room is full of energy." She swayed with her arms open as if basking in warmth, but then stopped abruptly. "Bad energy. Very bad." She floated around the room and gently allowed her fingers to contour a variety of items, including a pen on the desk, then the back of the desk chair. "This is where Mr. Drake, Vinton, would sit to do his work. He spent many an hour toiling here." Vieve shot a questioning expression to Harlan. He raised his eyebrows and shrugged.

An odd table sat in one corner, butting against the shelving. Light from the five helmets danced about the room, but the addition of Vieve and Harlan's candles lit it low and evenly. Harlan examined the table. It was tall with a padded leather top. "Perhaps it isn't a table at all," he muttered to himself. It was long, had a joint in the middle to elevate half the surface, and bore caster wheels on its legs.

La Claire rounded the desk and came again to its front. She slid her fingers along its surface, then moved her hand to the back of the smaller chair set before the desk. "Hmm." She then dropped into the chair. "Ohh! This, yes the magician, Kamrar, sat here. He and Vinton spoke. No, they quarreled. Kamrar rose." La Claire stood. She then moved over and took the other seat. "Money, debt, property, secrets; Vinton was angry, but..." She quieted, concentrating.

Ax scanned the room repeatedly with the camera though the screen only showed green-hued images of the other contestants. Audrey's EMF readings were equally unremarkable. Harlan placed his candelabrum on the desk and proceeded to skim the titles in the shelves.

"Ouch!" Everyone looked as La Claire doubled over, clutching her stomach, as if in pain. "A knife. He was stabbed. Vinton was stabbed here by Kamrar." She sprang to her feet, knocking the chair over backward. Enlivened, Ax and Audrey doubled their efforts scanning the room. Ax switched to monitoring his thermometer and elated at a temperature parody. Audrey rushed to see for herself, but La Claire fell to the floor.

"He bled, he bled here. Warm blood soaked his clothes. He was too drained to yell, but he tried." She reached toward the door and spoke with a strained, deflated whisper. "Martha, Martha my love. Danger! Get the children! Leave me. Leave me behind. Take the children away." She curled into a fetal position. "Martha, I love you." Her breathing was heavy and exhausted. Both Audrey and Vieve were drawn in, focused on La Claire exclusively. La Claire rose to one knee. Vieve and Audrey helped her stand. La Claire stepped backward, guiding them out of the spot where she had laid. "Kamrar stood, here. Vinton's words were too soft to reach anyone else. This is where Kamrar watched Vinton die." Shivers moved up and down both Vieve and Audrey's spines.

Ax switched his cam to thermal detection mode. On screen, the features of the room became defined in a red, orange, and yellow pallet. Ax could see a decidedly cooler spot in blue and violet surrounding the entry. "Something's drawing all the heat at the door."

La Claire looked to the door. "The killer moved to the kitchen next." She marched out, across the living room and toward the kitchen. Everyone followed.

As they moved, Harlan asked, "Ax, by chance do you carry an ultraviolet light in your kit?"

"Nah."

Harlan shrugged. "I'm too ignorant in forensics to know if blood would show up after 80 years anyway. It might be worth coming back and checking that area with all of your gear though, to see if any readings confirm Galva's"—he searched for an appropriate word—"supposition."

Ax had forgotten his disfavor for Harlan in the excitement as he agreed it was a good idea. Audrey waited for Ax. She was thrilled. Ax put a hand on her back to move into the kitchen together.

"Vieve," Harlan called. She let him catch her. "Half the books in there had to do with medicine: surgery, anatomy, diagnostics. Do you know why they'd have had a library like that?"

"Yes, actually. Many of the coal workers used to call him Dr.

Drake. You know, he was a medic in World War One, and I guess he had a year or so of med school. He didn't go back to get a degree or anything, but apparently he used to handle all the first aid and emergencies in the mine himself and even opened a hospital for the town. He supposedly carried a medical bag everywhere he went. It can be seen in many photos of him in and around the mine, and if there was a cave-in or an accident and someone was hurt, he'd treat them. So many of the workers were uneducated. They probably just figured he was a genuine doctor, and of course there weren't any alternatives if you were injured down in the mine. Most couldn't afford a real doctor anyway. An experienced medic with a year of school was better than nothing, I suppose. I guess he must have continued his medical study independently." She grinned. "That or he bought all those books just to keep up appearances."

"Thanks." Harlan smiled. He and Vieve were last to enter the kitchen.

The room looked more like the heart of a home once it was lit by the candles that Harlan and Vieve toted. La Claire was already across the room. She stood before the sinks with her hands on the counter's edge. "Martha was here. She was preparing coffee for her husband's guest." The medium traced objects with her fingers just as before. "But she got a sickening feeling, like something was wrong." La Claire scanned the counter tops. Within arm's reach was a block of knives. "She noticed one of the knives was missing. That's when she knew...no." La Claire appeared puzzled for a moment. Ax followed her with his camera.

"Her first thought was for the children. She feared one had taken the knife. Then she heard a sound, heavy breathing." La Claire turned quickly. "Kamrar was there and on her in a matter of seconds." La Claire fell back but caught herself on the counter's edge in front of the sinks. "He plunged the blade into her shoulder, aiming for her heart. She was paralyzed in fear. His rage was animalistic, savage. He withdrew the knife and planted it directly in his target the second time."

La Claire broke from her trance and spoke to the others directly.

"At least her death was quick compared to Vinton's. She didn't have to suffer bleeding out." La Claire stepped away from the spot but stopped and turned back. She closed her eyes and placed her index fingers on her temples. "As she fell, she grasped for a hold, grasped for life, and she reached a cabinet door with her hand." La Claire stepped forward and lifted her hand slowly to a cupboard door near the sink. Audrey and Vieve hung on her words. Harlan was reserved while Ax swung his camera back to her and zoomed in closer, switching between the thermal and night-vision variations of image.

When La Claire opened the cabinet, a metallic object flickered in the sparse light. A long carving knife slammed down, lodging tip first into the countertop. La Claire gasped and winced as she covered a nick on her hand. She scrambled backward. Vieve and Audrey caught her from behind.

"Oh, my God," Audrey exclaimed. "Did you see that? It nearly took her head off!" Ax dashed over and took readings inside the cabinet.

"That's impossible." Vieve looked to Harlan. "Harlan, we were just in here. You opened this very cabinet half an hour ago, and that knife wasn't there, was it?"

Harlan's was calm. "No, it wasn't there." Vieve was irritated by Harlan's lack of reaction. She held La Claire's hand up and diagnosed the wound in the direct light from her helmet.

"It's the spirit," La Claire said. "The family is here in the house, but so is Malvern. It's as if they're his prisoners. Enslaved by the unresolved mystery and bound by Malvern's hold. He was the one warning me not to enter the study when the others begged me to go. I believe he steered the knife. Malvern doesn't want us to uncover the truth. He doesn't want to let them go. That's why he tried to kill me. He knows that I'm the one who can expose him." Vieve, Audrey, and Ax were motionless, watching La Claire with awe.

Harlan interrupted, "That or she planted the knife." All four looked to him with contempt.

"You were right here watching just like the rest of us, Harlan." Vieve was curt. "It nearly killed her. How could she have planted that, and why?"

"She was the first in here before the rest of us, and the knives were right there. All she had to do was squeeze it in between the door and a shelf, and let it out when the time was right. That or she slid it up her sleeve and let it drop when she had her arm up. She wouldn't be the first supposed medium to use basic sleight-of-hand to fake evidence of spirits and powers. You have to admit it conveniently helps to support her story, which there's not one other bit of evidence for."

"Well something I can't explain just happened here." Vieve turned her back on Harlan.

"Spirits can hurt or even kill whether you believe in them or not, Harlan," La Claire added.

Harlan became irritated. "It's not even a difficult trick. You don't have to be Harry Blackstone to palm a knife in the dark with your back to the audience." He stepped up to the knife in the counter. "I don't even think gravity alone could force the blade into the counter from only a two-foot fall." He struggled to dislodge the blade. "Did you actually see the knife fall, here in the dimly lit room, or did you just see some reflective object up there, then see her pull her hand back and then see the knife in the counter a split second later? It's no different from a magician's disappearing trick. She has all of our attention on her hand as she moves it up to the cupboard." He mimicked with his hand up. "Meanwhile in the hand we're not paying attention to she pulls the knife from concealment in her clothes, then as she shrieks and winces with the extended hand"—he whipped his hand backward and at the same time slammed the blade back into the countertop—"she plants the knife with a loud thud. All she had to do was give her hand a little nick before she performed the trick, and everyone thinks the knife flew by." Harlan turned to find the others had walked out on him. Exasperated, he removed his helmet and turned the lens to his face. "Well, I hope you at least got that."

Outside, Walter watched the live broadcast on a flat-screen monitor in the corner of his oversized trailer, along with several executives. He was deep in conversation when Jason burst in without bothering to knock. He toted a laptop under his arm. Jason spoke before Walter could scold him.

"Two million sir, we're up to two million unique online visitors, and they're averaging over 50 minutes on us." He plopped the computer down and flipped up the screen. The browser window had dozens of thumbnail-sized video frames. Most bore motionless images inside the house with only a few showing activity from the contestants. Beside the mural of video feeds a larger frame showed Harlan's helmet cam focused on his face, after which it returned to the angle of view from atop Harlan's head. Everything on screen was framed in advertising banners and promotional links. There was a counter near the bottom that read 2,113,995. "See, another hundred thousand since I headed this way."

"That's fantastic." Walter socked Jason in the arm, forgetting he wanted to lecture him about knocking. Several of the others congratulated Walter as they crowded around the computer. The viewer total continued to gain. "Just imagine the ratings." Walter looked back up to the telecast monitor, after which he checked his watch and then proceeded to exit the trailer hurriedly and without uttering another word.

In the broadcast truck, everyone was on the edge of their seats following the action. Walter stepped into the truck and cleared his throat. "Nora, you know you're five minutes past your scheduled commercial break."

Nora glanced to him briefly. "We'll have to double up next break, Walt. I'm not cutting away from this for anything."

La Claire led Vieve, Audrey, and Ax back across the living room, leaving Harlan behind. Her next impressions came from upstairs. She insisted that the choir of voices beckoned her there. At the top of the steps, they were met with another camera pillar. La Claire moved, often closing her eyes, as if she heard something that no one else could, but couldn't quite determine its source. She had to turn her ears to each door they passed to test whether these voices grew in intensity. They passed a pair of bedrooms followed by a washroom and closet opposite one another in the hall. Both doors were open.

The next set of doors had another bedroom to one side and a closed door to the other. La Claire put her ear to the door and listened.

Vieve, Audrey, and Ax quieted themselves, allowing her to concentrate. She grasped the doorknob and turned it slowly. An unsettling metallic grinding resonated. "It was here," she said as she peeked in through the cracked doorway. The door swung with a creaking wail as she opened it further and revealed a child's bedroom. As they entered, Harlan rejoined the group.

"Be careful," Vieve said. "No telling where another knife or something heavy and blunt could drop from." La Claire acknowledged her warmly.

To Harlan, this was the saddest room so far. The beds were half sized and neatly made while a dozen wooden toys, a horse, a car, army men, and a train engine, were spread out on the floor. Pajamas for a toddler were even laid out. Everything was coated in the dust of nearly a century. "It bears the clearest impression of absence and tragedy."

La Claire probed and sensed the room along with its contents, and then walked the others through her perception. She told them that the middle child, a son, was watching the other boy, the youngest, while the oldest child, the girl, prepared a bath. She even mentioned that when the Drakes had company, the girl would often take over for the mother and attend the other two kids, though that night was odd because the nanny wasn't there as she normally would have been. La Claire described how Malvern crept to the door and watched for a moment while the two boys played, but he waited too long and they noticed him. They ran and hid under the bed, but Malvern was able to reach under and drag them out, slitting each one across the neck mercilessly. She also recounted that with the water running in the bathtub, the older girl didn't hear. Malvern was able to move from room to room, striking each member of the family without alerting any of the others.

La Claire pushed past the others mid-description to a passage that adjoined the washroom next door. It was slightly ajar. She kicked the door in, producing a loud strike followed by a tremendous thud as the door collided with the sink inside. La Claire stormed in and pantomimed, grabbing the girl from her knees before the bathtub, lifting her to her feet by her hair, and then mercilessly slaying her. Everyone but Harlan raced to the doorframe to witness her demonstration. La Claire looked up from the envisioned body's resting place.

"All that remained was to dispose of the bodies and evidence. Kamrar knew a thing or two about making people disappear. He could have burned them, buried them, he had the whole place to himself after that. He cleaned the blood away, put the kitchen and study back in order, made the children's beds, and that was that." Vieve, Audrey, and Ax nodded their understanding. Again, Ax surveyed with his equipment. La Claire smiled with satisfaction.

"What about Malvern himself?" Harlan asked. "You said his spirit was here jailing the others, but it sounds like he made it out just fine. How do you account for that?"

"I'm glad you asked." La Claire's eyes gleamed. "It's true he committed his crimes perfectly and without injury, but he didn't make it out at all. I noticed that first thing when we entered the house."

Everyone returned to the front entryway downstairs. With eyes closed, La Claire began again. "Kamrar was very proud of himself, overly confident, and didn't even hurry to get away. He took his time. Not only was he careful about his cleanup, he basked in his deeds, sitting in Vinton's chair, lying in one of the children's beds. He even went through many of their possessions in hopes of taking something valuable, but that couldn't be traced back should he sell it. However, suddenly he became very uncomfortable. The spirits of his victims were awakening, and he could sense it."

La Claire put her hands on the wall as if information were streaming from it. "He decided to get out and rushed to here, but he found he couldn't open the door. You see, in death the family had powers that he could not match. He panicked. In a sweaty fury he checked every window and door, each time met with resistance from the spirits, and each time growing further out of his wits. By the time he returned here, to try this door again in desperation, he was verging on insanity. Perhaps he was insane to begin with to have massacred a family in this way, but now he was hysterical and the spirits kept pushing him."

La Claire took a long pause, as if taken aback by something the wall had told her. She stroked her hand across it, and then moved her fingers to the frame of a painting that hung askew nearby. "Kamrar took his own life in the end." Vieve and Audrey gasped. "It's sad, really. The spirits of the family were enraged by their murders just as you or I would be, but in driving him to suicide, they invited him into the world of their powers. If they'd let him leave, perhaps he would have been caught, maybe he would have left a confession upon his own natural death, or maybe someone like myself would have come sooner. In any of those cases with the tragic mystery uncovered, they could have been freed, but instead they brought Kamrar over, and with the rage of his own gruesome death the balance of power was shifted to his advantage again. He was left in control and has been so ever since." La Claire opened her eyes and shook her head with pity.

Everyone was convinced but Harlan. "Assuming Malvern expertly disposed of the family's bodies and left no evidence, what happened to Malvern's remains? Why haven't they surfaced? Wouldn't they be right here?"

La Claire shook her head. "His control depends on maintaining the mystery. Most spirits want their bodies found so they can finally rest. Kamrar needs the mystery, so his powers live on. Kamrar's spirit hid his own remains. Perhaps if we were to tear this place apart down to every last board and brick, it could be discovered. Then again, time may have done away with it completely by now."

"And the other deaths?" Harlan asked. "How do you explain the two policemen killed, the nanny poisoned, and the couple that were electrocuted?"

"Innocent bystanders. I don't sense their spirits here. Kamrar couldn't have them uncover the truth, so he dispensed with them, much as he tried to do with me in the kitchen."

Harlan frowned. "Are the spirits going to be gone now that you've solved the case? I mean, we're all safe now, right?"

"No one is safe." La Claire's tone was grave. "No, the spirits remain. It's going to be a fight to get rid of them, a fight with Kamrar. The house must be exorcised. It will take a number of people, joined in ceremony, and led by an intuitive, such as myself, in order to force Kamrar's spirit out. I believe that once Kamrar is gone, the others will cross over on their own. Of course, I'd be willing to return and see to the cleansing, and to help these poor trapped souls."

The on-air monitor in the broadcast truck held a camera view centered on La Claire. Her conclusion aired like a plea to the public. The crew was quiet. The exciting sequence seemed to have climaxed. After another moment, Nora faded the screen to black and then cut to commercial.

Harlan turned to Ax. "What were your readings in the rooms we just visited? Did you pick up any figures or anomalies?"

Ax shrugged. "Ya' know, there were a few cold spots, a couple other places I'd like to test further."

"Just out of curiosity, were they consistent with the spots Galva identified as particularly significant?"

Ax sighed and glanced to Audrey who looked at him with anticipation. "Not exclusively."

"Hmm," Harlan voiced.

As Ax went on, he spoke toward Audrey, not to Harlan. "The spirits themselves are constantly moving, though. I need to do a thorough and systematic search of every room to identify them conclusively and locate their current whereabouts." Audrey was satisfied.

"Very well. Where to next?" Harlan asked.

Before Ax could make a suggestion, La Claire imposed, "I'm very exhausted." She leaned her weight on the wall and reached one hand toward Audrey. Audrey helped to steady her. "Communing with the dead is a draining task. I think I need to rest for a bit." Ax moved to her and took her other arm. Together Audrey and Ax helped her toward the living room.

"A break for dinner then?" Again Harlan didn't display the empathy for La Claire as everyone else. He and Vieve followed the others. Harlan spoke softly to Vieve, "Are you buying all of this?"

"I don't know what to believe, Harlan." She quickened her steps to separate from him, and she entered the living room alone. Harlan let her go.

Ax and Audrey helped La Claire to the couch. "We might as well have a bite to eat while we rest, hadn't we?" Ax slid another seat up to the central table. Harlan retrieved Vinton's journal while the other four gathered and perused the sealed ration packages. He sat at a distance and flipped the volume open to the second chapter.

For Those Who Wish to Follow In My Footsteps:
What I Discovered Part 2

The last time I visited the alleyway was at the same hour the following night, "4 a.m." Intuition told me I would find no tent or usher, and only a locked door, but the same curiosity that took me down those stairs initially insisted I investigate just the same. "A man has to fill his time, anyway." The alley was deserted and so deprived of light that I only discovered the padlocked doorway on the ground when I caught my toe and fell over it.

I'd returned to that place earlier in the daylight, around noon. The streets were active, and service trucks blocked the alleyway. From the front street, I located a decrepit structure I estimated to be above the theater. It was neighbored on both sides by active factory buildings, but its own doors and windows were boarded over. Many of the factory workers were out on the street taking their lunches.

Sweaty, greasy, crude, and cursing, for better or for worse, I doubted they would consider me a social peer. Leery, their lips tightened when I approached. I broke the silence when I sat and shared some admiring, though lewd, words for an attractive woman on the opposite sidewalk. "Excuse me, did I say that out loud? I have a bad habit of talking to myself." Eliciting several smiles, I proceeded to invite them to share my cigarettes, after which most were willing to answer my questions.

Years ago the entire block was tenanted by a motion picture company. The larger buildings were empty in back, ground to roof, through three floors and built with no windows for use as filming stages. They'd build large sets inside. The smaller building between them, atop the theater, housed the studio offices. The window offices in front were for executives, directors, producers and general big shots while the rear was designed for film developing and editing, again built windowless.

Though generous with information, the workers knew nothing of the basement theater. None had been inside. The movie studio vacated and moved westward long ago. The larger buildings were retrofitted to manufacture munitions during the war and recently again for domestic products. The office building remained empty.

This, my final visit to the old studio building, is under the cover of night once more, and I've come fully equipped to investigate. After scanning to ensure I'll be alone, I enter the alley with flashlight drawn. At the end, I withdraw a set of bolt cutters and a crow bar from under my coat. It's clear, upon close inspection. "The doors have been pried open before." After cutting the lock away, the doors open, "More easily than anticipated." The latches inside are already broken and dangling off the doors as I draw them open. The space below is totally devoid of light. Before entering, I slide my hand into my front coat pocket confirming the presence of my pistol, a military issue Colt M1911. I flip the slide safety off, and back on again, to be certain the precautionary mechanism is, in fact, engaged. "An old habit."

After closing the doors behind me, albeit counter-instinctual to close myself in, I traverse the nineteen steps on faith and not on actual vision of the surroundings. The floor and walls are painted black, rendering my flashlight mostly ineffective. With my sight better adjusted to the virtual pitch-black surroundings, I continue down the hallway beyond, slowly searching the darkness for threats. The night is warm, but the air below is cold. Further in, the sounds of the world fall away. "Deathly silent." My voice breaks the quiet, but I'm startled and spin to my rear when it echoes intelligibly back. The hair on my neck and arms stands on end as I approach the theater door. Inside, my light dissipates into broad emptiness. I recall the placement of the light switches.

The bulbs heat slowly. Light gradually fills the room revealing I am indeed quite alone. "Assuming that no one is hiding behind the lowered curtain." I return to the theater door to close it, once again restricting my escape route in favor of preventing any surprise followers. However, with the theater lights up, I notice a second door off the hallway wall, immediately outside the theater. "I hadn't noticed that before." Shining my light reveals the door handle is sunk in and flush with the wall, not protruding. "Easy to miss."

I find the door unlocked. Briefly, I point my light back toward the steps leading out to be sure I am still alone. Inside, I find a small chamber behind the theater, with two windows in the wall between the two rooms. A pair of film projectors is crowded into the far end corner. I've no doubt they were meant to occupy the windows. "Perhaps they projected their spot lights from here," though there are no such lights or any mechanism for manipulating the appearance of shadows. This room confirms my suspicion that the theater itself was originally a screening facility for the once tenanting film company. Besides the projection equipment, the room contains a rack for film reels and a few wall-mounted switches.

Experimentation reveals one switch raises the floor lighting on the stage and another, the curtain. The final switch raises a faint light inside the projection room. After another quick survey for anything relevant, I head back into the theater and close both doors behind me.

Removing my jacket, I move the pistol to my pants pocket then place the jacket and my tools in a corner near the stage front, closer to me than the door, "Just in case." When I climb on stage, my eyes linger on the bloodstain at the center. The rest of my inspection proceeds quickly. With the lights fully bright, I closely examine the three sides enclosing the stage and discover only solid brick walls with no indication of doorways, secret or otherwise. The bricks are offset, crack free, and all the mortar appears intact. As I'd assumed, the stage floor seems to be hollow below, yet it is flawless, sans the remnants of the pooled blood. It's solid wood, with no suggestion of a hinged or removable section.

My search turns next to the area above the stage, though it is mere ceiling, just a continuation from the rest of the room. Besides a few light fixtures identical to all the house lights and a small motor to raise the curtain, there are no other standouts. No joist, or openings are present, and it's barely above the reach of my extended arm. "Built for watching films, not for live performances."

Content with my appraisal of the stage, I have only one more objective. "Let's get on with it then." I hop down, retrieve my crowbar and with considerable force dig it into the stage-front wall at the corner. Prying out a substantial section, I move a foot down the wall and stab again, taking an even larger slab. The sum result of my destruction is a hole into the under-stage area wide enough for me to squeeze in. I kick the debris away, place the crowbar back at rest, and shimmy under the stage with my back on the floor and flashlight in hand.

The clearance is low. Rafters supporting the stage floor fill most of the space. The air is putrid. "It smells like a rotting corpse." I push further in, scanning above for any indication of access up to the stage. It's difficult to breathe or to see. Suddenly, my focus is ripped away when I hear a loud slam out in the theater. I stop moving and control my breath as I listen closely. Nothing further can be heard. As soon as I decide to continue my search I am abruptly diverted once more as an icy sensation clasps the back of my neck. It's like a cold hand just in from a winter day, or as it troubles me to imagine, the chill of a lifeless appendage. At first I'm petrified, motionless as the feeling spreads. My response is sudden and instinctual when I finally react, springing away and in the process rapping my forehead forcefully against one of the floor joists. I'm knocked temporarily delirious and am once again lying motionless on my back. My light rolls away from my hand. Its beam slowly progresses through the space independently.

When I return to full awareness, my thoughts are of personal defense. My fear is still restrained as I've trained myself. I avoid the desire to pull my weapon, which would have been an awkward and time-wasting effort in this tight of space. Instead, I favor the heft of the flashlight. I roll over toward the light and shrink into a protective position facing the perceived danger. In the same motion, I retrieve the light and point it ahead; however, several passes uncover nothing other than myself in the darkness. With the chill still clutching my body, I reach back to my neck and discover it covered in liquid. I hold my hand to the light; it's almost black in appearance, blood. The effect is again momentarily stunning. As I fight back impending hysteria, I search myself internally for a sense of pain to indicate where the wound is and how severe.

Thought eventually overtakes instinct, and it occurs to me that this blood is ice cold. My blood would be warm. The blood must have been the source of the assault on my neck and not the result. Crawling forward, and watching the ground with my light, my reasoning is confirmed. There's a pooling of blood on the ground near the center of the under-stage area, dry on the edges but still damp in the middle. Further traces of the blood's progression from the stage-floor, onto the substructure and eventually into the puddle are evident. This must be a result of the blood above seeping down, yet for a portion to still be liquid seems improbable. I suppose if a man were heavily drugged with a blood-thinning toxin, dangerously intoxicated with alcohol, or both, it would be possible that the blood would never clot, but for the puddle to furthermore resist simple evaporation this crawl space would need to be virtually airtight. Even that seems impossible. Though the notion is an affront to common sense, it would explain the concentration of foul smell. I suppose years of varnish and paint layers could create an airtight cavity accessible only by the permeability of the wood above. It would also imply that there's no access door between the stage and the under area. Again, this seems far-fetched, yet here lies the blood pool as evidence. Avoiding the blood, I finish my visual sweep from below, finding nothing but brick walls continuing down and confirming my hypothesis. "No trap door."

I flip to my stomach and army crawl toward my custom opening. "This takes me back." Near the hole, I slow and proceed cautiously. I have no confirmation that the earlier noise was benign. I peer into the theater and watch for movement or shadows. Detecting none, I exit feet first, favoring an attack to the legs over one to the head should some blow await me.

I emerge unscathed and find my crowbar on the floor, having fallen away from the wall. "Careless," but reasonable to infer as the source of the earlier commotion. Stepping forward, I confirm the area behind the theater seating is clear. "Let's be certain." Next, I return to collect my tools and breathe a relieved sigh. Finally, I open the door a few inches to peer down the hallway before I commit to exiting. Seeing nothing, I continue out. There will be little doubt someone has been inside given the hole which I have no intention of taking the time to mask or repair; thus it seems pointless to return to the projection room or bother with any of the lights whatsoever. I'm satisfied with my investigation, for its thoroughness, not for any uncovered answers. With the advantage of light spilling from the theater, I check the hallway one last time for any other previously unnoticed door handles. Finding none I take my leave, dropping the cumbersome tools once I've cleared the outside door. Before vacating the alley, I return my pistol to my jacket pocket and flip the safety off and back on once more, "Just in case."

Days later, I find myself dining late in the evening in a secluded bistro. I sit in the back corner at the only occupied table in the restaurant, finishing a bottle of wine while reflecting on the recent events, going over the circumstances, details, and minimal answers repeatedly, and occasionally jotting down a note. The staff is finishing the dishes, collecting the flatware and cutlery, and stacking chairs on the tables to clean the floor. Across the room at a small bar, the manager and kitchen staff enjoy an after-hours cocktail, as they usually do. I make it in here several times a week. It's one of only a few worthwhile restaurants that aren't either excessively crowded or in a dry district. They're used to my presence and I'm used to watching them close the place. The waiter pulls me from my thoughts, notifying me they'll be locking up in ten minutes as he drops off the change from my bill. When I look up to confirm my intended compliance, a couple enters the establishment. They're barely noteworthy. I expect they'll be turned away. Preparing to go, I tuck my notepad and money into my pockets.

To my surprise the maître d' makes his way to the bar hastily. With only a few words the entire staff bolts into action. The chef's team returns to the kitchen, the tables in the front window is restored with seats and table settings, and within only a few moments the couple, a man and woman dressed to imply a social status of wealth, are seated across the way. "They must be important."

The waiter comes from their table to mine. "Sir, it looks like we'll be remaining open just a little longer than I had thought. Is there anything else I can get for you?"

I glance at the new table. Naturally I don't have any particular interest in this couple, but the fact is I have nowhere else to be and am unlikely to find my bed for hours yet. Just as well that I spent that time here rather than strolling dark streets and alleys. "A brandy and a coffee, please."

"Very good, sir," he speeds to the bar and then to the newcomers. After barely enough time to withdraw my notes and remind myself of what I'd been thinking, the waiter interrupts again.

"Excuse me, sir." I glance up. The waiter has my beverages in tote. "The gentleman asked to buy your drink." The man and woman both hold glasses of wine. When I look over, the man lifts his glass to me. "He also would like to invite you to join them." My eyes glance back and forth between the couple and the waiter. It's my usual practice to avoid socializing, especially with high society. "Shall I take your brandy to their table?"

I had to ponder what the couple could be interested in. "I certainly don't present myself as a socialite."

"Excuse me, sir?"

"Please thank them on my behalf, but kindly decline." The waiter serves the coffee mug and snifter to my table.

"Very well, sir, he thought you might not recognize him but he said he was sure you had attended the same performance a few nights ago."

He turns to go but I grab his jacket sleeve. "Saturday night?" My gaze darts back to the front table. Excitement begins to manifest as I try to place the couple's faces in my memory of Malvern's show.

"I believe that's what he said, sir."

"On second thought, I've decided I will join them."

The waiter places the coffee and brandy back on his tray. "Excellent, sir." He escorts me over. One setting awaits. The gentleman speaks before I'm seated.

"Good evening, delighted you could join us."

"The pleasure's mine."

The woman nods and smiles, then leans over to her companion. "See, Norwalk, I told you it was the doctor from the show." He adjusts his glasses to see me through the other half of bifocals.

"Oh yes. I wasn't sure from across the room, but now I can see it for certain. Let me introduce my wife, Tiffin. I'm Norwalk." He waves to the waiter. "Bring us the bottle of whatever our friend is having and two more glasses."

"Right away."

"A damn tantalizing show, was it not? I'd be interested to hear a doctor's opinion on the spectacle."

"I'm no doctor, I'm afraid, just basic medic training. Vinton Drake." I offer my hand across the table. "It was a most intriguing performance indeed."

"Is that of the Drakes?"

"I suppose so."

Norwalk turns to his wife. "Honey, the company does all of our banking with his family's institution."

"Really?" She's as bored with this direction of the conversation as am I.

"Warren Drake handled our first account personally."

I feign a smile. "My father."

"Well now, where's he off to lately? I haven't seen him in ages."

"We've made a large investment in Iowan mining. He's been overseeing operations and the development of rail infrastructure."

"Coal? Isn't that something?" The conversation pauses as the waiter delivers the bottle and glasses. After pouring for the couple, he freshens my glass. Norwalk swirls his drink and takes a deep sniff before tasting. He notices Tiffin is distant. "Now, let's cut to matters of genuine interest. Do you think a man died that night?"

"Sir, I've pondered that nearly every moment since. Common sense tells me no. I saw the man alive before we left, but my feelings, my guts say a man laid dead on that stage."

We've reclaimed Tiffin's attention. With a devilish grin, she leans forward and whispers, "We have friends in several cities where Malvern has put on these shows—"

"That's how the show was recommended to us," Norwalk inserts.

"We've heard that they snatch bums or drunkards off the streets in each city. Lord knows there are plenty around, then they drug them up and during the show they switch the magician out for the unsuspecting fool. And then—" She mimes an ax chopping and squeals with giddy delight. "Isn't that positively ghoulish?"

"After that, they just swap the magician back in, no different from your average magic act where the magician and his assistant change places before your very eyes, only this assistant gets a little more than a curtain call." Norwalk grins as well. "It's curtains."

With the details of their theory, I re-imagine the events of that night. I uncovered no indication of a method with which to exchange a substitute for Malvern, be it victim or prop. Furthermore, I never took my hands off him, or so I thought.

The couple perceives my moment of internal thought for distress over their glee. Tiffin's smile fades. "That's just what we've heard, you understand. No telling how they manage it."

"You must admit, they're surely up to something fishy having secret shows, at ungodly hours, for one thousand dollars a seat. That's twenty-five, thirty thousand a show. Who's going to miss one beggar, or even notice for that matter?" I nod in agreement with Norwalk's notion, not the morality. "That's the beauty of it. Suppose they were offing the unsuspected. At a thousand a seat you can be sure everyone in that room is wealthy or affluent and would be losing prestigious positions or giving up fortunes if they were caught participating in"—he checks that no one aside from us three is within earshot, then whispers—"murder. No one would dream of squealing. What would a person tell anyway? There's no evidence of a crime."

"Aside from a possible missing person," I say.

"Sure, but the show's in town only one night. One has to wait longer than that to even file a missing person's report. Besides, even if the police had an inkling of what was going on, and somehow found out the details of where and when the show was happening, I doubt they'd be able to secure a warrant or a thousand bucks to go see for themselves. Based on what? A rumor?"

"That's why their invitations come with only a time, place, location, and instructions to 'Destroy After Reading' in the mailbox with just one day's notice," Tiffin adds. "If you hadn't heard of the show by word of mouth, you would never dream of going to some dark alley in the middle of the night with pockets full of cash, just because some mysterious green and white striped envelope showed up in your mailbox with no return address, stamp, or postmark, and told you to do so."

An interesting means of promotion, and amazing luck that I should stumble into it at all. "Have you been spreading recommendations to your circle of friends?"

"Heavens no. Not us. Have you?" She doesn't allow for me to answer. "We hadn't breathed a word to anyone, not until we saw you this evening. Maybe our closest friends, but I'd be afraid for most of our casual friends to know what we'd been a part of. You can never tell how someone might react. We have to maintain a certain status in town."

"How is it then, that you heard about the event?"

Norwalk replies, "Same as you, I'm sure. We had good friends in from down state. They hadn't been to the show; they'd just heard an alleged story from another couple over in Cincinnati. They only mentioned it anecdotally. Of course, it seemed preposterous until that invitation showed up. Hell, I half expected to go down to the show and find our friends waiting for us, laughing right up until the curtain raised."

They both smile. I feign laughter. "How do you suppose that you, I mean we, were selected as recipients of invitations?"

"That's another thing I can't quite figure." He gestures to the waiter for the bill. "I suppose if you hadn't heard anything about the show, you'd just throw out a strange, unmarked invitation. Besides, that eerie doorman is there to keep out anyone who might come across the show without prior knowledge."

"One would think," I add. The waiter arrives and before Norwalk can, I snatch up the check. "It's been very interesting running into the two of you again. Please allow me." They nod graciously. It's the least I can do in payment for the legwork they've saved me. After I've fed the waiter several bills we all stand to leave.

"I wonder where Malvern will show up next." Again my predilection for speaking to myself surfaces. I have no intention of revealing the extent of my investigation to these two.

"Wherever the carnival goes, I imagine. It was along with the carnival that the couple in Cincinnati caught the act, and again after the carnival came through Champaign that our friends spoke of it. I assume he's attached himself to it." Norwalk shoots me one last devilish grin. "You have friends you'd like to notify?" I return his smile without answering as I exit.

I don't waste a single moment making my way from the restaurant to the police station across town. "Captain O'Brian," I bellow to the uniform at the front desk, but he informs me, of course, that O'Brian is long gone for the evening. The nearby clock reads 3:00AM. "How silly of me," I mutter as I slink away. I've grown oblivious to unusual hours. "Accustomed, at least."

I'm too immersed in this mystery to slow down or even to sleep. I return to the station early the following morning, finding a new young officer manning the desk. Again, I ask for O'Brian. He plugs a phone into a small switchboard then relays the request. "Who should I say is asking?"

"Just tell him I've something for him that he left in Europe." My response is met with puzzlement, which was expected, as he tentatively repeats the gist of my message back into the phone.

He nods as he hangs up. "Go on back, it's the last office on the right." I know the location as I nod and pass. Making my way there, I hurry to roll up one of my sleeves and expose my arm from the shoulder down.

The office door is closed. My knock is met with a muffled, "Yeah, come in." I open the door only a few inches. I let my hand go limp on the exposed arm and use my other hand to dangle the arm in through the doorway, allowing the wall to mask my body.

"I heard you've been looking for this," I shout in toward the office, my face brimming with glee, though I manage to hold back my laughter.

"Yeah, I needed some target practice; now hold still."

Giving up my jest, I head in. At the desk sits a burly, red-haired man with a tie that matches his suspenders, and a revolver pointed directly at my head. Ignoring it, I casually take the seat at the front of the desk. "Did you finally devise a way to load that thing?"

"You really are an asshole, Drake." He stows the weapon in the desk's top drawer. To my surprise he actually has to uncock the hammer. Corporal Philip O'Brian, as I knew him originally, was a force to be reckoned with before he lost an arm, but he still managed to place third in the policemen's boxing league this year. "I know I owe you my life, but you sure make it hard to like you."

"I don't need a friend, I just need a favor."

10:00PM

Harlan looked up from Vinton's journal to find Vieve had moved behind him to read over his shoulder. She smiled. The others were mid conversation. Harlan folded the book.

"In the paranormal shows I've worked on, I've always been behind the scenes, heading up the technical or doing advance scouting, all the hard work, ya' know, but never getting the screen time. After tonight, that's all gonna change. They'll be beggin' me to head up my own team." Ax winked at Audrey. "A couple hundred grand ain't gonna hurt in gettin' that ball rolling either." His smile grew wider. "What about you, Hollywood? What are your plans? What are you gonna do with your cut?"

Audrey fluffed her hair. "I've had lead roles in a number of fantastic horror films. They've done well in festivals and in the cult horror niche market, but they're not quite in the 'opening on a thousand screens' category. My agent is absolutely convinced that the national audience this show should bring in will help get me in the conversation for casting either in a big-budget blockbuster or for a network TV gig. I've been called the next Lucy Liu in a few reviews."

"A superstar in the making, huh?"

"You know it."

"What about the money?" Vieve stepped out from behind Harlan and took a seat in the conversation.

"I have a friend in Houston, a writer-director who's trying to get a project off the ground. It's a romantic comedy. The script is just dynamite for a little independent." She feigned coyness. "If I were to accept the lead, and bring in a chunk of the budget with my share, I'm sure the project would take off. It'd really help show my range."

Ax nodded. "Nothin' but business."

Audrey turned toward Vieve. "How about you, Genevieve? You just live here, right, so..." She smirked.

"No, I grew up here. My family lives here. I just graduated from the University of Iowa with my B.S., where I was also a scholarship soccer player on a full ride, and I was accepted into med school at Washington University." Vieve noticed she sounded defensive. Audrey's smirk had faded. Vieve eased off. "I've always planned to go into family practice but the reality of the medical field is that if you rack up a couple hundred thousand in student loans putting yourself through school, by the time you're ready to work, once you factor in malpractice insurance and other expenses, many new grads can't afford to choose family practice, especially returning to a smaller community like Shadows Bend. Specialists make significantly more money. That's why so many doctors go that route. Some people say there's an impending shortage of family doctors on the horizon. However, since the family doctor is the first step for most ailments, having the best physicians possible in that position is the key to better health overall. If I walk away with a cut of the million, I'll just put it toward med school so I can graduate without a huge debt. If not, I'll have to think seriously about," she shrugged, "cardiology, maybe."

"That's really noble and thoughtful." Harlan leaned forward.

"I didn't realize you were still over there, buddy," Ax said.

Audrey saw that Ax's attention had shifted to Vieve. "So what was it like growing up around this place?" Audrey asked. "Made you want to get the heck out of town, huh?"

"Not at all. I loved growing up here. My family has been around for generations. My father's a police officer, and so was my grandfather, and his father actually. My great-grandfather was on the force when the Drake family disappearance occurred. He knew the two officers that died here." Both Ax and Harlan listened carefully. "I never really found this place intimidating. It was here my whole life so it just seemed like a normal part of living in the town. High school kids used to sneak over the fence and drink beer in the courtyard. I suppose I can admit I did a few times myself."

"Did anybody ever sneak in the house?" Ax asked.

"I don't think so, not that I heard of anyway. Guys would dare each other to go look through a window, but most would chicken out. I think they pulled them out before this show started, but all the doors and windows all used to be nailed shut and boarded over. They really didn't want people breaking in."

"Did you ever hear or see anything spooky?" Ax's eyebrows rose.

Vieve glanced at each of the others' faces. "You've probably heard how people say they've seen all sorts of supposed persons or spirit figures in the attic window at dawn, right? And about the noises? One time, when I'd jumped the fence with a few friends, we were clear over in the far corner of the lot. I don't remember what we were talking about, but we were all laughing about something, and then I started to hear this...rumble I guess. I thought it sounded like someone's stomach growling. I asked everyone 'Who was hungry?' As everyone got quiet we all heard the sound, and it got louder and louder until it seemed like you could feel it as much as hear it, like really low bass sounds." All four followed Vieve's story closely.

"I wouldn't call it a growl, scream, or a howl like other stories do; it didn't sound like a person or even an animal. It was definitely more than the creaking and settling of an old house, and we all heard it."

"What'd you do?" Audrey asked.

"We all bolted the hell out of there."

"Did you tell anybody?"

"Are you kidding? I'd have been locked up forever if my dad found out I was in there. The town was serious about keeping this place locked up tight. It wouldn't do at all for a cop's daughter to be caught on the grounds. It'd have made the front page of the paper." Vieve paused and looked directly into the lens of the closest pillar camera. "Sorry, Dad." The others laughed.

"Did you ever see anything in the attic window, like others report?" Harlan asked.

Vieve's voice grew mysterious. "I was freaked after I heard that rumble, but curious too. The next morning, I snuck out of our house before dawn, walked to the mansion, and waited as the sun came up." Everyone was deeply enthralled. "I took a pair of binoculars and watched the attic window the whole time. I couldn't see much of anything at first, when the sun's glow was barely creeping over the horizon, but then as the sun gradually rose the windows of the house slowly lit, and then, do you know what I saw?"

Audrey was eager. "No, what?" Vieve took a long, deep breath. "Come on."

"Nothing." The others sighed in disappointment. "Not a thing, that morning. But wait just a second. I did see a figure in the window a few times after that, when I wasn't trying to spot it but just happened to be nearby at the right time."

Ax leaned back, folded his arms, and shook his head. "So what did ya' see, man, woman, or child?"

"I couldn't tell. It was more like movement than a shape, and it looked different every time."

"It may be different each time. There are six individual entities here." La Claire's interjection quieted the conversation.

Harlan filled the silence. "Why do you think the police never investigated further? Did your dad or grandpa ever talk about that?"

"No bodies, no evidence of a crime. They were just missing persons, so the police investigated that. They watched for travel records, communication to relatives, bank activity, but with nothing surfacing that directly indicated foul play, they couldn't tear the house apart like a murder investigation. Then without any evidence, without any solid leads, and with a real cost in human life—two officers and three civilians—they had to close it down. For all the same reasons, they could never reopen the case, not without new evidence, and frankly the town committed to keeping the place sealed up and a lid on the mystery. The ordinance was for 100 years, which was enforced without exception for more then 80. I was astonished when I heard of this TV thing was in the works and even more floored when they called me."

"What changed, then? Why do you think they agreed to let us in here years early, or at all for that matter, and not just let us in but let them televise it nationally? It doesn't seem in line."

Vieve shrugged. "It's money, pure and simple. Mining was essentially played out around the state by the forties. Shadows Bend was lucky enough to pull in two large factories about that time that hired up all the same workers. One later grew into a Fortune-Five-Hundred company, but they didn't have their offices here only manufacturing. That's why our airport has a runway long enough for large planes and jets. They used to fly bigwigs into our little municipal airport all the time. The thing is, neither of the factories expanded their workforce after the seventies. They were rolling back through the eighties and nineties. After 2000, one moved to another state for lower minimum wage and the other closed down completely. Farming has always been important to the community, but it doesn't offer nearly the number of jobs it once did. The town has been steadily shrinking my entire life, before even. What I've heard is that the city, the mayor, and city council jumped at the proposal from the TV network. I'm sure they're hoping this will become a nationally known landmark and bring in some much-needed tourist dollars."

"I presumed as much," Harlan said.

"It's been disheartening to watch businesses close and people move away, but it'll be a disappointment to see the town overrun with cheap souvenir stands, T-shirt shops, and theme motels." Harlan nodded. A warm smile crept across Vieve's face. "We haven't heard from you, Harlan. What's your plan after tonight? What do you want to do with the money?"

"First, I'll head back to school and hopefully graduate by the end of next semester. I've already passed my comps, but I still have plenty to do before I submit and defend my dissertation. After that, I'll look for a post-doc position and then hopefully get on a tenure track."

"No ambitions for riding the wake of TV success into stardom?" Vieve jested.

"I may write a paper. That's about it." He smiled. "Maybe someone will publish my dissertation. The story and lore about this house will definitely factor into my work now. I'm considering adding an entire section on this Malvern Kamrar."

"I've never known much about the magician. Apparently, Vinton Drake knew him before the night of their disappearance, but I just learned that tonight." Ax and Audrey looked to Vieve with questioning expressions, but La Claire smiled with pride. "Vinton's said so in his journal." La Claire's smile faded. "I don't think anyone ever knew for certain that they had a previous connection. What else can you fill in about Kamrar?"

Harlan pulled his backpack closer and removed his notepad. "No birth date, but I'm assuming Malvern Kamrar is an assumed name. I haven't uncovered his real name." Harlan flipped to a page marked by a sticky note. "Let's see. He first shows up as a street magician in New York around 1918. He was mentioned in a news article when he was questioned in connection with a series of scams where wealthy victims fell into staged accidents in which they appeared to have killed or seriously injured a person and were subsequently asked to bribe a witness or were extorted after the fact. No formal charges ever came of it, and the article only gave his stage name." Harlan tapped a finger on Vinton's journal. "Apparently after that, he started performing underground in a series of 'death shows' with high-priced admission. That explains why I couldn't find another printed word about him prior to 1925. It also clears up the source of his reputation."

"What do you mean?" Vieve asked.

"After 1925, he went legit and began booking extended gigs in big-city vaudeville theaters, as well as the traveling shows later on, but the advertisements and the articles often refer to him as"—Harlan read from his notes—"the Indestructible Man, the Unkillable Man, the Resurrected Man, the Undead, the Cheater of Death, and even Master of Life Itself." He looked up. "I'll have to look into it further, but it seems logical now that the word-of-mouth buzz from his underground shows spilled over into his mainstream persona, though his official stage moniker was simply the Master of Shadows."

"He sounds pretty shady." Harlan chuckled at Audrey's pun, but quickly realized it was inadvertent.

"He was. But he had a fair amount of success and even ended up as a subject for three short films near the end of the silent era. Back then people would walk into films whenever they wanted, not necessarily at the beginning, and most films played with complementary material, news reels, comedy shorts, animations, and such. Malvern's magic act films played for about 15 minutes each, before the features. He was gaining real notoriety up until his disappearance. Frankly he might have been on his way to national stardom had his career not been cut short. He was a talent magician, ahead of his time."

Harlan dropped his notes. "I'm just speculating here, but we now understand Vinton Drake knew Malvern personally. With his star rising but his questionable and possibly criminal past, I have to wonder if Vinton had something on Kamrar; something to hold over him —information worth killing over. Some bit of evidence or knowledge that could sink Malvern's career. Perhaps that brought the situation to the climax, whatever ending they all met."

"So what makes you the authority on all the magic stuff?" Ax asked.

"I don't consider myself an authority. My research deals heavily with charlatan mystics and popular misbeliefs as well as their impact on society." Both Ax and La Claire soured at Harlan's answer. "Listen, whether you believe in the existence or possibility of a genuine psychic or spiritualist or not, it's difficult to ignore the fact that there have been many fakes, frauds, and con men throughout history, and the odds are there are still frauds around today. Right?" Ax softened slightly.

"To understand the bag of tricks the charlatan uses, you have to educate yourself as best you can on the legitimate tricks out there, which come from the field of conjuring—a better term than magic. Also, one finds with only cursory research that for the most part, whether it's a psychic fraud versus a mentalist, or telekinesis fakes versus sleight-of-hand artists, the only difference is the conjurers are up front that they are performing tricks while the charlatans claim spirits give them powers. The tricks are the same. While I wouldn't consider myself an authority on magic or conjuring, I have done significant research in the field, and of course I've been involved with the SMSF for years, which further calls upon me to educate myself on the subject."

"SMSF?" Vieve asked.

"The Scientist, Magician, Skeptic Foundation."

La Claire tisked and shook her head in disgust. Harlan took pause. "Madam Galva, are you going to defend every storefront psychic; that every single one has the same powers you believe you possess? That no one out there is trying to dupe people out of their money by taking advantage of their trust in mediums?"

La Claire clenched her jaw and said nothing.

Vieve sensed the tension. "You didn't say what your plans were for your prize money, Harlan?"

He relaxed. "I've benefited greatly from an SMSF scholarship, so I'd like to reciprocate by donating my winnings back to the foundation. Maybe with a couple hundred thousand extra in the bank we can expand the million-dollar test."

"The what?" Audrey asked. La Claire sighed loudly.

"It's called the Million Dollar Paranormal Test. It seems you may have heard of it, Galva. What about you, Ax?" Ax shook his head. "It's a prize that is offered to anyone who can demonstrate evidence of any paranormal, supernatural, or occult power or event, under scientific observing conditions. Essentially, if you have a supposed power beyond that of our normal human senses and abilities, and will submit to testing it under mutually agreed upon terms that remove or virtually eliminate the possibility of falsifying the results, then you can win one million dollars." Ax was intrigued and Vieve was impressed.

"Wow. What do you have to do?" Audrey asked.

"Applicants have to state what they can do, under what conditions, and with what accuracy. They also need an affidavit from someone familiar with the scientific method, stating that they have witnessed this ability and are convinced it's genuine. It can be a researcher from a nearby college, a person in a science career, a doctor maybe." Harlan nodded toward Vieve. "After that, we try to agree on terms for testing the ability while taking out any means by which the applicant could skew the results. For instance, if their ability were psychic, then we would want to make sure they were doing readings on people they don't already know, right?"

La Claire erupted, "It's bullshit. They just try to embarrass people. The conditions are impossible. They see to that."

"They're not. We're interested in finding an authentic example if it exists. The fact is many people apply with claims that cannot be tested. If you claim you can bend wire hangers into animal shapes with your mind but that you can only do it in your own house, in the dark, with no one else around and with no cameras on you, and you propose the testers bring some hangers by in the evening and come back in the morning and give you the money if they're bent up, that simply won't work because we can't in any way be sure you didn't simply bend them with your hands. Wouldn't you agree?"

"So what would an agreed-upon test be like?" Ax asked.

"As an example, have you ever heard of psychics who can supposedly hold a picture of a missing person, sense it, and then help police, families, or investigators by telling them if the person is alive or dead, and maybe give them a clue as to where the person is, near water, in an abandoned building, etc.? It's certainly a popular idea in TV dramas."

Ax, Vieve, and Audrey all agreed. La Claire refused to answer.

"Let's say you claim to have this power, and you even have examples where you were given a missing person's photo, you said, 'I sense they're dead already,' and you ended up being correct, that would suggest your claim is true. My first thought as a skeptic would be to ask if you had any advanced information about the case. If the newspapers already reported the victim's blood was found in a large pool where he or she was last seen, and a bloody knife was found a few blocks away, then the psychic might just be playing the odds to guess the victim is dead." Everyone but La Claire followed along.

"My second thought would then be the simple fact that you, the psychic, are only being presented with a person's photo when they're already missing. He or she is already very likely the subject of a crime, so again whatever prediction you make, dead, abandoned, lost, or captive, your chances of being right by guessing alone are improved. No one brings you photos of people who aren't in trouble. It would be reasonable to infer that if your power is genuine, then if you are given a random photo, and told nothing about it, that it wasn't necessarily a person missing, just a photo of a person, then you would be able to sense whether they were living or dead. Since that is a binary choice with 50-50 odds like calling a coin toss, I would then organize a test where you had to diagnose 20 random photos, living or dead. Odds would say that, by chance alone, you might come up with as many as 10 correct answers or half. With a little luck, you may get another 2 or 3, but if you can get all of them right, or 19 out of 20 right, then that would substantiate your claim. If you could replicate the same 95 percent or even 85 percent accuracy for a couple hundred random photos, then that would be grounds for awarding you the million."

"Has anyone ever won?" Audrey asked.

Harlan shook his head. "No one has even made it past the preliminary round of testing. Most of the time people with these claimed powers don't even score as high as you'd expect from guessing alone."

"See, their conditions are unwinnable," La Claire finally rejoined the conversation.

"You have to consider the possibility that none of these people have the ability they claim. It's true, the SMSF has tested hundreds of so-called psychics, dowsers, spiritualists, and para-investigators, and no one has even come close to replicating their supposed results and accuracy under unbiased testing conditions, the implication certainly being that such powers do not exist."

Ax frowned. La Claire scoffed, "Unbiased?"

Vieve stepped between them. "We've all given our plans for after tonight but you, Madam La Claire. What's your next step? What will you do with the money?"

"No plans, young lady. I'm just interested in using my gift to help others. That's what I do with my online readings, I help people put their lost loved ones finally to rest, and that's why I'm here. Nothing more."

Everyone nodded but Harlan. "That's very generous, Galva. I assume your online services are completely free then, aren't they? You wouldn't dream of charging for sharing your gift."

La Claire shot him a glare and abstained from answering.

"What will you do with the money?" Audrey reminded.

"Charity, I'll give my winnings to charity."

Harlan remained distrustful. "What charity specifically? I'm curious."

La Claire turned away.

"The SMSF's million dollars would go a long way for your charity interests, wouldn't it?" Harlan asked.

Walter leaned over the director's chair. "Now, that's great TV tension. La Claire looks like she's fuming. Maybe this skeptic kid is finally paying off."

Jason stepped into the truck. "You have to see this, Mr. Resnick." He gestured to outside. Walter joined him at the steps and was immediately taken back. Just beyond the officers stationed at one of the property entrances, thousands of people were crowded in the street. Each carried a lit candle. Walter grabbed Jason's arm and bee-lined toward the people.

"Call the local news. See if they'll cover us for the 11 o'clock." He checked his watch. "It'll be close. And get a camera out here, ASAP"

Jason dashed away but turned back after a few yards. "Internet traffic is above 6 million." Though Walter didn't turn around, he grinned broadly.

At the gate, Walter beckoned one of the crowd members over, a middle-aged woman. "What are you folks doing out here?"

"We're here for Madam La Claire, to offer her spiritual support for casting out the negative entity."

"You're all her online clients?"

"Some of us are, but I only found out about her tonight, on this show." The woman held up a cellphone that was streaming the online broadcast. "I was compelled to help immediately, along with my spiritual sisters." She pointed to a group of five other similarly aged women nearby.

"Come in. All of you, come in." Walter pushed the gates open. "Let everyone in," he told the officers, then shouted to the crowd. "You're all welcome to assemble at the back of the property. Right this way."

From above the grounds a fluid-like mass of light appeared to pour into the property as the candle-toting congregation filed in.

11:00PM

"I'm sure you could do it, Madam La Claire," Audrey said. "If anyone could. We've seen you in action."

"I don't have anything to prove to anyone, and I don't need the money. I have my loyal patrons, tens of thousands of them. That is all I require."

Harlan was calm. "First, if I had such a power, I'd be outraged by all the fakers. I'd want to prove it, and challenge others to do the same, and expose the frauds. Second, if I had psychic power, I'd take the million-dollar test, simply because the media coverage would be unstoppable if I were successful. You'd have more people than you could ever dream of accommodating seeking you out for readings. To the press largely, you'd be the only proven psychic in the world. Isn't that worth taking a shot?"

"Intuitive. I prefer to be called an intuitive, not psychic."

"Excuse me, Joyce." Vieve, Audrey, and Ax looked to him curiously. Harlan feigned an apologetic tone. "Joyce Hill, that's just her real name." La Claire frowned. "The only proven 'intuitive' in the world, then."

"I routinely have several thousand people join in on my weekly public online readings. I need neither the money nor the press."

"So how do those readings work, anyway? I think it'd be hard to get a good 'connection' over the internet?" Harlan asked. La Claire didn't answer.

"I'd like to know too, Galva. What kind of readings do you do?" Audrey asked.

La Claire hesitated, and then spoke toward Audrey only, "Online, everyone joins in a chat room where they can see me on video, and type messages back." She closed her eyes and lifted her hands as if a keyboard was before her. "We begin by asking the spirits to join us. All the viewers should do this at home along with me. We invite any spirits with messages for any of the viewers to come to me and speak through me. You see, the spirits are not bound to the world as we are." She tilted her head toward Harlan. "We use the internet to communicate between living people, the spirits have no such need."

La Claire turned back toward Audrey. "After that, I open myself up to the spirits and simply convey what I can understand from them. They try to tell me their names or little messages to identify them. Not everything is always clear; there is a fog of sorts to it, but normally I can make out a general age, gender, and at least part of a name. I give that information and then all those viewers who suspect the spirit is trying to reach them specifically come forward through the online messages. I have assistants to monitor this and read significant messages to me. Sometimes though, as you can imagine, almost everyone has a grandfather in his 80s who passed away, so we narrow with what I can tell of his name, what he may have done for a living, where he lived, and all the details the spirits choose to communicate to me in order to hone in on their specific loved one."

La Claire opened her eyes. "When it is your loved one, people just tend to know." She smiled warmly to Audrey. "So my assistants watch until the details have brought out the one person the spirit is looking for. At that point, if they have video or audio capability we bring them up right from home, beside me on screen for everyone else to share in the reading. If not, we at least let everyone see the person's text posts. Then, I simply try to give them the messages the spirit intends for them. Again there is a fog involved with communicating across plains; it's not as simple as a conversation between the living. If you want an apple, you can say, 'May I have an apple,' but a spirit has to send me thoughts of the smell, of the taste of the apple, memories of when and where they enjoyed apples, and only then can I conclude their message has to do with an apple. It also can come like a flood of thoughts. All the information at once and it's difficult to know what is most important. Do you understand?" Audrey nodded.

"The other hurdle is that the message may not make sense to me. It's intended for the viewer; the spirit's loved one. The message may only make sense between the two of them, so it is then for the viewer to interpret the clues I can relay. That's why the conversation between the viewer and me is just as important as my connection with the spirit. The viewer has to help steer me toward what is helpful and what is important for me to look for."

"Conveniently," Harlan interrupted.

La Claire and Audrey both shot him glares. "They can also ask direct questions," La Claire continued, "which is helpful for me and the spirit to be focusing on the same thing. Usually though, between the three of us we're able to get the messages across, and of course it is easy to spot messages like 'I miss you,' or 'I love you; I'm watching over you.' These are unmistakable expressions of love."

"How long do these readings last?" Vieve asked.

"Only 15 minutes, unfortunately. I could continue for hours with a single spirit if I wanted, but as you have seen, this communication is very taxing, so I am only able to open myself up for a couple hours at a time. In the interest of helping more than one or two of the thousands of viewers per session, I limit the time to 15 minutes. We shoot for letting at least 10 spirits in, and of course we invite those spirits that did not get their turn to join us again next time." Audrey smiled warmly.

"So if a viewer wants to talk to their loved one for longer than their time limit, what can they do, just hope they get in again in a couple of weeks?" Harlan knew the answer to his question.

"Oh, we're very aware that some people have more extensive needs." La Claire was respondent to Harlan. "That's why we only have public readings once a week. The rest of the time we are open to private appointments for one or two hours, reserved for a single viewer."

"For a nominal fee," Harlan added. Then La Claire gave him the sour look he had expected.

"That is truly amazing," Audrey said. "You've really taken the psychic…I mean intuitive experience that I picture as in person at a shop or event, and made it accessible for everyone."

La Claire smiled. "That is exactly what our hopes were. Sometimes the people who need our help the most cannot afford to travel to see me, or another intuitive. They may even be elderly or bedridden, where they simply can't manage to leave the house at all. These are the people I feel we help the most."

"Are spirit, um, readings all you do, or can you do like tarot, palms, or…" Audrey trailed off.

"Yes. I do read people's futures. I rely on the spirits though, not on devices like tarot cards. Those of course, are just a tool, like choosing to phone or to email. The power is not in the cards but in the reader. I have a very powerful spirit guide, who is my usher into the other realm. There she has the power to see into the past, present, and the future and can share it with me. She is my tool. She's probably the reason Kamrar's knife didn't kill me, by the way. She watches over me."

Audrey shifted in her seat excitedly. "I'd love to have you give me a reading sometime."

La Claire smiled but before she could answer, Harlan interrupted. "I'd love to see that too, Joyce, I mean Galva."

Now she hesitated. "Well, I'm not sure—"

"Oh, don't let Mr. Spoilsport over there stop you." Vieve gave Harlan a playful wink. "I'd very much like to see this as well."

"Oh, all right, just a quick one." Audrey squealed. La Claire put her hands out, palms up. Audrey placed hers on top. La Claire closed her eyes. "My guide likes to look into your past to get to know you, you'll see, and it helps to be sure we're looking at the right track. Then we look at you today. That helps you to confirm the accuracy of the reading. We wouldn't want you to make any decisions based on the reading unless you are comfortable that the information given could only be known through the spirit world." Audrey agreed.

After a moment of internal searching, La Claire began, "You're a person who had a very warm and comfortable home, and yet you felt the need to break free. To spread your wings and fly on your own." Audrey nodded confirmation, though La Claire's eyes remained closed. "It does look like there may have been some tense times with your parents. You had to prove yourself and your plan for life to them most of all. But they love you. You've never doubted that, even if they wanted to control your choices a little too much."

Audrey smiled. "Yes."

"You are a self-starter and like to do things your own way, create your own path through life, not walk the path of others. When you were first starting out, there was a time when it looked as though you would not succeed. There were many struggles, and one time in particular when all the signs pointed to failure. But when others would have given up and gone back to the nest you stayed and prevailed no matter what it took."

Audrey grew more emotional as she confirmed each statement. "As a result, you have a life and career that is climbing high. You feel stronger, like you can overcome anything because of the hurdles you've already conquered. I'm also seeing that you enjoy the beautiful things in life, gourmet cuisine, fine art, great music, and you surround yourself with it. You recognize great art in all its forms, and you also make great art, for in your heart, you are an artist, whether it's in your profession, in the way you arrange your home, or simply the clothes you wear."

Audrey was ecstatic. "This is, it's just amazing." Ax watched Audrey while Vieve and Harlan's attentions were on La Claire.

"Hmm," La Claire murmured. "The love in your life is somewhat cloudy? It's not that there is none or little love, it's just extremely unfocused. Perhaps this shows you put romance in the back seat behind your career goals? It could also mean there are many objects of your affection, that there are a number of people you have your eye on, and no one stands out as the love of your life at this time." Audrey continued to agree to everything La Claire said. "That is your past and present. Now, for the future. I see bright days ahead. You are rapidly getting the things you want. Make no mistake, they are not simply coming to you. You are working hard to see to it that you get what you want. Ultimately, your star is rising and very soon you will be on top. I think it is then, when you don't have anything left to prove, that you find a true love." La Claire grinned. "But he is different because he doesn't see you for the glamor and allure of your career; he is blunt and cuts right to the heart of the situation. He sees you for what you really are." La Claire opened her eyes and looked into Audrey's. "And he likes what he sees. By chance, he is a handsome fellow as well." Audrey smiled and laughed but a single tear rolled down her cheek. La Claire squeezed Audrey's hands and pulled her in closer. "There you go, child. Good things ahead."

Audrey could only whisper, "Thank you." Everyone else was quiet. Audrey turned to Harlan. "Surely you can't doubt that. Nobody could know those things about me."

Harlan contemplated silently. Vieve teased, "He's speechless?"

Harlan shook his head. "I'd like to give it a try."

Everyone was surprised. "You want a reading?" Vieve asked.

"No. I'd like to give one. Can I give you a reading, Audrey?" Now they were puzzled. "I don't brag about it, but I do have some experience with this and I'd like to give it a shot."

"Umm, I guess so," Audrey said.

"Great." Harlan stood and moved over to the couch. "May I?" He gestured for La Claire to allow him to trade seats. She watched Harlan suspiciously. Audrey hung her hands out where Harlan could hold them. "No, I believe the messages come from deep inside of the subject. While a connection can be made through any touch, such as holding a hand, a much deeper connection is required for superior results."

"OK?"

"Your heart. That is the spiritual source." Harlan slid a little closer. As Audrey let her arms drop he placed both his hands near her chest, not quite touching. "Will this be OK?"

"Hey, this looks like a pile of crap. What are you trying to do?" Ax interrupted.

"I understand if you're uncomfortable, but it's how I work." Harlan feigned embarrassment and withdrew his hands. "Maybe we should just forget it. I don't want to..." He strategically mumbled coyly, hoping Audrey would interrupt him.

"No, it's OK. I'm really curious now. It'll be fine." Audrey pulled Harlan's hands back. Ax was vexed.

"Are you sure?" Harlan asked. Audrey nodded. "OK." He placed his hands on Audrey's upper chest, palms down, very near, but not quite cupping her breasts. Vieve rolled her eyes. Harlan closed his. La Claire sneered disapproval. "Hmm, yes. That is spectacular." He opened one eye. "The connection I mean, not the, ah..." He indicated to her chest with his eyes before he closed them again and continued. "Let's see. I'm getting a lot more coming through concerning your childhood. Which parent was it that put all the pressure on you? That pushed you toward perfection? Your mother?"

"Yes." Audrey was leery.

Harlan lowered his brow. "Unfortunately, I'm seeing some ugliness there. Pulling a young girl's hair to untangle it with irritation instead of a gentle hand, forcing the girl to wear makeup and take dance lessons at a young age when the child, you, would have rather had more freedom to play, to socialize with other children. It seems she often put beauty and appearances over your relationship; that the outward impression of a perfect mother and a perfect daughter was more important than just being a mother to you. She wasn't abusive, but the pressure of her expectations was high and relentless." Harlan's expression became distraught. "Ouch! I even see a scar, still there, on your leg. Did she knock you down and drag you when you didn't want to go?"

"Wow. That's...that's right." Audrey still withheld her trust.

Harlan's tone softened. He smiled. "Then there's your father. It looks like he was the one you trusted the most. His love was abundant, and he was usually there to limit how much your mother could press you."

"Yes, he was, he is." Audrey's faith grew.

"Now I can see you in school, older, in high school I believe." Harlan grinned. "I also see a number of boys. You got significant attention from the young men in school, didn't you?" Audrey smiled as well. "Now, forgive me if this gets a little too personal, but I'm seeing one boy in particular. He's older than you by a year or two and I think, again forgive me, what I see is steered by you as much as by me, but I think he is the man you lost your virginity to."

Both Ax and Vieve shifted, uneasy. La Claire watched Harlan with palpable irritation. Audrey was again leery, but had to again verify Harlan's accuracy. "Now it seems that you feel you were a little young when it happened, maybe you wish you'd waited; another year perhaps?" Harlan's tone lightened. "But you loved him. It may have been naive, but you thought you were in love. He, however, proved not to be reliable, or the man you thought he was. It cost you some of your friends, or showed you who was really your friend and who wasn't." Harlan opened his eyes and looked at Audrey. Her cheeks were red but she nodded agreement. "I think I'll keep the rest here between us if that's OK with you. I suspect you would prefer what remains of that story to go unsaid."

Audrey shed a couple of tears and whispered, "Yes, thank you."

"I believe, however, you're revealing this to me subconsciously because it shows even earlier in life, before you were acting, where your strength to overcome was born. We all have parts of our past we'd like to forget, but were it not for those events we also wouldn't be the people we are." Harlan closed his eyes again and adjusted his physical connection to Audrey, and adjusted again, and again. She was too enthralled to notice. "Now, moving forward, I see that you're a very proud adult. You blossomed into a fine woman. At the same time, though, internally I sense there is a seed of fear. You exude confidence. With anyone around you, you'd never show an ounce of intimidation, but when you're alone, when it's just you and your thoughts, there's still a part of you that questions yourself, that wonders if you really have the talent, if you'll be able to put your accomplishments where your mouth is, so to speak. Outwardly you're unstoppable. Internally you torture yourself."

"It's true." More tears trickled from Audrey.

"However that is natural and really it's healthy. It would be easy to be overly confident, which could harm the integrity of your work, but when you constantly need to prove your talent, not to others, but to yourself, then you hold yourself to a higher and uncompromising standard. Right? That's good. It means you put the same amount of time into a bit part in a no-budget movie as you would for a lead role in a blockbuster. Incidentally, this attitude comes from your relationship with your mother, and therefore, while she wasn't as warm as she should have been, she did help in shaping you into the dedicated performer that you are."

Audrey resisted sobbing.

"For the future, Audrey, I will warn you not to let the voice of doubt take over when you land a big role in a movie that flops. You'll want to blame yourself, but remember, there are many factors involved in the success of a film. The film's success and your personal success are not necessarily the same. If you can remember that, and you can see your talent is real, then you'll move on to conquer the industry." Harlan patted her twice on her chest, opened his eyes, and smiled before releasing her. Ax and Vieve were impressed. La Claire flopped back in her seat in disbelief.

Audrey wiped her tears away. "That was just amazing, Harlan. You're truly gifted."

"Why don't you try to win that million dollars yourself?" Vieve asked.

"I couldn't win, Vieve. I owe you an apology, Audrey." She was puzzled. "I have in a way taken advantage of you, for you see, I was totally faking."

"No." Audrey became cross.

"I knew it." Ax was relieved.

"You couldn't know those things. No one could just know that," Audrey said.

"It's tricks of mentalism." Harlan shrugged. "I'm sorry to make you look foolish or prey on your emotions, but that's all it is, trickery. While my demonstration may not be proof Galva used the same, established techniques, it should at least show you how a person might be fooled without any legitimate psychic powers at work." La Claire scoffed as she stood and stormed out into the hallway.

"That's really cold, bro." Ax frowned. Vieve pushed Harlan off the couch and comforted Audrey who was still tearful. Harlan didn't wish to hurt anyone's feeling further. He found it humorous that half an hour earlier Vieve and Audrey clashed egos, but in the face of his perceived mistreatment they now huddled in unity. He kept the observation to himself.

"Maybe you're wrong, Harlan," Audrey said between sniffles. "Maybe you have a special gift and you don't even know you're using it."

"I assure you that I do not. It's the well-known method of cold reading. Not even cold reading, it's lukewarm reading. I know what you do so I can make statements specifically relating to an actress, I know where you were from, I can see you're attractive so I can make guesses about what childhood was like for a good-looking teen. These are nothing more than educated guesses, which, by the way, I made strategically vague. Besides that, I used what's known as the Forer Effect, or the Barnum Effect, which are statements that anyone can identify with. Galva did the same thing, I mean, telling someone they appreciate beauty, good food, good music, who would disagree with that? Who would say, no, no, I only like bad music and crappy food?"

Ax and Vieve continued to console Audrey, shaking their heads.

"The only other thing I did, just the same as Galva I suspect, was to tell you what you wanted to hear. Praising your accomplishments, your talent, and telling you there's a bright future for you. It's difficult, if you're even slightly convinced by the reading, to question it when it ends with exactly what you wanted."

Harlan appealed directly to Audrey. "Look, I'm sorry I needed you in order to make my point, but if I simply told you all how I thought Galva did her reading, what tricks and methods she'd used, you'd blow off my explanation. Showing you how it's done, how easily it's done, and how everyone can be fooled is the only way to cast scrutiny on predators who use these methods to misrepresent themselves and exploit others. I'll go a step further in saying not all psychic frauds are deliberate. Certainly there are some people who so believe in their own psychic powers that they are blind to the deceptive methods they're employing. They can be as much a victim of their own performance as those around them whom they convince of their ability. I have an opinion on where Galva falls in that spectrum, but in either case the world needs to be educated on how these kinds of hoaxes are accomplished."

Audrey regained her composure. She nodded and even smiled. "I just feel really stupid."

"Do you see how Galva might have been faking it too?"

"I don't know."

"Well, everybody can be fooled, Audrey. I mean it, professor, doctor, president, or regular Joe, myself included. We can all be fooled when someone is willing to prey viciously on our emotions." Harlan paused. "Also, I was childish with putting my hands on your chest. I owe you another apology for that too. I was pushing it too far, I'll admit, for the sake of the cameras." Ax nodded agreement. Harlan smiled at Audrey, and she smiled back. "They are spectacular, though."

Ax and Vieve were shocked. Ax expected Audrey to slap Harlan, but she laughed. "Oh, I know they are." She winked. Vieve hit Harlan in the arm, halfheartedly.

Audrey squinted with a notion. "So, how could Madam La Claire do her speaking to the dead: her online intuitive readings? I mean, if she's faking her power?"

"Very good question," Harlan said. "I've never seen her online sessions, so I can't comment with complete accuracy. That said, I have a damn good idea of what she does, much like other big-venue, commune-with-the-dead psychic-frauds. First, notice that they don't single out a person and say, 'Greg, your father who died nine years ago at the age of eighty-one is here to speak to you.' Instead they say, 'A man, an older man with the initial G, does that mean anything to you? And they let you fill in the actual information." Harlan sat.

"What they do, and what Galva probably does, is a combination of cold reading, using vague and high-probability statements, and shotgun reading. It's crucial they use a large crowd. If the medium told one person, 'I'm seeing a Matthew,' it might mean nothing to the person, but when you have 100 people in an audience, there are likely to be several with passed loved ones with that name. Next they get more specific and say, 'He was a grandfather.' OK, so some had brothers, uncles and such, so only a few are left with grandfathers named Matthew. Then they say, 'He passed from cancer,' for example, and so on until they narrow it down to one person with a grandfather named Matthew who died from cancer. Now that person says wow, the psychic knew my grandfather had passed, his name, and what he died from, when in truth the psychic just threw out common names, relationships, and ailments until it narrowed."

"Think about this. There are about 5 million Johns in the US, and another 5 million James's out of our approximately 300 million people. Let's say half are men, so roughly 1 in 15 men is named James or John. If every person in an audience has a father, two grandfathers, four great grandfathers, and likely a few brothers, uncles, and great uncles, on average everyone has 10 males within a few generations of bloodline. At one in fifteen, that means on average saying 'I'm getting a James or a John' is going to net 66 hits out of 100 people. With thousands, as Galva claims her audience is, that's over 600 hits. If you say I'm seeing a man with the initial J, that adds in 5 million Josephs, Jasons, Jeffreys, Joshuas, Jerrys, and so on, even Jose and Juan add over 1.4 million in this country alone. Easy to get at least one hit on every audience member just with the letter J. For women, the initial M starts off with over 10 million possible Marys, Margarets, and Michelles. If a medium starts off saying they're seeing an initial, either a J or an M, it's a strong indicator right away that they're playing the percentages."

The three nodded in understanding. "Mediums play the odds with vague and common names and increase the odds of a hit with larger and larger audiences. Once they've narrowed it down to one person who already thinks the medium has 3 or 4 impossible guesses right, they cold read the person, bombarding him or her with statements, 20 or 30 a minute, only focusing on what they get right and ignoring, or bending and re-qualifying, all the wrong guesses, until they manipulate them into seeming correct. Once the subject is thoroughly convinced, they use the same reading techniques as I did, only about the dead person, and of course they only tell you trivial details: he loves you, he's watching over you, and never that he had a locked box with thousands of dollars he never told anyone about. The most critical element to the entire charade is that all these audiences come in with a need to hear from their lost loved ones. They're already predisposed to believing anyone who offers them a link to that person they lost, and we've all lost someone. It's that preying on emotions that infuriates me."

"They can't all be fakes," Audrey said.

"If they're not, then prove it." Harlan looked directly into Audrey's helmet camera. "If there is a single psychic out there who is authentic then please come to the SMSF and prove it so we can dispense with the thousands of fakes and move forward with only those genuinely capable."

"La Claire says she does individual readings for people, not just the large readings. How would she fake that?" Vieve asked.

"Easily. Others who fake this sort of power do single readings by appointment. Since the psychic has so many customers, it seems reasonable to have to schedule ahead. They take your name, then they have a few days, a week, or even a month to find information on you. That's one way to sow the seeds of belief, or since you're there for one reason, usually, to talk to your dead loved one, they ask you that upfront. Who do you want to connect with? Either way they begin with a portion of information in hand, after that the technique doesn't change. Vague general statements, messages of love, or specifics of life that are common to everyone. Bending the misses roughly until they sound more like hits, making hundreds of statements, only a portion of which are right, and so on and so on."

"So what's the big deal? If people feel comforted by it, what's the harm?" Ax asked.

"When people believe lies they will get hurt. That's the battle we fight every day. The problem with believing someone can speak with your dead loved one is that people dwell on the past and don't move on with their lives. Some mediums just want to sell tickets and books to make their fortune off the misfortune of others, but others really get ahold of subjects and drain bank accounts, tear families apart, give false hopes, and in extreme cases cause physical harm and death. Certain mediums claim spirits can cure illness and ask subjects to abandon modern medicine. In a book he wrote called *A Magician Among the Spirits*, Harry Houdini compared commune-with-the-dead psychics with vultures, after which he immediately apologized to vultures."

Harlan grew further impassioned. "My grandfather died when I was a kid. Shortly after, my grandmother began visiting a medium that claimed he could contact my grandpa. You might not think it was a big issue, but she started seeing the medium three times a week. The only thing he ever told her was how grandpa loved her and missed her, and was with her; nothing relevant at all. Even I thought it was odd. Somehow he never told her he wanted her to move on with her life. That message might have stopped her from coming back. At that time I was five years old. I'd sit on the floor while she'd have her readings. I could see the medium was using noisemaking and vibration machines triggered under the table. I would tell my grandmother, trying to expose him. At five, I could see it was a sham."

Harlan's face flushed. "Still, there was no dissuading her. She started struggling to pay her bills because she gave her retirement and Social Security money to the medium. My parents stepped in eventually and tried to force her to stop. Instead of listening to them, she stopped speaking with my parents and all the rest of her family, the ones who actually loved her and had her best interests in mind.

The medium became her only emotional support. Money quickly became so tight she couldn't afford her medications. She never told us, and never stopped seeing the medium. In fact, the medium began performing spiritual healing in place of the medicine. Sadly she only lived a few short months after that. She died broke and alone, years too soon, instead of comfortable and surrounded by loved ones, all because this particular vulture used her as a meal ticket."

The others were quiet. Vieve stretched over and placed a hand on Harlan's knee. "Families write the foundation with similar stories all the time. That's why we have to keep challenging them." He looked up to Vieve with damp eyes. Vieve's face was warm and empathetic when their eyes met for a long moment.

"So what about La Claire's visions of what happened here? How would she know all that?" Audrey asked.

"Bullshit." Harlan composed himself. "Malvern may very well have been the killer, but I don't think a bit of what Galva gave us was any more than fiction. Sadly, the likelihood of solving this case after 80 years is slim. She's counting on that so her story will go down as the popularly believed answer to the mystery. People like La Claire are very strategic, researched, and rehearsed in their performance. What they construct is often great fun to believe in, and in most cases it's far more exciting than the plain truth. It's a dangerous combination that has kept them around throughout history."

"A phony psychic doesn't mean spirits don't exist," Ax said. "Something may happen to us when we die."

"True. Just because certain people prey on our belief in an afterlife doesn't preclude the existence of one. Then again, I want to see evidence before I'll believe in that either. Whether it's a groundbreaking scientific discovery or a spiritual idea, I'm perfectly willing to be shown something new but only when it is based on evidence and reliable experiments, and not just feelings, faith, and mythology."

Audrey sighed. "This is very heavy. I could use a drink."

Harlan relaxed. He looked to Vieve and they both grinned. "I think that could be arranged. You're in for a treat." From near his bag, Harlan retrieved the Prohibition-era whiskey bottle he'd discovered earlier. "Did they pack any cups in the supply crate?" Vieve, Ax and Audrey all crowded.

With no cups to be found, they drank straight from the bottle. "Mmm, that's good," Vieve said as she passed the bottle to Audrey. Everyone agreed.

Harlan leaned back and put his feet up. Vieve slid in beside him with Vinton's journal in hand.

For Those Who Wish to Follow In My Footsteps:
What I Discovered Part 3

I leave O'Brian and the precinct with a stack of reports and "a promise." I make my way around the corner to a little café and dive into the files in tote. "Missing persons," escapes my lips as I open the first, but it is a young woman. "Not you." The next is an elderly man. "Or you." The third is a dark-skinned man. The right approximate height, weight, and age, but "not a likely substitute for Malvern." Not up close, as I was. "None of them are."

After four cups of coffee and dozens of failed candidates, I press the papers back into a neat stack and signal to the owner for one last cup. "They have the best coffee in town." All the missing person reports since a week before Malvern's show, but not one likely candidate.

"Not altogether surprising." I figured it was a long shot that if Malvern is using kidnapped stand-ins, it is unlikely they would be missed; that anyone would feel their absence enough to warrant the effort of filing a report. It's better just the same to be doing something rather than nothing while I wait to hear back from O'Brian.

As I savor the mug of strong black coffee, I watch a vagrant man outside cross the café windows. He barely infiltrates my thoughts at first, then something occurs to me.

Rushing out, I flop the coin contents of my pockets onto the table. The owner will curse me, no doubt, but he'll likely receive triple the dollar I owe. "Wait," I nearly abandoned the files. I scramble back, retrieve them, and the glass door doesn't even return to close before I dash out.

While I'm in a hurry, the vagrant man is not, and has progressed merely a building down the sidewalk. I close the distance quickly, but take care not to run which would certainly alarm him. His clothes are made of heavy-duty fabrics, but with several mended tears and even more unattended ones. Dusty and dirty, he also bears brown leaves clinging to the back of his jacket and seat of his pants. At one time, this was the uniform of a factory worker or tradesman; a welder, if I had to hazard a guess. Now they've seen a number of cold nights on the ground. His face is unshaven and his hair uncombed.

I reach him. "Excuse me, sir." He ignores me. "Excuse me, friend." My second beckon draws his notice.

He turns his head but maintains his steady pace forward. "Uh-huh."

"Can I persuade you to stop for a moment? I'd like to ask you a few questions."

He says nothing and locks his gaze forward in the direction of travel. His speed increases, but just to a normal walking pace. I stay alongside him with ease. "Leave me alone, cop. I ain't done nothin'." Deep-chest coughing follows his words.

I should have expected this perception; questions from a stranger, dressed as I am, and reeking of coffee. I didn't have time to strategize my approach. I acted on impulse, something I've been doing more and more these days. "I assure you I am not a police officer. I just want to ask about anything you've noticed out of the ordinary."

He walks even faster. It becomes difficult to speak clearly without gasping for air. The pace has grown rapid enough to accelerate my breathing, and his. The vagrant coughs on nearly every exhale. He takes a sudden corner into an alley to shake me. I have to stumble my stride to match his new course. "I'm trying to find—"

"I got nothing to say to you, copper." As a last effort, I overtake his stride and put my torso in front of his with an arm extended. The resulting collision forces him to stop. In the impact, the files are knocked from my other arm and strewn across the alleyway. He stares at me, surprised.

"Will you let me finish a sentence?" He eyes the scattered papers. Inconvenient for my purposes now; almost every page is marked with the Chicago Police Department seal.

"Not a cop, huh?" He speeds away again.

I stay with the pages. "I'm not a cop." I have to yell as the distance grows. "I'm just rich." He slows and looks back. "I just wanted to hire you for an hour." He stops, leery but interested. "If you haven't done anything, you don't have any reason not to make an honest buck, even if I am a cop, which I'm not, so all the better for you."

He returns cautiously. "You ain't gonna make me answer no questions."

"I can't make you do anything. I just want to hire you to accompany me for an hour. How does ten dollars sound? Now, I might do some talking, but I can't make you say one word back." When he's near, I start collecting my pages. "I'll do the talking, you do the listening, and if you're so compelled you can help me out with what you might have seen. If not, a thank you will suffice and an hour from now you'll have ten bucks in your pocket."

The vagrant man assists in scooping up the rest of the files. "Where did you say we were going?"

I grin. "Coincidentally, the same place you were going before I interrupted you."

I pay him five dollars up front to show that I'm serious. His fist is tight on the bill, but his tongue loosens. I accompany him several blocks toward an industrial part of town, finally arriving at a campsite of sorts under a railway bridge. Several men and even women linger there, all similarly squalid in appearance. He continues to call me copper, though I urge against it. I crack a few jokes, candidly share details about myself, and start earning everybody's trust. I find that honesty about coming from money, when one is careful neither to brag nor denounce it, is far more productive than avoiding or hiding the fact. After being introduced as such, all the others address me as 'copper' as well, in spite of my protests. Eventually, I concede to the nickname.

They ask if I've ever been yachting or met the president.

"Truth be told, gentlemen, I haven't had the pleasure. Some years ago, though, I was in my father's office when he received a phone call from none other than President Wilson himself." A few others wander over to listen.

"The president invited my father to Washington to play a round of golf. Wilson is an avid golf enthusiast, you understand. My father, on the other hand, is not. He pondered a moment before he replied." Now many are crowded around. I have them hooked. "As matter-of-factly as if testifying in court, he responded, 'I'm sorry, Mister President, but I haven't the time. Some of us must work for a living.' This is the god's honest truth." The crowd of vagrants burst with laughter.

"You're all right with me, copper," and other similar remarks are elicited. Once I've earned their favor, I shift to my purpose: explaining that while not an officer, I am investigating an incident involving a possible missing person or persons who may have fallen into a terrible demise, and that this person would likely have been on the edge of society with little family or formal contacts such as a home or employment.

"Has anyone noticed anything unusual or anyone missing from the streets?" The smiles that lingered from my joke fade into frowns and diverting eyes. "Don't mistake me, gentlemen, my intention, were I to uncover wrongdoing, is to expose it for the appropriate authorities, and certainly any information provided here would be completely confidential." The stragglers drift away just as quickly as they had come.

I scan their faces. Eventually, my focus turns solely to my original contact, now just as timid as the others but unlikely to withdraw given the money still owed to him. Feeling my eyes on him, he looks to the ground, but soon realizes that my attention is unwavering.

"Well, copper, there have been a couple of guys…um…that haven't been around for a while." He looks up to see if I'm pleased.

"When did they go missing?"

"One about a week ago, the other a week before that." Some of the others now return to the conversation, ready to contribute, but pleased to have not been the first.

"What were their names?"

A woman speaks up. Though her hair and clothes don't give her away, her lack of a beard does. "Jimmy Windsor, or James Windsor. I remember he always used to say his family were decedents of royalty." She snickers.

"And the other man?"

"Don't know. Everybody just called him Kansas City. I guess he drifted up from there." She shouts. "Any of you ever get a name for Kansas City?" Most shake their heads.

"Where were they last seen?"

Another man pipes in. "There's this warehouse building, just off the tracks, near the water."

"Both were there before they went missing?" I ask. They nod. "What goes on at this place?"

The men speak over one another. "There's a couple of guys that have this place. They don't mind opening it up for people like us to…you know…come in and warm up a bit," says one.

"Maybe have a bite to eat if something's around, nothing special though," says a second.

"A nip of the bottle too some evenings. It's hard to find a place in the city anymore, especially when you're down on your luck," says a third.

"And listen to the radio. They've usually got some music playing, that's if there isn't a game or race on. They play every game, any kind of sport, you name it," says yet another.

"And they don't charge you anything? They let you come in and enjoy a few basic comforts for free, like a charity?" I ask.

My original contact responds. "Like charity, but the city houses and churches wouldn't letcha' play a game of cards or have a bit of gin."

"The saints running this place, do they operate any kind of business there, store anything in the warehouse? Do they ask anything from you, like sweeping up or loading trucks, some kind of job in return?"

"No, they're swell guys. I've had 'em ask me to pick up or drop off a package once in a while, you know, if I was going downtown anyway and give you a buck for your trouble, that sort of thing. Nothing I'd call a job, more like a favor for a friend."

"Me too once or twice," says a new voice.

The picture is becoming clear. "This is the last place you saw the missing men?"

"Well, yeah, but you never know, maybe they caught a break and got back on their feet. Maybe they slept in the wrong place and got thrown in the county lockup, could be anything."

This wouldn't explain their initial apprehension with the subject. One way or another there's more to this story than what they're sharing. You couldn't blame them for wanting to turn a blind eye to wrongdoing in favor of keeping the last few pleasures they could muster.

Tempting and manipulating the destitute with what they do not have is hardly a challenge. I've done it myself with ten bucks and perhaps more so by treating them as my equals in conversation. Respect, no doubt, is in as short a supply as anything for their sort. Now, I find myself wondering what questionable motives the proprietors of this vagrant clubhouse have in wanting to surround themselves with these poor gentlemen and ladies.

"Take me there." As before, eyes shift and faces disappear. "Let me rephrase that. Twenty dollars to each and every man or woman who'll guide me in the direction of and point out this warehouse." Many of the vagrants seem sickly, thin, coughing, and weak, but apparently not one of them is suffering in their hearing. I set out for the warehouse with 23 chaperones.

The vagrants lead me on a short tour of the less appealing parts of

Chicago: used-up industry buildings, abandoned demolition lots, a landfill, working-class commercial boat docks, even a filthy coal distribution station just off a rail line bearing my own namesake: Drake. I've never seen it before, but then again these are far from the beaten path of high living or regular tourism. You wouldn't pass here on the way to Municipal Pier, or to the theater. Most of our trek follows the industrial rail line, eventually making our way to a waterfront warehouse area—dozens of buildings, each butted within a few feet of the next. Most are only designated by building number. Those few with company signs are so faded you couldn't tell Western Wheel from Bugmobile.

When my guides identify the building, one whose numbers are even worn into blurs, we hold back and observe from behind some shrubbery lining the tracks. There's nothing divulging about the building's appearance. It's rather generic with light-brown brick, two stories high, and with no windows save for a line of small panes contouring beneath the roof's overhang, "for ventilation, I imagine." I can see two wood doors, front and side, as well as a truck entry, but each lacks windows. Ruling out the vents, 20 feet off the ground, it will be impossible to get a look inside without entering directly. Within moments of arriving, the vagrants shrewdly insist on the promised payments. I'm happy to oblige, handing out bills from a wad in my pocket, but taking care not to show the entire roll; I can't rule out them jumping me. Desperation encourages uncharacteristic behavior, a fact I have witnessed on more than a few occasions.

After pocketing the money, one vagrant informs me the warehouse usually isn't open this early. No sooner than he completes his thought, a black automobile stops near a door and three men unload. All three are dressed in dark suits. To my astonishment, I recognize one. The man from the front passenger seat is the same black-suited gentleman with the mangled nose from Malvern's audience, the man who stood out as the only other calm soul while panic struck all others.

Initially I'm confused, even alarmed, but with a second thought, "It makes only too much sense." The driver unlocks the warehouse door and the flat-nosed man follows him in. The third fellow stops before entering, turns, and surveys the area. I'm noticeably excited to see the connection forming. Distracted would be another appropriate description as I fail to notice one of my vagrant guides step out and wave to the lingering man. I'd have preferred to observe for a while longer. The suit beckons him over. Without hesitation, the entire posse follows.

The flat-nosed man and the other suit step back out to greet the vagrants. I'm faced with a split-second decision to either turn and hide or to join the group. I'm reluctant, but see no other way to examine the building than to walk through the front door, and I suspect I'd be far less welcome on my own than with my present company. Besides, I have no reason to believe the men haven't seen me by now anyway. I reach into my pocket, finding my trusty M1911 pistol in place. I flip its safety off and back on, "just to be sure." I then jump in behind the group, ditching my police files beneath a bush at the rail. I wouldn't want them to misrepresent me. Again.

"Come on in guys." Flat Nose grins. "We were just turning the lights on." He scans the group counting to himself. "Jesus, were you guys coming over for a drink or are we putting together a football team and nobody told me?" He laughs. The other two suits take that as a cue for them to laugh as well. As we approach, my mind races to invent a plausible ruse for my presence. I don't think I can pass for a bum. A newly bankrupt CEO? That'd be very weak. Some city worker, like a census worker accounting for the fringe of society, perhaps? I think not. I wouldn't want to associate myself with the government if I expect to make it very far.

"I've got it!" I bite my tongue but no one noticed my eruption. A volunteer physician; I could claim I'm a doctor wanting to look the group over out of charity, but that I needed a shelter to work in, that my office was too small, that it might turn off my regular patients, and that one of the vagrants thought these fine gentleman wouldn't mind opening their doors as a makeshift clinic occasionally. I certainly can pull that off to a layman. If Flat Nose happens to remember me, all he would know is that I was a medic in the war.

I'll come off smug, no doubt, since I don't want to mix the bums with my upstanding clientele. Exactly what they'd expect from a young, well-to-do city doctor. They may suspect I'm doing this not out of concern for the men, but out of wishing to pat myself on the back for my philanthropy. Likely, they won't even go for it, but whether they do or do not, it seems a strong enough excuse to get me through the doors and speaking with them while I get a glimpse inside.

I've sized these men up as gangsters. The details of their criminal pursuits are as of yet unclear, but I suspect arrogance and ignorance will be the best way to get in and out smoothly. The vagrants file in. The gangsters stand aside allowing them entry. I represent the caboose of the group. The men eye me up and down, as I too draw near. Up close, the flat-nosed man is dwarfed in size by the other two, his muscle. Before I can introduce myself, one of the heavies speaks first. "You're no bum."

"Thank you for the keen observation, my friend." The superiority in my tone is strategic. I extend my arm, offering a handshake, but again fail to introduce myself before Flat Nose cuts me off.

"I recognize you. Yeah, I know you from somewhere, let me see." All the vagrants have entered. I stand alone with the criminals.

"Your face rings a bell as well. Perhaps at the theater, a play if I remember correctly?" The seed is planted for him to make the connection to Malvern's audience, while presenting myself as indifferent, and keeping my intentions disguised. "My name is Doctor—"

I'm interrupted yet again when the original vagrant I hired returns from inside. "This is my friend...officer, ahh...Copper." I'm devastated! "We just call him Copper."

Flat Nose and the other gangsters' faces instantly flare red. "He's all right." The vagrant turns and, unaware of the disservice and possible condemnation he has done me, whistles a little tune as he swaggers back inside.

"It's a nickname," is all I manage to eke out before one of the large fellows lands a solid right hook on my jaw. He and the other move for my arms. I have my piece, but assuming these three are armed as well, my chances would be slim. I'll have to concede to a little roughing up. They restrain and quickly haul me inside. My heels drag on the pavement. The door is quickly shut behind us.

The vagrants sit around a few tables inside. They watch but do nothing. "Take him in back. Get him away from these guys." The thugs do as Flat Nose commands. I've nothing to gain by resisting. Instead, I take those few moments to survey the building. It's primarily wide open with concrete floors, at least the front two-thirds. There's a door into some back sections that I take it we're headed for. Impressions on the floor suggest there used to be more walls and large machinery of some kind. My heels bounce on worn ridges and a couple of floor drains. Everything has been moved out. A half dozen round tables are spread out, each surrounded with chairs. Besides that a bar made from the scrap wood of shipping pallets has been constructed in a corner, and there are a few chalkboards thrown up on the back wall.

Somewhat unsettling is a series of rather ominous hooks on rails crisscrossing the ceiling. There original purpose becomes evident when we enter a short hallway with an industrial-sized cooler on either side. This place must have been a meatpacking plant, a remnant of the meat industry that exploded in the city during the Civil War. The building might date back that far, but it would've been a plant with longevity to last long enough to see mechanical coolers installed. Perhaps a recent relocation, merger, or bankruptcy left the building for the wolves, so to speak, now the hideaway of a gang of street criminals.

My imagination can't help but conjecture that these criminals operate in body trade. They lure in hobos, people no one will miss, pick one off when needed, store them in the livestock-sized freezers, and sell them to buyers like the magician Kamrar for use in his act, and for an exorbitant price. I shudder as a picture comes to mind of the vagrant men hanging lifeless from the hooks in the main room.

Past the coolers into old offices, the thugs toss me into a chair. One moves behind me and drops his enormous hands on my shoulders, suspending me in place. Down the hall I hear Flat Nose. I cannot make out his words but his tone is soothing as if pacifying the bums.

I collect my thoughts and push the wild ones aside. My eyes drift to a desk, which is adorned with a small pad of paper, a blackboard full of charted figures, and a grossly excessive number of telephones. Reassessing, a different picture begins to form. There's no sound from the coolers; their motors and condensers would be massive. The tables and bar are well suited for card playing, a radio with races and ball games, the chalk boards; this in no slaughter house, not anymore at least. It's a numbers joint for illegal gambling.

They probably use the vagrants to make collections and payoffs. The police would barely notice a bum walking into a barbershop, restaurant, or hotel to settle a bet anywhere in town. Better yet, standing on the corner awaiting payment from some loser, who appears to be generously helping out the beggar. The vagrants are always hanging around to keep out of the cold, heat, rain, or snow, and to get a nip off the bottle. Give them a few bucks now and then, and they do your dirty work. It's quite brilliant. Rather than sending some well-dressed mafioso, send a bum. Frankly, most people, including police, go out of their way not to see them at all, and a transaction on the street between a suit and bum is far less suspicious than between two well-dressed men.

I can write off Flat Nose's presence at Malvern's show, assuming he's making quite a living for himself taking the city's bets. Furthermore, he's likely well connected through offering his services to high society, especially the well-off types who would also patronize that morbid attraction. He probably attended the show as the rest of us did, but he kept his calm simply because he's no stranger to violence, a hazard of his chosen profession. Darkness seeps back into the picture when my thoughts return to the missing men, this Jimmy and Kansas City. If Flat Nose and his crew are not supplying Malvern with bodies, then what happened to those bums? Did they get wise, or rather get ambitious and try to skim bigger payoffs out of the gambling take? Maybe one ran off with a large sum and these two hotheads had to go after him.

I'm fairly convinced these men have nothing to do with my investigation into Malvern. It's coincidence that led me here. An unfortunate one, though, as I am still on the bad side of three probable murderers. Down the hall Flat Nose's murmurs are replaced by music, laughter, and the clanking of drink glasses and bottles. Soon, footsteps traverse the cooler passage.

Flat Nose enters calm, not heated like his thugs. He closes the door, controlled, allowing it to latch with a faint click. "Turn out his pockets." One thug continues to restrain me as the second goes through my jacket. I only see one way to play this, cool and calm. If I were a cop, which to my benefit, slightly, I am in fact not. But were I, I would be insane or unbelievably bold to try to waltz in here so directly and all on my own. On the other hand, if I'm someone else, then he would have to think I'm fairly bold anyway. However, if I remain cool and calm as if I am sure the situation will turn out in my favor, I have a chance, maybe not a good one, but a chance of turning the tables. I restrain the feelings of panic and fear that are burning to surface and counter their symptoms one by one. Keeping my heart rate down, keeping from shaking or sweating, and telling myself that I've been in tighter jams. No reason to lose my cool.

The thug finds my pistol first. "A-ha." He waves it in my face then in the air toward Flat Nose. "What's this then, copper?" I don't react in the slightest. I don't even look at the thug or the gun. I lock my eyes on Flat Nose and push confidence ahead of every other feeling. He sees it too. He shares my stare and doesn't break for the gun. However, his is an expression of curiosity. In another pocket, the thug uncovers the only other article I carry on me, my bankroll, over two thousand, I estimate. He's confused when he pulls it out and turns to show it to Flat Nose, who smirks. The thug finishes checking every other pocket. "That's it."

"No badge?" the thug on my shoulders asks. I feel his grip wavering slightly.

The first shakes his head.

Flat Nose moves in close and looks my face up and down. "So what do you have to say for yourself, slick? Are you a cop?"

"An unfortunate misunderstanding. I am not a cop." I'm starting on the right foot if he's willing to hear my explication.

"And the pistol?"

"For personal protection. When I'm carrying around large sums and associating with bums and gangsters I feel a need to carry some pocket insurance." I've formulated a new story, but I'll have bet my life on my recent deductions.

Flat Nose addresses his men. "Cops don't usually carry around rolls like this, and now I know where I saw you before. You were at that magic show a few nights ago. You got on stage with that Kamrar." He starts to laugh. "Hell of a thing, wasn't it?" I'm relieved to hear his recollection. It will aid my escape strategy. I fight showing my relief on my face. "He ain't no cop fellas. Nobody in that crowd is supposed to be from the law. You have to pay a grand just to get in the door. No cop I ever heard of could cover that, 'cept maybe a crooked one, but they're all on our payroll." He laughs again. This time, the thug behind me follows suit, while the other who searched me remains on edge. The hands on my shoulders further loosen. "No precinct's gonna cover it for an investigation either. So what's your name, guy?"

I present the most boastful tone I can muster. "Vinton Drake, of the Drakes."

Flat Nose whistles. "Well, what do you know? We've got Chicago royalty in our midst, boys." He waves off the hands of the thug behind me. "So what brings you to our little establishment?" This is the pinnacle moment. I must commit fully in my charade. If I've guessed correctly about the nature of their dealings, then I figure I'm safe. If I'm wrong, well, I wonder if anyone will report me missing?

"For fun, gentlemen," I smirk. "I just got into town, after an extended stay overseas, and with some back allowance burning a hole in my pocket." I wink and Flat Nose grins. "One of the chaps at my club mentioned I could catch a card game, bet on a few races, or raise the stakes on a Cubs game if I wanted some excitement. I was told all I had to do was get a hold of you and that most of the bums in town could point me in the right direction. That didn't make much sense to me, but I threw a few bills at your patrons out there and here I am." Flat Nose nods in understanding.

The thug that searched me interjects. "So why they call you copper?"

My reply is instant. It's easy when it's the truth. "He didn't know me and started to run when I came up asking questions. I had to chase him half way down the street. It must have looked ridiculous." I chuckle, shaking my head. "When I caught up, he thought I was a cop after him. Makes sense, I guess, if he's working for you. Anyway, I convinced him and some of his friends that I wasn't and to lead me your way, which they did, but they just kept calling me Copper."

Flat Nose is satisfied. "Good enough for me."

"Boss, I don't—" Flat Nose cuts him off with a sharp glare.

"That's good enough for us." They share a stare. The thug folds. Flat Nose's expression softens as he offers his hand to pull me out of the chair. "Now let's see what we can do for you."

"When's the next card game?" My tone is more chummy than confident. The only remaining danger is to my pocketbook.

Flat Nose returns my money and my gun. "This weekend."

"All right then, do you have today's racing form?" He nods and puts his arm around my shoulders as he guides me back to the main room.

Flat Nose gets me a drink and shares a few anecdotes while I make selections from the equestrian lineup. He happens to be a charismatic fellow. I can imagine he mingles comfortably with the wealthy men around the city. Every joke goes over well with the vagrant crowd, with one of the thugs, who's gotten right into the mix of showing me a good time, and incites me to chuckle a bit too. The other thug, however, seems to be stewing in the corner, keeping watch with a sour face but not engaging with me or the others. His pride is hurt, no doubt, seeing me getting along so well with his boss after he lobbied the greatest against me.

Hours later I leave the place a little inebriated and about 900 bucks short. A small price to pay for my life, and who knows, I might get lucky on some long shots and turn a profit. A few steps out I spin back to Flat Nose, who is in the doorway. I continue the ruse to the last moment. "You have my hotel if I win, right? I don't want to have to come find you for my winnings." I pat my gun pocket with a smile.

"You got it, Drake. I'll just take it all back from you at the poker table this weekend." He waves, then closes the door.

Stumbling once or twice, I cross back over to the track to collect the files O'Brian lent me. Behind the bushes, the stack is where I'd left it. However, when I lean over to scoop them up I hear a voice. "I knew it."

12:00AM

Welcome back," Walter said from atop the mansion's front steps as the broadcast faded back from a commercial. "It's midnight here at the Drake mansion. We're just about halfway through the night with the investigation and some excitement, as well as some terror developing. Will all the contestants last until morning? Will further light be shown on the Drake family mystery? What else might show itself? Stay tuned to find out." Walter concluded with a smile as the broadcast cut away and returned inside the mansion.

After sulking on the bench near the front door, La Claire finally stood and sauntered back up the hallway. She passed the door to the living room with stealth. At the opposite end of the hallway, she noticed an odd door. It was thin with a flat profile and painted to match the walls identically. She opened it, expecting a closet, but found a narrow staircase. La Claire followed the steps up, through a half flight that cornered back and continued upward. She then opened another door at a midway landing that led to the back side of the second floor hallway. It occurred to her that these steps, so near the kitchen, and meant to blend in, were likely intended to conceal the coming and going of servants.

The steps continued to the third story, but at the bend in each flight was a small window facing the rear courtyard. La Claire returned to the lower window and used the sleeve of her shirt to wipe away a thick layer of dust inside. Though significant buildup remained on the outside, she managed to gain a view of the property. The broadcast camp appeared unchanged, but behind them was something odd; a glow. She wiped the glass again. Eventually, the crowd of candle-bearing onlookers became visible. The light from their collective flames shimmered, reflected in La Claire's eyes.

Walter shook hands with a local reporter just as a news cameraman packed his equipment into a van with a "Channel 7" logo in bright colors on its side. They stood at the edge of the candlelit crowd. Walter and the reporter turned toward the property gate just in time to see a second wave of visitors begin to stream in. As the reporter walked away, Jason sprinted up and crammed a sheet of paper into Walter's hand.

"The latest numbers." He struggled to catch his breath. "We're up another 2 million online, likely 30% broadcast. They're already getting calls in your trailer about syndicating a second airing."

Walter smiled. "It's a beautiful thing." He patted Jason on the back. "Let's get some of the loose equipment and cars pushed up from here. We're going to be getting plenty more visitors. Have the crew put up a rope line around this area?" The two headed back toward the production camp. They passed numerous new spectators along the way.

"Midnight." Ax checked the time on his laptop screen. "The ghost hunter's magic hour." He looked toward Audrey. "If we're going to get any evidence on record, this is the best time to investigate." Audrey hopped to her feet with excitement. Vieve looked toward Harlan.

"That's what we came here to do," Harlan said with a smile. "I'm interested in witnessing your full methods anyway, Ax." Folding the journal closed, he secured it back into his pack, dusted his hands, and stood ready to venture back out into the house. Harlan extinguished the three quarter-spent candles in one of the candelabra and replaced them with fresh ones. Vieve straightened her helmet cam and turned on the mounted flashlight. "What's the plan?"

Ax stood at the table prepping his gear. "I'd like to be systematic in my sweep of the house, floor by floor and room by room, so if anything is here it'll have to pass by us. I have no doubt this place has seen more than its share of mayhem. There have to be spirits here, and I'm not leaving without concrete evidence."

"Concrete evidence? Defined loosely."

Ax ignored Harlan. Already he was outfitting Audrey with a few devices. He then turned to Vieve. "Can I count on you to run a couple pieces of equipment?"

"I'll try." She stepped toward him with a smile.

"This will be simple." Ax handed her one of the devices.

Harlan joined them at the table. "Anything you'd like me to carry?"

"I think we got it covered." Ax booted a program on his laptop, bringing up a screen full of digital gauges. All initially read zero, or no reading. Next, he turned on the device in Vieve's hand. "This is the EVP recorder. It catches spirit noises. The microphone is here on the front, so point it away from yourself." Ax selected a second gadget. "This is a white-noise generator. Just hold it out with the other hand." After tapping a button, a soft, yet nerve-rattling scramble of tones filled the air. Ax turned to the computer screen and made a few adjustments, then one of the readings came online with bouncing audio levels. "Check, check," he said leaning over into the microphone. At the same time, the levels on the screen jumped into the red. Ax was proud of himself. "I've modified everything so I can simultaneously record all readings and images here, time stamped."

Audrey carried the EMF detector and Ax's instant-read thermometer. "Can you turn those on, Audrey?" As she did, one and then the other, the screen lit up with a temperature reading in one corner and the three electromagnetic frequency readings in another.

"Great." Now he snapped two additional pieces onto the top of his digital camera, an ion generator and the infrared light emitter. When he touched a few more buttons on the computer, a large image appeared in the center of the screen and showed his handheld camera view in the green hues of night vision. He adjusted the camera, making the image shift to thermal vision and back. Finally, Ax pulled out a compact computer tablet. After booting the screen, in a few seconds he brought up an identical image of the laptop readouts. "This way I can monitor everything as we go. Another mod that I came up with, and coded myself." Grinning, he clipped on a wireless earpiece and inserted its receiver into the tablet. "Let's start back in the office."

"Wait just a sec." Vieve crossed to the open doorway to the hall and hollered, "Galva!" She waited a moment. No reply. "Galva, we're going to do some more exploring." She searched the dark, empty hall with her eyes and listened keenly. Nothing. "Madam La Claire?" Again, no answer. Finally, Vieve shrugged and returned to the others.

Loaded with gear, Ax led Audrey and Vieve. Harlan following behind them unencumbered except for his candelabrum. In the office, Audrey and Vieve lingered near the door. Ax swept the room with the camera, watching the tablet screen as he panned. The girls followed his lead and fanned their gadgets through the air. Moving farther into the room, Ax swept the entryway. He signaled the others to get behind him. The green-tinted features of the room flew by, unimpressively. After a few more passes, Ax switched the camera to the thermal imaging, or heat vision, mode. Immediately, he almost fell over, stumbling with giddiness. "Look, look," he whispered.

The ladies leaned in behind him to see the tablet screen. In the middle, a tall, slender figure in red became visible as if inside the wall. The shape seemed to have two slowly flailing arms, as it crept from right to left. When it drew closer, it appeared to gain a third arm. Ax pulsed with excitement as the figure approached the doorway. Even Harlan glanced back and forth from the wall to the screen with puzzlement. Ax double-checked the monitor was recording a timecode of the readings and dropped a numbered digital marker in the timeline. "The doorway, that's where the cold spot was before."

Ax spoke under his breath. Everyone was statuesque as the figure closed to a few feet outside the door.

Something dawned on Harlan. He whispered to Vieve. "Can you turn off the noise maker for a moment?" Ax looked back with scorn. Vieve didn't act as she watched Ax for a cue of approval. Undiscouraged, Harlan reached over and tapped the button on the white noise generator, pausing its sound. Ax hung his head in disappointment as the hum of a motor took over in the now quieted space. In another moment, one of the camera pillars crested the doorway. Its top-mounted lights waved back and forth as it searched for them. Harlan smiled while Vieve and Audrey let out deep sighs of relief, breathing for the first time in almost a minute.

"I'm gettin' nothing in here, man." Ax lowered his camera. "Even the cold zone from earlier is gone."

"Nothing new on the desk area, where Galva intuited Vinton Drake's murder?" Harlan asked.

Ax shook his head, "Nothin'." He pointed his camera at the floor below the desk and toggled the sensor modes once more. "Let's cover the living room next." On his cue, the ladies followed Ax back to the main room. Again, Harlan brought up the rear. Immediately inside, Ax reached over to the white noise generator in Vieve's hand and activated it.

As before, Ax, Audrey, and Vieve scanned the room with their respective equipment. Ax watched his camera first, but discovering no anomalies, he lowered the camcorder and followed the other readings on his portable screen. After a moment, he got a curious expression. "Hold still for a sec, Audrey." She did as asked. "Now turn to your right." She moved sharply. "No, no, um, go slowly." Audrey was very near the center of the room and faced the junction to the hallway. She reset her previous position and panned both devices with a slow turn to her right. As she completed a quarter revolution, she found she now faced the doorway back to the office. "Hmm, now go back the other way."

"OK." Audrey spun back to face the hallway and then continued her spin until she faced the dining room entryway.

"I'm not seein' it now."

"What about back here?" Audrey rapidly moved to face the outside wall with the fireplace.

"Woah! There it is. There's a drop in temp, almost ten degrees. Take a couple of steps forward." Audrey obliged. As her steps waved the thermometer back and forth slightly, the temperature reading on Ax's display fluctuated between 60 and 55 degrees. "Yeah, it's a really cold spot. Something's gobblin' up all the heat energy." Audrey shared in his excitement as Vieve and Harlan paused their own endeavors to watch. Audrey and Ax honed in on the center of the cold spot. It was soon clear that the mantle was the focus.

Audrey scanned the same photos Harlan and Vieve had earlier. "Do you think one of the spirits is here with these old photos?" Ax joined her. "I wonder if they're trying to show us something?" Ax nodded agreement as he too examined a few of the framed images. Harlan stepped up and put his hands over the fireplace below. With arms extended, he looked over to an approaching Vieve and gave her a smile and a wink. Vieve took a knee right next to the others and leaned over to peer up the chimney.

"The flue's open." She reached in and pulled a handle. Nothing happened at first. The others watched her. "It's good and stuck." She handed Harlan the devices she was carrying and with both hands used all her strength to pull the handle again. This time a rickety metallic noise emanated from within the masonry. Flakes of soot and chunks of built-up leaves and dirt dropped into the fireplace from above. She stood back up and dusted the filth off her hands. "Brrr, it's cold down there." She shot a smile back to Harlan. Ax turned away, irritated, while Audrey lingered. It took a few moments before she correlated cold readings and the open airway to the outdoors. By then, Ax and Vieve were back to surveying with their respective devices.

Ax hid quietly in his scanning, but after another minute, Audrey called for everyone's attention again. "There's another cold spot here." She pointed to a spot on the floor just in front of the staircase. "Here, see for yourself." She extended the thermometer out toward

Harlan. Ax swooped in, surveying the area.

"Wow, a solid ten-degree drop." He took a knee and, trusting his camera to one hand, placed his other hand palm down on the floor. "Definitely. Check it out—you can feel it," he said to Harlan.

Harlan approached and placed both hands palm down as Ax had, then he withdrew and performed the same test on a portion of the floor a few feet away. "It seems true."

"You got an explanation for this one?" Ax asked.

"Water under the foundation, perhaps? Nothing's for sure, but I'd think there could be a number of practical explanations for heat lost through a floor, ranging from construction design, to materials, to age and damage." He paused and looked around, taking scope of the entire room. "This is close to the one area where the nails weren't sticking out when we first came in. Maybe this section was replaced with different wood for some reason or another?"

Ax shrugged. "Looks like the same wood to me. I think a spirit has been lingering here recently." His eyes lit up and moved to Audrey, who was enthralled. Harlan made an annoyed humph. Ax, pleased with himself, used the tablet to drop another digital marker on the timeline near discovering the temperature anomaly and then resumed his scans of the room.

After another few moments, Ax concluded his sweep. "There aren't any other readings of interest here." Everyone nodded. "Let's keep movin'." He pointed to the dining room doorway. Once there, the four continued to examine the room without noteworthy results.

Before leaving, Audrey moved to the middle of the room and hushed the others. "Spirits," she called out to the walls, slowly altering her direction as she spoke. "Spirits, if you are there, show yourself." Ax zoomed his camera on Audrey's face. From the night-vision mode, her features were less defined and hued in green while her eyes produced washed-out reflective circles that shifted from side to side. "We mean you no harm. We're here to help you if we can. Please show yourselves." Ax moved his camera back to scanning the room. Vieve and Harlan waited quietly as all listened and watched. The total lack of voice or movement reestablished the sheer chill and eeriness that the dilapidated mansion exuded. The stale, musty air of the house registered now more than ever for Harlan. A minute passed in silence. Nothing.

Next, they moved to the kitchen and took extra care to not only survey the room for anomalies but to examine in particular the location of La Claire's perceived crime scene. Again the readings showed nothing that stood out as extraordinary. Harlan even led Ax to scan the pantry and Vinton's back-room workshop, which may have otherwise gone unnoticed. However, even in the workshop Ax's chosen set of metrics all came up as consistently unremarkable. In spite of the lack of developments, Ax was undiscouraged. "There's a whole other half down here we ain't even set foot in yet." He guided the group back through the kitchen and into the front hallway.

In the hallway, Vieve noticed the thin door to the servant stairway for the first time. It was ajar. "This wasn't open before." Both Ax and Harlan approached. Ax scanned the door and beckoned Audrey to do the same.

"Wow, did it open itself?" Audrey asked. "Maybe the spirits were trying to answer me?"

Harlan opened the door and looked up the empty steps. "We have no idea where Galva has gone or what doors she may have opened."

"Probably La Claire," Ax said. "No unusual readings on the door."

Across the hallway from the living room was a double, sliding-door entryway into another area. Both were slightly open, allowing a thin view into the room at first, but only enough to see a small amount of the wood floor. Ax opened them further, revealing only a deep emptiness as far as they could see, only black. Ax went in first, though he inspected the floorboards for protruding nails before he committed fully. With a few steps, Ax disappeared around the wall. Audrey and Vieve hesitated in the doorway, but after a few seconds they heard Ax. "Holy shit, you have to come see this."

Vieve proceeded into the dark boldly with Harlan right behind her. Audrey was still leery and proceeded slowly. They searched first with the beams from their helmets, enhanced with the cast from Harlan's candles. An ornate ceiling, along with lavishly decorated walls, were exposed. As Vieve and Harlan caught up to Ax, they passed under a chandelier even larger and more grand than the one that dangled in the living room. The hanging decoration bore thousands of long, sharply pointed crystals facing downward. Harlan pulled out his handheld flashlight and directed it into the cornucopia of prisms, casting a galaxy of rainbow-streaked trapezoids onto the ceiling, floor, and walls. He waved the light in a small circle and the emitted spots danced and flickered in response.

"Disco." Vieve laughed.

"Looks like this was a ballroom. Ahead of its time," Harlan lowered his flashlight and scanned the outside wall, opposite the doorway. Long, heavy, velvet curtains framed several large windows. They reached Ax and noticed that he was elated.

"Here, look at this." Ax handed Harlan the tablet screen, the center of which still showed, in real time, what Ax's camera captured. Harlan set his candelabrum down nearby to manage the tablet. The image was in thermal mode. "So heat rises, right?" Ax directed his camera at the floor under a second grand chandelier, identical to the first. The image on the screen was unimpressive, showing a flat surface in orange tones with faint parallel lines from the floor joints. "That's why ya' might expect the ceiling in a room to be slightly warmer than the floor, or at least the same temp, but watch this." Ax slowly panned the camera upward, first to the chandelier. The image onscreen gave the shapes of the crystals, though they were only slightly visible. Their temperature was nearly the same as the ambient temperature in the room. Finally, Ax's camera pan reached the ceiling, just above the ornament. Vieve and Harlan were taken back by a dark spot on the ceiling through the camera. It was purplish on its edges and faded to pitch black at its center. "Something is sucking in all the nearby heat right at this point."

One of the mobile camera pillars appeared in the doorway and continued to glide into the room. Its lights expanded the dim illumination in the room and shined brightly on Audrey, creeping her way to the others. "You need to get some temp readings on this, Audrey," Ax said. She moved more rapidly.

Audrey scanned the area from ten feet away. Harlan followed on the tablet readout. "Your EMF is bouncing as well, Ax."

Ax looked over with a smile. Harlan turned the screen toward him. With a nod, Ax pivoted back to the camera. "It's suckin' up all kinds of energy. I'd say this is an area where one of the spirits, or hell maybe all of them, have recently passed through the ceiling to the floor upstairs. Now look at this." Ax held the camera over his head. Vieve and Harlan followed again on the tablet screen. Ax waved the camera from the dark spot back toward the door to the room, and a narrow strip of purple could be seen standing out from the orange ceiling image, trailing all the way across. "Maybe the spirit moved from there"—he whipped the camera back to the large cool spot—"to over there." Quickly he retraced the purple line. "I bet it was movin' upstairs, so it was just barely leavin' a trail on the floor, and down here it came through as this narrow track." He grinned.

"Maybe that spot is where the spirit was waiting around for a long time upstairs." Audrey said.

"Yeah, maybe." Ax nodded to her. With the camera centered again on the cold area, Ax walked a half circle, arching around the chandelier a couple steps back. The spot remained on screen as the room turned around it. Once on the other side, he panned the camera along the ceiling in the opposite direction, but no matching trail of cold was detected. "See, it's localized to just that one absorption point, and the trail away from it is in a single direction. Somethin' definitely was movin' there." Vieve looked over to Harlan, expecting a debate; however, Harlan was too focused, looking from the image to the ceiling and back, to notice.

Ax broke from the spot and surveyed the back end of the ballroom. A third chandelier lied in line with the other. There were more windows, walls, and artwork, but nothing that captured Ax's attention. Content that there was nothing of further interest, Ax returned his focus to the cold spot. Back under the center chandelier, Ax moved in closer. This time he slowly zoomed the camera in tighter until the purple and black of the cold area were the only portions in frame. Harlan continued to observe on the read-out screen. Vieve and Audrey often checked over his shoulder.

With the camera zoomed to such an extreme, the screen blurred with the slightest movement of Ax's hands. For a brief second he managed to steady his hands, and suddenly an intricate pattern flashed on the screen. Straight lines, perfect circles, square corners, and a bevy of shapes sprang out of the black as pencil-thin lines in the violet spectrum, but just whispers of them, as slight of an impression as one could detect, and then they disappeared just as quickly into the blur of Ax's unsteady camera work.

"What was that?" Audrey asked, inadvertently screaming directly into Harlan's ear.

"I don't know." Ax nearly fumbled the camera with excitement. "I saw it too, though." He regained control of his equipment and brought it back to the spot, but he couldn't replicate the steadiness needed. He moved the camera away. Everyone's helmet lights overlapped on the area, but no indication of the shapes could be seen, only a uniform plaster ceiling.

"Let's try this." Ax knelt just outside the chandelier's coverage. Next, he rested the camera on his knee and steered it back to the ceiling. Further away, the frame of the screen captured a large portion of the ceiling outside the cool spot. Ax zoomed the camera as far in as it would go to isolate the spot again. However, the stability gained was defeated by the reactiveness of the increased zoom, only giving more blurred images.

"Hold on a sec." Ax jumped back to his feet. He rushed to the door and dodged the camera pillar that blocked the way. Ax returned in a few moments with a wooden chair from the dining room in tow. He placed the chair near the chandelier and stepped up on the seat. Now he could pull the camera zoom out all the way and move the camera itself in toward the cool spot to examine it closer.

"Yeah, that's a little better," Harlan said. Ax had to hold the camera at full arm's extension over the top of the chandelier. The screen was still largely shaking and blurred, but periodically, for only a second, the intricate lines and shapes from inside the spot emerged. Ax, however, could not hold the camera out at length and observe what it was picking up on screen simultaneously. Frustrated, he jumped down from the chair and dragged it to just under the very center of the chandelier. He had to duck the hanging crystals as he returned to his perch atop the seat. Finally, Ax snaked the camera and his body up through the decoration.

Ax had to lean far backward to get around a structural part of the chandelier, and in doing so, the chair began to tip. Harlan noticed. "Be careful up there."

"Yeah, hold on." Ax continued to struggle to get set between pieces of the ornament. He leaned too far and the chair started to flip on him, but he managed to correct himself in time and the chair slammed back down to all four feet on the floor. The stomp was followed by an eerie creak in the floorboards that lingered oddly for several seconds.

"What was that?" Audrey said. Harlan hushed her and concentrated on what could be heard. Ax found the position he wanted, then re-centered his weight, distributing it evenly on the seat. The trace cracking sound continued, emanating from the floor.

Harlan's face showed concern. "Ax, maybe you should come down."

"No man, just gimme a minute." Ax placed the camera very near the ceiling where the cold spot had been and then adjusted the lens to focus. Again, the purple and black spot was framed exclusively, only this time the details of the shapes beyond it came out very clear and held for several seconds. Now, Ax could hold the camera and examine the image. Harlan traced the features on screen with a finger. There were long rods, hinges, and gears, in his estimation. The composition puzzled him and Ax both.

Another crack sounded from the floor, much louder than before. Ax ignored it, enamored by the image on the camera screen. Harlan looked down and noticed one leg of the chair seemed to be pushing into the floor as if the wood was giving way. When he looked back to the monitor screen, he was surprised to see several of the features in the ceiling were now in motion. A hum became audible from the ceiling in the same moment.

Ax was unwavering in his focus on the spectacle, but Harlan was alarmed. He thought for a moment but the hum grew louder. Harlan sprang forward instinctually. He tossed the screen in Vieve's direction. She managed to catch it as Harlan dashed to Ax and tackled him, mid-body, pulling him off the chair and out from under the chandelier and flinging both their bodies several feet away. A split second later the chandelier dropped from its hanging position and crashed to the floor with the thud of a boulder falling, overlapped with the shimmering sound of a thousand needles dropped in unison.

Audrey screamed and scrambled backward to the doorway. Ax was dumbfounded. He stared first at the chandelier, which was flat on the floor, and then stared into Harlan's face with utter disbelief. Vieve rounded the mess and helped both men to their feet.

"Christ, thanks man." Ax finally spoke.

Harlan dusted himself off and rubbed one shoulder. "No worries." As the three of them inspected the damage, Audrey returned. Not only had the chair been reduced to splinters, crushed under the heft of the chandelier, but also several individual crystals stood upright, their downward points penetrating the floor like the tips of darts.

Ax was quiet, no longer stunned, but embarrassed. Vieve attempted to look him over, but he pushed her away. "I'm fine, I'm fine." He noticed his camera had been knocked out and slid away. Ax retrieved it. "Hey, didn't even break the camera."

"That was too close." Vieve said. "Is anyone else wondering if we really should be in here? I mean, is the house even structurally sound?"

"You do what ya' want. Nobody's forcin' anyone to stay, but I'm just gettin' started." Ax gestured with his head to the pile that once was a beautiful chandelier. "Tells me we're on the right track."

As everyone's adrenaline waned, the four made another survey of both the chandelier and the cool spot. Vieve's eyes lingered for a long moment on Harlan with a smile of admiration. On the camera's screen, the purple and black coloration remained on the ceiling.

Their silent examination was interrupted by a voice in the darkness. "No one is hurt, I hope." They all turned, but the lights on the camera pillar hid the speaker. "No new spirits to speak to?" It was La Claire.

"That is damn exciting television." Walter's were the only words uttered in the otherwise enthralled broadcast truck. "I think it's safe to cut to commercial now." No one moved. Walter tapped Nora on the shoulder to break her trance. She rubbed her eyes, then faded the broadcast out.

1:00AM

A digital tone echoed through the expansive room from Harlan's watch. Ax checked his own briefly. Still embarrassed, Ax was eager to move on. "Times a wastin'. Looks like there's another room up front we haven't checked." With nods from the others, Ax collected the tablet from Vieve and proceeded to a closed set of French doors on the far end of the ballroom. Harlan reclaimed his candelabrum.

"Where'd you go?" Audrey asked La Claire, who was now following along with the others. "You shouldn't run off alone; this place is dangerous. Did you get in touch with any other spirits?" La Claire just shook her head.

The doors held large glass collages, each section of which was either frosted or textured so that the composition was translucent, but not transparent. They disappeared into the walls as Ax opened and unmasked a front parlor. The first in, Ax surveyed the room alone. The front wall and one side wall both bore large windows to the outside, which lit up with the cast from the production camp on the lawn. Though they were too grimy to peer out, they cast a medium glow on the rest of the room. Its dimensions, as well as door and window placement, were a mirror reflection of the front office.

Vieve and Audrey entered next. There were several elegant chairs, side tables, one table with a chessboard, another table bearing a half-sized roulette wheel, and there was even a small bar in the corner. Vieve spun the roulette wheel. "Probably a hub for getting drinks, sitting, or having a smoke when the Drakes hosted parties."

The first thing Harlan noticed was an overturned and broken cabinet cloaked in shadows behind the bar. Its contents were scattered on the floor around it. Dozens of wine bottles and scores of glasses had been reduced to shards, pulverized under the heft of thick mahogany shelves. Harlan sifted into the rubble with his shoe. "Supposedly one of the tragedy locations," Vieve said as she approached from behind.

He turned to her with a look of query. "One of the investigating officers?"

Vieve nodded. "Yeah, I think so. They said he was searching the house and ran into prohibited substances, and while collecting them was crushed in a freak collapse of the cabinet."

"I guess that isn't all too uncommon in this house."

"People speculated the cabinet was engineered to destroy its contents should it get searched in a raid. A prohibition booby trap, I guess, but who knows?"

"If Vinton made his furniture custom himself, I guess that's a firm possibility," Harlan agreed.

"He probably never dreamed it would kill someone." She sighed. Harlan nodded. They both silently imagined the long-past incident, until Audrey butted in.

"What if the magician's spirit led the officer into that trap so he wouldn't uncover the truth, just as he tried to kill Madam La Claire?" In the corner, La Claire smiled. Reading Vieve's contempt, Harlan could see she took the policemen's deaths more personally and was far less open, at that moment, to spiritual conjecture. He signaled Audrey to back off with a shake of his head. Audrey hung her head, turned, and then began waving her given gadgets around the room.

After scanning 360-degrees with both sensor modes, which resulted in nothing noteworthy, Ax turned his attention exclusively to the ceiling. His excitement returned. Harlan and Vieve's attention was drawn to Ax's giddiness. Vieve realized she had neglected the devices Ax assigned her. She snapped to work, moving the equipment about the room. Harlan stepped over to get a glimpse of the video feed on the tablet. The image at the center of the readout showed the room in the familiar hues of the thermal-vision mode. Just as in the ballroom, there was a large purple to black concentration of cold. Ax's focus was on the area of the ceiling directly above the crashed cabinet however, this time as he panned away from it, the rest of the ceiling bore a network of similar yet smaller cool spots.

"Tons of spirit activity here," Ax said. "There must be somethin' important about this area because the spirits are movin' through here like mad." He continued to pan the ceiling in a full-circle pivot.

Harlan furrowed his brow. "You realize the supposed spirit movement in the ballroom ended up correlating to an actual, physical, and of-this-world anomaly in the ceiling, which housed hidden mechanisms? Is it outlandish to speculate for a moment on whether some similar physical explanation might exist in here?" Ax ignored him. "I wouldn't recommend going in for a close and in-depth inspection this time." Harlan mumbled to himself, but Vieve struck an amused smirk.

"This is great. Let's keep movin'. I have a feeling there's more to come." The group followed Ax out a second side doorway directly into the front hallway. Ax led them back toward the center of the house.

Harlan hollered from the back of the group. "Wait a minute, Ax." Ax paused and looked back. "Can we spend a minute up here at the entryway? If you'll recall, Joyce, I mean Galva, proposed it was an important point where the spirits of the family drove Malvern to kill himself in a fit of insanity. I'd be interested to see what your readings gather here." Ax reluctantly agreed and walked back. All five crammed into the small portion of the hall. Ax's camera readings, however, revealed nothing, even on the ceiling. After a couple of passes, Ax turned his attention to the readout numbers from the other sensors.

"I'm gettin' nothin'."

La Claire rolled her eyes and scoffed as Audrey looked expectantly from Ax to her. "As usual, technology falls short of nature."

"I personally think science reveals the flaws of nature." Ax turned his back on La Claire and returned to his path through the house. "One room left on this floor, I think. Who's comin'?"

Harlan chuckled. He spoke only loud enough for Vieve to hear. "Flaws, yes. Science, I think not." Vieve shook her head with a laugh as they followed Ax.

The final room on the ground floor was a spectacular lavatory, just across the hallway from the kitchen and dining room, tucked between the back of the ballroom and the back wall of the house. The counter tops were marble. The room had fine porcelain amenities, a pair of large, arching faucets with nickel finish, tarnished by years of neglect, and each wall bore elegant, hand-painted tiles. There was no bathtub. Harlan concluded that particular need would have been limited to the upstairs bathrooms, not there, where guests would have been frequent.

"Whoa, did you see that?" Ax said moments into his scan. He jostled his camera as he balanced it and the tablet screen hurriedly. "A shape, there was a figure there, like a person." He pointed to the sink area. "It was, like, standing inside the countertop and up." Audrey paid careful attention.

"Are you sure it wasn't one of the camera pillars behind the wall?" Harlan asked.

Ax scowled. "No, it was different." He used the tablet to replay the moment in question. On screen, the room appeared in the florescent green shades of night-vision. When the video panned across the room, as claimed, an odd shape popped up near the sink as a green flare, brighter than anything else, but only on the very edge of the frame. It was far from strictly human shaped, and it was only present for a split second. "There, there, did you see it?" Audrey nodded excitedly. Ax panned the area again. He spoke toward Harlan. "It's gone now, but something was definitely there."

"It could be a camera glitch, a digital inconsistency as you move the camera," Harlan said. "Since you're shining extra infrared light, it could be a partially reflected flare off the mirror that you can't replicate."

Ax shrugged as he and Audrey inspected the area closely. "Wow, I think I can feel something. It's like a sensation in my stomach." Audrey smiled to Ax as she touched the countertop with her fingertips. "I've got goose bumps." After continuing for several minutes with no new anomalous readings, Ax indicated the search would be moving upstairs.

They returned to the second floor by way of the living room staircase. One of the camera pillars met them at the top of the steps. The contestants came first to a pair of bedrooms on either side of the floor's central hallway. Earlier, La Claire passed these rooms by.

Ax decided they'd search this floor systematically front to back. The left door was open. From the hall, they could see a large shape draped like a tent in the middle of the room with poles at four corners and a sagging shroud between them. It seemed clear that it was a large, decorated bed. Ax judged it to be the master bedroom. He elected to search that room first. Within the bedroom, Harlan moved to uncloak the bed. In a gray cloud of particulates, he revealed intricate and hand-carved head and foot boards including the tall, wooden corner posts framing the bed. Matching wood chests of drawers and bedside tables completed the layout, complemented by green walls and a matching bed cover. The room was orderly, though covered in a lifetime of dust. There were several personal items neatly laid before a dressing mirror: a hairbrush, perfume, jewelry box, an ornate hand mirror, and a few other beauty items. Nothing appeared to be out of place or disrupted.

After an initial sweep, Ax showed the others more cold spots adorning the ceiling. There were no large central portions as in the ballroom or parlor, but a smaller and repetitive network, just as Ax noticed in the majority of the front parlor, was consistent throughout. Ax was convinced it was further evidence of spirit activity. Without a word, his face conveyed his elation to the others, particularly to

Audrey, who shared in his interpretation. The rest of the room seemed to offer little out of the ordinary.

Across the hall, another smaller, less ornate bed was covered. The furniture in the second room was more basic. The color palette of walls, bedding, and drapery was in blue shades. There was another dressing mirror, but with no belongings. "It's very generic," Vieve said. "This must have been a guest bedroom." As they searched the room with Ax's gizmos, the results were the same as before. Only the ceiling showed abnormalities, the same pattern of cool areas.

They moved down to the next set of doors, which were the bathroom and a large walk-in closet opposite it. Ax's method seemed to grow less and less diligent. He tended to begin with a search of the ceiling in thermal camera mode, his sweeps of the lower half of the rooms were brief, and he paid little to no attention to the readouts from the other sensing equipment. His focus was almost exclusively on the ceiling anomalies.

The bathroom and the closet both bore the same patterns in his thermal images. Continuing down the hall, the boys' bedroom was next. As the four followed Ax, so did the camera pillar. The children's room wasn't exceptional through Ax's technical perceptions. It did contain the same cold spots as the other rooms on this story; however, there were no other readings to add any credence to La Claire's version of the heated and gruesome events that occurred there or her revelation of a concentration of spirit activity in this location. Harlan pointed out that fact once Ax's search had concluded, but La Claire didn't bother to comment or protest this time.

The bedroom across from the children's was much like the guest room, in its furniture and arrangement, though its hues were maroons and reds. It also had a few personal touches. "The daughter's room," Audrey said. She lifted a hand mirror, much simpler than the one in the master bedroom, and examined herself in it, straightening her hair. "So sad."

In this room, Ax trained his camera view on the floor. "Look here." They crowded around to see over Ax's shoulder. The screen revealed another large, cold spot, but this time on the floor of the room.

"It's the same spot as in the ballroom," Harlan said. "We're just seeing it from above now."

Ax nodded with a satisfied smile. "We might just be uncovering the single best example of specter presence, influence, and trans vallum ever recorded." His voice was overrun with delight.

"Trans vallum?" Vieve repeated.

Ax grinned, but Harlan spoke before Ax could respond. "From Latin I presume. 'Trans' for across and 'vallum' for wall. I've never heard that, very apt, and clever." Ax just smiled again.

Satisfied they'd covered the room, Ax moved to the end of the hall and to the final pair of rooms on the second floor. Both were additional bedrooms, each done up in its own color scheme, but both lacked the personal touches of a permanent resident. They scanned the rooms with their respective instruments. The smaller ceiling cold spots were consistently present while nothing else of note emerged.

At last, Ax declared the second-story search was complete. "All the spirits seem to be moving upstairs." He spoke toward Audrey. "Away from us? Maybe. Or, there just might be something earth-shattering up there." He feigned an eerie voice and winked at Audrey. "I guess we won't find out from down here though, huh?" Ax began to walk back up the hall toward the main stairs, which continued up another floor.

La Claire spoke for the first time since they'd come up. "There are steps here." She opened the narrow door at the back end of the hallway, again painted and masked to blend into the wall, which revealed the servant stairway both up and down. "If you like." Ax gave her a nod and moved to the back stairwell. La Claire spoke under her breath as he passed. "You may want to run your little toys back here anyway, to be thorough." Caught off guard, Ax struggled to find a retort. Conceding this time, he said nothing and proceeded up.

As the others filed in, Vieve spotted the field of light through the window. "What the heck is all that?" She looked more closely. Ax barely noticed while Audrey, Harlan, and La Claire crowded in to share the vantage point. Harlan and Audrey were as puzzled as Vieve.

They struggled with the dirty glass. The crowd outside had more than doubled in an hour, and was now packed so tightly together it was impossible to distinguish a single figure.

"It's candles. Thousands of them," La Claire said. "I think we're developing a crowd of fans."

"All those people out there are coming to see us?" Audrey asked. "To see what happens?"

"To follow at least one of us." La Claire's tone was boastful.

Outside the house, the gathering was even larger than could be seen from the window. Besides the candle vigil, now nearly 5,000 strong, other pockets of the property were filling with teenage and college-aged gawkers. Some held signs with messages of encouragement for the contestants while others dressed in costumes of popular movie ghosts, monsters, and even fictional ghost-capturing emergency responders, complete with prop backpacks and faux equipment. The crowd spilled out of the property and filled every street leading to the entry gate. Outside the property, along with the crowd, local restaurants brought catering trucks, grills, or folding tables and sold refreshments to the growing flock. Other vendors offered piles of T-shirts bearing the town's name, camp chairs, warm clothes, and even candles.

As Walter looked out over the setting, Jason imagined cartoon dollar signs spinning in his eyes. The two-lane highways leading into town from the North and South were both at standstills, jammed with more prospective enthusiasts hoping to join the affair.

The five emerged from the servant stairwell, reaching the third floor at last. The third-story hallway was long with only two doors, one on each side, both closed, midway down. At the front end of the house, the hall simply opened into a large, doorless room. Their view, however, was obstructed by yet another of the camera pillars.

They proceeded to the set of doors. The first door selected lead into living quarters; a large room set up to function as a small bedroom, mini living room, kitchenette, and bath, with only the bath isolated by walls.

"This must have served as a small apartment for house staff," Harlan said. "They can sleep, cook, and do their own living here, so they're never more than a moment away if needed."

Ax used his camera to diagnose the room. Similar to the second floor, the ceilings here again bore the pattern of cold abnormalities. Nothing else seemed to stand out about the space. Harlan checked some drawers and kitchen cupboards but found virtually nothing. He concluded these quarters were empty at the time of the Drake's disappearance. Soon after entering, the group proceeded to the room across the hall.

The second door led to a mirror reflection of the first living quarters with all amenities squeezed into a single room. This time, however, when Harlan inspected the cupboard and drawers, he found dishes, old dry goods, clothes, shoes and more. The beds on this floor were never covered with dust cloths as most downstairs had been, so the bedding appeared gray with dust.

There was a small table with a seat and mirror near the bed. It bore some personal possessions: makeup, perfume, and a small jewelry box. Ax noticed another of the large concentrated cold spots like that of the fallen chandelier and broken cabinet. This spot was centered directly above the dressing station Harlan perused. "You may not want to stand there, bro," Ax smirked. When Harlan looked over, the camera was pointed above him. Ax flashed the tablet screen showing the cold spot.

Vieve joined Ax and Harlan while Audrey and La Claire explored. "If these were quarters for the nanny, then she was here supposedly collecting her things when she met an untimely end as well."

Ax pointed to the ceiling. "Probably why so much spirit activity is centered there."

Ax completed his search and led the others out and started toward the room at the front of the floor. "What about this," Harlan called from behind. The others turned to find Harlan pointing upward. On the ceiling was a rectangle frame of wood set flush in the surface. "Presumably the attic access."

Ax pushed back past the others and over to Harlan. "We can't open it until morning, remember?"

Harlan nodded. "I thought you might want to scan the area anyway, for the sake of thoroughness." Ax was perturbed with his oversight and more so with the fact that Harlan was the one to point it out. He reluctantly aimed his camera lens up toward the hallway ceiling and attic entrance. Many of the same small cold spot patterns continued, but the hatch to the attic was completely trimmed with the dark, cold appearance. For the first time, the streaking lines of purple that Ax observed near the ballroom chandelier appeared again, emanating in several directions from the hatch.

Harlan expected Ax to be brimming with glee. Instead, Ax was solemn. "I guess there must be somethin' up there. We won't find out for a few more hours, though." He turned his back on Harlan, moved past the women, and resumed course for the front.

Where the hallway ended, or began, the space opened into a wide area, essentially one-third of the entire floor. There were large windows on three sides. "Probably a very bright space during the daytime," Vieve said.

The room's furnishings were sparse with a sewing machine in the center, a wooden chair set before it, and a cupboard along the back wall. Other than that, there was a small table with a lamp, and another chair set in a corner. Just to the side of the hallway junction, the main set of stairs came up through the floor. "Maybe this was Mrs. Drake's personal area? Someplace she could come, away from the main living space where she could sew, or just look out at the view of the town?" Audrey sat in the sewing seat and imagined a spectacular panorama vantage when the house was used.

Ax pointed out one of the large, cold spots was centered above the sewing seat. Audrey reflexively jumped up and away. Ax continued to point out that the rest of the ceiling had several smaller, cool spots, just as many other rooms, but there was a second point of larger concentration above the top of the stairway.

"The last spot of tragedy." Everyone looked to Vieve. "The second officer that died in the house. They think he was heading down these stairs and a loose step gave way. He slammed his head on the edge of the opening in the floor, and they found him sprawled out at the bottom of the steps with cranial hematoma and a fracture to the cervical vertebrae." No one responded. Each examined the stairwell with their eyes and imagined the tragedy.

Ax scanned the room once more, then powered down the camera. "This has been very enlightening." Ax turned off the devices that Audrey and Vieve carried as well.

"That's it?" Harlan asked. "What now?"

"Now we go back downstairs and look back over the data. Ya' almost always catch new aberrations when you look back. Sometimes, you just can't take it all in at once. Other times the signs are so slight, you miss them in real time. Plus, sometimes the spirits interfere with the data stream between the equipment and the recording computer. That's another way to spot evidence of their influence."

"What's it all mean, though?" Audrey asked. "All these cold spots and the evidence, what does it amount to?"

Harlan smiled. "A damn fine question." He looked to Ax.

"Man, it all paints an interesting picture," Ax's tone was matter-of-fact. "There's no doubt the spirits are here. We can assume they remain due to the causes of their deaths being gruesome and unresolved. That leads us to conclude they were killed in the house." He paced as he spoke. The others followed along. La Claire nodded agreement thus far. "Now, with the abundant traces of the spirits' movement, if we draw a correlation that they would tend to dwell near the points of interest tied to their own murders, we can start to piece together what happened more clearly." Audrey was captivated. Harlan made objective notes internally. Vieve was reserved.

"I believe the spot in the front parlor, where we know the first officer died, means his spirit is here along with the family. He frequents the spot of his death, but I believe he was killed due to coming close to uncoverin' the truth, way back then. That's why the other spirit activity is there, plus in the ballroom. Something up in that area could have given the mystery away, but instead the officer was killed. I think the magician Kamrar killed Vinton there; it was a long and drawn-out quarrel that moved about the parlor and into the ballroom where Vinton was finally offed near the chandelier. One of the spirits tried to attack me with the chandelier to keep it covered."

"Not in Vinton's office?" Harlan asked.

"No, there's no scientific evidence to suggest anything happened there." Galva rolled her eyes. Harlan rolled his eyes at the same instance, though his grievance was with the words "scientific evidence."

"It doesn't seem anything else happened downstairs," Ax said.

"What about the bathroom thing?" Vieve asked.

"I think that was an actual spirit, following us and breakin' its normal routine. So, I'd say the rest of the family was upstairs when Kamrar killed Vinton. Now, the second floor had activity all over. I'd bet the children were there in one room, but they ran, scattered, and hid. Kamrar had to chase them down all over the place, one of them might even have made it up to the third floor before Kamrar caught and eventually killed them. That's why they seem to move evenly all around on the second. We know that the nanny died in her room, and we can see she was sitting at her dresser when it happened. It's not clear how exactly, but that was the spot. We also know the other cop died right here on the steps. It's his spirit activity creating the cold spot there."

"Both their spirits are here too?" Audrey asked.

"Oh, definitely."

"If the family is trapped by the mystery of their deaths, as you seem to think and as Galva suggested, why would they be attacking the police and the nanny?" Harlan asked. "Wouldn't they want the crime solved? Wouldn't they have protected the officers, or is Malvern's spirit that powerful in your estimation?"

"I'll get to that. Now, where was I? Oh yeah, so Kamrar chased at least one of the children up here and around the entire third floor. We know because of all the even spirit activity around this floor. Finally, here at the sewing machine, the only other large, cold spot, Mrs. Drake was the last to die."

Harlan was expecting more. After a moment's pause, he broke the silence. "Why would she just sit there while Malvern murdered her husband and her children? Wouldn't she be trying to help them? Wouldn't the kids be running to her?"

Ax pondered for a moment. "Maybe she knew it was gonna happen. Maybe she wanted Kamrar to do it so that they could be together, and he simply double-crossed her at the last moment." Audrey gasped. Harlan was unsatisfied. Galva and Vieve both shook their heads.

"Wait a second! I've got it!" Everyone looked to Audrey. "Let's say Ax is right. The magician killed Mr. Drake down in the ballroom. What if the children and Mrs. Drake all ran upstairs, but the magician followed them, and while the children hid, Mrs. Drake came here to get a pair of scissors or something, but she was too slow and he killed her before she could fight back, here like you thought, but as the second victim." Ax nodded along. "OK, so then only the kids are left and he chases them all over this floor and even back downstairs to the second floor and, well, you know, eventually gets them."

"I like it better than his story," Harlan said. Vieve smiled.

La Claire huffed. "I'm detecting no such thing up here." The others ignored her.

"Yeah, that could be it." Ax touched Audrey's arm. "You have a real knack for this." Audrey smiled warmly. La Claire wandered to the stairs and toed the top step.

"OK, but you never got back to the other deaths," Harlan said. "What about Malvern? Nothing you said suggests what happened to him, or if Galva's notion of spirit-fueled suicide played in?"

"Malvern killed the others, the cops, and the nanny. He was the only one interested in coverin' up the crimes, as you said. So he saw to killing anyone who got close, but..." Ax paused. Audrey brimmed with anticipation. "But he wasn't dead. A spirit couldn't have pulled off those murders. No, he just hid here, I think, to sabotage the investigation, and when the coast was clear he split. There's no other place where it appears anyone was killed, and I don't really think spirits can do that kind of thing. I mean, they can freak us out, maybe move stuff, or trip someone, but I don't think they can execute three additional murders from beyond. Kamrar probably died rich in Mexico or somethin'." Audrey nodded and smiled. Now, let's go check out all the data we got."

Harlan stopped Ax. "One last thing, the attic. It has all the same, supposed signs of spirit activity. No one included that in their explanations." Ax and Audrey looked at one another.

"I bet one of the children was caught there under the attic door," Audrey said.

"Or, maybe all the spirits like to move up to the highest point to see the rest of the town, or to try to draw attention." Ax shrugged.

The group moved toward the main stairwell. Audrey, Vieve, and La Claire traversed the upper flight, each of them eyeing the steps, the edge of the floor, and the railing, picturing the second officer's demise. Ax followed. Harlan waited for Ax to clear the steps, but the third step down snapped loose and flipped up, tilting forward when Ax's foot was upon it, and with all his weight in motion forward. He was thrown headfirst. His nose was on vector to collide with the sharp edge of the floor-level opening.

The women panicked and clutched one another's hands as first they heard, and then turned and saw, the incident. Harlan reacted quickly. He dashed forward, sliding with one knee on the floor and the other leg on the steps. He grabbed Ax by the back of his shirt, choking him incidentally, but pulled him back and slowed his fall enough for Ax to stumble and get his footing on the next couple steps. Ax bore a shocked expression as he envisioned the blow he'd avoided against the solid wood corner mere inches from his face. He looked up to Harlan. The incident with the nails in the living room, his near fall in the ballroom, and this narrowly avoided accident all rushed through his mind.

"Don't mention it," Harlan said with a smile. Vieve helped Ax steady himself as Harlan released the shirt. He pushed the askew step back in its proper place.

"Just like the cop!" Audrey's panic waned.

La Claire was calm. "Are you still certain that Kamrar's spirit isn't capable of making attempts on our lives?" Fear and adrenaline subsided in Ax, and embarrassment took their place. He pushed past the others and continued down. Audrey's eyes darted back and forth between Ax and La Claire several times with a confused expression.

The others returned to the living room but moved cautiously. Ax had already begun reviewing readings at his computer. Audrey looked between him and La Claire again. La Claire smiled at her warmly. After a moment, Audrey joined Ax at the computer. La Claire's smile turned to a look of disappointment as she took a seat isolated from the others. Harlan noticed she was upset. Ax had won Audrey's admiration. With Vieve leaning increasingly toward skepticism, no one was left to buy into her explanation, no one inside the house at least. Harlan took a seat himself and returned to the only source he felt had provided legitimate clues and insight, Vinton's journal. Seeing him open it, Vieve eagerly joined him.

For Those Who Wish to Follow In My Footsteps:
What I Discovered Part 4

"I knew it," echoes in my ears. Flat Nose's other thug must have slipped out when I hadn't noticed and discovered the files marked with the police seal. Before I can turn, he's on me. He flips a cord over my neck, but I manage to get my thumb hooked under before he clinches down. He's strong. As he pulls tighter, he lifts me off my feet. Before I know it, I'm hanging like a rag doll across his chest with both hands up countering the constriction on my neck.

This might be it, "But I'm not going without putting up one hell of a fight." My distorted words would be hard to distinguish from a gurgled exhale. After what seemed like minutes, though probably mere seconds of struggling instinctively, I manage to reclaim a vestige of logical thinking. Thus far, I've managed to work a couple of fingers from my other hand under the cord. My pistol remains in my pocket, but when the thug grabbed me, my jacket folded back. The gun is pinned between us, pressing into my back and his chest. I'm beginning to regret the libations I'd indulged in, but adrenaline beats back the haze of alcohol remarkably.

The tracks below us consist of steel rails, spikes, wood planks, and mostly loose, jagged rock. The thug has all his weight shifted to his back, countering my mass. If I can throw the both of us backward, fortune might reward me with a substantial blow to his head from the terrain, or he may reflexively release the cord to break his fall with his hands. Either way I'd land on his massive body and stay relatively unscathed. Though, I'll have to concede my progress on the cord to pull it off. The calculation takes only a fraction of a second.

First I drop one arm from the noose, leaving only the one thumb defending my throat. The constriction increases. In the same moment, I pull my knees to my chest and press my free hand between us. Pushing off of his chest, I roll my body up so my center of gravity rises up to his head. The shift of forces induces the desired reaction. The thug is thrown off balance. He futilely shuffles back trying to center the weight, then crashes over backward like a toppling tree. As we drop, I let my body unroll, flattening mine against his. He doesn't release the cord, but his body takes 100 percent of the blow, cushioning mine as planned.

The thug's head strikes a plank and he lets out a bellow of pain. Unfortunately, the blow wasn't devastating. He maintains his hold. As the pain no doubt subsides, he growls angrily, and is invigorated with newfound strength. He lies flat on his back, with my body parallel across his chest. If I survive, I may laugh in retrospect, imagining someone at a distance hearing our grunts, seeing our bodies pressed together, and mistaking this for a venereal spectacle.

The thug makes predictable moves, trying to roll and gain the top position. My thumb throbs with pain. My limited breaths are insufficient. I won't hold out much longer. To my benefit, we're centered in the tracks. When he rolls left, I press my left leg against the rail, preventing us from rolling over. When he attempts to turn us the other way, I wedge my leg against the right rail for the same result.

He alternates trying to roll one way then the other, but I counter each move. Then I hear an unusual sound. I can't quite recognize it, though I fear my senses are faltering from oxygen depravity. It must have alarmed the thug because the constriction falters for a moment. Everything I've done has been intended to gain that opening. Instantly, I slide my palm under the cord and quickly breathe a half dozen gasping, but deep breaths. The sound comes again. This time it's unmistakable—a train whistle.

His focus returns and the cord constriction grows tighter than ever, adrenaline aiding his strength. The whistle warns us again, louder this time. We wrestle on a curved section of track. The operator won't see us until it is far too late. The rails begin to vibrate, and the pulsing of the engine can be heard as well. I surmise I only have time for one more effort to free myself.

I concede the last defense on my throat and draw both hands behind my back. The pain on my neck grows nearly unbearable. Simultaneously I roll my body up, and again use one hand to push off the thug's chest to further separate my back from his front. This time my other arm is free, however, to reach for my pistol. All of this comes in under a second, but the layers of material surrounding my gun work against me, and thoughtlessly I'm trying to reach into the right hand pocket behind my back using my left hand. This takes time, and my air supply is completely cut off. Each moment brings tighter and tighter sensation. Already darkness creeps into the edges of my frame of vision, leaving only a tunnel of forward sight. Oddly, it feels more like my head will pop off than that I'll suffocate.

At last, I reach the firearm. One round is already chambered. I flip the safety off with my thumb then move it to cock the hammer. I expect to take a wild shot at a steep angle into the thug's abdomen and probably burn my own back or take a painful jab from the slide action. I'm surprised when the cord goes limp. He must have heard the hammer click. The thug lets go and tries to throw me off and gain his feet. I'm fast, though. I roll my weight to the same side he tries to push me to. Our combined efforts essentially catapulted me to my feet, just outside the rail. Twisting mid-leap, I manage to land facing him with the gun pointed forward.

"You win," he utters, but it is too late. My mind and body function sluggishly. It seems I have a perceivable moment to reconsider, but the command has already been issued, mind to body, slowed through an exhausted nervous system, but unstoppable. I watch helplessly as my finger squeezes and the pistol fires.

I'm an excellent marksman, but my shot finds no flesh, only metal: the steel of the train engine's wheels. It's probably for the better. I need neither Flat Nose's crew nor the police investigating me for his death even if it was unmistakably self-defense.

I linger until the train passes, actually open to rendering aid should the thug have miraculously been spared fatal wounds. However, far too little of him remains to check for a pulse. The scene is grotesque, but little shocks me in human carnage anymore.

Killing, I've often heard, is a haunting experience. Oddly, I find that I look back on that event almost never.

I watch the warehouse doors for reaction to the gunfire. Seeing none after several minutes, it's reasonable to conclude the train drowned out the shot. I slide the pistol into my pocket and flip the safety off and on, "Just to be sure." Next, I step over to the shrubs, secure the police files, and follow the tracks back the way I'd come.

Returning to my suite, I pause at the desk. Across the counter sits Mrs. Davis. I've spoken with her a number of times. She's a widow in her late fifties. Her husband died before the war. He didn't leave money, but he left her this twenty-room hotel in the middle of the city. Looking past the modest wrinkles, gray hair, and consequences of gravity, I see the bust, legs, and smile of a temptress once upon a time. "Good morning, Mrs. Davis. Any messages for me?"

She flashes a charming simper. "As a matter of fact, there was, Mr. Drake." She pulls out a note. "A Mr., excuse me, Captain O'Brian phoned, and asked that you call him back immediately. I hope you're not in any sort of trouble." She winks.

"No more than I can handle."

She pulls the telephone up to the counter. "Shall I?"

"Please." She proceeds to ask the operator for the police precinct, and then to ask the station clerk for the captain. Finally, she passes the receiver. "What have you got for me, Phil?"

"Hello to you too, Drake." His cynical tone comes as no surprise. "I put in a few calls. An officer I know in Moline said your carnival came through there, just stopping overnight en route to Des Moines. He also said he had an unusual influx of burglaries reported that night."

"Go figure."

"Precisely what I said. I checked with the force in Iowa next. They told me the show had been and gone but thought they were moving on to Minneapolis. That's as much as I could dig up."

"A sufficient effort, Phil. Perhaps I'll see you when I return from Minnesota." My omission of gratitude is intentional. I wouldn't want O'Brian thinking this made us even.

"You're welcome, Vinton. You son of a—" I hear him cursing me as I hang the receiver.

"Thank you, Mrs. Davis." There's no reason not to be forthcoming with appreciation for her.

"My pleasure." I step toward the stairway but she stops me. "Will you be leaving us then? I couldn't help but overhear."

"Not for long I hope. I see no reason to check out if that's what you mean, unless you think you'll need the room?" I ask knowing she hasn't had more than half occupancy in the several months I've been staying. "If you'd like, I can pay a week in advance in case I don't make it back as quickly as expected."

She rewards me with that endearing smile. "No need."

"Can we just consider my room reservation to be standing indefinitely for the foreseeable future?"

"That will be no trouble at all. Will there be anything else?"

"One last thing," I remember at that very moment. "I need these files returned to the police precinct, but I won't have the time before my trip. Could you have your bellman run them over?" I flop the pile onto the counter.

She draws them over, stacking them neatly. "Happy to, Mr. Drake."

Only an hour later, I board a train destined for the Twin Cities. I'd have preferred a cabin to myself, but the only availability was in a shared one. As I push through the log-jammed aisles of a coach car, I hope to myself that the cabin isn't too crowded. I check my pocket several times as I squeeze by person after person, each time ensuring my pistol hasn't dislodged, and each time pushing the safety rapidly off and back on, "just to be sure."

Barring any unforeseen delays, "I should be there late this evening." Other passengers look up to see if I am speaking to them as I pass. Let's see, Saturday was the night I caught the secret show, "or Sunday morning, technically." It's Friday now, and the carnival is probably up and running for the weekend.

I enter my cabin and find a couple of men in cheap suits across from a woman dressed very plainly, with a long skirt, glasses, and three books in her lap. I've no doubt the men are in sales; a thoroughly stale topic. "Do you teach?" I ask the woman. Looking up from the pages of one of the texts, she smiles and nods. "Three books, for such a short trip?"

"Yes." She leans forward. "I love to read, it's practically all I do."

Waiting a moment, I deliberately allow my eyes to drift downward, contouring her figure, first her bust, then her legs. "Pity." I turn and close my eyes, surely leaving either a denigrated or bewildered look on her face. There'll be no stunning conversation from these three. At least I'll get some sleep before the long nights ahead. I hope to have until after midnight tomorrow to uncover Malvern's next "death show." The words slip under my breath.

Opening my eyes slightly, I glance side to side. The men are consumed in boasting to one another, but the woman has heard me. She continues to stare at her pages but her body is tense. The men's chatter is biting on the ears, but soon the train is underway and the metronome-like sounds of the wheels on the track take dominance. It's rhythmic and, to me, soporific. My eyes drop closed as I allow my mind to clear and for sleep to creep in.

Let me diverge for a moment to reflect on the terrible oddness of the world, that fate should twist and turn and lead me to marry that very same homely bookworm from the train less than a year later.

The conductor announces arrival in Minneapolis. I assume that we made several stops along the way, but I find it easy to disregard irrelevant information and maintain slumber. The salesmen hurry out, leaving just her and I. When I stand, I offer to help the woman lift her bag from the storage above. I brought none of my own.

Her unease is compounded when my pistol slips out while my hands are over my head. Cavalier to the incident, I continue to lower the suitcase, then scoop up the gun, check its safety visually, and replace it in my coat pocket, all before disembarking. The station clock reads around 11 p.m. "No time to waste." I hail the first driver outside. "Take me to the ritziest lounge the city has to offer."

Dozens of well-dressed socialites occupy the windows when we pull up. Many fortunes were made here in the flour-milling business. I find a table and a glass of rye in the back corner and begin studying the patrons. After a second drink, I notice a couple across the bar that strike me as ideal targets. Both are dressed expensively, but their mannerisms and way of speaking are less polished than the rest of the room. In short, they're not snobs. They're well off, but not from wealthy families. Most important, they're young.

I estimate he has chosen a high-paying career, but he's not likely at the top of his field; a vice president in finance, junior partner in law, or physician with fewer than five years practicing. He may also simply be a successful entrepreneur. Whichever the case, I'm certain he's in the situation of seeking out people of higher and more established positions in hopes that a casual conversation might one day ease his own ascension up the "social food chain." Buying these two a few rounds and implying that I have such a revered position, whether it's true or not, is my best shot for permeating the local hierarchy in one night.

Precisely as predicted my company is welcomed and soon the young gentleman wraps his arm around my shoulder as he leans in to deliver the punch line of a humorous story about the infidelities of a senator he clerked for. His execution is rehearsed; no doubt it's a story that he's utilized on more than a few occasions. I have to force myself to laugh, not because he isn't humorous, but because I'm moderately inebriated and focusing on keeping him from leaning too much of his weight on me and discovering my pistol in the pocket between us. As the evening winds down for the bar, the couple finally makes the offer I've been banking on: to keep the night alive back at their apartment.

"Green and white stripes," the envelope is just as described, calling to me from under a stack of letters by the front door of the couple's home. It's so distinct I spotted it before we stepped inside. It's untouched.

I'm sure the couple has spoken to me, but my anticipation of this instant, the un-extinguishing curiosity that has been festering, leading me to this moment, has paralyzed me. My strategies with the couple, my investigation, and O'Brian's lead have fully paid off. When I finally turn my attention back to the couple, the woman has excused herself to the lavatory. The gentleman fixes three drinks. One minute in the apartment and already I pocket the invitation. I stay for one cocktail. I'm elated with success. It deserves some celebration. After that, I bid them goodnight.

The following evening I find the carnival on the outskirts of the city. The same rides and attractions litter the streets. I have a room rented, but I can barely sit still, let alone sleep, or even eat. I keep walking back and forth down the long, main stretch. The families come and go, leaving only the younger adults to see the carnival to its end. After that, the workers start breaking down the equipment, and I still have hours until the show.

A thick pine forest borders the edge of town, mere yards behind the carnival trailers, and continues into acres of wilderness. The hour nears. I can't attest of the rumors of Malvern's shows apart from the one I witnessed, but this seems a drastic departure. The invitation doesn't list the address of a theater or abandoned warehouse, as I anticipated. Rather, it gives an "X"-marks-the-spot map of walking trails starting at the forest's edge and leading to a small lake a half-mile in. I'd planned to stake out the location in advance this morning, but given the obscurely remote venue, I dared not risk being discovered.

The dark-soaked woods remain undisturbed until three in the morning. A light appears deep in the thick of the trees, the flame of a lantern. Over the next hour that flame drifts back and forth and spawns into dozens more, twinkling like stars in the sky. When the street finally wanes to virtually no activity, the first haughty attendees appear. Armed with their map they enter the woods. I watch from the shadows. As they move between the trees, I step into the forest a hundred feet away. I pace myself to stay even while maintaining the same distance. As they follow the twists and turns of the trail, I contour on my own original path. When a small creek interrupts my progress, I lose the first group, but soon the next set of Malvern's esteemed patrons takes their place on the trail and I continue.

My path is untamed. It's necessary to trade repeatedly to successive packs of exhibition goers, but my progress is steady. I estimate that I've covered about three quarters of the distance when a gateman appears on the established course: the stoic, scheming-eyed, sinister, and pompous man whom I encountered before. I crouch down and observe.

The usher stands between two oil lanterns dangling from overhanging branches. Behind him, a cord has been tied to two trees and a curtain hung, blocking the path, though it would be easy to circumvent. "Theatrics are everything," I whisper.

Next to the usher sits the same thin table and cash box as before. The approaching guests stop and engage him. Their voices are detectable, but not discernible as the trees and the distance claim most of the sound. The group hands off their cash admittance and, with the curtain pulled for them, continue past. Periodic lamps accentuate the path forward from there. The group disappears into the depths. The usher stores the till in his box and returns to a lifeless posture.

Now with lights to dictate my way, I decide to proceed without anyone opposite me on the provided path. However, when I stand, shifting my weight to one foot, a branch snaps. A sizable crack emanates across the underbrush. The usher's attention whips in my direction. I dare not move a muscle. He reaches to the lantern above and pulls it down, bending the branch and redirecting its cast. The two of us, separated by only a short span, spend a long moment motionless. The giggles of distant conversation fill the air. The usher finally returns his gaze to the path. Several couples emerge from the night.

With his attention misplaced, I hustle to further distance myself, and make my way forward. At its end, the trail opens into a lakeside clearing. A large portion of the shore is defined by a lantern-marked perimeter. In that half circle, several long benches have been placed with two large pillars before them. Beyond that is the rim of the water. Half of the benches are occupied. The next group that appears on the trail proceeds to further fill the seats. I find a spot along the edge where the trees are still dense and hunker into the darkness.

The trail of lights in the woods behind us grows shorter and shorter, with the extinguishing of the most distant flames one after the other. "It must be nearly show time." Again, my voice is nothing more than a wisp of breath. A few more people emerge, taking all but two of the remaining openings. After that, the last of the path's lamps is extinguished. Carrying one lantern to light his way, the usher steps out from the now pitch-dark trail.

He crosses before the crowd to the pillars and holds the light up to one's top. Immediately a flame ignites and rapidly spreads, covering the top of the column, illuminating the area around it. He sets the second pillar ablaze so the area of shore before the crowd is now brightly lit. The oval of light extends greatly onto the water's surface as well, though there is one ominous void in its cast. The source is a tarp-covered box set back from the pillars, almost in the water.

The water is still with only gentle ripples. Though it's warm, a soft breeze crosses the lake and gives a cooling sensation on the face, delivering the aroma of an earthy and damp, yet refreshing locale. The pillars' brightness contrasts the wilderness so drastically that, other than the first few rows of trees, the darkness is absolute.

Many in the audience are talkative. The usher moves to the covered box and begins reeling a long chain out from under the tarp, foot by foot. The crowd's murmurs fade away. Some resist initially, but the usher proceeds to shackle one ankle of every guest to the chain. I'm in awe of the spectacle but too far away to hear what he said to either earn or force their compliance. Once the first several cooperate, the usher receives no further objections. The chain is not affixed to any stake or post. When he's done, everyone is linked in one continuous strand. Finally, the usher returns to the trail and disappears into the night.

There's a long delay in the action. The crowd grows restless, evident in the ever-increasing rattle of chain links. The noise is humorous, but not nearly as amusing as the consequence will be, if the chain's purpose is what I suspect. I can't help but smile.

Malvern emerges from the trees far to one side. At first only a few notice. Soon, silence falls again. Everyone's eyes follow him. He centers himself in the throw of the pillars. Two shadows of his body are cast to the ground and continue onto the water. They dance erratically between the flames and the gentle waves, but soon coalesce into perfect projections of him, though the edges of the light and the water continue to flurry.

He speaks in a calm but well projected voice. "I am Malvern Kamrar..." the rest fades into mere tones. I'm too distant to fluidly understand him. In spite of my patience up to this point, I grow restless at missing his oration and resolve to creep around the scene, staying just behind the trees and out of sight as I work my way from the back toward the side where Malvern started.

Gasps uttered in unison by the crowd beg for my attention as I move. Malvern's shadow contortion seems to be the origin; first into castle towers, later into waving flags. I still cannot hear the story they punctuate. By the time I've moved to the edge, where it's more poorly lit so that I could sneak in a little closer, Malvern's speech has concluded. He rushes to the covered box. I stop dead and hunker down again.

Malvern pulls back the tarp. A few metal parts protrude from the top, but whatever is inside is still mostly hidden. Next, he pulls two pins allowing the back side of the box to drop, followed by the left and right sides. Still, the object within is largely concealed. Finally, he drops the front of the box. In the center is a mangled collection of metal pieces with gears, hinges, shining blades, and all manner of parts, but nothing recognizable.

The magician draws a piece toward him that is attached to others. Joints move, latches click and soon a pedestal with a crank is formed. He turns the crank and a giant mechanism unfolds ten feet into the air, complete with a ladder on one side and a long piece of steel angling down across the rest. The crank comes to a stop and one final metallic clack signals the device is locked in.

Malvern walks completely around it, then while grabbing one metal crossbeam, circles again, with the device turning as well. The ladder has a flat seat at the apex, not unlike the top of a slide, but as the smooth steel slide travels down, it becomes narrower. Two-thirds of the way down it's virtually width-less so that the final third of the slide is literally a blade edge. The entire run must be fifteen feet. I shudder in awe, "Imagining the capabilities of the contrivance."

He speaks again as he turns the device a second rotation, bringing it to a stop with the ladder toward the lake and the razor end facing the audience directly. Malvern grabs the discarded tarp from the ground and wads it into a ball. Next, he places the ball at the top of the slide and allows it to drop. The angle of the slide is dramatic. The tarp-ball picks up speed and when it nears the bottom it is sliced with virtually no friction. The breeze picks up the halves before they reach the ground, unfolding them as they are flutter over the spectators. "Awws" punctuate the demonstration.

Now, Malvern spins the machine half circle, reversing its direction so the ladder faces the audience. He takes a bow. His final words resonate, "Without further ado."

He climbs the ladder, sits on the slide, and waits, allowing one last dramatic pause. His flexing arms are the only things combating gravity's pull. I feel the crowd's tension even from far away. It seems the crickets and the wind have silenced for this moment. Malvern releases his grasp. His body falls. No sound emanates, no audible hint of what has happened until the very end of the blade when half a man drops right and half a man falls left, both into the water. The splash is the first noise, the screams are the second.

The crowd members spring to their feet and instinctively attempt to run in all directions, forgetting the shackles. Everyone tumbles to the ground, but the result doesn't elicit the laugh from me I had pictured. The surreality of what has transpired has forestalled my sense of humor. Many gasp or scream as they claw their way to their feet, though when one individual makes it up, he drags another back down. The trail of blood on the blade appears black in the narrow light spectrum of the flames.

My own reaction is mixed with terror, but I've spoken before of my ability to repress such distractions in support of clear actions. I focus on the spot where Malvern's body lay. It's unlikely that he could have swapped a body between the bottom and the top of the ladder. After a small eternity, likely less than a minute, a living and complete figure stands in the water and wades the short distance back to the shore.

"Be calm. Please calm down, everyone." It is Malvern. He brings the crowd to order. I hear only part of his words and surmise the rest. He explains that the shackles were precautions to prevent anyone from being injured in the state of panic and to ensure that everyone could see he had survived the exhibition.

There'll be nothing more to see of the show, and I doubt that I'll get a chance to examine the scene any closer before it's packed and gone. Instead, I turn my attention to the woods. Malvern emerged near the point where I now stand. I'll have a little time to look around while they unchain all of those people. I slip into the trees several yards then scan for any anomalies.

There's a hint of a path, far less worn than the one leading to the lake from the city. I can't be certain that this was Malvern's course, but given the remote chances of finding anything more relevant in my brief window of opportunity, I focus my search there. Unfortunately, in the pitch black, "I'm about as likely to stumble over something as I am to see it."

The words barely escape my lips before pain surges through my legs followed by the cold wet of the earth on my cheek. Some unnatural obstruction has planted me face first on the ground. I roll over so that I'm seated on the forest floor. A large crate sits before me. The outside of the box bears ornate carvings in hard wood, which is stained a deep blue hue. "Very unusual." The top of the crate dealt the blow to my thigh and was dislodged in the process. Back on my feet, I step up and peer inside, but I can barely see to the end of my arm out here, let alone to the bottom of a tall, mostly covered box.

The lid is difficult to move, somewhat heavy but also secured in places with nails or screws. Pausing a moment, I hold my breath and listen. I can hear several voices. There's still a commotion from the lakeside. I scramble to find a stick and shimmy it under the lid. As I pull up with all my might, the branch splits in half. I forage for another, a larger one, and use it to finally pry the cover off the crate.

The sky is cloudless with only a sliver of a waning crescent moon. "If only there'd been a little more light, or if I had a match." Only traces of starlight make it down through the leaves, insufficient even now to see into the bottom of the box. I can tell that something is inside, but I've no resource for determining what.

I pause to listen again. The voices at the lake have dissipated. I've little time remaining. Hanging over the side of the box, I lean in and search with my fingers. I feel some clothes at first, then discover something solid below them. I try pulling it out, but it's tethered. I bring it into a sliver of starlight and can see only for a second, a human hand held in my own.

The arm drops back into the crate, "Coffin," when I release it. Quickly, I move to replace the top but I make it only a step and never have a chance to pull my weapon before the stoic, scheming-eyed, sinister, pompous, and apparently church-mouse quiet usher issues me an incapacitating strike to the side of my head. My legs give way. All I can see is the leafy underbrush racing toward my face. I've not been knocked unconscious, but the usher soon rectifies that. The sounds of crumpling leaves and the smell of something sweet are the last sensations I can decipher before I'm out. "Ether."

2:00AM

Vieve and Harlan turned the page. "My heart is pounding," Vieve said, but before they read on, Audrey rushed over.

"Come here, you guys. You have to come see this. La Claire, you have to come quick." Audrey grabbed Vieve by the arm and pulled her toward Ax at the computer. She waved for Harlan and La Claire to follow. Ax beckoned with equal effervescence. Vieve complied. Soon Harlan tucked the journal away and followed. La Claire didn't bother.

At the computer, Ax sat with a pair of headphones. One side was over his ear while the other was askew to afford him partial hearing of the room. On the computer screen, one of the thermal image videos was frozen. An array of orange, red, and yellow shapes outlined the living room. "Take a look at this." He pressed the space bar and the image jumped to action. Audrey, Vieve, and Harlan were all huddled, looking over Ax's shoulders. With another keystroke, the image became full-screen. "Here's my thermal pan of this room." Ax's enthusiasm was barely contained. "Remember, we were noticing some temperature variations, so I spent most of the time in this room lookin' at thermal."

The footage moved around the room. The cool features of the fireplace were followed by a cool spot near the stairs, and the camera lingered on each. They watched for almost a minute before Harlan spoke. "I don't see anything. Nothing different from before, at least."

"Exactly." Ax struck a few keys, the laptop dropped out of full screen, the video stopped, and another video replaced it, all in shades of green. "Now watch this." He rolled the footage, again in full-screen. This time, in night-vision mode, the camera view panned the living room, as before, but after a moment there was a flicker at the edge of the frame. Audrey squealed with delight as Ax stopped the video. "There, did ya' catch it?"

Vieve shook her head while Harlan continued to examine the screen. "OK, let me roll it again, but I'll slow it down this time." With another stroke of the keyboard, the video jumped back ten seconds and proceeded to roll forward at one-quarter speed. The shot moved across the wall with the door to Vinton's office, then the staircase to the second floor entered the left edge of the frame. The moment the steps were fully in the shot a bright, rectangular spot flared on screen, just at the foot of the stairs. It lasted less than a second, even in slow motion, but it appeared three times in rapid succession. Once the last had faded the image returned to normal, and Ax stopped it there. "Did ya' catch it that time?"

"Pretty freaky, right?" Audrey asked. Harlan shrugged.

"What was it?" Vieve asked.

"Hard to say for sure, but look again with each flash frozen." Ax danced his fingers on the keys once more and brought up one of the anomalous frames as a still image. "You can see the rectangle shape, but here with some closer attention to detail you can also see inconsistencies inside the shape, lighter and darker spots." Harlan and Vieve both leaned toward the screen. There were swirls of dark and light green, along with some simple blacked-out spots within the shape. "Now look at the next." Ax pressed an arrow key and the image shifted. The shape had identical boundaries but appeared further into the image frame as the camera's pan had progressed further along the wall. "Now you can see the same basic types of patterns, but they're spread out in different ways. And look, the spots are moved around." Ax flipped back and forth between both images, exemplifying the changes. "Same thing on the third." He moved to yet another still frame. "The pattern shifts a little bit more and this frame only has one of those spots."

"So what are you telling us it is?" Harlan asked.

Ax looked to Audrey and both smiled. "A map. Look, there are one, two, three separate images, just like there's a first, second, and third floor." Ax's eyebrows rose. "The shape is a rectangle, just like the shape of the house, and we think those spots were intended to show us where to look for evidence. See?" He flipped back to the first image and pointed to one of the black spots. "It's near the ballroom-to-parlor doorway, obviously showing us that it's a point of interest."

"Someone or something was trying to send us an advanced roadmap of where to look," Audrey added.

Ax nodded. "What about all these other spots?" Harlan pointed to several more in the first image. Ax shrugged.

"Places where we might have missed somethin' I guess, or more likely just couldn't detect it with the limitations of the equipment, but obviously not as important." Harlan sighed. Ax moved to the second image. "This would have to be the second floor, and look, there's spots all over the place, just like all the evidence we found."

Harlan shook his head. "So, all these spots roughly correspond to the many points in the second floor where you found supposed evidence. That suggests to you not only is your interpretation confirmed, but something tried to tell you this before you even went up there?"

"Exactly." Ax nodded.

Harlan rubbed his brow. "But on the first floor, where there are virtually as many spots, all except one do not correspond to the evidence you found down here. That doesn't bother you, or make you wonder if it's all purely coincidence?"

"No. Like I said, we missed somethin', or don't have the right equipment to detect it. Plus, this information is being passed basically from the mind of a spirit into our equipment. It's not a perfect line of communication." Harlan closed his eyes, frustrated. "Plus look at the third, the third floor." He moved on to the last still image. Harlan opened his eyes again. "One spot, exactly where we found the largest anomalies up there, in the front sewing room."

"It looks closer to the middle of the whole floor to me," Harlan said.

Ax turned away and took a moment to calm down, and then spoke with his back to Harlan. "Yeah, well, like I said, it ain't a perfect system. It's pretty damn good, considering."

Silence followed until a huge grin dawned on Audrey lips. "Show them the other thing, Ax. Show them the face." Vieve looked from Audrey to Ax curiously. Harlan's expression remained perturbed. Ax moved his hands back to the keyboard. This time, instead of smooth manipulation, Ax slammed his fingers down one at a time. Each key signaled his anger.

In a few strokes, a new video segment opened. "OK, by the time we were finishin' up on the second floor most of our focus was on the thermal images, but I did keep doing quick pans of each room in night vision." Ax played the video. In green shades, the frame showed the end of a 360-degree pan of the last bedroom on the second floor, after which the camera moved to the hallway and toward the front staircases. Suddenly the camera stopped and turned back the opposite way. "This is when La Claire pointed out the back stairs." Ax's elation returned. "So we went up. That's when we noticed the crowd outside. I think this was when we were all lookin' out the windows, and that's why I missed it. Watch."

The camera dropped from level at shoulder-high down to waist-high and angled upward capturing the last half flight of steps.

"Look at the top." Audrey pointed. Parallel green lines defined the ascending staircase, with the narrow walls, and the door at the peak. After a moment, a dark mass formed at the top of the steps, obscuring the sight of the door. The shape quivered. It grew in some areas while it shrank in others, its edges in constant flux. After five-seconds, it faded away. Ax paused the footage. He and Audrey look to

Harlan and Vieve, but both were contemplating silently.

"See, it helps to go back and look at it frame by frame, but here are a few we thought were the most telling." Ax loaded another series of three still images taken from the video. The first came up showing the blob of black at its largest in the upper half of the frame, while in the lower half, it had shrunk to a very thin column with a split in the middle, which looked like two merged segments.

"Legs," Audrey said. Ax nodded as he switched to the second image. This time, the bottom half had blurred and widened into an amorphous blob, while most of the upper half had narrowed into an upside-down pear shape, though it had gotten shorter. "Looks like a torso, right?" Audrey grinned. Ax switched to the final still frame. In it, the area was wider, yet fainter, and with a small, dark concentrated sphere, separate from the rest at the top. "Zoom in like you did before."

Ax obliged, and framed the small sphere alone on screen. With greater details revealed, Audrey proceeded to point out a few curved lines. "See, here is a nose and here is a mouth." She traced them with her finger. Harlan had to squint, but could see a few horizontal lines near the bottom of the shape and another couple of vertical lines clustered near the center. Audrey's hand moved to the top. Two bright spots were there. One was higher than the other, which was also far to the side, almost escaping the limits of the shape. "The eyes!" Vieve leaned in close to see the faint features.

"A little bit of a stretch, don't you think?" Harlan asked.

"Take Genevieve's helmet cam," Walter barked to the crew in the broadcast truck, "we don't want to miss this." With her view up in the on-air monitor everyone could see the shapes on Ax's computer screen, reframed by Vieve's shaky point of view. "Can we get one of the pillar cams on this for a steadier shot?" Walter asked the operators at controls in one corner. An instant later, Vieve turned to Harlan, and the images in question were out of frame on every camera in the house. "Damn, we should have thought to patch into his computer screen before we started."

"Now show them that thing you did before," Audrey said to Ax. He switched to a new program. On a blank, digital canvas, Ax layered all three images. He proceeded to crop the first to only the lower portion, trim the second to its middle, and cut the last to only the upper piece. When he stacked them one on top of the other, he tweaked the positioning and sizing of each until the distortion shape merged seamlessly between each image.

The resulting assemblage was a distinct, human-shaped figure. Its legs narrowed as they moved toward the floor, coming to points that kissed the surface. The hovering body was larger on top and in the head, as if it leaned from the top of the steps over the staircase and loomed over the camera, or over where the contestants stood when the footage was taken. Behind the figure, the stairwell was fractured and contorted, clearly segmented by the three separate images, giving even more of an unnatural appearance than the green color palette already created.

"Try shaking your head at that." Ax pointed to the screen with smirk, but Harlan did just that. "Come on, man, what will it take for you? That is a spirit, caught on tape, right in front of your face, and you still deny it?" Ax sighed. "It's right there lookin' back at you."

Audrey and Vieve looked to Harlan, who held one hand over his forehead as if pained by his thoughts. "That is absolutely not what I see, Ax. What you have is a collage of separate and distinct inconsistencies that you have cut, sized, and adjusted to make look like a person. It's a work of art by Baxter Cruz, not evidence of spirits."

"It's a difficult thing for a spirit to materialize, man. Maybe it can only do it partially at any given moment, so it did only part of its body at a time, but together we could see its entire form. Did that ever occur to you?"

"Then where's the limit?" Harlan asked. "How many pieces are too many in your estimation to be beyond the scope of intention and fall into merely a desired image? If it took ten pieces to get the shape you wanted, or a hundred, would it still be evidence to you?"

La Claire called across from her seat. "It does seem tough to swallow when it takes a dozen steps to put together the thing you claim backs up your story."

Ax looked to her with scorn. "At least my work has evidence, Galva. Your bullshit is just made up off the top of your head." Harlan chuckled, before Ax whipped his attention back. "Hey, we didn't make up these shapes in the video, those just appeared there. You can't dismiss those as my creations."

"No, but they rely on the programmed interpretation of trace amounts of visible light along with a spectrum of light that people can't see. You're taking something abstract, distorting and translating it into an approximate visual form, and then acting surprised when it looks weird and unnatural. Oh, and you're using a spectrum, by the way, which you are greatly supplementing with an emitter, further exaggerating the gap between a natural sight and your abstraction. In that hallway, you've got light coming in through dirty and clouded windows and even more light shining from an emitter that is bouncing around with every movement of your body. Is it possible that it was reflecting off of glass? Is it possible at some point you or something nearby was in front of the emitter, blocking it partially?" Harlan was just as heated as Ax. "There are any number of ways for this convoluted system you rely on to fail in accuracy."

"Convoluted system? This is"—he turned and gestured to the array of equipment laid on the table nearby—"these are tested and proven scientific methods for detecting the paranormal. It's science."

"You're kidding yourself, Ax. What you do is far from science. You may use scientific words and try to utilize unusual resources, which appear to be scientific, but that doesn't make what you do science. Science depends on one thing, the scientific method, and that is most certainly not a part of your process."

Ax slammed the top of the laptop closed. "OK, Mr. Know-it-all, enlighten us. Scientifically, what created each of these anomalies, huh? What evidence do you have that proves these are not paranormal? How can you prove absolutely that there are no ghosts or spirits here?"

"That's not the point, Ax. The point is, you see something strange, and all so-called paranormal investigators do this. You see something odd, and when a logical reason for it is not easily available, not that it isn't there, but it isn't readily evident, then you conclude it must be paranormal. That isn't scientific. A witchdoctor saying an ill or even a schizophrenic person is possessed by spirits because they can't explain their ailments or odd behavior is not science. When uneducated civilizations determine anything they can't explain, the movement of the sun and moon, the tides of the sea, the changing of seasons, whatever, are the acts of gods and spirits because they don't understand the orbit of the earth, the tilt of the earth, and gravity, that is the opposite of science. That is what you're doing. You can't explain it, therefore, it must be paranormal, and that is flawed. If a scientist happens upon unexpected results and anomalies, they would first try to investigate any factors that might affect the results, which haven't been accounted for. Are there inconsistencies in the ceiling and structure of the house that could be creating the cold spots? What else in the room and the environment could be producing or manipulating the infrared spectrum? Those are the questions you should have. Then a scientist would try to reproduce the phenomena under experimental controls. Of course, I think you and I both know you would never do that because your results would always be the same —that you could not recreate the anomalies. But, in the event you did, scientists would then conclude they didn't have the right information for evaluating the situation. Either they needed to investigate further and deeper, or the scientific understanding at this time is not developed enough to evaluate this fully. You couldn't fully understand microscopic organisms or particles before the microscope was developed. No, Ax, you see what you want to see. You jump to absurd conclusions at the slightest suggestion of the unexplained, and then you manipulate the data to skew it toward the results you want. That is anything but science."

Silently, Ax boiled with rage. Harlan didn't let up for a second. "Isn't it rather convenient that the readings paranormal investigators rely on as evidence come from such a hugely diverse range of sensors and tactics, and so rarely do any two or more of them confirm a result?"

Ax's teeth remained clenched as he spoke. "Every situation is different. Spirits can reveal themselves in a great number of ways at any single moment. Their power is limited."

"As I said, convenient. It seems if you take enough readings, with enough obscure equipment, while you yourself are supplementing the noise and light, you're bound to find something odd. If you go to the doctor feeling fine but you have X-rays, an MRI, a CT scan, an ultrasound, and other scans, and they all came back as perfectly fine, except one of them has some little anomaly that doesn't look normal but doesn't look exactly like a tumor or any other known problems either, would you jump to the conclusion that there is something gravely wrong with you, or would you say to yourself, well, 5 out of 6 scans showed a clean bill of health so this other one must just be a fluke?" Neither Ax nor Audrey responded. "Do you see what I'm saying? If you do enough scans you're bound to come up with something out of the ordinary eventually, but that doesn't mean something is there. Do you rush into surgery, or do you say, well, without a single additional confirmation of a problem I think it's best to write this one off?"

Audrey moved behind Ax, showing her allegiance. "What about statistics, Harlan?" Ax reopened the computer, his tone derisive. "We're not talkin' about some blob, were talkin' about a person-shaped mass. You called these failures of my detection system or somethin' like that. You claim they just happen to look like the parts of a body, and not just one, but an entire body, including a head with a face?" Ax changed the screen back to showing the close-up still of the head-shaped figure. "Don't ya' think statistically that is extremely unlikely? And that statistic would suggest there is some design here and not randomness? Surely you'll admit at least that?"

Harlan sighed. The others watched as he pulled a chair out from the other end of the equipment table and took a seat. "There is actually a simple principle called apophenia. Apophenia is a psychological phenomenon in which human beings tend to interpret random stimulus as being significant. We inherently seek patterns in everything, even in truly random nature. Pareidolia is a specific type of apophenia that pertains to sights and sounds. Essentially, when humans see random shapes, we turn them into objects. Thus, we see random rock shapes as possible animal fossils, we see Rorschach ink blots, if you're familiar with them, as various projected objects supposedly reflecting our psyche, and we even see the faces of deities in grilled cheese sandwiches. In fact, we are particularly wired to see faces in this way. Likewise, we interpret random sounds as voices such as electronic voice phenomena, or when people play albums backward and think they hear a secret message. When we hear a jumble of random sounds, we make them into words and voices." He pointed at the face shape on the screen. "This is a digital Rorschach, and you want to see spirits so you think you see a face, or parts of a ghost's body, nothing more."

"Bullshit. I'm fed up." Ax knocked his chair over as he stood stomped out to the hallway. The others stayed quiet. Harlan held his tongue and watched as Ax disappeared into the darkness.

"Maybe we should all cool off a bit," Vieve said.

Audrey ignored her. "I don't buy that, I mean, if that's the case, and we just imagined this face, then, like, the map, the cold spots around the house, everything could be just in our heads?"

Harlan nodded. "Precisely!"

"It can't all be made up. They're not all faces or the shapes of people. They're all sorts of stuff."

Harlan thought for a moment. "Look, have you ever laid on the ground, watched clouds in the sky, and pointed out when their shapes resembled objects or animals?"

"Yeah, I guess so."

"OK, but when you see a bunny in the sky do you assume some rabbit spirit is out there trying to contact you?"

Audrey was reluctant. "No, I suppose not."

"On top of that, if we all looked at the same cloud, we might all see different things, don't you think? You see a bunny, I see a Volkswagen, and Vieve sees an upside-down boat." Audrey nodded. "It's the randomness of our imaginations, but it might also be reflections of our desires or, at the very least, what we're thinking about right then. One person likes fuzzy animals, so theirs is a bunny, another is a gear head, so their interpretation is a car."

Ax heard Harlan's voice muffled through the wall as he paced. After a moment, he stopped and smiled. He peeked into the living room and found the others were all involved in conversation, or in La Claire's case, in her own world and paid no attention to the others or to him. He quickly crossed the doorway and moved to the entrance of the back steps. As he went up, Harlan's voice faded away.

Audrey pointed to the computer screen. "Yeah, but these shapes aren't all random and all over the place, they all pertain to the house being haunted, and we all, at least Ax and I, see the same things in them."

"If I just lost my grandmother, I might see some clouds and think one looks like a pine tree, and my grandma's house always smelled like pine, and I'd think it's more than a coincidence. Likewise, I see another as a pan, and think my grandmother always made great food for me, and I see a big car-shaped cloud and think my grandma drove a big, old boat of an Oldsmobile, and I might conclude she is up in heaven sending me these clouds as signals that she's watching over me, but really I'd just be projecting it. I'm seeing a projection of what I want to see, what I'm thinking about, and of what I want to believe. Get it?" Audrey nodded. "So you and Ax are both here looking for ghosts, wanting to find them. Doesn't it make sense you'd both project similar significance to random shapes? Or realistically, one of you would make that projection and the other would be extremely likely to accept it as your own interpretation since it supports your common assumption?"

Audrey shook her head with confusion. "My mind is swimming."

Harlan reached and put a hand on top of her shoulder. "It's simple. When you see something like this, some shape you think looks like a spirit or paranormal communication, just stop and ask yourself two questions. Am I just seeing this because it's what I want to see?

And, is there any other possible explanation?"

For a moment, Audrey's face lit up as if having an epiphany. Harlan was hopeful. After another second, she shook her head. "No, no, no. See, that would preclude any sort of spirits ever. Any communication from beyond could be dismissed by your explanation, so if there were a real ghost, we'd never know it. We'd ignore it. Who's to say you are an actual person, and not just a blob that I think looks like a person, and a bunch of random noises I think sound like a voice?"

"There might be some grounds for a deep philosophical discussion of what you just said, but for practical purposes, the difference is I'm here all the time, not just parts of my body for split seconds, and I speak in complete sentences with coherent thoughts and streaming conversation, not single and barely audible words. Plus, I'll show up in your vision, in her vision, on camera, in thermal sensors, on a microphone recording, and virtually any detection method you would like—all at the same time. If we all saw a figure in person, and heard it, and saw it on camera, and recorded its voice, then we'd be talking about something very different. But all this"—he waved a hand at all the equipment and the computer—"it's just desperation, taking any tiny inconsistency and calling it a huge discovery."

Ax crossed from the back to the front of the second floor in almost complete darkness. As he neared the front steps, traces of light seeped up. He was careful to step softly, without making noise. Harlan's voice was faintly detectable again, and grew louder with every step closer to the stairwell. Ax stopped at the top of the steps, listening and watching. Below, just a few feet away from the bottom step, he could see a part of a couch where La Claire had laid down on her side. Only her shoulders and head were within Ax's view, which was limited by the shape of the stairwell opening. After he watched for a long moment, Ax turned and headed back toward the rear staircase.

Harlan continued. "As for the statistics Ax mentioned, the question is not how likely it is for random blobs and masses to closely resemble recognizable shapes and patterns. The question is, when a person is presented with truly random shapes, how often do they perceive a recognizable pattern in them? And the answer is almost always."

Audrey contemplated for a moment. "Nope, I'm not buying it." Harlan hung his head and sighed. Vieve couldn't help but quietly snicker at his letdown.

3:00AM

The Mansion had fallen back to calm. La Claire dozed on the sofa. "Just a few more hours now, huh?" Vieve said with a yawn. Harlan checked his watch then nodded.

La Claire's terror-filled scream seized Harlan's attention, although a crash had preceded it. At the couch, an object struck inches away from La Claire's head. There was a crisp crack against the edge of the sofa, followed by brittle fracturing and a dull thud on the floor. La Claire jumped off, twisted in midair, and landed on all fours facing back toward the sofa. Both Vieve and Audrey were roused from their own drowsy states.

Harlan dashed toward the disturbance, placing himself in front of the others. All four surged with adrenaline. There, just beside the sofa, lay the fancy hand mirror from the master bedroom upstairs. It faced downward.

"Shit." Vieve broke the silence. A long moment followed before she uttered another word. "It just flew down from up the staircase. I saw it from the corner of my eye." Audrey and Vieve crept closer but stayed behind Harlan. La Claire backed further away.

"It came right for you, Madam La Claire." Audrey turned to her. "Just like the knife in the kitchen, you were the target." Audrey began to tremble. Harlan looked to La Claire as well. Her hands quaked, her eyes were wide and sweat built on her brow. She shook her head in disbelief. Harlan noted she was far more apprehensive now than with the knife incident. To him, it was obvious she truly had no anticipation of the attack. Her arrogance had vanished as she cowered away. His mistrust of La Claire turned to empathy.

The faint creaking sound of a floorboard drew Harlan's attention. It seemed to be above them. Harlan listened for it to repeat. He scanned the others, but no one else had heard it.

"Was that a bat?" Jason asked from a corner seat. He was the only one to notice something fly across one of the small screens. However, with the mirror's crash on the sofa and floor, several screens sprang to life. Nora was lethargic from the lull in activity. At first, she struggled to bring up a better shot in the on-air monitor.

Walter said nothing. He and everyone else in the broadcast truck were equally stupefied. The large screen finally cut to a wide shot of the room from one of the pillars' cams. It showed all four reacting. "At least something lively happened; it's been a while," Walter said.

Jason watched another of the small monitors with a puzzled expression. It was Ax's helmet view. Ax appeared to be gazing through the window from the back stairwell, where the mob of fans continued to grow. What Ax saw didn't perplex Jason as much as why Ax simply stared out the window, motionless, amidst all the other commotion in the house. Jason watched Ax's cam for 30 unmoving seconds. When Jason opened his mouth to point it out, Ax's cam whipped away and dashed back toward the living room. He reacted a full minute after the incident occurred.

La Claire gasped a deep breath, her first since the mirror fell. Her muscles finally unclenched, and she collapsed to a nearby seat. With her eyes closed, she covered her heart with both hands as if trying to keep it from escaping her chest. One of the camera pillars moved to frame the group. Audrey and Vieve rushed over to La Claire, but fright overtook Audrey and she began to shudder uncontrollably. Harlan placed a hand on Audrey's shoulder. "Everything's going to be all right. I'm quite certain that whoever tossed that mirror had no intention of hurting you."

Audrey looked up, confused at first. However, Harlan's confidence was reassuring. She reached up and squeezed Harlan's hand. He lingered for a long moment, then returned to the mirror and sofa.

Ax burst through the doorway from the hall. "Is everyone OK? What the hell happened?"

"La Claire nearly bit it," Audrey said. "Martha's mirror, you know, from up in her bedroom? Something flung it down the stairs and straight for Galva." Ax looked shocked. "The spirits really don't want us here." Audrey still seemed shaken. Ax approached and reached to comfort her, but she pulled away from his hand.

Harlan watched Ax. "What took you so long to get back? Where'd you go?"

Ax raised his eyebrows. "Me? I was out in the hall, cooling off mostly, but I stepped up in the back to look out at the crowd on the lawn. It's gotten bigger. Anyway, I thought I heard some movement upstairs, so I went halfway up, and I guess the door closed and I couldn't hear much. I didn't hear a crash, but I did hear the scream. I just wasn't sure if it came from downstairs or up. It took a minute to figure." He smiled and turned to Audrey. "I'm just glad you're all OK." Audrey shrugged. Ax's smile faded.

Harlan stepped over the mirror and climbed half of the front stairway. He looked back and imagined the angle the mirror might have traveled.

Audrey softened to Ax. "I'm starting to wonder if we should really be here. That was only an inch or two from causing a serious injury, and it could have been any of us."

"What do you think, Galva?" Ax asked. "Do you believe we're in danger? Should we be thinking about gettin' out of here?"

La Claire looked up. Traces of tears lined her cheeks. "I...I don't know what is going on here now. I...we may be in danger, but..." Her eyes moved away from Ax and stared off into the dark beyond the living room door.

"Hmm." Ax's gaze moved back to Audrey. "With only a little over three hours to go, it'd be a shame for you to go, Audrey, with all your plans for the reward money, your carrier and everything." Audrey's adrenaline waned and she signaled agreement. Finally, she took Ax's hand, squeezed, and sent a somber smile toward Ax.

Harlan traversed the rest of the steps to the second floor. He peered down and found that the end of the couch, where La Claire's head rested, was just within the view the stairs opening allowed. Below, the mirror remained where it had landed.

Having composed herself, La Claire moved to her feet. "Take it easy, Galva." La Claire waved off Vieve's concerns. She crossed back to the sofa. Looming over the mirror, she smirked as she reached down and collected it. When she flipped it over, the reflection surface was a spider's web of jagged shards. La Claire gazed at her reflection. Her image was dissected into a hundred segments. She shook her head.

"Galva?" Vieve asked. La Claire didn't respond. "Madam La Claire?"

"We shouldn't be here," La Claire whispered under her breath.

Vieve put her hand on La Claire's shoulder, startling her out of the trance. "Galva, are you all right?" As La Claire turned her face, Vieve could see tears had returned to her eyes, but at that moment several of the candles Harlan had lit overhead extinguished, burned down to nubs. Vieve could no longer see La Claire's face clearly. Within minutes, several other candles flickered and died. The entire room returned to its original dark and silent state. "Perhaps now would be a good time to think about getting some rest."

Harlan landed at the bottom of the steps just as Vieve finished her thought. "That's probably a good idea. There are plenty of beds up there. We could all probably do with an hour or so, to clear our heads. Do you want to help her up to one of the rooms?"

Vieve took La Claire's hand and walked her to the steps. La Claire clenched the small mirror with her other hand. Vieve struggled to pry it away, and eventually discarded it to a nearby end table.

Harlan grabbed one of the candelabra, swapped in fresh sticks, and lit them as he returned to Vieve and La Claire. "Take this."

"I don't think I can even close my eyes," La Claire said.

"I'll be up in a moment to look around, and one of us will be right next door." Harlan stepped away. Candles in hand, Vieve and La Claire proceeded up.

Thumps of footsteps sounded above, followed by the creaking of an opening door. Harlan glared toward Ax. He and Audrey exchanged words, too quietly for Harlan to hear. He gathered that Ax was encouraging Audrey to move upstairs with the others, while Audrey was reluctant. Soon they looked up and came toward him.

"I think we're gonna go try to relax for a bit too, man." Harlan said nothing as Ax passed by with Audrey and started up the steps. When they were halfway up, Harlan stopped them.

"Ax, can I speak with you for a moment?" Ax was surprised when he turned and found Harlan waiting at the bottom step.

"Ah, sure, go on up and I'll come check on you in a sec." Audrey barely acknowledged his words as she proceeded up. Ax went back down a couple of steps, but not all the way. With three steps between them, Ax towered over Harlan. "What's up?"

"The mirror. That was you, wasn't it?"

Ax grinned. "What are ya' talkin' about, bro?"

"You threw that mirror." Harlan looked to the top of the steps. "You tossed it from up there, with a perfectly clear line right down to the end of the couch."

Ax threw his hands up, signaling innocence. "Hey, man, I don't know nothin' about that. All I know is whatever tossed that mirror did us two favors." He stuck a figure into Harlan's chest. "You and me."

"I don't follow."

"How I see it, the way Madam Galva flipped out over the attempt to attack her makes it damn clear she orchestrated the knife attack in the kitchen. Why so apprehensive now, and so calm about it then, right? That means she was full of shit. Whether we agree on the science of my investigations or not, we both know she's full of it, and whatever happened to send that mirror down here proves that." Ax smiled, expecting a reaction from Harlan, but receiving none. "Besides that there's the money. If one person gets too freaked out and leaves that means an extra 50 G's for both of us. She's on the verge, and if she leaves early we'd all owe a thank you to the person who threw that mirror." He winked. "Good for you, and good for me." Ax patted Harlan on the shoulder as he pivoted and continued up to the second floor.

Harlan lingered downstairs alone. He was torn. Ax's actions were underhanded and contemptible, but had supported Harlan's efforts to exposes La Claire. Exposing Ax meant defending La Claire. He wasn't sure he was prepared to do that, but felt guilty for considering not.

Vieve tossed off the bedspread along with years of dust buildup, most of it anyway. La Claire rested her head on the pillow and drew her feet up onto the bed. Vieve and Audrey stayed by the bed until La Claire dosed off. It took only a few moments. Ax waited outside the door. Vieve and Audrey joined him in the hall. This room was opposite the master. Harlan crested the top of the steps, garnishing freshly plated candles for everyone.

"Which room are you heading to?" Harlan asked Vieve.

Vieve looked toward the master bedroom. "Not this one."

"No more dangerous than anywhere else in the house, right Ax?" Ax said nothing.

"No reason to take any chances." Vieve smirked.

"I don't think anyone's going to want to sleep in the children's beds, so I guess I can take this room." Harlan walked Vieve along with Ax and Audrey past the next set of doors to the other sets of bedrooms. "Through Galva and Ax's investigations, we've been everywhere in the house, except the attic, which is where those small windows are that people claim to have seen spirits in, right? I don't think we want to miss it by all falling asleep once we're finally permitted to take a peek, so I propose we reconvene at ten-to-five, so we have as much time as possible to go open that access door and get up to the attic. I for one want to be there as the sun rises to see for myself. It'll be a great way to end this ordeal, I suspect. Probably what the producers had in mind anyway. Are we all agreed?" He received no argument.

Ax poked his head into the next bedroom, on the same side as the closet. "This'll do, I guess." He lingered in the doorway as the other three went on. At the end of the hall, Harlan saw Vieve into the last door on the right. She wished good night to both him and Audrey and then closed the door. Audrey moved to the last remaining bedroom on the floor, opposite Vieve's. Harlan turned and headed back up the hall, but Audrey stopped him.

"Thank you for your reassurances back there. I really needed to hear that. You've been so calm through everything and in control, you know? I just, I'm glad you're here."

Harlan was surprised with Audrey's new attitude. "Don't mention it. Disagreements aside, I certainly want everyone to make it through the night safely."

She smiled warmly and whispered so that only Harlan could hear. "You know, you don't have to sleep alone if you don't want to, Harlan." He was caught off guard and hesitated. He wondered if Audrey could detect his shock though he tried to remain poised. Ax still hovered at the door of his room. He watched Audrey and Harlan with suspicion and jealousy on his face. He couldn't hear everything word for word but gathered the general idea of what was occurring. He'd expected to be the subject of such an invitation himself.

"No, Audrey, I think I'll be fine. Thank you." Harlan then had to awkwardly turn and walk away while Audrey watched. He passed the dumbfounded Ax, without so much as a look in Ax's direction. Audrey's door soon shut. Behind the closed door, Audrey's graceful expression turned to a bothered look. When she offered herself to men, she wasn't accustomed to being turned down. She shook her head, shaking off her agitation, then took a seat on the bed.

Ax, still confused, entered his room and slammed the door closed. Audrey smirked when she heard the strike. Her confidence was reinvigorated. Down the hallway, in the same instant, Harlan arrived at the master bedroom. Without hesitation, he crossed the threshold and closed the door behind himself. The house was now in absolute silence.

Walter scanned every screen on the monitor wall of the broadcast truck. Each was dark and motionless. Even the crowd outside was lethargic. Nora cut from one camera to another, and another, inside and out, through several dozen views using rapid-fire cutting in place of on-screen action, but generating no excitement. "Should we cut back and review some recorded shots from earlier?" Nora asked.

"No. Hold off for just a minute." Walter looked to the helmet cams and mumbled to himself. "OK, sweetheart, this is the time. Let's get something lively going. We've got to keep up viewership. It's on your shoulders now." Everyone in the booth watched the screens, each searching for any sort of excitement, but finding none. "Bring up the best shot we have on the actress." Nora looked at Audrey's helmet cam and then to Walter, puzzled. Seeing the conviction on his face, she punched up Audrey's view. Audrey was still, but just for a few seconds. Soon she sprang from the bed, and with a candle in tow moved to face the wall mirror in the room. Now her own camera was centered on the reflection of her face and figure.

"All right, everyone out there, I hope you're still watching." Audrey's demeanor was as audacious as ever before. In the mirror, she straightened her clothes and primped what hair hung from under the helmet. Next, she pressed her breasts up and together, blew herself a kiss, and then marched out into the hallway, where one of the camera pillars awaited her. She strutted to the next room down the hall, Ax's, and rapped at the door. Without an immediate response, though no more than a few seconds, she knocked again, longer and louder.

When Ax finally answered, Audrey sprang forward, wrapping her arms around his neck. She pulled herself up to his lips for a kiss while leaping and wrapped her legs around him. The two stumbled awkwardly back into the room while their bodies remained entangled. Ax managed to swipe the door back toward closed, but the camera pillar breached the doorway first, taking a minuscule blow from the door but also prevented it from closing as the unit continued into the room.

After prolonged kissing, Ax pulled back for a breath. Audrey fell away from him and landed on the bed with a laugh. "What about that stuff with Harlan in the—" Audrey ignored his words as she reached up, grabbed Ax, and pulled him down to the bed. He was again dumbfounded, but quickly overcome with excitement and desire, forgetting his objection. After another moment of passion, he jumped up, took a single leap that spanned the entire room, and closed the door, securely this time, so that he, Audrey, and the cameras had the room to themselves.

Ax returned to the bed. Audrey removed her helmet and placed it on the bedside table, but with the lens precisely pointed back toward her. With Ax back in her embrace, she slid his helmet off and discarded it to the floor.

The broadcast truck now teamed with activity. The couple, gently lit by candlelight, was intertwined on the bed. Walter smiled with deep satisfaction. Nora cut between the pillar cam, and Audrey's helmet, but soon the couple pulled the bed sheets over their bodies, obstructing the view. The entity under the linens continued to twist, roll, and contort. The movement of arms across backs, legs running up the other's and heads shifting from one side to the other in prolonged kissing were all unmistakable. One hand managed to escape the covering, off the side of the bed. Nora cut to Ax's helmet cam, albeit framed upside-down, just in time to catch an article of clothing fall to the floor, followed by another, and then another. Walter glanced from the steamy action to Jason who was focused on his laptop. Jason grinned, turned to Walter, and gave a thumbs-up, then pointed a finger skyward and silently mouthed, "Through the roof."

Vieve sat silently on the side of her bed. She'd heard the commotion of knocking and doors closing from her fellow contestants. The house had fallen silent again, though she paid keen attention, listening for more disruption. She was concerned for La Claire.

She decided the disturbances had concluded. She closed her eyes and laid back on the bed but was interrupted once again. Another door's latch released. Its hinges scraped as it swung open. This time it was from a more distant room and was followed by footfalls that moved down the staircase. Silence returned, but Vieve's curiosity was piqued, as well as her paranoia. She abandoned her bed, tiptoed to her door and listened as best she could.

For a long moment there was nothing, but soon footfalls on a staircase returned, coming up instead of down. The thumps continued in the hallway, drawing closer and closer to her own bedroom, louder and louder. Finally they stopped, again silence, but the last were very nearby. She leaned even closer, her ear grazing the wood. Nothing. She hesitated to even breathe. She was startled and sent to the floor by a soft knock at her door. Her spine shivered with anxiety as she stared at the door, unsure of what had happened. Her fear subsided and she breathed more easily when the next knock was followed with a whisper. "Vieve, it's me, Harlan."

She shook off her anxiety and opened the door. Harlan stood there with his hands behind his back. Vieve covered her jitters. "Scared to sleep alone?"

Harlan brought one hand forward with the remaining half bottle of rye whisky, then the other hand, Vinton's journal. "I couldn't keep my mind from racing, thinking of what else might be in here. Any interest?" Vieve grinned and beckoned him in.

They sat on the edge of the bed and Harlan opened the book. "Wait." Vieve placed a hand on top of the diary, drawing Harlan's attention to her face. She looked him in the eyes but was silent for a moment. Harlan's expression grew puzzled. "I just wanted to say I'm sorry, Harlan."

"Sorry for what?"

"For not trusting you, I guess; for siding against you." Harlan still didn't understand. "Earlier tonight with Galva in the kitchen. I was mad, I wasn't very fair to you, and I just wanted to apologize."

Harlan smiled. "Consider it forgotten." She smiled back and allowed her fingers to graze Harlan's palm as she withdrew her hand from the pages.

For Those Who Wish to Follow In My Footsteps: What I Discovered Part 5

I wake to warm, wet air pulsing against my cheek. My eyes struggle to focus on the face of the usher, only inches from my own. "He's awake."

I'm surprised to find myself not abandoned in the woods or a ditch somewhere. "I'm a little surprised to find myself waking up at all." My throat is dry, and my words are feeble whispers. The usher makes a humph as he backs away. I'm seated on a wood chair. My sight is still hazy, the effects of the knockout persisting. As my eyes clear I make out a narrow room with a small kitchen on one wall, some seats and a table across from that, and a bunk at the far end. It's there that I spot the fuzzy figure of another person. "Malvern?"

A calm voice echoes from across the trailer. "Vinton." He stands and hands me a glass of water. Sensation and control have not yet spread to all of my extremities. I'd assumed my hands were bound, but discover otherwise as I take the glass and sip from it.

Malvern sits at another nearby chair. "I was alarmed to see you among my audience in Chicago, Drake." There's a single light above, but Malvern's face is just out of its cast. "I've been traveling for some time now. You were the first person I've come across from" he searches for words—"my previous life."

"I didn't think you recognized me, Leon." I use the name I knew him by, and buried him under: Leon Carroll. He ignores it.

"I assumed it was unlikely any of my war acquaintances would ever turn up among my millionaires. You've proved that mistaken, but you always were contrary, to say the least."

"You're looking quite smashing, Leon. Perhaps not so great for the living, but for the deceased you're top notch." Again he carries on as if deaf to me.

"Imagine my surprise when Jerome found you lurking out of sight at our show tonight and snooping through our possessions, only one week after you surfaced in our affairs. Jerome here thinks that you're an investigator. Luckily, I intercepted him and informed him of our history. I'll tell you, detaining you here was all I could do to prevent Jerome from doing unspeakable things to you."

"I once used the story of my fallen brother of the battlefield to elicit the sympathy of a beautiful young woman in order to bed her. I'm comfortable with being a pity-monger, but now I find that I was a liar as well."

"What is it you think is going on here, Drake?" That is one hell of a question. I have my theory, but if I'm right it would be foolish, no, unfathomable for two killers to allow me to leave with substantial and verifiable knowledge of their dealings. On the other hand, if my suspicions are correct, it's unlikely that I'll be leaving here alive anyway, and I, unlike Malvern, have no confidence in my ability to continue my lifestyle postmortem. The only approach I have left to employ is candor. Perhaps frankness and confidence will, at the very least, suggest I'm not acting without constituents, such as law enforcement, and force them to belabor what to do with me.

"I postulate that you're drugging and kidnapping unsuspecting persons, substituting them in place for yourself, and ultimately profiting handsomely off their gruesome murders and the morbid desires of the affluent individuals who attend. Furthermore, I surmise that your death in combat was fraudulent and came similarly at the expense of an innocent victim. The ample mayhem of battle provided the cover, just as your illusion prowess does now, for you to perpetrate such a ruse."

Malvern contemplates, then leans in, allowing the light to disclose his face. His expression is warm, as is his voice. "That's not it at all, Drake. Your claims, those are the illusions, and my illusions are the reality. It's true that we take advantage of the curiosity of mortality and even allow the rumors of implied crimes to bolster our profits, but I'm no murderer."

"I felt your heartbeat, Leon, or the heartbeat of whoever lay in that guillotine. I could feel the warmth and vigor in the flesh of a living man, and then before my eyes and in my hands that pulse was terminated, and life cut short. You know as I do what that feels like. We both saw it routinely. I'll admit that there are likely ways to fake the dismemberment of a body that I'm not privy to, but I know of no method of instantly ending a heartbeat, sans death, and certainly no way to resurrect it thereafter. How can you tell me you didn't kill someone in that device?"

While I'm fiery, Malvern is cool. "I'm an illusionist, Vinton. I've studied this as an art, Asia, Europe, Africa, around the world, far before our service together. It's a strategy as old as the discipline, to make that which seems to be the illusion real, and that which seems real, to be the illusion." He reads the dissatisfaction in my face. "Perhaps it's simpler to fake a heartbeat than to fake stopping one. It's like showing an audience an object, then making it disappear. Everyone thinks you somehow moved it off the stage or are covering it from view, so they look for trap doors and screens or mirrors, all along it never occurring to them that the object was never there in the first place."

I ruminate silently. His implication is believable, but my feelings scream that there is much more to this.

"I wish you could trust me, Drake."

"Trust you? How can I with what I've witnessed?"

"If I were the killer you accuse, I'd be a fool to let you leave here alive." I reluctantly nod agreement. "If innocent, you still pose the danger of a cornered animal, ready to bare teeth and claws regardless of my intent. Thus, why would I allow you to retain the piece in your pocket?" It hadn't occurred to me that they'd left my pistol. Instantly, I squeeze my arm inward, pinching the metal to confirm.

"If it weren't you, Drake, I wouldn't be having this conversation at all, but I trust you. Why can you not extend me that faith?"

Now I remember my most recent discovery, how could I have forgotten? "The body." The notion that Malvern could use cadavers as stand-ins enters my mind. That would be a significant improvement over cold-blooded murder, but this, too, seems to be an unfulfilling and incomplete explanation. "How do you explain the body that lay in your box out in the woods? With only limited medical education along with my basic medic training, I won't claim to be a medical expert, but I'm confident that I can tell the difference between a dummy, a corpse, and a living person. It was neither a dummy nor a cadaver on your stage in Chicago, and it was certainly no dummy in that box tonight."

Malvern is quiet, organizing his mind. Finally, he sighs. He turns to the usher, Jerome, who until now has lingered back in the dimly lit corner. Malvern gestures for him to give us privacy. Only after we are alone does he begin again.

"I suppose you've forced my hand, Vinton. I'd have preferred not to open this door. It's good to see you, truthfully. I have no one now to call family or friend, but I surely wish I'd never run into you again. My options are limited to either harming you, totally discrediting you, or against my better judgment, being truthful. It's only out of my admiration for you, your bravery on the battlefield, and for the friendship that we once had that I'm willing to share the truth of this matter. I only hope you understand the trust that I'm granting you."

He has my unwavering attention. He waits as if reassessing his decision internally before speaking. "It was my body you found in that crate. It was my cold lifeless body, inanimate since the day vitality was drained from it in your very arms. What you saw was no trick or swindle, that was the day that Leon Carroll died, the day Malvern Kamrar was born."

"How can this be? What are you telling me?"

"I'm dead, Drake. That shell in the crate is but evidence of a life that once was. Before you now is the continuation of a consciousness clinging to existence."

"You're a ghost? Is that what you're saying?"

"No, energy. The same energy that animates the body, just disjointed from the body."

I grab Malvern. Were my hands to pass through him I might believe, but I latch on to both his arms successfully.

"I'm still bound by physics. Energy and mass. I can neither defy gravity nor Newton's laws, but I exist when others would not."

I jerk him closer. "How, Leon? How can you sit there and make this claim earnestly?" He waits for my grip to loosen, then he pushes back to a comfortable separation.

"When you were attending injuries on the field, how many men do you think lived because of you? How many more fatal casualties would there have been if you hadn't stopped blood loss, kept men's insides from coming out, then dragged them out and sent them to hospitals?"

I've thought of this many times. "Hundreds."

"And how many men perished in your care? How many were beyond your saving as I was?"

Not a figure I think of as often. "Twice as many, at least."

"Now, how many of the lives you saved required you risking your own life to aid them?"

"Practically all of them. You know that."

"Suppose you, or any medic for that matter, were rewarded for every man that died, not rewarded for saving men, but for allowing them to die; one hundred dollars or more per man, not for killing, but for allowing death to occur, for not intervening. Do you think your success would have been compromised?"

I have no answer. It's obvious that it would and requires no confirmation from me.

"This is the danger that lurks in what I'm to tell you, Drake. Remember this as a warning of how this knowledge can affect, can change a person." Silence claims the room. Malvern's head lowers and his body droops into a defeated position. "It is possible to capture the force of a man's life, the vestige of existence, at the moment of death. When someone dies, this spark fades into nothingness, but it can be collected by another."

Naturally this is preposterous. From a logical viewpoint, I would scarcely consider humoring such a notion. But this is an unnatural person sitting before me, and I'm solely driven by emotion now, not by reason. "Are you talking about souls? You collect men's souls?"

"No, not souls. I don't really believe in such a thing. A soul would suggest there is consciousness, feelings, or memories within. None of these are present in this effervescence radiated at the moment of passing. It's as though every person, every living thing, has a driving source of life-power inside, which separates biology from mere chemistry. Perhaps it's qualifiable energy, not unlike electricity, that human beings haven't yet discovered a way to measure. But the emissions of others can be harnessed and added to one's own surplus, essentially super-invigorating your own ability to exist."

Malvern sounds relieved, as if a weight has lifted from his shoulders. "It's not unlike ingesting sustenance. Just as food is dismantled and calories appropriated to perpetuate the life-function of an animal, this power is absorbed and devoted to the preservation of existence."

"I don't understand, Leon. How does this explain your body laying out in that coffin while you're here as lively and tangible as I?"

"This is the dangerous part. It's simple and it's complicated. When you take on this excess of life, it enhances your own, at first just as a feeling of elevated power, like you're more resistant to the attrition of life. But if you collect more, the effects are expanded. You age more slowly, your body mends more rapidly, and you gain exceptional vigor. I was nearly 90 when we first met, Drake."

One would think at this point, as I speak with a dead man, little more would surprise me. Yet his admission of advanced years raises my eyebrows.

"There's more. As you collect greater and greater numbers, it's possible for your life-force to essentially outgrow your body. Nearing that point you have the ability to ward off your own death. If a collector is killed when body and energy are in equilibrium, then it is possible to greatly resist fading away for many, many years. But if the amount of energy collected vastly exceeds the body, then it is achievable for the consciousness to go on when the body cannot. Indefinitely."

Malvern's tone becomes boastful. "I reached such a state, Drake. In my travels and education as an illusionist, I met a man who taught me of such matters. Afterward, I collected life-energy whenever I could. You can see why this information is so dangerous, can't you? The Great War was not the first where I served. War is an ideal place to position oneself to benefit from deaths already bound to occur. On the battlefield with you, I continued to collect whenever I could. I'd like to think I performed my duty faithfully and saved as many men as I could have, but when men died, as so often they did, I was there to collect their energy as well."

"How many, Leon?"

"That's how the trick is done. My consciousness is the person before you, not my body. So it's my consciousness that is subjected to the abuse of the performance, and consciousness cannot be injured. I can no longer suffer physical harm. I simply reconstitute my appearance and thus am perceived to have died and been resurrected before your very eyes. Here." He extends his arm towards me. "Feel for my heartbeat. You'll find that there is none until I decide to imitate one."

I refuse the offer. "How many people did you have to watch die to grant yourself this power?"

Malvern's excitement fades, his expression saddens and his speaking grows distant. "You'd be wise to forget me, and all this when you leave here. Part of me hopes you won't believe a word I tell you. You'll laugh, and it will slip from mind never to return." He sighs. "The pursuit of eternal life is a selfish one, as selfish a purpose as exists, you see? Reaching it means facing death again and again. Both are capable of turning a person into something ugly, Drake; a monster through another's eyes."

I only stare, still awaiting an answer.

"Thousands."

I find myself shaking my head, not in judgment but in disbelief.

"Understand, not everyone's level of life-force is the same. Sick people, elderly individuals, their energies are already diminished. By the time they pass, it's nearly insignificant. But young men, such as soldiers, vibrant lives cut short by violence, they have magnitudes more power to give. I didn't know until well after I began amassing. Perhaps it could have been far fewer. There's no clear number to reach, only a threshold, a feeling of critical mass."

"Where does the blood come from? I assume that neither your corpse nor your pulse-less apparition require circulation. Is the blood a manifestation as well?"

Malvern's expression lightens. "That we fake the old-fashioned way. We use animal blood for authenticity, both in color and odor, with chemicals added that prevent coagulating, so it can be dispensed on command. Simple theatrics, I'm afraid."

I nod slightly. This is a much better explanation of the frigid pool I uncovered under the stage than my original theory. "Then why keep the body? What use is it to you now, worth toting across the Atlantic and from stop to stop?"

"I'd like to say it was sentimental, as morbid as that may be. Unfortunately, though, I am tethered to it. Perhaps it is unwise to fill you in on the limitations of my situation." He smirks. Perhaps he is quite right, but I only smile and feign coy intrigue. "I'm not completely clear on this matter." Malvern stands and paces. "The man who gave me the knowledge of collecting this power did not himself amass enough to overtake his own quietus. I can only relate that which I have experienced, and it seems I am bound to my remains. Where I wish to go, so too must they."

"Like an animal on a leash," I say. Malvern drifts to the opposite side of the trailer.

"I prefer to think of my body as a battery, storage for the energy I've amassed, and that I'm merely limited to proximity of my source."

"What becomes of you when your body, as I presume it inevitably must, decays away completely?"

"A very logical question, and one to which I've given significant thought. Perhaps I'll at last be unleashed completely. Maybe that's just a part of the process, the evolution of existence? Mere speculation, however. I'm afraid I've run out of answers."

Malvern gazes out a window and into the night. I stand and step toward him. "I've one more question, Leon." He continues to stare outside. "How is this done? How is the energy you describe extracted, or absorbed? How do I, or does a person, learn to do this?"

Malvern turns and slowly draws his eyes from my feet to my face. "Haven't you figured it out? I'd be disappointed if you didn't at least suspect it." I look at him with puzzlement. "You already have."

This concludes my accounting of the events that transpired regarding my uncovering of the truth about Malvern Kamrar.

4:00AM

Harlan glanced up, astounded. Vieve's jaw literally hung open. They stared at one another in silence until Harlan shook his head. "There has to be more." Vieve watched in virtually intolerable suspense as Harlan turned to the next chapter, but before they read on, their attention was stolen by a thunderous, room-encompassing groan.

It was low at first but grew to nearly ear shattering in a matter of seconds. Both Harlan's and Vieve's eyes darted wildly, desperately trying to identify the orientation of the sound. After a minute of duration, the sound faded just as quickly as it began. Harlan paused, only a moment, to ensure Vieve was unharmed. He then dashed to the hallway, searching for further symptoms of the event.

Audrey and Ax lay side by side covered to their shoulders by the bed sheet. The features of their nude figures were traceable through the thin draping. The contour of Ax's arm extended across Audrey with his hand spread on her stomach. When the house-wide roar began, Audrey instinctually grabbed and dug her fingernails into Ax's arm. He leaned up and tried to assess the sound. Audrey was thrown into a state of fright. She rolled toward Ax and tucked her face into his chest. When the noise subsided, Ax moved to desert the bed but was tethered by Audrey.

"Don't go."

"I have to go check this out. If it's dangerous I need to find out before it threatens you, right?"

Audrey was satisfied, whether Ax was genuine or not. Ax dressed as best he could while he scrambled to the door. He fumbled with the latch but eventually managed to open it and sprinted into the hallway, still putting on one shoe and with no shirt. Harlan was already by the front stairwell. Vieve stood in the open doorway of her room. Ax watched, but Harlan was doing nothing but listening.

"What the hell was that?" Ax asked. Harlan held up a hand for quiet. By this time, Audrey had crept to the doorway too, wrapped only in the bed sheet. After Ax had quieted, they heard a soft rumble seemingly from below them. The noise increased volume exponentially. This time at its peak, everyone had to cover their ears and it literally shook the floor below them. Vieve and Audrey braced themselves in their respective doorjambs. With both hands steadying her, Audrey's covering fell away, exposing her fully. No one noticed. Harlan and Ax simultaneously lost balance and stumbled to their hands and knees. A camera pillar nearby was upended.

In the broadcast truck, Walter and the crew were puzzled as they watched the contestants scrambling. Soon, however, the howl from the house not only filled every audio recording device inside the mansion but echoed outside the truck itself, emanating from the building. An empty coffee cup tumbled off of one operator's station. Outside of the house, the shaking seemed little more than the typical rocking of a person stepping onto the stairs of the truck. The noise, however, was far more imposing. When the disturbance passed, Walter stuck his head out the truck's door. A hush had fallen over the congregation at the back of the property. "Did that just happen?" Walter asked rhetorically. After a moment of quiet, the gathered mass began softly chanting in unison, though the message was too distant and overlapping for him to decipher.

The second episode lasted twice as long as the first. When the sound finally waned the trembles remained for a few moments longer. Harlan and Ax climbed back to their feet.

Audrey quickly replaced her covering. "Is that the howling you've heard before, Genevieve?" She asked." The growls that people around here tell stories about?"

"No, nothing like that. What I've heard was more like an animal in the house, not like an animal about to eat the house, and I've never heard anything about physical shaking. This...this is totally new."

"Maybe we should go look around downstairs," Ax said.

"Good idea, Ax, but let's give Audrey a moment to fix her wardrobe." In spite of the events, Harlan still saw the humor. "You better put your helmet back on too, Ax. Anything could have shaken loose, clothes, chandeliers, you name it." Harlan grinned. Ax glared. Audrey retreated to the room to redress, but Ax didn't move a muscle. "We'll want your helmet cam anyway. This is live TV, after all." Ax begrudgingly agreed and retrieved his helmet and his shirt.

Harlan stepped over to the downed camera unit. He struggled at first with its heft, but managed to lift it back upright. "Not sure if anything was damaged, but at least you're back on your feet," he said into the closest camera.

A minute later the four gathered back in the hallway. "We need to get to my equipment first thing when we get down there," Ax said.

"We better check on Galva before we do anything." La Claire's door opened just as Harlan swung his fist to knock. Harlan stepped back, surprised as La Claire emerged. Her movements were odd as if she struggled to take each step. Both Harlan and Vieve presumed she was hurt. They rushed toward her. When the lights of their helmets shown on her face, they halted. Her eyes were tightly closed and she turned her head with abrupt adjustments as if tuning into some faint noise.

"Get out," she whispered. Her voice was different, low and rough.

"Get out," she repeated louder, and then dropped her face downward. Now she whispered again only with an exaggerated high pitch. "Help us. Free us." The others could only stare in wonder. "Get out." She voiced again, in the low, gravelly tone, this time yelling it, followed by another verse in the high pitch. "You have to help us, please." La Claire made one final statement in the deep, ugly voice. "This is your last warning. Leave now or die here." Upon finishing these words, La Claire's eyes snapped open, then her body collapsed to the floor.

Vieve dove to her aid but failed to soften her fall. She lifted La Claire's head and gently roused her awake. "What, what happened?" La Claire struggled to speak.

"You don't remember?" Vieve asked.

"No, I..." La Claire noticed Ax, Audrey, and Harlan, hovering over her. "I was just...resting my eyes in the bedroom." Suddenly her muscles tightened. She strained looking back at the open door behind her. "How'd I get out here?" Harlan's expression, amid the legitimate recent danger, was of genuine concern for La Claire's well-being, but this faded into disdain as he detected the hallmarks of performance from La Claire.

La Claire tried to stand. While helping her, Vieve reached for Harlan's arm. For Vieve, he offered it and guided both women to their feet. La Claire threw one arm over Harlan's shoulder without warning, to his discomfort, but Vieve slid her head under La Claire's other arm. Harlan complied. He and Vieve supported La Claire to the stairwell.

Once on the move, Ax sprinted ahead. While Vieve, Harlan, and La Claire slowly navigated the stairs together, Ax began to power up his devices. When the trio reached the bottom of the staircase, the house's growl softly began again.

"Sit, sit," Harlan ordered. The three only needed to lean back to find their bottoms on the steps. Behind them, Audrey sat on the stairs halfway up. She braced herself on the banister. Ax, however, was stranded in the middle of the room with no walls, doorways, or relevant supports nearby. As before, the groan grew loud and shook vigorously. The floorboards of the living room jumped and quivered in place accompanied by cracking and slamming sounds. Ax bent his knees to keep upright while he steadied his gadgets, but the convulsing overtook him.

"Oww, goddamn it." Ax hit the floor. Harlan noticed the small section of boards directly at their feet, the bottom of the steps, didn't shift and gyrate like the rest of the room. After over a minute, the phenomenon relented. Ax stood with several bloodied cuts on his forearms and legs. "These damn nails."

As Harlan and Vieve brought La Claire back to her feet, Harlan scanned the floor with the light from his helmet. The nails of almost every board were protruding back up, not as pronounced, but similar to when they first entered. Again, the section near the steps, where they now stood, appeared to be untouched by the problem. Harlan's thoughts were disrupted when La Claire pulled him forcefully in her direction, nearly toppling all three of them.

"That's it. We have to leave this place. It isn't safe. We need to go."

"I ain't going nowhere." Ax returned to his equipment. La Claire looked first to Vieve and then to Harlan but found no agreement. Disappointed, she turned to Audrey. Audrey shook her head.

"Well I can't...I just can't stay here." She pulled away from Harlan and Vieve, stormed to the couch, and hastily collected her few possessions.

Walter sprang from his chair. "Stay on this. Stay on this." He flew out the door. Several crewmembers were scattered near the broadcast truck. "Camera, camera." He shouted to each, most shook their heads, but soon a crewman with a shoulder camera stepped forward. "Get to the door. Now, now, go, go, go." Walter grabbed the man by the arm and ushered him at a sprinting pace. "I want a tight shot on her face when she comes out. I want to see the emotion, the fear."

La Claire proceeded to march through the hallway, rapidly toward the front door. Audrey, Vieve, and Harlan watched from the living room doorway. Ax stayed at the table, smiling. Before La Claire reached the door, Harlan dashed behind and stopped her. "Ax threw that mirror, La Claire, not a spirit."

She touched Harlan's arm. "No matter."

As Walter and the crewman waited outside the front door, a disturbance began far behind them.

In the mass of spectators, many still followed the live web stream through mobile devices. One shouted, "She's coming out," and the message was repeated again and again by others nearby. Word spread throughout the crowd, nearly 10,000 strong. Most of the town's police, and even reserve officers, had been mobilized to control the growing audience, but when the spectators collectively decided to move forward there was nothing the limited force could do to stop them. The mass streamed toward the mansion. All the officers and the crew could do was get out of their way.

When La Claire finally breached the doorway, Walter and the crewman captured her exit only briefly before the mob overtook them and surrounded La Claire. They cheered for her. With nowhere left to go the crowd stopped, but not before every foot of space between trailers, trucks, and the front of the mansion was filled with people. "Thank, you. Thank you for your support," La Claire projected out to the masses, with tears building in her eyes. "Thank you for coming to share our experiences here, and I hope you can help me. Help to rid this house of this awful evil and free the tragic victims' souls." The crowd cheered again. La Claire beamed elation.

Walter pointed the crewman to the top of the steps where the area was clear. From there, the crewman framed La Claire on camera with the crowd behind her. Walter struggled and pushed his way back through the people until he reached the broadcast truck.

From inside, Harlan, Vieve, and Audrey watched the spectacle with amazement. When Harlan closed the door, muffled cheering permeated the walls.

"Hip, hip, hooray, woo hoo," Ax chanted sarcastically from the living room. The others returned to the main area. "Three cheers for

Madam La Claire." Ax looked over at the others. "Why aren't you cheering?" He received only questioning looks. "Madam La Claire just gave each of us 50K. Isn't that worth cheering for?" Vieve and Audrey frowned.

Harlan ignored Ax. "I'm sure many people are going to interpret these noises as outbursts from the spirits, but all beliefs and theories aside I think we should strongly consider a scientific interpretation which would be that there are legitimately life-threatening structural issues with this house."

"Go ahead and take off Harlan. Be my guest. We'll take your share of the money too." Ax raised his readied gear. "All right, where should we start?"

Harlan glanced over to Audrey who nodded determination. Vieve shrugged. "If they're staying, I'm staying."

"As long as we're all aware of the risk we're taking." Harlan's tone grew inquisitive. "The noise seemed to be all around us, but there's a patch on the floor that doesn't jump up and rumble like the rest. The same spot over there didn't have its nails sticking out when we arrived. I think it's as good a place to start as any." Audrey and Vieve nodded agreement. Ax offered nothing. Harlan moved to the patch of floorboards. All the candles remained upstairs. Harlan retrieved the extra flashlight from his bag, dropped to his hands and knees, and used the flashlight, along with the beam from his helmet, to inspect the floor closely. When he looked up, he was grinning. "This section is totally different from the rest. Look." He pointed as he spoke. "Most of the flooring is worn round in all the seams, probably from years of traffic, but here it has crisp corners, like it was installed nearer to when the house was abandoned."

Vieve crouched to look. Ax followed along from behind his camera, capturing Harlan's actions. "Now look here. Like most wood floors, the end-to-end joints between boards are staggered from row to row, but in this little patch up on this end, and down here at this end, those joints are aligned for nine or ten rows. Isn't that odd?" He pointed to the strips that squared off a perfect rectangle between them. "Oh, and there's a big wedge or knot broken out right here outside the rectangle." A divide over an inch deep, four inches across, and angled downward was illuminated by Harlan's lights. It was on the outside edge of the section, directly in the middle of one side. Inside the cavity, there were several smaller gashes. "Repeated abrasions." Harlan surmised.

"That's the identical spot where we captured the message from the spirits. The maps." Excitement mounted in Ax's voice. "That same shape, there's got to be something to it." Ax and Audrey both crowded in closer.

Harlan scanned again with his nose an inch off the floor. "Wait a second." He spun around and scanned the other end, and then again in the middle as the others watched. "A-ha, look. There aren't any nails in this section at all. At least not hammered in from the top." While the others were puzzled, a look of epiphany struck Harlan's face. He sprang to his feet. With his eyes locked on the patch, he backed away. "I'm starting to think this isn't just a section of floor."

"Huh?" Audrey shook her head.

"Give me a minute." Harlan dashed across the room and into the dining room. He continued to sprint straight through to the kitchen. Vieve walked to the dining room doorway to see where he had gone, but by the time she reached it, Harlan was nowhere to be found. She proceeded into the kitchen but found it empty as well. Harlan had already run through the large pantry and proceeded into Vinton's back workshop through the concealed doorway he'd discovered early in the evening.

"I know I saw it earlier," Harlan mumbled to himself as he searched the workbench. He swiped several rusty tools out of the way, making a large ruckus. When the clanking noises faded, however, Harlan heard an odd sound at the far end of the room. He whipped his attention in the perceived direction, but his lights fell only on the large mine poster on the wall. After a moment, he realized it was voices from the crowd outside, still seeping through the walls. Harlan turned back to the tools. This time he spotted it immediately.

Harlan ran back just as quickly as he'd come, navigating through the door to the pantry and then into the kitchen. Just as he emerged, however, he was taken off guard by a shriek from Vieve, followed by the impact of their bodies. She had stepped into the door just as he dashed out. Harlan caught her from falling to the floor as she was knocked backward. In his effort to save her, he dropped the newly procured crowbar to the floor, resulting in a racket of metal striking tile, one end, then the other, and then the first back and forth like a teeter-totter. It resonated through the room, taking many seconds to come to rest. Both Harlan and Vieve held their breath awaiting silence, with Vieve wrapped in Harlan's arms.

"What were you—" Harlan began.

Vieve spoke at the same instant, "I was just—" she paused as well. Harlan indicated for her to speak first. "I was just coming to see where you went. None of us should be running around alone in here." Harlan nodded with a smile. Just as he released her the house's growl returned. The two of them clutched one another as they fought the quaking that accompanied the noise. They managed to stay upright. When the disturbance faded, they were left silently holding one another again. Harlan looked into Vieve's eyes with a smile, which she returned. The embrace lasted a few more moments.

Harlan broke the quiet. "We should get back in there." Vieve nodded. Harlan released her and retrieved the crowbar. They hurried back to the living room.

"I have a good idea about what caused this damage." Harlan jammed the straight wedge end of the crowbar into the divide in the floor. With surprising ease, the front end of the joint became offset. Not only did the adjacent floorboard rise with little resistance, but the entire section, ten boards across, lifted simultaneously. The others were in awe. From the first pivot point, Harlan could only lift the area about an inch on one side, but with that gap, he slid the bar deeper into the joint. With his second attempt he hoisted the floor section half a foot off the ground.

"It's like a door or a hatch," Vieve said.

"I thought this place didn't have a basement. There must be a crawl space or a cellar of some sort underneath here."

With the wider gap between the dislodged boards and the rest of the floor, Harlan could get both hands into the opening. He lifted the section completely and then pulled it out, leaving a half-door size portal to some space below the house. Vieve and Audrey helped Harlan stow the section out of the way. Ax continued observing through his camera.

With the hatch removed, cold air and a musty aroma filled the room. Audrey held her nose. "Wow, that's nasty."

Vieve smiled. "Hasn't been opened in more than 80 years, I imagine. That will make for some stale air."

"It could be that the family's bodies are under the floor, too." Harlan dusted his hands off. Audrey gagged. Harlan pointed his lights down below. "I can't see any bottom to it; not with this light, but there's a ladder attached here." The first several feet down were walled with boards, making a wood-sided corridor. The ladder was secured at the bottom of the wood on one side. The rungs lead down and disappeared into darkness.

"What's down there?" Audrey crept up to the opening.

"There's one way to find out." Harlan smiled.

"Why didn't we know about this?" Walter flipped through his scripts and papers with anger. Everyone in the truck leaned forward as Harlan stepped into the hole. His feet found the first rung of the ladder and proceeded on to the second. Half of Harlan's body was submerged. "We need coverage on this," Walter shouted toward the pillar operators. "Can we get a better perspective, something down there with him?"

"Just the helmet cams, sir," one of the operators said. Walter slammed his fist on a counter as he turned back to the monitors. On another screen, a shot from outside the mansion showed La Claire among the crowd, down away from the front steps. The image was silent, but she could be seen shouting toward the building, after which the crowd around her did the same.

When the group spoke, the sound infiltrated the truck through closed doors and windows. "Be gone, evil spirits. Leave this place. Let there be peace." Just as they completed their appeal, the howl of the house began, as if in rebuttal. The ground quaking followed, more violently than ever before. Several crowd members close to the house were thrown to the ground. Many bounced off one another, trailers, and equipment before they reached the grass.

The truck rocked. Walter braced himself as he watched the screens. On the on-air monitor, only Harlan's shoulders and head could be seen protruding from the passageway.

With the floor open, it was unmistakable. The howling was originating down below the house. Harlan grasped at the floor, and the edges of the hole, trying to steady himself. Audrey dove into the sofa. Ax looped his arms in the stairway railing and continued to shoot video. Scrambling, Harlan grabbed the crowbar and tried to hook its curved end into the floor. He couldn't outlast the quaking. His legs slipped out, but he managed to grab the top rung with one hand. Only his head remained in sight. Vieve was on all fours nearby. She laid out, flattening her body to the floor as she stretched an arm toward Harlan. Her efforts were too late. Harlan dropped away below the opening.

"No!" Vieve screamed. Soon after, the sound and vibrations subsided. Vieve crawled to the edge of the opening and shouted down. "Harlan! Harlan!"

Vieve stared into the cold, motionless abyss. After a long moment, she called again. "Harlan!" This time, she heard a tapping sound. She was puzzled until a beam of light struck in the darkness. It was still for a moment at the then visible bottom of the ladder, some twenty-five feet down, then it started to move. The light landed on one of the camera helmets.

The sound of coughing came next, after which a voice finally emerged from the pit. "I'm all right." It was Harlan. His words echoed. "I caught myself near the bottom, before I fell off, but I'm OK, I think." Vieve sighed. Harlan's helmet light turned on as well.

"What's down there, Harlan? What are you seeing?" Vieve waited as two beams scanned a full circle.

"Rock," Harlan shouted back, "the walls are tall and made of rock. It's more like a cavern down here than a basement, except the walls are mostly flat and they're square with the ground. I don't know what this is." Vieve looked to Audrey and Ax, puzzled. "You guys have to come down here."

Harlan's helmet cam was on the on-air monitor. Only the narrow circle that his light hit was visible. The edges of the frame were pitch black. The view moved side to side and found more rock everywhere it turned. Since the camera and light were affixed together, the spot was always in the center of the screen. The resulting effect looked like the rock face was warping or oozing rather than the camera moving. Where light fell showed only dark, stratified, rocky surfaces. "This is amazing. Go, go, go," Walter shouted toward the monitors holding Ax, Vieve, and Audrey views. "We need more cameras down there." He glanced to another screen showing the mansion grounds. Walter expected the crowd to be thinning, alarmed by the disturbances. To his surprise, they were even more invigorated.

Outside, the crowd members helped each other to their feet. La Claire repositioned herself at the head of the congregation. Many still toted flickering candles.

"Do not be detoured by the tantrums of the devil here. Hold your ground." La Claire turned from the crowd to the house. "Be gone, evil spirits"—her shouts were forceful as if she put every bit of herself into each word—"leave this place. Let there be peace."

The gathered followers recited her supplication. "Be gone, evil spirits—" The voice of the crowd resonated across the entire town.

"I'm here at the bottom. I've got you," Harlan said as Vieve moved her feet to the top rung of the ladder. "Let's hurry, though. The sooner you're off the ladder, the better." Vieve descended rapidly. When she reached the bottom, her feet splashed in shallow water. She looked around. Her light landed on the rocky surface of a wall right beside them. More distant walls met in corners to the left and right, though, in the fourth direction her light simply faded into distant darkness.

"What's down there?" Her light fell on Harlan. The back of his shirt and pants were both saturated with water.

"I haven't explored anything yet."

"Are you ready?" Audrey shouted. Both looked up to see Audrey at the top of the ladder.

"Yeah, go ahead," Vieve answered. While Harlan held the bottom of the ladder, he had to shield his eyes to avoid looking directly up Audrey's short skirt. A minute later, both Audrey and Ax had reached the bottom, though Ax struggled to climb down while carrying his camera.

With all of their lights shining, the chamber's attributes became clearer. They were surrounded on three sides by cut-rock walls, the rough texture broken only occasionally by a vertical, steel support beam. The area was about twenty-five feet wide and enclosed by the wall at their end. In the fourth direction the chamber narrowed into a corridor, which continued further than their lights could reach. Other than a stack of thick wood planks in one corner, the area was empty. "No storage or mechanics," Vieve said. "Nothing to suggest this was a functioning part of the household.

Harlan led the pack toward the open end. "I wonder if this will disqualify us for the million. I mean, technically we all left the house." His calm eased everyone's nerves.

"Thanks for mentioning that after we all came down." Ax's anger was half-hearted. They searched the walls with their lights as they moved forward.

"There's a light grade in the floor," Harlan said.

"What's that?" Audrey asked.

"The ground is angling up as we move away from the ladder." When they got several yards down the corridor, the rock of the walls disappeared on both sides. There were two openings like doors off a hallway. Harlan directed everyone to one side. With their beams compiled, a spur chamber was revealed through the opening. They found an identical room of rock on the other side. Both were barren except for a few more piles of loose wood beams. Past these doorways, the hallway of stone resumed.

As the floor rose, they left the water behind except for a thin trickle that snaked down the middle of the corridor. After another twenty feet, a second pair of chamber doorways came into view. Audrey, Vieve, and Ax moved toward one room, but Harlan hesitated. They turned to him. "You know, I think I've seen something like this before."

"Where?" Vieve asked.

"On Vinton's workshop wall. Do you remember? You called it room and pillar?"

Vieve nodded and looked side to side. "You might be right, Harlan. It's definitely man-made, with chamber after chamber off of a central hallway. Yeah, it seems like a mine." She stepped close to one wall and examined the surface. "These might even be veins of coal in here."

"So there's a coal mine under the house?" Ax asked.

Vieve turned back. "Looks that way."

"What if that map on Vinton's wall wasn't just of one of the company mines?" Harlan pointed his light up and down the corridor. "What if it was of these chambers?"

Vieve grinned. "I guess it's not crazy a house would be over the top of a mine. There are networks of abandoned mines under several parts of town, but I don't understand why there would be an entryway to down here from inside the house. They wouldn't have hauled coal up through there. Why have it?"

Harlan pondered for a moment, until his attention was pulled away.

"Look, look." Audrey stood in the doorway into one of the nearby chambers. "There's something in this one." The others rushed to her. The chamber lit up and in the center sat a wooden crate. They all moved to it. The box was covered with dark, sooty dust. Harlan used his hands to clear a spot and revealed a smooth, hard wood surface that bore complex carvings. Seeing this, Vieve and Audrey began clearing with their hands as well. Soon, the entire top of the box was exposed.

"This is beautiful." Vieve traced a portion of the carvings with her fingers.

Something occurred to Harlan. "Step back." The others complied. "Now, shine all your lights right here on one side." With one small area brightly lit, Harlan examined it closely. "Does this look blue to you?"

Vieve was ecstatic. "Yes, yes, it's blue."

"I don't understand?" Audrey looked to Ax. Ax shrugged.

"It was in Vinton's journal." Vieve touched the box again. "He wrote about a blue wood box, just like this. It can't be a coincidence."

"So what was in the box?" Ax asked.

"It was..." Vieve pulled her hand off the box and looked back to the others. "It was a coffin, I guess."

"Let's open it." No one moved to assist Harlan. He proceeded to dislodge the top using the crowbar he still carried. It took his entire strength to move it the first inch. After a moment of rest, Harlan heaved into it again and pried the cover halfway off. He glanced inside and smiled.

The others tentatively crept to the edge of the box. Vieve gasped. "Legs! Just like Vinton discovered, a body." The lower half of a skeleton was exposed at the bottom of the crate. The leg bones were wrapped in tattered, dark clothing. Audrey covered her eyes and retreated to the wall. Ax smiled, drew his camera up, and shot the sight with his enhanced spectrums.

Harlan leaned over the box, pressed on the edge of the lid, and pushed it completely off. When it slammed to the floor, Vieve jumped, her heart racing. Audrey let out a panicked yelp in the same moment. The rest of the body was revealed. The time-shredded clothing partially concealed the chest and arms. One arm was folded over the torso while the other lay beside it.

Vieve shivered, remembering that in his journal Vinton had pulled one hand up out of the box. Enough of the clothing remained to identify it as a military dress uniform, complete with collar, tie, and an array of rank and accomplishment emblems, as well as a medic's insignia. Above the collar, the dark empty sockets of a skull stared straight upward. "This is Kamrar's body," Vieve said to Harlan. "Just like Vinton detailed, taken from its burial in World War I." Ax and Audrey both looked puzzled.

Harlan's eyes stayed on the body as he spoke. "Vinton wrote all about this in his journal." Harlan walked a half circle around the box until he stood over the skull. After a moment of contemplation, he chuckled.

"What's funny?" Vieve asked.

Harlan stepped back to the bottom of the box. He reached in, pulled one leg of the remains up, and inspected it closely. "Just as I thought. The knees and pelvis are the wrong shape. My paleontology expertise is limited, but I'd guess these are the lower extremities of a chimpanzee or an orangutan. I can say they're definitively not human." Now Vieve was as confused as Ax and Audrey. Harlan released the bones, and they fell back into the crate with a thud. Audrey shrieked again.

Next, Harlan stepped to midway along one edge, leaned in, and lifted an arm. "Ah, I believe this is the arm of a different ape, a bonobo or an adolescent chimpanzee. Intended to more appropriately proportion its length with that of a human."

"I don't understand?" Vieve leaned in and looked closer. "Is...is that a chimp skull, too?"

"No." Harlan's smile dropped. "It would have larger and sharper teeth, and a smaller brain. The skull looks human." He moved to the top of the coffin and lifted the skull out. Audrey cringed. Harlan held it up, shining both his helmet and flashlight on it. He turned it side to side. Finally, he shook his head and sighed. "This isn't even bone. It's a ceramic replica." When he dropped the skull back into the crate, it fractured into pieces. Vieve still stared at Harlan with a confused expression. "I suppose Kamrar, or Leon rather, may have died on the battlefield, or have used another body to stage his own death, but in either case these remains are a hoax, pure and simple. Someone just assembled them and made them up in a uniform to look like Kamrar's."

"Man, this is too freaky," Ax said.

Harlan dusted his hands off, and then moved to the chamber doorway. "It looks like there is plenty more corridor to explore, and more rooms as well if that map upstairs was accurate. Should we get moving?" The others were slow to respond. Eventually, Vieve and Audrey followed Harlan.

"Hold up." They turned to Ax. "I need to go back up and get the rest of my equipment. This is too intense to cover half-assed. Will you wait a few minutes?"

Harlan nodded. "I suppose we still have a few hours." Ax smiled. He trusted his camera to Audrey, and then sprinted out.

Audrey looked toward the box. "Can we wait outside of this room?" With a nod from Harlan, the three stepped into the hallway.

"Since we have some time to kill." Harlan grinned and pulled Vinton's journal out from tucked in his waistband and held it for Vieve to see. "I managed to keep it from getting wet. I think it's clear that the only reliable resource for insight into these mysteries will be found here. What do you say we dig a little further?"

The manic events and discoveries of the last hour still flustered Vieve, but she took a deep breath and answered with resolute conviction. "I think that's a great idea."

For Those Who Wish to Follow In My Footsteps: How I Became Immortal Part 1

Reader,

For the remainder of these memoirs I must sacrifice richness in favor of potency. I'll limit my recollections more precisely to my actions, experiences, and thoughts across many years, which have the greatest relevance toward understanding the course of my life and accomplishments after my uncovering of Leon Carroll's circumstances.

V.D.

Following my confrontation with Leon, the world was a very different place. I couldn't escape his final words to me. Had I inherited this life energy from casualties in the war incidentally, just as Leon had collected them purposefully? Or was it something else? The face of the thug I'd seen to his end lingered in my mind. Not with guilt but with curiosity. Was the exhilaration I felt upon the conclusion of our bout the very infusion of life energy that Leon described? If so, how could he have known anything of the circumstances and outcome of that situation? Was the benefit of collecting his energy radiating from me to the point that Leon could detect it unmistakably?

The trifles of daily life seemed barely worth a thought with this new perspective, the awareness of so much greater an existence. I had sought something exceptional for my life as long as I could remember. That, I suspect, was why I rejected the path my father and family had laid out for me, priming me to take over the business empire they had built. It's why I first turned to medicine, and then to war. It's probably what compelled me to investigate a mysterious magician to any end, at any cost. Yes, a thirst for the extraordinary has certainly been the driving force for my life. Now, before me was a potential I'd never dreamed of, the possibility of eternal life.

One couldn't help but hypothesize about the existence of others like Leon in history. How many legends, such as a vampire that lives eternally by feeding on the living, might have been exaggerations of the real-life existence of a "collector?" Furthermore, what religious icons believed to have lived exceptionally long lives, or to have been resurrected from death, might also have been individuals who reached the plane of immortality through these means? I could imagine how a being of this nature might become the subject of worship, or the subject of fear on a mythological scale. It was interesting and delightful to reflect on.

On my train back to Chicago, by chance, I was seated next to the same homely, shy teacher with whom I'd shared a cabin just the day before last. In retrospect, it was good fortune, but I didn't know it at that moment. This time the opposite seats were vacant. "We have the place to ourselves," she chattered nervously as the train pulled out.

I can't say what came over me. It would be untrue to say I saw something different in her than before, something that impressed me or called for attention whatsoever. No, I think I was simply on a high from my recent accomplishment and discovery, my body surging with adrenaline and endorphins, and she was, to put it bluntly, easy prey.

I began by asking again about the books she carried, feigning greater interest this time. It was clear, just as I'd expected, that she was deprived of the attention of men and quite eager to receive it. We conversed about her name and career. They barely registered in memory. I shared trivial bits of my own life: war heroism, med school, and wealth, all along keeping details vague and reserved on my end. She didn't show the same discretion. I was briefly interested when she spoke of her family. Her father was a land tycoon in Iowa. She had no brothers, no sisters, and of course was unwed. I artfully kept my boredom concealed.

After prolonged conversation, I finally moved on her. "So in this book, is there any sex?" Her cheeks grew red with the mere mention of the word. Silently, she nodded the affirmative. "Is that something that you often find appealing in literature? Not to be too forward, but I personally find literary romances so enthralling. I imagine and relate myself more to those parts than any others. Is that foolish?" I emulated her shyness. She shook her head, comforting me, silently. It wasn't foolish to her. "I hesitate to share this, but after I finish a book, I often go back and reread the steamy bits two or three times." I finished with a smile.

"Me too." She was enthusiastic.

"Do you ever dream that someone will write about you in a scene like that?" I stroked my fingers through her hair and leaned in closely while pulling my voice back to a near whisper. "Strangers meet briefly on a train. It happens every day." She closed her eyes. "Happenstance strikes, and they find themselves in each other's company again. Maybe it's fate, but this time they're alone." I placed my other hand on her lap. "They soon strike up conversation and find they have more in common than either ever dreamed." I wrapped both arms around her. "They fall into one another's arms." Next, I leaned in toward her lips, my breath warming her cheek as she tilted her head to receive me. "They make love, then and there, aboard the train." I kissed her. If there was any further conversation between us, then or after, I don't recall it. My mind continued to race regarding immortality, even during coitus. The idea of receiving another human's essence of life is not mutually exclusive from sexuality. You take from another for your own pleasure, or at the very least both are deeply intimate events. When I left the train, I never expected to see Martha again.

By the time I reached my hotel, I'd already resolved to walk a new path. I would dedicate the rest of my natural life to achieving that which Leon had accomplished. The first step would be to position myself to acquire further life energies, great quantities of them. I'd need to situate myself in a circumstance where the death of youthful individuals was routine. It occurred to me that my more sinister hypotheses about Leon, now proven unlikely, could serve to advance my goal, such as kidnapping and slaughtering vagrants. If a man were willing to do anything to extend his own life, that would be one approach. One problem, among many with that notion, is the anything-but-clear number of captures needed. One thousand is far too great for a murder spree. Quickly I abandon that course of thinking.

War medic, I realized, was a perfect cover for this agenda. There were current conflicts in the war aftermath in the Ottoman Empire, unrest with the Irish, and with the Soviets, but none seemed a practical placement to insert myself, and I wouldn't expect another world war any time soon. The key to my future dawned on me days after returning while reading a newspaper in the hotel lobby. A small headline read, "Nine Killed in Mine Collapse." The story went on to divulge the details of the incident.

I researched further. Reported rates revealed that in just one mining operation of my family's, where the workers numbered 1,000 or stronger, one could expect several accidental fatalities each year. This endeavor would be a test of patience, a long game of strategy, not a singular conquest. My mind raced with ideas, statistics, and calculations. In our mining towns, our business didn't simply employ a workforce; we were for all practical purposes the town itself. Our company ran the shops, schools, hospital, we owned everything. For every thousand workers there might be five thousand residents. Each year brings waves of age, illness, and deaths. Each year would bear nearly one hundred births, complete with more than one in eighteen infant mortalities, and almost one in thirty maternal mortalities; ripe fruit for plucking. People die. That's a fundamental fact of life. Why shouldn't I reap the benefits of tragedies that are bound to occur whether I'm there or not? In a way, I'd be adding value to each life lost, making them part of a greater cause instead of dying in vain. In the closed community of the mining town, I'd stand to benefit from every passing. The grin lasted for days on my face; satisfaction with my clever plans.

Aside from brief written correspondence, I hadn't spoken with my father, Warren, in years. Money came from both sides of my family. My father couldn't deny me the substantial trust provided for my subsistence by my grandparents. He had no leverage with which to force me to comply with his will once I was an adult, and it irritated him greatly.

If he was surprised that I arrived at his office unannounced, he didn't show it. When I told him I'd come to involve myself in our family's dealings, I'd hoped for a warm reception, one that showed he'd been eagerly awaiting my reversal, to satisfy his family and legacy desires. I was prepared for a wrathful reaction as well. I hadn't anticipated he'd be apathetic.

He coldly stared across the expansive desk that kept visitors ten feet from him. "What's in it for me?" I was at a loss for words. "Are you here to tell me that you can deliver greater profits for our businesses? That your expertise could advance our company interests in ways that we couldn't without you?" Again, I was silent. "Perhaps you feel your management will be better than my own?" He waited again for an answer.

"Vinton, there was a time when you simply taking over what I've built would have delighted me, whether you could control it as well as I have or not, but I'm afraid that will no longer suffice. You're too late. I expected you to show up here one day. I thought you'd be in to ask for money, for startup capital to begin some grand business of your own imagining. While that wouldn't have been in line with my original hopes, I could have understood it as a man. As a businessman, I could have given you the same consideration I would give any other business proposal. If I thought there was merit, that it could generate revenue, I'd put feelings aside and support you, but showing up with nothing—"

"Are you familiar with Ely Stanton?" When the words left my mouth it came as a surprise even to me. Warren was silent, confounded. "I understand he owns a great deal of land in Iowa. Isn't that where most of your mineral assets are coming from?" I rather unsettlingly considered for a moment that my subconscious had become capable of scheming without me. But I chose to follow this course to an end.

Warren was hesitant. "At this point, yes, it is. The fact is I've gone head to head with that bullheaded bastard more times than I can count." I raised my eyebrows, beckoning him to go on. "He's dirt rich, not wealthy. He doesn't understand the first thing about business. He's sitting on piles of cash underneath all that farmland. He doesn't do a thing with it, but he won't deal with developers, and he won't sell a single acre. It's curious; he has no problem with knocking down a forest or leveling a prairie to plant a few more plots of corn, but when you talk about digging, he clams up and hides behind land conservation." I smiled. The pieces fell into place. "If you have some kind of pull with Stanton, maybe this conversation hasn't been a complete waste of time."

"Not with Ely. With his daughter and only heir." Warren raised a single eyebrow. "What's your best prospect for mining on Stanton's land? What would be the most desirable deal to strike with him?" He searched my face, hesitant to share sensitive business details. "I may not have been the greatest supporter or contributor to family business matters, father, but I've never done anything to compete with or to undermine your dealings."

"There's a little town called Shadows Bend. The town sits on top of some of the largest and purest coal deposits we've identified. There's already a rail line going through town and bisecting the county, with a straight shot to Chicago, so the investment in infrastructure to develop those deposits would be minimal. On top of that, there are another dozen promising prospects all around the county, but Stanton owns nearly everything in the damn county and the town. No one in the area is willing to cut a deal if he won't." Warren leaned forward on his desk. "Figuratively, it's a gold mine if we can get our hands on it."

"If I were to marry Stanton's daughter, I imagine he'd be more liable to open the door to doing business. Don't you think? I could then spearhead negotiations for that development. He'd have common interests in our shared prosperity, at least in mine and Martha's, and maybe a grandchild or two. Perhaps after that the road would be clear to the entire state. If not, it would only be a matter of time before the old man passed and the land bequeathed to Martha"—I pause strategically—"and to me, I suppose." I grin.

Warren glared suspiciously. "And you're in love with this girl?" I said nothing; desperation, behavior, and all that. It took only seconds of my silent smirk for Warren to understand. "Cut to it then, Vinton. What do you want in return, vice president, a seat on the board?"

"Not that much even. I just want to be put in charge of the Shadows Bend development." I leaned in as well. "I'll spearhead operations there for reasonable pay, we'll make our home there, I'll be introduced to the family business, and the Drake empire reaps the benefits."

Warren searched my face with untrusting eyes, then got a sinister smile, much like my own. An inherited trait, I realized for the first time. He extended an arm across the desk and I stretched to meet him, which was no small distance to cover. "If you can deliver all that, you've got the position without question." We shook hands with mirrored pleasure. "You getting married and joining the company. Your mother will think she's died and gone to heaven."

Martha was most receptive when I showed up that very evening, flowers in hand, on her doorstep. The courtship was brief. With me on my best behavior, Martha swooned over the fortune of me stumbling into her life, "Just when I'd given up on finding love," she'd say. The wedding would follow two months later, rushed, but the circumstances warranted it. Our first child was born seven months after that. Ely Stanton's only stipulation over dealing with the Drakes was a verbal commitment to deliver a grandson as soon as possible. We were surveying for mining development in Shadows Bend before the year was out. Everything was moving forward as perfectly as I'd envisioned it.

It'd be impossible to continue my formal medical education with these affairs forging ahead. I felt, however, that expanding my knowledge and experience in health would serve my clandestine objective. I needed to understand death as deeply as possible in order to master it. It would serve to further position myself to appear innocently surrounded by mortality. I began studying medicine independently, in private lessons from practicing physicians.

In the first year of operations, I opened four mines around Shadows Bend, and another three in the county. The labor force exceeded 3,000 workers. The town swelled with nearly 12,000 new residents. I was in our temporary offices just outside the entrance to mine #2 when the first significant mining accident occurred. Part of the ceiling in mine #2 had been damaged during pre-shift blasting in a different branch. When workers entered, unaware of the impairment, the ceiling gave way, striking and trapping fourteen.

Reports were ushered out to the mine boss, and I was at his side. I grabbed my medic bag, and we rushed down. The other workers were clearing the rubble when we arrived. Two men were already freed and slumped against a wall. They hadn't been injured severely. The others were less fortunate. One was killed instantly. Six were in poor condition but could be treated and survive. I tended to them before anything else, rendering first aid. The other five were too badly harmed—blood loss, critical spine damage, brain trauma—no one could have gotten them out of that mine and to a hospital in time to make a difference. I witnessed each of their passings.

One man quivered uncontrollably. I couldn't tell if his wounds caused involuntary nerve responses or if he trembled in fear. I held his hand and looked into his eyes, comforting him as he expired, something I'd never done during the war. In his last breath, his eyes glazed over, but there was an implication in them, as if he wished to thank me for my presence. "No, thank you," I whispered. He went limp. I slide my hand over his face to close his lifeless eyes, then a feeling surged within me. It started as a warmth in the ends of my extremities, a heat that expanded to fill my body and soon turned to fire, no, electricity, which invigorated and revitalized every cell inside and out. My heart sped as I, for lack of a better description, digested the power. It was glorious.

When the rush faded, I turned to the next, and the next, and the next, collecting the vitality of each. When all five fatal victims had extinguished, I stood from their bodies and ordered an office worker to see to their remains and to their families, then I escorted the injured survivors out of the mine to seek further treatment. The workers who witnessed the ordeal applauded my actions as I left.

This incident was just the beginning. Soon, I set up a first stop medical office in the same building as the permanent administrative offices. All workers and their families, be it illness or injury, would pass through there before any other doctor or hospital. My services, along with a small staff, were provided without cost for Drake mine employees. Word of the facility circulated and soon it was regarded as groundbreaking in commitment to the well-being of the labor force. Even the governor visited to express his admiration for our benevolence.

My reach grew past mine workers. The boom of population required huge forces of construction workers, the rail station grew by a factor of ten, and a dozen other derivative labor pools developed, many with their own inherent risk of bodily harm. At the year's end, my count exceeded 60, 60 deaths, each occurring in my own two arms, albeit a dozen were elderly or infants, which yielded reduced quantities of life energy. At any rate, it was a magnificent start. I was so empowered I floated on a high. I wondered if my feet ever really touched the ground.

By the second year, the town population grew by another 5,000 and I was personally administrating the town's newly built primary hospital as well as overseeing the mines. An explosion early in the year brought the deaths of ten men and set the pace for an even more prosperous year than the first. I found that even arriving several minutes after a death, I was still able to reap most of the spark from a departed individual. Mine business was booming. Several new prospects were identified in the area. We were set to continue this pace for another 20 years. When one mine was depleted, we moved the labor to another within a few miles and continued with virtually no interruption in productivity.

My father was reveling. He negotiated a dozen other joint ventures of mining with Stanton. Martha's and my second child was soon on the way: the grandson Ely had requested. Though we built an extravagant home for Martha and the family, I was barely ever there. Between the mines and the hospital, my time was in high demand. That made it much easier to hide the nature of my objectives from Martha, and it left only an hour or so in an average day in which I had to maintain my ruse of interest in her, in our business, in our home, or in our family. Martha gave up school teaching, something I'm sure was just to fill her time in the first place. She saw to the house, the staff, and the children while I worked. On weekends, I would occupy myself with medical reading and even trifled with carpentry. I kept myself present but distant.

The passing years and two childbirths did nothing to improve Martha's looks. By the time our third child was on the way, it occurred to me that the timing didn't coincide with my participation in any sort of love life, as I'd decided to relieve myself of that burden months prior. I mused at the thought of Martha taking a lover. I suppose money can blind a man. Was it someone who worked at the house or a serviceman? Perhaps she ran out for errands a few times a week to meet with some power-hungry merchant or foreman who hoped to use her to advance his own circumstances. I didn't find the thought of my own mining subordinates engaged in such infidelity to be humorous. The notion of a man staring me in the face and believing he had some embracing secret to lord over me enraged me, in fact.

It was no matter, I told myself, for she will age, wither, and pass as all others, while I will have mastered life itself —as long as her escapades do nothing to interfere with business. And business raged on, thriving and growing, both mining and the business of collecting.

Five years brought a tally nearing 400 in this, my vocation of death and immortality, on track to match Leon's accomplishment.

I wondered whether Leon might find my endeavors threatening, rivaling himself, if he'd see my eventual success as diminishing his own. It would be several more years before I'd witness the exact nature of his reaction.

5:00AM

Vieve and Harlan bore grave expressions. "Leon. That's the magician, Malvern Kamrar?" Audrey asked. Vieve and Harlan both nodded. Ax fumbled with several gadgets while navigating down the ladder. The racket pulled everyone's attention from the journal.

All three moved up the corridor to help Ax. Once he was set, the four returned to where they had left off in exploring the subterranean space. They passed the chamber with Malvern's blue crate to a third set of rooms. One of the rooms was open and empty, but the other was boarded over with heavy lumber as thick as the supports used in mining. The planks were laid horizontally and stacked one on top of the next, each bolted directly into the rock that framed the chamber doorway.

"I don't think these bolts are going anywhere." Harlan leaned onto the edge of one board. It held firmly. "But much of the wood is rotten." He held the crowbar like a baseball bat with the hook at the far end, drew back, and with a great swing buried it into a soggy portion of a plank in the middle of the barrier. Harlan put one foot flat against the wooden surface and pulled, bringing the crowbar out of the wall and a large chunk of the wood with it.

An arm-size opening into the chamber resulted. Harlan discarded the wood scraps and swung again, and again. While he whittled away, Audrey and Vieve wandered further down the corridor. They returned a few minutes later.

"The hallway ends, just down there a ways. It looks like there are two more open doorways after these, and another pair at the end. But the last pair are boarded up just like this," Vieve said. Breathing heavily, Harlan rolled his eyes at the thought of breaking down two more walls.

By the time Harlan had fully exhausted himself, he'd opened a two-foot wide by four-foot tall hole in the wall. Harlan dropped the crowbar, caught his breath, and then stepped up to the opening. "Step back." Harlan extended one leg into the chamber, but it found something other than flat floor. He probed with the tip of his shoe.

"What is it?" Vieve asked.

"I'm not certain. There's something just inside the door." He withdrew his foot, knelt on one knee, and reached inside with his hand. Ax stood back, running video and other metrics of the others while Vieve and Audrey both leaned over Harlan's shoulder. Their helmet lights, along with Harlan's, only slightly penetrated the opening, but as they leaned closer, the lights grew more focused. Harlan's arm was fully stretched into the hole. "There it is." He tugged with all his might, but it didn't move.

Audrey leaned even closer. "What do you think it is?"

Harlan didn't answer. He stretched his other arm in and gripped the slender object with both hands. He stood as he pulled again, using his leg strength. The object remained in place at first, then suddenly gave way. Harlan was thrown backward as a skeleton surged forward from the hole. The skull butted Audrey's head and knocked her to the ground. She screamed at the top of her lungs. Ax broke from recording and offered Audrey a hand up.

As Harlan returned to his feet, and Audrey calmed herself, the four of them eyed the skeleton. It lay face down, with its feet still in the hole, positioned as if it were crawling out. The bones were held together by traces of dried tissue and adorned with a deteriorated suit. Vieve thought that the arms of the jacket looked odd. She poked at them, first with her foot, and then with a hand. She grabbed the end of one sleeve, lifted it, and revealed the material was limp. "There are no arms inside." Harlan grabbed the other sleeve. Its arm was missing as well. He then grabbed the torso and flipped the entire skeleton over.

Audrey shrieked when its face turned upward. "Is that...is that a monkey or whatever, too?"

Harlan surveyed the corpse with his light. "No. It's human."

"Who is it...who was it?" Ax asked. Harlan didn't answer.

"Malvern Kamrar," Vieve said. "Or at least his clothes. I recognize that suit from the posters for his show. I've seen them a thousand times."

Harlan pulled a kerchief from its pocket, embroidered with an M and a K. "We can't be certain about the body, but she's right. It's Malvern's clothes."

Walter watched from the door of the broadcast truck. Harlan's view was on air. Jason looked from the screens to Walter. "That pretty well destroys Madam La Claire's theory."

Walter smiled and looked outside. The crowd, as large, loud, and impassioned as ever, still followed La Claire's lead. "If they're following along, it doesn't seem like they care." Walter laughed. He looked back at the screen, now close-up on the face of the skeleton. "This is better than I'd ever imagined. We couldn't script a show this compelling. They'll be re-airing this for years."

Everyone hovered over the body. "Someone entombed him in there?" Vieve asked.

No one answered. "What happened to his arms?' Audrey looked up to the barricade. "Was he dead when they sealed it up?"

"I don't know about the arms, but if you were closing up a dead body, wouldn't it be lying on the floor, not leaning against the wall from the inside?" Harlan gestured toward the hole. "I grabbed his leg at the bottom, and when I pulled him free, his head came through at the top. He was standing, somehow the corpse was standing." Harlan shook his head. "Malvern or not, he must have been shut in alive. Audrey shivered. Harlan looked up at her. His expression grew concerned. "Do you know there's blood on your face?"

Audrey was alarmed. "No."

Harlan shined his light on Audrey's face. She squinted. "The hit from his skull must have cut your cheek."

Audrey turned to Vieve with tears mounting in her eyes. "Does it look like something that will scar?"

Before Vieve could check, a soft, rumbling noise mounted distantly. All four turned to the corridor's far end. As the roar grew, it drew closer. The progression was slower than in the previous occurrences, but continued to grow louder and nearer. The ground below their feet started to tremble. Soon, the quaking and full-volume growl surrounded them. All four were knocked off their feet.

This disturbance lasted longer and shook more violently than ever. Cracking and splitting sounds of rock above them accompanied the growl. Harlan wondered if the ceiling might cave in, but everyone was frozen. A series of rocks began to drop. The first could be heard crashing, but was too distant to be seen. The next was directly between Harlan and Vieve. It scattered pebbles on impact. Dozens more fell all around them. Audrey squealed with each strike, though her hands covered her ears tightly. Then everyone's fear was realized. A sizable rock dropped on Ax's legs. He let out a bellow.

Vieve and Harlan both moved toward Ax, but the shaking limited progress. After several more strikes in the darkness in both directions, the rumble and quaking finally subsided. As soon as the disturbance passed, all three rushed to Ax. Harlan pulled the boulder off.

"Are you all right?" Audrey asked.

Ax bit down and struggled to speak. "No...I think my leg is broken." He groaned in anguish.

"It'll be all right, Ax. We'll get you up and out of here." Harlan braced Ax's upper body while Vieve inspected the injury.

Ax grabbed Harlan's shoulder, squeezed, and pulled him down.

"No, no ya can't. We're almost to the end." Agony overtook him, and he released another moan. "It's almost over, man. I have to last to the end."

"That would be exceptionally dangerous, Ax." Vieve looked up from his leg. "It's severe." She reached for Harlan to hand her his flashlight. Once illuminated, Vieve put her fingers into a hole in Ax's jeans and tore it wide open. Everyone, including Ax, could see the two sides of a broken tibia protruding from his flesh. Audrey turned, unable to stomach the sight. Ax began to hyperventilate.

Harlan held Ax from squirming and injuring himself further. "It's OK. You'll be OK."

Ax composed himself briefly. "Look, I gotta stay." His eyes pleaded to Harlan. "Just leave me here and when the sun's up send the paramedics down."

Vieve's hands were soaked in red. "You're losing blood. It isn't safe. This could get infected. You could lose the leg, or worse. You could bleed out. We have to get you to the ambulance outside." Ax shook his head, wincing in pain.

"Don't be stupid, Ax," Audrey said.

"We can't risk leaving you here. The next episode might crush you completely." Harlan smiled. "Don't sweat it. You're going to be a big star after this anyway, right? Believe me, you'll probably have your own show in a couple months, just like you wanted. The money isn't worth the danger now. It isn't worth your life. "Ax sighed and nodded.

Harlan, Vieve, and Audrey lifted Ax. He could maneuver on one leg, with his arms around Harlan and Vieve. At the ladder they pushed Ax halfway up from below, then Harlan scaled the rungs around him, got to the top, and then lifted Ax the rest of the way from above.

Paramedics were standing by at the front door with a gurney. Cameras were waiting as well. As they secured Ax to the bed, he blew Audrey a kiss. There was a small pocket in the crowd, free of candles, where youthful onlookers dressed in movie costumes waved signs. They cheered Ax's name as he was wheeled from the house and loaded into the back of the ambulance. Ax waved to them. They roared even louder.

Galva was still at the head of her followers. They were packed tightly in virtually every open inch of grass near the mansion and most of the rest of the property. The back-most quarter was the sparsest, but more people streamed in from the street with every passing minute. Their chants grew louder and louder as they continued to exorcise the property.

Vieve, Harlan, and Audrey watched from the doorway. The ambulance disappeared off the grounds. Audrey wiped a tear from her face. She glanced down. There were streaks of blood on her palm. She looked up with unease, turned and stared fearfully into the cold, dark house. She looked at the blood on her hand again and sighed. "I can't do this. I don't think I can go on." Both Harlan and Vieve turned to her, surprised. "If that happened to me or my face was cut worse, my career could be over. I... I just can't."

"Wait!" Vieve's plea was too late. Audrey dashed out. Vieve and Harlan watched, shocked as Audrey disappeared into the frenzy outside.

Vieve looked to Harlan. "Are you going to stay?"

Harlan's face showed determination. "I'm going back down there."

"You know it's too dangerous. Why not stay here and play it safe to the end?"

"I didn't come here for the money. I came to get to the bottom of what happened, or at least curtail all the false conclusions. If I stop here, all those people watching will take Galva's, or Ax's, completely unfounded versions of the story for granted. I'm sure investigations will follow and the truth will come out, but not to an audience in the millions. The only way to reach everyone is to finish the story for them, right now, with the actual evidence. And now, there is finally evidence. The answers are back down there." He pointed to the floor. "I don't expect you to join me. It's probably not a good idea, but I have to."

"I hoped you'd feel that way. I'm going too." Vieve closed the door. "You're not going to get all the credit for solving this mystery." She stepped toward the living room but smirked and spoke over her shoulder. "And you might just need me."

"Wait a second. Hold it right there." Harlan stepped up to Vieve and placed his hands on her shoulders, putting the two of them intimately close. Vieve smiled, closed her eyes and puckered her lips. "Walter." Vieve opened her eyes, baffled. Harlan spoke into the camera on her helmet. "I'm sure you're following this. Send us in an ax. There's got to be one on the fire truck out there. If we're going to break into two more chambers down below, we need something heavy duty. A power saw would be better if you have one, and if you want more than two cameras down there you better send the other three helmets back in here too."

Harlan dropped his hands and turned toward the front door, but just as quickly, he spun back to facing Vieve. "Don't think I didn't notice." He smiled. Vieve remained puzzled, but Harlan wrapped his arms around her, tilted her back, and proceeded to kiss her passionately. The kiss only ended when a banging on the front door drew both of them from it. They looked into one another's eyes for a long moment, and then with a mutual smile stepped back to the front door. A fireman's ax was leaned up in the doorway with the helmets beside it.

Harlan and Vieve returned to the barricaded doorway they'd already broken through. Harlan dropped one of the helmets onto the ground and tilted it up, so both the light and the lens were aimed at the opening. He and Vieve proceeded through the rupture and searched the room. It was completely empty.

"No furniture or provisions. Nothing to suggest this was a prison." Harlan looked to Vieve. "It was a tomb." When they turned to leave, they discovered the missing appendages. Malvern's arms were suspended at shoulder level on the inside of the barricade, strung together by what remained of shirtsleeves. The wood was both dented, as if beaten with a rock, and scratched by fingernails. The skeleton's hands were dug into the cracks between planks.

Vieve eyed the arms. "You must have separated the shoulder

joints when you pulled the rest of the skeleton through." With the slightest touch, one of the arms fell apart, scattering the bones. Vieve felt the markings on the boards, then placed her fingers in the wall crevices, where Malvern's arms hung, matching their position. "He was alive when they boarded this up. He died standing here trying to break out." Harlan solemnly nodded.

The two moved back into the corridor and continued in the unexplored direction. As was described, there was another open set of chambers, which were completely empty, and one final set of chamber doors, both covered with bolted lumber. With closer inspection, the hallway didn't end at a wall. It appeared the corridor continued but had been filled in with rock and debris. "Either these chambers used to go on, or this was the mining entrance and they backfilled it when they were done digging this all out." Harlan shined a light back toward the entrance from the mansion living room, though the light only traveled 15 yards of the 100-yard-long hallway. He turned again to the rocks. "I wonder how much farther this might go? We're probably already near the back end of the Mansion's property."

"No telling." Vieve touched one of the large boulders blocking the way. "We won't be getting through this, though."

Harlan shined his light to the ceiling. "They didn't put any support beams down here."

"I'm not sure you need them with this mining method. They may have put them in, up under the mansion, because of the extra weight above."

Harlan placed the other two abandoned helmets on the floor with their beams crisscrossing, illuminating the last two chamber entrances. "Stand back." Harlan buried the fireman's ax in one of the boarded doorways. This time he made faster work of carving a passage through the rotted barricade.

Harlan felt for another body at the door, but discovered none. He led the way in with Vieve following closely. Just inside the chamber another corpse was revealed. The skeleton was in a seated position at one of the front corners. What was left of its clothes appeared to belong to a male of that period. Harlan watched as Vieve sat next to the body, mimicking its shape. "It's hard to tell when he's all balled up like this, but"—Vieve extended an arm to compare length with the forearm on the body—"he was very short. Almost a foot shorter than I am." Vieve looked up but Harlan had wandered farther into the chamber. Vieve returned to her feet. "Maybe this was the Drake's oldest son?"

"I don't think so."

Vieve went to Harlan. He had to block his eyes from her helmet light. "What makes you say that?" she asked. Harlan pointed towards the wall nearby. As they both looked over their beams met on the wall. Vieve gasped. Bodies surrounded them. The skeletal remains of more than a dozen men lined the walls. Each was in a similar seated position, resting their backs on the wall of the chamber. Harlan paced down one line of bodies.

"Tools, a pick ax, lunch boxes, lanterns." He moved to the opposite wall. "They were miners. Twenty in total. No obvious bone injuries, though. Nothing to plainly suggest what caused their deaths."

"Killed in some sort of accident, maybe? Not a cave-in, I suppose, but perhaps the chamber filled with noxious gas?"

"Could be." Harlan shined his light back at the door's barricade. "But why seal them in?"

"Just like with Malvern, this place is giving me chills. Let's go take a look at that other room. The sooner we get out of here the better." Harlan agreed.

Back in the corridor, Harlan set to breaking into the final chamber. This time when he planted the ax in a central plank, he pulled back and the entire board, end to end, along with two others above it, fell back at him. Harlan was knocked backward by his own momentum and fell to the ground. The three loose planks crashed down, narrowly missing him. Vieve shrieked, then rushed to Harlan and pulled him to his feet.

Harlan shook his head as he dusted himself off. "These weren't as securely affixed as the others." He examined the wall. "There are only a few bolts in, and just on this one side. Several are just freely stacked."

"Why the deviation?"

"Either this one wasn't as important or there wasn't time to finish it." Harlan abandoned the ax. One plank hung at head height with a gap below. It tilted from a single bolt that held it at one end. Two others rested on top of it, leading to the top of the doorway. Harlan grabbed the plank at the loose end and swung it back and forth. The bolt pried free. It and the lumber above all fell away. Three planks remained blocking from the ground to his knee, but only two were remotely secured. Harlan knocked all of them out with a few strikes from his heel. Vieve dragged the planks out of the way. Now the doorway was completely open.

"Last one. Shall we?" Harlan gestured for Vieve to follow, but she clutched his hand and squeezed tightly. Harlan squeezed back as he led the way in.

Vieve's light fell on the skeletal remains of another body in the middle of the floor, near the doorway and laid out perpendicular to it. "I guess it's not surprising anymore."

Harlan squeezed Vieve's hand tighter, briefly, and then released. He stepped forward and touched the new remains' tattered clothing. "This appears to have been a dress."

Harlan walked a half circle around the body while Vieve remained near the door. On the other side, farther into the chamber, Harlan turned and revealed a second female corpse laid parallel to the first. This skeleton was smaller than the other, but it too wore a dress.

Vieve looked back at the open doorway. "They weren't really even sealed in like the others?"

"If they were alive, they could've knocked those planks out easily."

"They must have been dead before it was sealed."

Harlan passed the second body and explored deeper. Vieve remained still. She watched Harlan, not the bodies. For a long stretch of empty floor, Harlan found nothing. Then, at the rear of the chamber, he discovered two more bodies, both laid out as neatly as the first two: a smaller corpse in male clothing and a young boy. Harlan lingered a moment, and then returned to Vieve. She'd gathered enough to draw the same conclusion Harlan had, even from a distance. No words were necessary to communicate that they'd uncovered Martha and the Drake children.

"Just not Vinton," Vieve said.

"I'm not sure." Harlan aimed his light to one of the front corners and exposed two slumped skeletal remains. Both wore black suits with bow ties.

"How'd we miss that?"

"One of those might be Vinton," Harlan moved closer. "But why would someone take the time to lay those four out with such care while these two were just discarded to a corner?" He turned to Vieve. "And if one of these is Vinton, who's the other?"

Vieve shook her head. "What now?"

Harlan surveyed the room once more. "I don't think there's much left we can do down here. It's probably wise to get back upstairs before another tremor starts. We've been pushing our luck as it is." Vieve nodded. "There are still some pages left in Vinton's journal and another hour to go. We might as well see if there's more light to be shed there."

They left the fireman's ax, spare helmet cams, and all the skeletons where they lay and returned to below the living room.

Vieve ascended first. The moment Harlan stepped off the top rung and onto the living room floor, the howling and quaking of the house began again. They could hear the cracking of surfaces and smashing of falling rocks below. They braced themselves until the disturbance passed.

Vieve gazed at the opening. "All these years people have been claiming to hear howls or cries from this house. It makes sense that it was these cavernous rumbles they were mistaking for ghostly sounds." Vieve turned to Harlan. "No doubt those voids have been down there all along, but no one ever noticed the ground shaking. If the tremors were enough to shake things off the walls and knock objects over, wouldn't everything have been dislodged decades ago? I know it seems like Galva and Ax's stories are just that, stories, but if all the howling has been some natural phenomenon, coming from those caverns, consistently for 80 years, why has it gotten magnitudes worse tonight? Just since we got here?"

Harlan stared at Vinton's journal in contemplation. "Your implication being that our presence has upset something somehow? As if there was a consciousness to it?" He looked up.

Vieve shrugged. "All those bodies, after all these years, and the house's growls led us to them. It's also nearly injured all of us and chased three of us away."

Harlan thought for another moment. "I don't have the answer."

For Those Who Wish to Follow In My Footsteps:
How I Became Immortal Part 2

It was more than thirteen years after the events that began with Malvern Kamrar's magic show in the basement of an abandoned film studio and led to changing my life, that I encountered Leon Carroll again. Thirteen years since Leon enlightened me on the true nature of existence. For a dozen of those years, I've been steward of the town of Shadows Bend, and during such, I've ushered more than 1,000 individuals out of this world, claiming the vitality of each.

This time I sought Leon out. I'd seen his act advertised in a newspaper months before. He'd moved out of the underground and into legitimate public performance, touring the country. When I noticed his show would be in Chicago, I was compelled to attend and make contact. His performance had changed drastically. He was billed as "The Unkillable Man," yet there were no spectacles of death or gruesomeness.

His illusions were impressive as far as magicians go: they entailed disappearances, conjuring of items from thin air, escapism, and mentalism, but they lacked in the morbid noir that had reached the audience on such a deeper and soul-shaking level. The blue coffin made an appearance among the stage sets and props. He was elusive regarding its contents but alluded it held the source of his abilities. I'd consider this the only unique detail of the performance.

The crowd numbered in the hundreds with more children than adults. Altogether, it was very common. While his celebrity has grown considerably, and likely his profits, I found it saddening. Why would a man with an existence so exceptional, so above the common man, concern himself with such disgustingly average ambitions? Perhaps for Leon, with life everlasting comes ego unabating.

After the performance, the backstage of the theater was cramped with people. Besides the staff's resistance to allow me access, lack of privacy made it a poor candidate for engaging Leon in discussion. I pressed no further. Instead, I ventured to a nearby cafe, one I'd favored back when I was living there, and waited for the day's subsequent performances to elapse: four in total for a Saturday. The last concluded at midnight. The patrons streamed out. I made my way to the service entrance at the rear of the building. Leon emerged half an hour later, in coat and hat, but he was surround by a dozen others; theater management and show business types. Not one noticed my presence, concealed in the shadows. I checked my pocket to inspect the safety on my pistol several times before I consciously realized I hadn't brought the sidearm. The situation was bringing out old habits.

I thought it unwise to approach Leon with others around, given the subject I wished to discuss. I let them pass and disappear around a street corner, but it wasn't long before I did manage an audience with the magician again.

Leon's inclusion in the second phase of my final efforts was not coincidental. The theater in Shadows Bend was funded and built by the Drake Mining Corporation. With an offhand remark of my interest in a certain magic act I'd caught in Chicago, while in the presence of the theater manager, booking was immediate.

While returning from some errand, I noticed a poster affixed to a fence near the center of town. "Malvern Kamrar, Master of Shadows" was printed in extravagant letters with an artist's drawing of Leon at its center. "This Weekend Only" was printed below. When I had the car stopped to examine the poster, the children became excited by the fantastic magic show that it promised. Since I couldn't reach Leon, I had him brought to me. My plans were progressing marvelously.

Leon had no knowledge that I was in the town where he was performing. I excused myself from the family and stepped backstage near the end of the show. I was free to come and go as I pleased at this particular theater. With an ovation, Leon left the stage and retired to his dressing room. The door was ajar. When I knocked, it swung further open.

"All alone now, Leon?" He turned, but a bright light shone in his eyes. He masked the light to see my face. "No salute is necessary. That life is quite far behind both of us now, don't you think?" I stepped inside, eclipsing the light.

"Drake? Is that you?"

"You've changed the act since I saw it last."

"You noticed, did you?" He laughed and turned back to his mirror.

"For the better, I suppose, at least for popularity's sake." I stepped closer. "What's become of your stoic, scheming-eyed, sinister, pompous, and church-mouse quiet, assistant? Jerome, was it?"

"We've parted ways, unfortunately. His unpleasantness, while once beneficial, didn't serve as well with family oriented crowds. What brings you here, Drake? I have to say, I'm rather surprised to see you."

"My company owns this theater, but I came to speak with you, Leon."

"Please call me Malvern."

"Of course, Malvern. Are you heading to a hotel tonight? Can I give you a ride?" Leon was uneasy, which I found odd. A hundred men could jump him in an alley, and what would he have to fear? Then again, I had knowledge of him, which, if exposed, could adversely affect his career, now more than ever. Obviously it's important to him. "I just had some questions for you Le...Malvern. If it's a bad time, I'll return tomorrow."

He remained anxious, but then Martha and the children interrupted.

"There you are, Vinton. The children are getting restless. Will you be ready to go soon?"

"My family." I presented to Leon. "Look kids, it's the magician." Martha and the children were surprised and delighted that I was acquainted with him. They rushed past me to see him up close and shake his hand. Leon sprang from his chair and greeted the children graciously, after which he looked up to me with far more trusting eyes.

"Yes. I was heading to the hotel, Drake." He rubbed the boys' heads. "A ride would be appreciated."

When we exited the theater, the children and Martha headed in the direction of our car and usual driver, waiting up the block. "Wait, Martha. I've made other arrangements." I waved to a pair of gentlemen waiting in the other direction. On my cue, they pulled up with a larger vehicle, a company car. "I thought this would accommodate a larger party more comfortably." Martha thought this was odd, but complied. We loaded and disembarked.

"Say, Malvern, it's not that late in the evening. We need to get the children to bed but what would you say to a drink up at our house? Some supper, perhaps?" Leon turned down the offer, but with encouragement from Martha and cheers from the children he was eventually persuaded.

Martha took the young ones upstairs, after much protest. Leon and I sat down to a drink in the front office. "There are a number of topics I can't help but be curious about, Leon, excuse me, Malvern, since our previous conversation regarding the finer details of your achievement and altered existence." I stood and closed the door. "That's why I have sought you out, to query you."

He hesitated. "Have you shared that information with anyone, else Drake?" His expression appeared gravely concerned.

"Of course not. Your secret is safe with me, but surely you can understand how that information is difficult to simply put out of mind?

I assure you any further information you impart will be treated with equal confidentiality."

He smiled and relaxed. "I see your point. All right then, let's have it."

"The quantity you confessed was sizable, unbelievable, in fact. You also mentioned that the man who taught you of this possibility, of collecting, did not himself reach the state you have, before his death." Leon nodded. "You then described that prior to obtaining enough energy to outgrow one's bodily existence, a collector such as yourself would first reach an equilibrium where one could not live on freely, but where one could greatly resist fading away at the time of death, almost indefinitely." Leon continued to agree. "This is what has perplexed me. What existence would that person then have? A hell where they're trapped with their dead body, buried, discarded, but still conscious? And lasting forever? I can't imagine it."

Leon contemplated for a moment. "This is an interesting thought, Drake. I can't answer with certainty as this was not my experience, but I imagine at first, the person would be bound there in the physical space of the body. It wouldn't last forever, but for a long, long time, hundreds of years, maybe. Eventually, however, they would fade and finally cease to exist. Like death's final minutes, but spanning centuries."

"Can nothing change that fate once it has begun? It would be a great risk when you began collecting, if falling short meant enduring hundreds of years of torture."

"Ah, I see." He smiled. "Let me share a story I was told during my studies. Long ago, there was a Chinese man who endeavored to make himself immortal. He, just as you've described, reached a point where he could forestall succumbing to death but could not overcome it." Leon grew enlivened. "He lay in the ground for decades, a century. Long after he, and even the location of his grave were forgotten, a great battle occurred. Many men were slain above his resting place. The man absorbed the force of those new casualties and was pushed to the surplus he needed. He arose, finally freed. I was told he described it as a great slumber. He wasn't keenly aware of existence until he was awoken. It leads me to conclude that if he'd never been awoken, he would have faded away and would never have consciously known he outlasted his corporeal death. Imagine dying in your sleep, just a century-long sleep." Leon leaned back, pleased. "Does that satisfy your curiosity?"

"It confirms what I'd hoped was the case." Leon looked at me with puzzlement. "I've wondered about your physical remains as well, being tethered to them. I noticed your crate is still with you. I suppose the essence of my question is what range do you have from it?"

"Obviously the tether is none too tight." He gestured with a wave, indicating he wasn't very close to the box at the moment. "A few miles, five maybe. Tell me, Drake, what's stirred this up? After all these years, why did you decide to see me now?"

Then, I was the one who hesitated. "I'm ill, Leon." My tone was matter-of-fact. There was no point in avoidance or softening. "To the extent of my medical expertise, which has grown over the years, the condition is untreatable. I expect my time is short, six months maybe, probably less."

Leon stared at me, saying nothing. He was disheartened by the news but also puzzled. He failed to connect this information with the purpose of this visit. "The weaknesses of the body seem trivial given the level at which we understand life, but unfortunately, I've only been able to collect the force of little more than a thousand people, including many sick and elderly. I don't feel the critical mass as you once described it, and I fear I'll not reach such a milestone before disease takes my body."

He whispered with bewilderment. "You've collected?"

"Indeed. Now you can see why I was concerned with what my fate would be under the circumstances. You've given me great hope—"

Leon interrupted me. "Stop." I couldn't tell if he was responding with outrage or repulsion. Either confused me, but he was nonetheless flustered. "I have to be going." As he mumbled he stood and crossed to the door. Did it personally threaten his own accomplishment to find I'd nearly matched it? I had feared as much, but this conclusion to the conversation was perplexing.

He flung the office door open and hurried for the hallway. On his course, he had to cross a small rug before the stairwell in the living room. When he placed his weight on it, the rug collapsed, and Leon dropped through the floor and into the mine below. It was a simple trap, but remarkably effective. I stood above the opening. Leon was sprawled on the ground below. I withdrew the missing floor section, which I'd stashed in a closet, and calmly covered the opening.

After Chicago, my health declined even more rapid than predicted, but I'd never been more focused on the goal. It was necessary to accelerate the rate of collecting energy, beyond the natural events of the town. That was phase one of my final efforts. Few people, in the company or otherwise, were informed of the excavation I ordered under my home. There had already been an exploratory vein with a few spur chambers initiated before the house was built. The entrance was at the farthest corner of the property, in an earthy, barren spot. It was easy to reopen the mine and expand the chambers for what I'd envisioned.

I sent Martha, the children, and the help on an extended visit with Martha's father, Ely, while work was undertaken. So little coal was actually unearthed that it was easy to hide in the company accounts, and the miners were too intimidated to question my prerogative. My position of total control over the mines and the city made everything remarkably simple. I saw to it that everyone besides myself who was aware of the job was present when the work was finished.

I flooded the site with gas and knocked out all the miners inside. One by one I suffocated them. Unconscious, they were unable to resist. I handpicked each man; young, strong, and full of vitality. All were single and new to the crews. It wasn't uncommon for such workers to find that mining didn't suit them and to abandon the job and the town without warning. Since these men had been pulled from the regular sites for weeks, their disappearances were virtually unnoticed.

As I claimed their essences, the surge of invigoration was intoxicating and unparalleled by any previous collecting. I'd never taken

UNTIL THE SUN RISES

the energy of a man who wasn't ill, or already afflicted with mortal wounds. No words can sufficiently describe the splendor. When all twenty had been extinguished, I sealed the remains away and then concealed the entrance to the mine. Afterward, I still felt unfulfilled, short of what was required. This was but one of three final endeavors to secure my immortality.

By the night of Leon's show, I'd relinquished most of my duties, both to the mines and to the hospital. In fact, I was teetering on the cusp of my legs abandoning me from the disease. Time was short. I gave the staff the evening off, particularly our nanny. She was always leery of me and kept her distance, all while keeping the children close to her. While her vitality would have been prized, she'd be too difficult to control. I wanted her and the other help far away from us that night. This was the true reason we didn't take our usual driver home that evening.

With Leon captured, I had to move quickly. First, I called to Martha to come downstairs. When she reached the bottom, I sprang from behind her, wrapped a cord around her neck, and constricted. It was odd to be on the opposite end of this situation. She struggled. It took every ounce of my remaining strength to overcome her, but eventually my will prevailed. Her life essence was added to my own. In spite of the exhilaration from claiming her vitality, my body was wiped of energy. I rested, sitting on the steps. Martha's lifeless eyes stared at me as I gathered my strength. It was sad, I thought as I gazed upon her, sad that she would never know of the extraordinary cause for which she gave her life. Sad that she'd never feel satisfaction or pride for her contribution to my greatness. I finally caught my breath. Many physically exerting challenges remained.

All three of the children had fallen asleep playing, still dressed from the theater. I took my medical bag and injected each with an anesthetic, which prevented them from waking, struggling, becoming aware of their surroundings, or alerting the others. I extinguished each of them. Once finished, I moved their bodies down to join Martha's.

I opened the passage to the mine. Surprisingly, Malvern still lay motionless at the bottom. In my wood shop, I'd constructed a ladder to connect the mine to the house. Once I'd retrieved and installed it, I proceeded down to the underground chambers. Twenty rungs, I counted each as I descended.

When I inspected Malvern, he tried to raise and defend himself, but he was delirious. It was disconcerting to find Leon, given his state of being, still susceptible to physical damage and injury. Did further distance from his remains decrease his capabilities? There was no time, however, to reflect on the matter. Obviously my understanding of this elevated plane of existence was still incomplete. Perhaps, when I reach it, all the nuances will be clear. Forging ahead, I dragged him to an empty chamber and barricaded him in.

Next, I climbed back to the top of the ladder and proceeded to roll Martha's body through the opening. The sound of dead weight hitting the hard ground echoed through the stony corridor and resonated back. The bodies of the children followed. Returning to the bottom, I then placed their remains in another of the empty rooms, one farthest from the opening to the house, and with no time to spare, I might add.

Just as I extinguished the lamp I'd used to light the room below, I heard an aggressive rapping on a wooden surface. I stepped into the corridor. "Leon?"

"No, boss," I heard from behind me. "It's us." The far end of the mine was the primary access point, though it had been concealed, and gated from inside. I paused for a moment and slid my hand into my pocket to check the safety of my Colt. I'd decided to carry it that evening. I switched the safety off and then back on, "just in case." Quickly, I moved up the last few yards of hallway, retrieved the key from my pocket, and then unlatched and opened the swinging gates.

The same pair of company workers who had escorted us home was waiting. They were hard, burly men. Both were on the company payroll, but they didn't mine or work in the offices. They kept low profiles until needed. Messengers for the company, ambassadors even, or better yet, I'd say they were specialists in handling odds and ends and doing so as efficiently and quietly as possible. Best of all, they were quite accustomed to receiving strange orders without explanations, and they knew not to ask questions. They were an unspoken necessity of doing business that I'd learned from my father at an early age. In preparation for this evening, I asked them to attend the magic show as well. After they dropped Leon, the family, and me at the house, I gave them additional instructions.

"Do you have it?" Both were still dressed in their suits from the theater.

"Yes, in the truck." One pointed to a tarp-covered object on the flat bed of an auto.

"Did anyone see you?"

"No," the other answered. "We waited until everyone was gone before we went in."

"Excellent, bring it in." Moments later the large tarp-covered object was ushered through the door.

"Where do you want it, boss?" They asked almost in unison.

"Go toward the house, second set from the end, and put it in the room on the right." I followed them down. After they placed it I pulled back the tarp revealing Leon's ornate blue coffin. I admired it briefly then turned back to the men. "Did you bring the sledge hammers?"

"Yeah, in the cab of the truck."

"All right, go to each chamber and knock out the ceiling supports, then go back to the entrance and seal it off. Start at the fifth set of supports and work your way out. A few small charges are already in place to collapse it in. Once that's done, do your best to smooth out the dirt and rubble to mask it." They nodded understanding. "When you're finished, return the truck and meet me back up in the house." They turned to leave. "Oh, leave one hammer in here for me." They nodded again.

When I finished with them, I headed back up. "Twenty rungs." They proceeded in the other direction. I could hear the strikes on the wood supports, first in the chambers and then at the entrance. Next came the charges, just pops, very controlled, and followed by the tumbling of rock. Within a few moments, the entrance to the mine was thoroughly sealed with rock and debris.

One body, then the other. The sound of the weight falling from the house to the mine echoed, just as before. When my men came to the house, I already had three whiskeys poured, waiting to reward them for a job well done. The toxin I'd added extinguished the men. I dragged their bodies into the room with Martha and the children and sealed them away as well. The plan was nearly complete.

"Drake," I heard muffled and weak as I moved back toward the ladder. "Drake, let me out of here." This time it was Leon.

I stepped up to the barricaded doorway and shouted back. "I'm afraid I can't do that, Leon."

"Please let me out, Drake. You can't do this to me. I'm hurt. I need help."

"I think you'll be fine, Leon, and I need you here. You're the bait." He was silent for a long moment.

"Bait? For what?"

"For phase three of the plan. As I told you earlier, I'm ill and will not reach the necessary peak of life energy before my body defeats me. But I've collected so many I'm convinced I'll last a very long time before fading away."

"Drake?" His voice was a whimper.

"I've brought your remains down here as well, Leon. Don't you see? It's simple. I've taken in every source of life energy I could muster. Everyone around me. But, I feared that it wouldn't be enough, so I made appropriate preparations."

"Drake?"

I ignored his plea. "I'll be dead soon, but I've orchestrated a series of traps here in the mansion. Deadfalls as it were. After I'm gone, we, well you, must continue to draw people here. I'm certain that mystery will shroud our disappearances, and the events of this evening, for years to come. You lure them here, and when they die, I'll be poised to absorb their energy, and just like the Chinese fellow you mentioned, I'll awaken from death and join you in eternal life." I was rather satisfied with myself. Every point of my plan had gone perfectly.

"You'll stay here, tethered to your remains. No one will know what became of me, or of the family. No one will know of the mine below, but you'll remain. You'll maintain the mystery. I'm sure you'll escape these confines, but not in time to stop me. You could expose the truth of it all, but not without throwing away the career you hold so precious. Instead, to get your freedom back all you'll have to do is help me, Leon, just draw people here until I've collected enough. Help me to finish what I began." I awaited his reply.

"You're mad, Drake. It's crazy. There's no eternal life. It was a lie. A ruse that sold the legend and mystery. That's all." His vexed tone diminished into desperation. "The heartbeat. That sold it, right? It's a simple trick performed with a rubber ball under the arm. I faked my death each time, just like in the war." He seemed to be weeping. "You've, you've killed your family, haven't you?" I didn't respond. "You've gone too far, Drake." His reluctance to help me, and this ploy to confuse me, were both very disappointing.

"I understand your selfishness, Leon. Truly, I can relate. But you'll see that helping me is the best thing for you." I moved to the now filled-in mine entrance, and with the hammer left for me, began knocking out the remaining wood supports all the way until I reached the segment actually under the house with steel supports, which I left in place. Leon senselessly maintained his ruse and pleaded sorrowfully the entire time. "Desperation encourages uncharacteristic behavior," I mumbled to myself. With the work finished, I returned to the ladder, but called to him one last time. "I'll see you soon, Leon."

Atop the ladder's twenty rungs, I concealed the opening as it had been before and proceeded to finish with all the small details needed. I cleaned away the evidence of the night and set every mechanism for my traps into their final places. In the months since my diagnosis, I'd orchestrated more than a dozen. One I'm particularly proud of rests in wait of our nanny. She was so close to the children, and last Christmas they collaborated in getting her perfume as a gift. I've taken the liberty of adding a very potent toxin to that perfume in estimation that upon being separated from the children, she'll utilize the perfume, sentimentally, right here in the house. This, however, isn't even the grandest of my designs and insights. If all others fail to tip the scale of vitality in my favor, my masterpiece is sure to accommodate generously.

For this plan, I've also installed a series of pipelines, conducting channels, designed to cascade any released life energy directly to my resting place. Now, all that remains is to conclude the plan.

I pen this entry on the very night of my family's death and of my own disappearance. Once I've finished with the story up to this point, I'll take my place, ready to receive the pending vitality. When I raise from the grave my story, these notes, and my gift to the mankind, will be completed and ready for anyone worthy of following.

6:00AM

On the broadcast truck's wall of monitors, the on-air screen showed the inside of an ambulance. A cameraman rode with Ax as an EMT dressed his wound. Nora cut to another camera following Audrey. She sat exhausted in her trailer, but quickly primped her appearance, collected a stack of glossy portrait photos, then stepped outside and began signing autographs. Nora brought up another view centered on La Claire at the head of her flock. "Swing around the crowd." The view on screen slowly rotated and revealed seemingly endless masses of people gathered.

The open journal page was marked with fingerprints in blood. When Harlan and Vieve's eyes reached the bottom, both were transfixed, assimilating Vinton's disclosure.
Vieve broke the silence. "We drank the whiskey."
"We'd know by now."
Many pages remained in the journal. Harlan slid his finger under the pages' edge, but before he could turn it, the onset of another rumbling, quaking disturbance snatched their attention.

Both braced themselves. Vieve grasped Harlan's hand. Vinton's journal was knocked onto an empty part of the seat. Neither spoke until the shaking passed.

"Here I was, worried about mold and fungus coming into this," Vieve said, "little did I know whiplash was the real threat. I'll be glad when this is all over and we can get the heck out of here." Harlan laughed. "I don't understand the rubber ball comment from Kamrar, in the journal?"

"I gather it was a trick. James Randi and Jose Alvarez used a similar method during what's called the 'Carlos Hoax.' You put the ball in your armpit and when you squeeze down it constricts blood flow to the arm and gives the impression of no pulse. Malvern must have used it during his guillotine performance to fool Vinton."

Vieve grabbed Harlan's arm and pulled it over to read his watch. "We've got less than an hour to go." Harlan glanced at his timepiece.

"We're free to search the attic now. The sun will be rising shortly. Should we find our way to the summit?" The toll of a strenuous and manic night was evident on Vieve's face. She hesitated. Harlan could see she wasn't frightened or nervous, just mentally drained and exhausted. He stood and offered his hand to Vieve. "Like you said, it's almost over." Vieve was still unsure, but Harlan followed with an inviting smile. She took his hands. He led her toward the main stairwell. "You're going to be a half million dollars richer in less than an hour. That is, if another of Vinton's traps doesn't get us first." He laughed. Vieve halted, forcing Harlan to stop just ahead of her, still tethered by held hands.

"That's not funny to joke about." Vieve's face was stern. Harlan was lost for words, but Vieve's expression turned to a smile as she shook her head, rolled her eyes, and then resumed moving to the steps. "We should be very careful though, buddy," she punctuated with a playfully thrown elbow into Harlan's side.

A gentle glow had developed outside, the predecessor of sunrise. It cast a low but even light throughout the house and made Vieve and Harlan's navigation easier. Harlan retained his spare handheld flashlight just the same. The two climbed to the third floor, taking care to avoid the loose step near the top.

They passed Martha's sewing area and into the third story's main hallway. "We saw the attic access point when we were up here before." Harlan found the hatch. He stood below it and reached upward, but was short of reaching the attic door. There was no cord or low-hanging handle. Harlan turned back toward Vieve, but she was nowhere to be found. Before Harlan took a single step, Vieve appeared at the hallway entrance with a chair in tow.

"Let's see if this will be tall enough." Vieve placed the chair below the hatch. "Hopefully it's not rigged to collapse." She smiled. Harlan proceeded to inspect the chair. He used his body to test as much weight as possible on each of its four legs, all before he trusted the chair to be stood on. Once assuaged, Harlan stepped on the seat and stretched for the ceiling. This time he reached it, but with only a few inches to spare.

A long, rectangular frame separated the plaster ceiling from the white painted, wood panels of the attic hatch. However, close up, Harlan couldn't detect any openings, handles, hinges, or mechanisms whatsoever. He searched the perimeter of the hatch's frame inside and out with his fingertips. He checked and rechecked, but found nothing. Frustrated, he jumped and smashed his palm into the hatch on one end. The panel jumped, pushing up an inch or two, but immediately fell back into place. Harlan struck it again, more forcefully, but was no more effective. He tried again as hard as he could, but got the same result. The panel was restricted from moving any farther up and out of position. With jumping harder, Harlan also landed more forcefully. Both he and Vieve heard a cracking sound from the chair. Harlan dismounted hastily.

"Maybe we can find something long enough to push the panel," Harlan said.

Both stepped into Martha's sewing room. Vieve discovered a stout wood yardstick. Back, cautiously on top of the seat, Harlan used the stick to lift the panel. He could push it up a very small amount directly above him, but it would go no further and allowed no movement side to side. "It doesn't look like we're meant to just push it up out of the way." He retracted the yardstick. The panel fell back into place again.

"Try the other side," Vieve said. Harlan climbed down and moved the chair a few feet, to under the opposite end of the hatch. Once back up, he pressed the other edge and the panel lifted higher than before. He held that position and moved one hand down the stick, and then extended it farther up hand over hand. The panel moved higher and higher. The entire panel end to end lifted until it was nearly a foot out of place.

Harlan looked to Vieve, sharing a satisfied grin, then a mechanical click sounded. Both their smiles faded, and eyes shifted up. The edge of the panel above Harlan totally released and shot upward, pivoting from the other end. This side was now several feet up into the attic while the opposite side of the hatch still rested near the ceiling level. "Watch out, get back!" Harlan shouted. Vieve scrambled backward. With the panel at a steep angle, a section of ladder, which rested on rollers, rocketed downward. It slammed into place as it reached its full extension only halfway down. Harlan sprang from the chair, tipping it over, as he dashed down the hallway in the other direction. A second extension of rungs followed, telescoping past the first all the way to the floor. It struck forcefully, exactly where Vieve originally stood.

Harlan and Vieve stared at one another, and then in unison they both burst into laughter. "I don't think that was intended to kill anyone," Vieve said.

"It would have made for a rather unpleasant bump to the head or stubbed toe at least." Harlan squeezed past the ladder and joined Vieve on the access side. They looked up the flight of rungs, into what they could see of the space above.

"It's a shame the others are missing this. It's the only place people have claimed to actually see ghosts."

"Let's find out what they've really been seeing." Harlan grabbed a rung midway up and moved his foot to the first step. He searched for hazards as he climbed. Harlan hesitated before his head breached the opening. Vieve held her breathe. "Hmm." Harlan stretched up and turned to see behind him. He scrunched back down and then traced one side of the ladder to the rung just below his hands. "Aha." He smiled. "You crafty devil."

Harlan looked back toward Vieve. "Observe. This rung is firm enough when my hands are on it, when I'm essentially pulling against it." He demonstrated pulling on the rung, and then he climbed back down to the floor. "Step back now, and watch when I put my full weight in the downward direction, just as if someone had stepped on it." Vieve backed away. From underneath the ladder, Harlan gripped the same rung with both hands and lifted his feet off the floor. His entire body weight hung from the rung, pulling down instead of pushing down as a foot would.

The rung dropped an inch. It remained in the ladder, just out of place. A series of mechanical clicking sounds began, and then a heavy wood plank slammed down on the opening above. It crashed with such heft that it shook the ladder, the ceiling, and the walls. The trap stopped flush with the ceiling. It didn't collide with the ladder directly but rather filled the open area where Harlan's head and shoulders would have been had his foot triggered the mechanism. "Nothing would have stopped that from breaking my neck." He smirked nervously. "Close call."

Harlan checked each of the other rungs on the ladder. After, he climbed back up and with strain, pivoted the trap plank out of the way. Once it was clear, he double-checked the trigger rung. "It doesn't appear to have reset. I think it's safe."

"Be careful."

Vieve watched Harlan's feet disappear into the ceiling. She stepped up to the ladder and peered upward, finding only an empty space once again. Harlan's voice emanated from above. "Wow. What is this?" Vieve crept onto the first rung and continued to the second, but she was startled and jumped off the ladder when Harlan's head popped down. "You have to come see this." He disappeared again. Vieve took a deep breath, and then returned to the ladder.

The attic was an open space in the shape of an "X" with four equal-size wings. The entrance was located in one wing. Vieve's head poked through the floor. A window behind her gleamed with pre-dawn light. The ladder hatch, now inverted, blocked the light from shinning into the room. Vieve didn't see Harlan or even the cast from his lights. She stepped onto the attic floor, turned and peered out the window. She could barely see the front yard of the mansion. "Come over here." The words came from the darkness. "And watch your step."

Vieve had to walk around the hatch. As she did, her toe caught on something, and she fell to one knee. When she looked down, the light from her helmet highlighted a crystal pyramid protruding through the floorboards. "Are you okay?" Harlan appeared from the darkness. His helmet light was off.

"Yes. What, what is this?"

Harlan helped Vieve to her feet. "Look here." He flipped his flashlight back on and pointed toward the intersection of the four wings. His light revealed a densely packed mosaic of thousands of crystals hanging from the roof. Most were clear or white, but a few were colored. "Quartz, fluorite, amethyst." Harlan's light refracted on every surface it touched and sent rays in every direction, striking other crystals. Rainbow-colored and multi-shaped points of light were cast into every corner of the attic.

"What..." Vieve was mesmerized.

Harlan directed his light to the floor. "Watch out." He showed another pyramid, followed by another. "These are all over the place." He returned the beam to the crystal sculpture. They moved closer.

"What is this?" Vieve asked.

Together, all the crystals formed a downward pointing cone. It was over three feet wide at the top and came down to a single crystal point barely kissing the floor. No individual crystal was more than an inch wide or a few inches long, but they were so densely strung that the center was completely concealed. Vieve and Harlan couldn't see whether it was filled with stones through and through, or just at its edges. Vieve walked around the assemblage.

"I didn't see much else up here." Harlan briefly aimed the light down each of the other three wings. "But there are mirrors and stones scattered on the walls and ceilings, too." Vieve barely acknowledged the other details. She touched the surface of the sculpture. The crystals were hung by fine threads and dangled freely. She slid her hand from top to bottom, grazing the outer stones. Shapes danced on the wall behind her, refracted from her own helmet light.

When Vieve finally looked away, she found Harlan watching her silently. She blushed. "It's very intricate. Do you have any idea what this is all about?"

"Vinton's journal said he made changes to the house to channel the supposed life energy to him. I can only speculate everything up here has something to do with that."

Harlan pointed to the wing behind Vieve, across from the entrance wing. "That should be the back of the house, right?" Vieve nodded. He crossed to the window at its end. "So this is the window that witnesses have claimed to see strange figures in? The ghosts?"

"Yes, but not just it, all the attic windows." Vieve pointed to windows in both the adjacent wings. "Every side has one." Harlan returned to the wing where they came up.

"This one faces east. So that's where the morning light would come in." Predawn glow continued to mount, and shine inward. Harlan noticed the hatch panel eclipsed the rest of the room. Though the dirty window, Harlan could make out the town and the distinct horizon. He turned back to the attic entrance.

"What are you thinking?"

"The sun will be up soon and the hatch will block the light." Harlan moved to the hatch and pulls the extension ladder up, one section and then the other. The sections clicked into locked positions, and then with little force the inverted panel tilted parallel with the floor and proceeded to drop back into the closed position. Vieve watched. The unobstructed glow from the window now lit the attic evenly, and for the first time shined on the crystal cone. Many more rays refracted from the crystals, and in larger shapes, though they were fainter than from the flashlight. "Look." Harlan pointed to above the window.

Vieve looked up. There was a more concentrated spot of light, projecting through the window. "The sun will be up in a few minutes." Harlan stepped to Vieve, took her hand, and guided her to a corner out of the way. They watched the light. The golden shape moved steadily across the ceiling, drawing closer and closer to the crystals in the center.

Harlan dashed back to the eastern-facing window and aligned his flashlight with the spot above. "When the sun crests, the light will intensify and move across, reaching the crystals." He mocked the path along the ceiling with his light, and ending on the crystal sculpture. When his beam hit the stones, the refracted shapes brightened. They spanned every corner of the walls, floor, ceiling, and windows. Harlan moved his beam down the crystal sculpture. "The sun will continue to ascend, the light will level, and..." With the movement of his light, the shapes shimmered, shifted colors, and danced about the room.

Vieve watched in awe. "It's beautiful."

"I believe these are the images everyone's been mistaking for spirits." When Harlan dropped his light away, the shapes darted back and grew dim. "It just needs the sunrise." He smiled.

"Amazing."

Harlan crossed the attic to the west-facing window and polished the surface with his sleeve. As he pressed the window gave way. Pivoting from the top and bottom, the windowpane turned ninety degrees and opened the attic to the morning air. Harlan breathed deeply. Vieve joined him and indulged in the fresh air.

Now without obstruction, they could see in full perspective the mass of people gathered around the production camp and expanding to the far reaches of the property. The crowd's strength approached 15,000. Over one hundred uniformed police officers, city, county, and state, had joined the crowd-controlling forces. At the rear of the property, local news vans sat in a line waiting for space to open to enter the site. Several additional vendor trucks and police vehicles lined up behind that. Harlan and Vieve both shook their heads in awe. Vieve took Harlan's hand.

"Mystery solved, I guess," Vieve said. "No spirits, just dancing projections of sunlight from these crystals."

"I believe so."

"And the howling, just the acoustics of an unstable mine below."

Harlan began to nod but his smile faded, concern struck on his face. He looked back outside, surveying the massive crowd, after which he released Vieve's hand and dashed for the hatch on the floor.

"Harlan, what is it?"

Harlan brought one end of the hatch up and let the telescoping ladder sections shoot down. "Vinton's masterpiece."

"What are you talking about?"

Harlan descended the rungs. "In the journal, Vinton wrote about his traps, and he said if the others weren't enough to tip the scales, his masterpiece would." The last of Harlan's words were uttered with him out of sight and at the bottom of the ladder. His next sentence was shouted as he ran to the third-floor steps. "I've got to get out there. Everyone is in danger."

Vieve descended the ladder herself, though at a more controlled speed. By the time she reached the bottom, Harlan was gone.

As Harlan neared the bottom of the first floor steps, he pulled his helmet off and turned its camera to his face. "Walter! Anybody in the crew! You need to get all those people out of here. Tell the police to open all the gates and start clearing them." He sprinted through the living room and rounded the hallway corner toward the front door. "Walter, get up here ASAP, I'm coming out."

In the broadcast truck, the shaky image of Harlan's face was full screen in the on-air monitor. Walter stood behind the director's chair. All the truck operators looked to Walter for his reaction. He said nothing at first, then leaned in toward Nora and spoke quietly. "Make sure you're ready with an outside camera on the front door." She punched a button and the on-air screen cut to a stable shot centered on the front entry of the mansion. Seconds later, Harlan burst through. "And then there was one," Walter spoke under his breath. Harlan leapt several steps with one lunge. He dropped his helmet on the front stoop and bounding the remaining steps with his second stride. He proceeded toward the broadcast truck. Out a few yards from the steps, however, Harlan ran into a wall of people and was slowed to a crawling pace as he waded through.

Walter was finally enlivened. He dashed out of the truck and dove into the crowd himself. The gathered masses continued to chant messages of exorcism for the grounds. Harlan and Walter progressed slowly. "Walter!" Harlan shouted.

"Here, Harlan! Over here!" Walter waved his arms in the air. Harlan finally reached him.

"We have to get all these people out of here." Harlan still had to shout to overcome the noise of the crowd. His voice was strained by heavy breathing. "Where's the police chief?"

"What are you talking about, Harlan?"

"Everyone's in terrible danger. This entire yard is intended to collapse."

"We can't just—"

"The mine. It runs under the entire property, and Vinton took out all the supports before he died." Walter shook his head, confused. "He wanted a big crowd, or heavy equipment, anything that would bring many people and substantial weight onto the grounds. He wanted a big event here so the grounds could collapse with the very specific intention of killing as many people as possible." Harlan steered Walter back toward the broadcast truck. "Haven't you noticed the tremors getting bigger? We already saw rocks falling down there. It's all a new phenomenon, just since we showed up, and it's all by design."

Walter's expression grew concerned. Harlan awaited action, but Walter lingered, dumbfounded. Harlan grabbed Walter and shook him. "I know you want ratings, but you don't want a disaster with casualties in the thousands on your hands, right? The entire Drake property is a giant deathtrap, designed by Vinton to kill on a massive scale. We need to start evacuating. Now!"

Walter hesitated as he processed Harlan's words. He was nervous, speechless, frightened, and all around opposite in demeanor than the cool, collected persona he typically exuded. Harlan noticed him sweating. Then, the low, howling noise began to emanate from the mansion. The tremors followed, far more violently than ever before on the outside grounds. Harlan and Walter both watched as the entire crowd in a wave from back to front was knocked off balance, with many people swept off their feet.

Harlan's warning finally sunk in for Walter as the disturbance subsided. "Yes, yes we have to move these people. Follow me." Walter shouting to clear the way as they both pushed toward the broadcast truck. "We've got every gate closed right now."

They reached the truck's steps. Inside Walter grabbed a radio from Jason. "Chief, this is Walter." He waited for a reply, but there was none. "Does anyone have eyes on the police chief? Someone get him on the line ASAP. It's urgent." He listened again for a reply.

"Here, Walter. This is Chief Bahar," squawked from the radio.

"Chief, you need to have your men open up all the gates and evacuate the property immediately. We believe the mine tunnels below are in danger of collapsing with all the stress." Again they waited for a reply. The radio was silent. Harlan and Walter looked back and forth nervously.

At last, the voice on the radio responded. "Understood." The men shared a relieved breath. "But that's going to be easier said than done."

Walter and Harlan stepped back out to the top of the truck's stairs. Both surveyed the entrances they could see. Outside each closed gate, a large crowd of people and vehicles pushed forward, trying to gain entrance.

Rapid orders from the chief flew over the open radio channel to all the other officers. The gates at the side entrance started to open as a dozen officers tried to direct the nearby crowd members out. However, once open, the gate was rushed from outside and resulted in an addition of several hundred people inside, instead of the start of an evacuation.

When the rear gate opened, the same result was seen, only with a rush of vehicles entering the property. As Walter and Harlan watched, one van pushed in, then a second, but when the third pushed forward entering the grounds, it abruptly disappeared.

"Shit, oh shit," came over the radio. Crowd members screamed as they scrambled away from the van. They packed in more tightly in the surrounding area, which opened a void in the mass of people. The van's driver and another passenger climbed on top of the vehicle's roof and jumped to safer ground before they disappeared into the crowd. The van was below ground in the rocky far terminus of the mine corridor, now exposed by a hole to the surface. "That van, it just dropped. The ground just gave out and swallowed it," the radio voice continued. On the tails of the report, another rumble from the house began.

Harlan grabbed the radio. "Chief, Chief, you have to move everyone through the front gates. The front of the house is empty. Everyone is in the rear yard. The house still has supports down in the mine. It was meant to withstand the cave-in. Move everyone around the house and out through the front." Harlan listened for a reply. Another long moment passed.

"Did everyone hear that?" The Chief's voice finally came on the channel again. "The front is the evacuation point. Close the other gates again and every available officer move to the front to direct traffic out through that egress point. Go, go, go." Throughout his orders, the groan from the house was audible. When the subsequent quaking returned, the earth around the sunken van started to crumble away. It began there, and slowly expanded. Harlan and Walter could do nothing but watch. Panic struck part of the crowd as increasingly many people saw the threat.

When the shaking dwindled, the opening in the earth was five times as large as when it started, greater portions of the mine below having caved in. Many officers had made their way to the front and a small stream of evacuation was under way. "Hurry, hurry." Harlan pleaded under his breath. The open grass around the sinkhole continued to grow as the masses pushed away from it. The spectators closest to the hole tried hardest to move while all the people between them and the exit did nothing, unaware of the threat. Progress was slow, but Harlan could see a visible wave of hysteria move through the crowd back to front. He looked to the house. Vieve stood just inside the open front door. She watched with worry, teetering on coming out herself.

Harlan shouted toward her, "No, no, stay inside!" His voice just faded into the wails of the masses. He thought for a moment, then tossed the radio to Walter and dashed back into the chaos of people, carving a path toward the mansion entrance.

With increasing numbers of people exiting, the onlookers outside the gates were finally growing aware of the danger. The sinkhole was more visible than ever. Walter watched as the outsiders scattered. In another minute, the side and rear gates had completely cleared of people and traffic outside. He raised the radio. "The other gates are clearing now, Chief Bahar. You may be able to start directing traffic back through those." No reply came on the radio but soon the back and side entrances opened again. This time, people from inside the grounds rushed the gates and scrambled out.

The crowd pushed Harlan one way and then the other, like a wave crashing against him then pulling him back as it receded. He was constantly knocked off course for the mansion steps. Vieve was still at the doorway, nervously eyeing the action. Though Harlan had only made it halfway, he shouted again, "No, Vieve, go back inside. The house is the safest place." Vieve couldn't see or hear him.

With people streaming out three gates, the back of the property cleared rapidly. Walter returned to inside the broadcast truck. The crew were alarmed but remained at their stations. "Tell everyone out in that mess, who hasn't already, to get the hell out of here. Get everyone out of the VIP trailer. And all of you need to make your way out to safe ground." Nora relayed Walter's message over the crew communications, after which the entire truck was abandoned, except for Walter. He leapt into the empty director's chair. Jason popped his head back in the doorway. "Sir, aren't you—"

"Go Jason. Get your ass moving and get to safety." Walter didn't look over. His attention was focused on the monitor wall. Jason lingered only a moment, and then nodded and disappeared.

There were a number of cameras in the evacuation. Some were from crewmembers' shoulders that were already off the property. Others bore sideways views, abandoned somewhere on the grounds. Walter couldn't call for any changes to the shots, but he could cut between them.

When the next rumble and quaking began, the caved-in area at the rear of the property crumbled open farther and farther. It revealed more of the corridor below as well as the farthest set of chambers. Pieces of earth, equipment, and other debris fell in from the surface. The slant of the mine below ushered everything downhill into the still covered portion of the mine, and toward the underbelly of the mansion.

By now, the entire back third of the grounds were cleared. Vieve continued to watch from the door. With the heightened quaking, objects fell, boards split, and plaster cracked throughout the house. Vieve decided she'd be better off out in the stampede of people than inside. She backed up a few steps, then, with a running start, sped forward through the door. Right as she stepped outside, however, Harlan sprang from the mass of people. Intercepting Vieve, he wrapped his arms around her, and redirected them both back inside.

"We have to stay inside. It's safer here." Vieve looked at Harlan, shocked. "Vinton designed it so all the damage, all the casualties, would be ushered to under the house, but the house would stay standing." Harlan pushed them further inside, but Vieve resisted. "He wanted all the bodies underneath but wanted the house intact so he would be poised to collect them." Vieve said nothing. "Trust me." She finally relented. Harlan guided them farther inside to a central point in the hallway. From there, they could see the mine opening in the living room floor. Dust spouted up into the room from below. Minutes passed, then the quaking subsided.

Harlan released Vieve and ran to a window in the kitchen with a view of the rear property. The glass was dirt covered. Harlan grabbed a pan and smashed out the glass. The entire back third of the grounds had crumbled, but the crowd was ahead of it. No one could exit through the rear gate now, but the side and apparently the front were still streaming freely. Only the front third of the grounds still had people waiting to leave.

Vieve stepped in behind him. "Should we go?"

"No. I don't think it's over." Just as he spoke, the rumble returned. "Get back to the center. Get under a door frame."

A line spanned the property between what had caved in and what ground was intact. When the shaking returned, the edge pushed farther toward the house. When it reached the untouched carriage house near the back of the grounds, the building disappeared into the earth.

Walter struggled to remain upright in the chair as the broadcast truck shook violently. Equipment fell off other stations. The sideways camera view on the on-air screen showed the devastation line moving toward it, then the camera fell. Glimpses of tumbling earth and the dark mine followed before the camera crashed and went to static. Walter cut to another camera.

The destruction progress was slow but it eventually reached the camp of production vehicles. One by one, trailers and trucks tipped and dropped into the caving mine. The crowd continued to thin and stay ahead of the devastation. The boundary line eclipsed the side entrance to the grounds, leaving only the front gate passable. Before this quake subsided, the line of destruction reached right up to the back of the house. Many of the officers were the last of the crowd to go, but all managed to escape. Only one truck remained topside, though one axle had fallen into the crater. It was the broadcast truck.

Inside, more dust and debris shot up through the hole in the floor. Vieve shrieked, as the collisions below grew more thunderous and more frequent. She held her breath, convinced the house was about to crumble, but the disturbance finally diminished. Harlan crept over and looked down the opening. The entire space below was full of rocks and debris, right up to the floor level. Harlan turned to Vieve, who still trembled. "I think it's finished. The worst of it anyway." He sighed, and returned to Vieve with open arms. She met him for a long embrace. Harlan whispered into her ear. "It's over." Vieve nodded. She closed her eyes and reached up to Harlan with a passionate, cathartic kiss.

After Sunrise

Five minutes passed without a sound or vibration. Vieve and Harlan emerged from the mansion. The sun was in full view over the eastern horizon. They both had to shield their eyes from its bright light. Several additional ambulances had arrived on the street in front of the property. Most of the crowd had dispersed, but the crew, along with Audrey, was rallied around the medics. Bomber accounted for each member of his crew. Jeff and Brian were among them. Lenox sat on the rear of an ambulance as an EMT wrapped an arm injury. Nora patted her on the shoulder and they shared a smile. La Claire and a select group of her followers, nearly 100 in all, huddled in another spot.

Several emergency workers, police, fire, and EMT passed as Harlan and Vieve descended the front steps and rounded the corner of the house to survey the damage. Most of the property lay in ruins, though no fatal injuries were evident.

Walter still sat alone in the broadcast van, which rested at a downward angle due to the single, submerged axle. Harlan and Vieve were on screen, but they were framed sideways from an overturned camera that lay on the ground. Walter called out on the crew communication mic, "Anyone left out there?" He listened through a set of headphones. "Jason, excellent. Can you get to a camera?" Walter scanned all the small screens on the wall. Jason's face popped up on one, though it was out of focus. Walter brought that camera into the on-air view as the frame moved from Jason's face to the mansion and proceeded to find Vieve and Harlan.

They moved to the end of the broadcast truck and sat on the steps. From there, they could see the action on the front street, as well as the devastation in the rear. Two people pushed through the front gate and ran back inside, toward Harlan and Vieve. It was Vieve's parents. When they arrived, they embraced their daughter with sighs of relief. "Are you all right? Do you need to check in with a medic?"

She shook her head. "I'm all right. Physically at least." Another round of hugs followed.

Harlan watched, smiling. He only interjected when the emotions settled. "I think Walter has a million dollars somewhere around here with your name on it. That might ease any psychological injuries you may have sustained." Vieve looked at him with confusion. "I left. You were the only one that stayed in the house through to morning." Jason maintained the camera on their faces.

Vieve shook her head. "That's not fair—"

"It's not accurate either," Walter shouted from inside the truck. He kept his eyes on the screens but beckoned them in with one hand. Harlan and Vieve rose and stepped inside. Jason followed. "The contest was to last until sunrise, which I'm sure you know is the instant when the sun first appears on the horizon; 6:38 a.m. this morning at this latitude, to be precise. Our contracts had to be very specific. Now look at this." Walter pulled up a still frame, frozen from a video feed. It showed Harlan with one leg in the house, and one leg out, but not quite touching the steps, mid stride when he ran to alert Walter of the impending danger. At the bottom of the screen, a time code read 06:38:01. "I'd say that is you, still inside the house, one second after the end of the contest. You both won." Walter finally looked toward them and grinned.

Harlan nodded humbly. Vieve smiled. "I guess a half million will just have to do." She hugged Harlan.

When they stepped back outside, Harlan looked to the attic window. It danced with movement between muted dark and shimmering light. Harlan pointed, Vieve grinned and nodded. She hugged her mother one last time, then with Jason following, she and Harlan moved back to the house. They proceeded with no particular hurry. Harlan scooped up his discarded helmet and placed it back on his head. Next, they stepped inside, went up to the third floor, and on into the attic. Harlan stowed the ladder behind them. The sun's rays fully penetrated the window and lit the crystals. The projections from refraction and reflection were more glorious than before. All together the room was brightly lit. The beams shot into every other crystal on the walls and floor and bounced around the room further. Shapes and colors moved and overlapped, making a continuous kaleidoscope effect on every nook and cranny of the space. Harlan put an arm over Vieve's shoulder and basked in the quiet beauty.

After a moment, Vieve pulled away slightly so she could look Harlan in the face. "Harlan? If all these crystals are here to channel the life vitality to Vinton like you said before, and the entire house was set up to kill people inside, or underneath so he could absorb their life energy too, then where is Vinton? Where's his body?"

Harlan gestured toward some of the crystals along the floor and walls. "Ax's camera showed all those inconsistencies in the ceilings and floors, and we know Vinton made additions he thought would channel the energy. I'd be willing to bet we'd find more crystals, maybe pulverized and mixed into plaster all through the house. Maybe even conduits of water. There are many spiritual beliefs that assign fantastic qualities to pure water or specific minerals and crystal forms. Any of them might make the cool spots and lines that Ax saw. At any rate, it would seem everything is designed from the mine, through each floor, and up into the attic to usher the supposed energy to here." He pointed to the hanging crystal mosaic.

Harlan stepped up to the crystals. As Vieve had earlier, he

brushed the outer hanging stones with his hand, sending them swaying from their threads. Vieve joined him. "If it's all pointing here, then wouldn't that mean—" Before Vieve could finish her thought, Harlan abruptly surged both arms directly inward, his arms disappeared into the sculpture as if they'd been plunged into water. Without hesitation, he yanked his arms right back out, and with them emerged the shoulders and head of Vinton's mostly skeletal remains. Jason fumbled his camera as he lurched backward and stumbled on one of the floor's stones. Vinton's body continued to fall away. Eventually, it flopped on the floor, fully exposed.

Harlan helped Jason to his feet. Camera in hand, Jason panned the newfound body. It was the least decayed they'd seen through the course of the night. Its fine suit was mostly intact while the body itself was mummified in appearance, with much of the flesh preserved. Vieve looked away. Harlan went to her. "I don't think there's much left for us to do here. Let's get out of this nightmare for good." He took her hand and led her to the ladder. After he restored the steps, Vieve climbed down, Harlan and Jason followed.

"Be watchful," Harlan instructed Jason as they continued back down the stairs. "This step is loose. Plus, there could be other undiscovered deadfalls left, untriggered thus far. I wouldn't touch anything you don't have to." Jason took his eye out from behind the camera for a moment. He nodded to Harlan, and then scanned the area. When they landed on the first floor, they crossed the living room and headed to the hallway. Harlan stopped for a moment. Vieve noticed the separation between them after she took a few more steps. She spun to see what had caught Harlan's attention.

Harlan's eyes were fixed on Vinton's journal. He leaned over the back of the sofa, reached down, and retrieved the leather-bound volume. Tucking it under his arm, he smiled back at Vieve and rejoined her. They left the mansion for the last time.

Walter awaited Vieve and Harlan on the front steps. "Hold it here a moment, please." He beckoned both to stop with the doorway centered behind them. "Jason, hop down there and get a wide shot on us." Walter plugged a handheld microphone into a port on the side of the camera. "Actually, start close on me, and then zoom out to all three of us. Let me know when you're set." Jason gave a thumbs up to Walter. Even after all the adrenaline, worry, stress, and demands on him, Walter had no trouble summoning his superficial, on-air self.

Walter looked into the camera lens. "There you have it, folks. I'd like to thank all of our sponsors, and all of you who've tuned in, signed on, and stayed with us through the night. It's been one rollercoaster of excitement, from spooky noises in the dark to inexplicable technical readings, cold spots on the ceilings, hot spots between the sheets, and the entire collapse of a secret mine shaft under the property. There were plenty of bumps and bruises, but we're pleased to report there were no fatalities or life-threatening injuries. I'm also very happy to present to you, our winners. Ms. Freedman, Mr. Holt, you'll be splitting the million dollar purse." Walter stepped closer to Vieve and Harlan. "Genevieve, were you frightened during your night's stay at the Drake Mansion?"

Vieve's eyebrows rose. "Well, there were traps set specifically to kill anyone who came here. One of the other contestants was injured, while thousands of people were nearly caught in the cave-in. I think it's safe to say there were a few times I, very prudently, was fearful for my life."

"We certainly understand that, my dear." Walter smiled. "Well, now that you'll be collecting a cool 500K, have your plans changed? Will you still be putting it toward your education, or are convertibles and world vacations in your future?"

"After taxes, every bit will go to getting my medical degree."

Walter laughed. "Wonderful. Best of luck to you." Walter then stepped to the other side of Vieve, so he was between her and Harlan. "What about you, Harlan? Did the house get to you during the night?"

"I wouldn't put it that way. I'll admit when there was legitimate mortal danger I was appropriately and proportionally concerned about it."

"A tough guy to the bitter end, huh? I don't recall your preshow interview. Now that you've got a half million dollars coming your way, what will you do? Anything exciting?"

Harlan shook his head. "Just as I said when we started, I'll be donating my winnings to the Scientist, Magician, Skeptic Foundation. They're a nonprofit organization dedicated to skepticism and—" Walter cut Harlan off.

"Very admirable indeed. If I were in either of your shoes I think I'd splurge a little bit, but maybe that's just me. At any rate, again, congratulations to the victors." Walter bowed slightly to the two of them. On Walter's silent cue, Harlan and Vieve exited down the steps and out of frame. After that, Walter gestured for Jason to come in tight with the camera. Vieve and Harlan watched from behind.

"You saw it here, live, with us first, folks. After more than eight decades, we've witnessed in one night the unraveling of the Drake family mystery, the uncovering of a secret plot that led to the tragedy, and to the discovery of a slew of victims hidden on the grounds. With the cave-in, and near destruction of the property, it will likely take years to sort through all the events and evidence, but you got the inside look."

Harlan leaned toward Vieve and whispered, "He'd better not."

"Were these all the intricate plans—come to fruition—of a madman who died over 80 years ago? Or was this the work of the very much alive and active spirits, of the killer and the victims, desperate to resolve their earthly entanglements?" Harlan sighed and clinched his fist. He stormed away from the steps, toward the crew people just off the property. Vieve smirked as she spun and followed after him.

"Were greater forces at work here?" Walter paused, raised one eyebrow, and looked back at the mansion doors. "We may never know for sure. Perhaps there are no certain answers, but we've all seen the evidence—each of us will just have to make up our own minds. Once again we thank you for joining us on this adventure. I'm Walter Resnick, bidding you farewell from Drake Mansion." Walter cued Jason to cut the shot.

Harlan kicked a rock out of his way and sat down on an empty section of curb with his back to the mansion. Vieve caught up and slid in beside him. "What's wrong?"

"I knew he'd do it." Harlan stared toward the ground. "There wasn't a shred of legitimate evidence to suggest anything paranormal ever occurred here. In truth, what we witnessed was the real danger of believing in woo-woo."

Harlan looked up at Vieve. "Malvern Kamrar was an exceptional conjurer. He was ahead of his time with the death and resurrection tricks he orchestrated. However, Kamrar thought he could advance his career even more quickly by spreading the legend of his abilities being supernatural, like so many charlatans throughout history, to gain infamy. He went too far in convincing Vinton. Vinton, on the other hand, had severe, and today clinically diagnosable, personality disorder traits, which made him, among other things, fearless, selfish, self-important, delusional, guiltless, and virtually without empathy. When Kamrar gave Vinton the idea he could advance his self-interest through the demise and suffering of others, he unleashed a monster. The danger only compounded when Vinton faced an untimely death due to terminal illness. In his own words, 'desperation encourages uncharacteristic behavior,' and these were the explosive results." Harlan gestured to the destruction behind them.

Vieve said nothing but took Harlan's hand and squeezed it. After a moment, Walter walked by with a determined stride, a phone to his ear, and a huge smile. "Fantastic work in there." He passed quickly. Jason followed, now with a notepad instead of a camera. After a few more steps, Walter stopped and looked around with confusion.

Jason did the same for a moment, then dashed back over to Harlan and Vieve. "Have either of you seen Madam La Claire or Ax?"

Vieve pointed toward La Claire's circle of followers. "Galva's over there, but I imagine Ax is still at the hospital." Jason nodded and stepped back toward Walter.

Harlan stopped him. "Why?"

"The network loved this. They're considering launching a couple series." Jason continued away.

"With Galva and Ax?" Harlan had to shout to reach Jason.

"Yeah." Jason smiled as he found Walter and directed him down the street toward La Claire.

Harlan shook his head. "You were right. I'll bet in a year this entire block will be full of psychic readers, spells and potions shops, new-age bookstores, and a couple of services offering ghost tours of Shadows Bend." He waved indicating the block of houses across the street from the Mansion.

"Probably."

"It's just frustrating."

"Well, you converted me, and I'm sure I'm not the only one." Harlan looked back up to Vieve with a softened expression. "Maybe you can come visit me once they're both on the air, and we can share our outrage." She smiled brightly and leaned, knocking Harlan with her shoulder playfully.

Harlan returned the grin and put his arm over Vieve's shoulders. "You know what? You can count on it." After a shared moment of laughter, they kissed.

When the passion subsided, Vieve placed something in Harlan's hand. "You dropped this when you stormed off." Harlan looked down, it was Vinton's journal. He stared at the cover a moment, and then opened to the last few pages they hadn't had time to finish. Vieve couldn't see what he was reading over the cover. His eyes moved side to side. He flipped one more page and chuckled. Vieve was puzzled. "What could be so funny? The last few chapters were so grave."

"That says it all." Harlan handed her the book.

For Those Who Wish to Follow In My Footsteps:

The Posthumous Notes of Vinton Drake, After My Resurrection

About the Author

Born in Centerville, Iowa, Channing studied cinema, screenwriting, literature, and mathematics at the University of Iowa. He went on to work in the production of television news, independent films, and commercial videos as well as to write for websites, corporate media, and advertising. His nearly 10-year career in writing has taken Channing from Iowa, to Texas, Alaska, and currently to Oklahoma. In that time, Channing has also written and directed over 50 short films. The publication of this, his debut novel, comes in tandem with the production of his first feature screenplay, also in the mystery/thriller genre, slated for a 2015 release.

Made in the USA
Middletown, DE
11 April 2015